THE FRENCH
ATLANTIC
AFFAIR

THE FRENCH ATLANTIC AFFAIR

Ernest Lehman

M

ISBN 0 333 22315 2

First published in Great Britain 1977 by
MACMILLAN LONDON LIMITED
4 Little Essex Street London WC2R 3LF
and Basingstoke
Associated Companies in Delhi, Dublin,
Hong Kong, Johannesburg, Lagos, Melbourne,
New York, Singapore and Tokyo

Printed in Great Britain by
UNWIN BROTHERS LIMITED
The Gresham Press, Old Woking, Surrey
A member of the Staples Printing Group

To my wife, Jackie,

and to our fine young men, Roger and Alan,

with love and pride

BOOK ONE

THE PLAN

"I tell you the past is a bucket of ashes."
CARL SANDBURG

"Let's meet, and either do or die."
JOHN FLETCHER

CHAPTER ONE

─────────

H O W   H A D   I T   all started?

No one would ever know for sure.

A bitter joke perhaps, at which no one had laughed?

"Not very funny . . ."

Suck it in, hold it, let it out slowly.

"But y'know something? That may just be one hell of an idea . . . ?"

"What?"

"Uh-huh."

"Come on."

"I mean it."

"Come *on.*" And *now* the laughter. Because *that was* funny.

But maybe not such a bad idea at that, don't laugh.

Maybe it was their only hope.

At first there had been only the four of them: Craig Dunleavy and his wife Betty, and the Kleinfelds, Herb and Harriet, bound together by faded dreams, shared unemployment insurance, a love of martinis, and a seemingly inexhaustible repertoire of black-humored bitterness toward NASA, the U.S. Senate, the Pentagon, and any other agency of the establishment that could be held responsible for the devastating cutbacks in the space program.

Houston heroes and JPL hotshots cool fast when forcibly separated from their lives. So do their wives and lovers, who had been totally a part of those lives. The Dunleavys and Kleinfelds had simply never bothered to prepare themselves, either financially or emotionally, for the catastrophe that eventually overtook them, and for all the ludicrous humiliations that followed.

Oh, it wasn't just the last look at the house, and the first sight of (oh, *no*) the new apartment. It wasn't just the selling of (I *can't*) the things you loved, and the renting of things you didn't. It wasn't even (I don't believe it) the jobs you had to take, or the jobs (I don't believe it) that wouldn't take *you*. There was nothing so terrible about being, let's face it, poor. Practically everyone in the world was poor at *one* time or another.

But how many had put men on the moon, and probes on the planets? How many had lived and slept with those who *had* during the years they'd been doing it?

What had been lost forever was not what had been pridefully achieved and shared. What *was* gone forever, irretrievably dead— God, *how* many months has it been? How many *years?*—was the reasonable hope that they would ever have the chance to do it, or share in it, again.

That was truly the worst of it. The rest was just merely awful, the stark reality that there was no place to go with the years of training, no rate of exchange for the unique expertise. The newspaper clippings, the résumés, the past glories, were nothing but an acute embarrassment to others.

I'm sorry, I hear what you're saying, sir, but I wouldn't feel *right* knowing who it is out there pumping gas for me and cleaning windshields. I hope you understand, sir . . .

I just can't do it, man. I couldn't stand watching someone like you behind a checkout counter, understand what I mean?

Sure they understood.

They were the living dead.

They would lie on the beach at Venice, Craig and Betty, Herb and Harriet, and let the California sun cover their paranoia with a year-round golden tan, because how could you feel your despair when the mirror (and everyone else) kept telling you how great you looked? How could you hear the panic inside of you when the breaking waves made such a noise you couldn't even hear yourself *think* (unless you sprawled out a couple of hundred feet back from the shoreline, which you almost never did)?

They'd have a late lunch at the Brown Bagger or the Cheese and the Olive, always getting a table in the sun, and let the cold chablis sink in and dissolve the lurking anxiety, and sometimes Betty Dunleavy and Herb Kleinfeld would look into each other's eyes and wonder what it would. be like together, while Craig and Harriet were playing the same game, and that would make it even better later, when they went home to their own apartments and lay down in their rightful beds and made lovely love and slept off the wine until it was dark and time for dinner at Jay's and some good work on the real booze then, and maybe a flick afterward, or just sitting around watching the tube and listening to music and getting stoned out of their minds before going to bed, never all in one bed, though they joked about it a lot, and that's how they'd finish the day, not making lovely love but fucking like animals before falling into a dreamless stupor.

Oh, they always knew when the dough was running out, no way you couldn't know *that,* but *doing* something about it temporarily, something wretched and degrading, became more and more unfaceable, and that was what probably led finally to the ridiculous idea, and the obsession with it. And the more they talked about it, the more real it became to them, until there came that day, that night, that moment when they no longer knew that they had slipped over the edge into insanity.

Of *course* it was insane.

But it felt so beautiful to them. It would be like rebirth. A new beginning. Another gorgeous chance. *Christ* what an idea hey watch it of *course* we can do it Jesus *brilliant* you're spilling Vermouth all over my left tit all right gin then but *fantastic really* give us a kiss . . .

Insanity.

The first outsider on whom Craig Dunleavy dared to try out the idea was a total stranger, an unemployed supermarket manager he was sitting next to at a bar in Hermosa Beach while waiting for a broken fan belt to be replaced in his car. He felt safe, because the man was pissed, had no idea who Craig was, and would never see him again. Also, Craig told the man the ship was the *QE 2.*

Immediately, he was sorry he had spoken. Later, he would be grateful for the reassurance the incident had given him. But there at the bar in Hermosa Beach that rainy afternoon, he wondered how he was ever going to shake the guy.

"Don't take me so seriously, for Christ's sake." Craig laughed at him. "Come on, I'll buy you another drink."

"I don't *want* another drink, I want *in*."

Dunleavy looked at the coarse-featured stranger for a moment, then said, "Okay, write your name and address on this book of matches . . ."

"Crazy."

"And don't forget your phone number in case I get delayed or something."

"Don't worry, I'll be waiting."

Dunleavy took the match folder and glanced at it. "Marty Josias?"

"Apartment 4C," the stranger said.

"Joe Smalley," Craig Dunleavy said, letting the man shake his hand.

"You're a fuckin' genius, Joe. You know that?"

Dunleavy smiled and walked out.

When he got to the garage, the car was ready for him. He threw the match folder away and drove north, leaving Hermosa Beach and Marty Josias far behind him as fast as he could.

Yep, they *had* something all right. And it was not going to be all that difficult to sell it to others. If there was one thing Craig Dunleavy had always known how to do, it was to get other people to dream his dreams.

Everyone who knew him, as far back as high school, had been certain he'd become outstanding some day. The only question had been whether he'd make his mark in business, in science, or in a federal prison. Today, at forty-one, he had the same lean, well-tanned, boyish good looks that used to fool the folks around Long Beach and San Diego back in the days when he was using their trust in him to buy up small real estate holding companies and fledgling research-and-development outfits in the instrument packaging field and run them swiftly into bankruptcy, while growing mysteriously well-heeled in the process, all before the age of twenty-six. The horn-rimmed glasses, the soft voice, the ever-burning pipe, and the smoothly understated, button-down style of dress camouflaged a heart filled with joyous larceny. The fact that he could have been a brilliant aerospace engineer was totally irrelevant to him at the time. He simply could not understand how some men could get such a charge out of working their asses off in the pursuit of honest bucks when it was obviously so much more fun to *steal* the dough. He did it with sleight-of-hand corporate funding and artful siphoning, followed by lamentations all the way to the safety deposit box when the companies inevitably went belly up.

It was only after his second marriage went the way of his first, and he was picked up at the Luau in Beverly Hills by a striking blonde named Betty Wilkerson, two days fresh from *her* divorce, that his life veered sharply to the right. He didn't like merely fucking the girl, he also liked to talk to her until five in the morning and look at her, every part of her, constantly, and listen to her, how he loved to listen to her and think about her, she was all he thought about, and then he wanted nothing but to marry her, because he would have had to kill any other man who got her, and that's when she told him she didn't really want to be with him any more because he was, let's face it, a thief by any other name but still a thief.

He had no choice. He took his masters at Stanford, then got his doctorate at M.I.T. (she lived with him in Boston), and they stopped off at Las Vegas long enough to get married, and long enough for Craig to beat a sweating, rage-filled blackjack dealer out of $11,000, before flying down to Cocoa Beach to go house-hunting, with NASA, of course, picking up the tab and training him, too.

For the next eight years, half of them at Cape Kennedy, the rest at Houston, years during which he rose to Technical Liaison between Vehicle Systems and Mission Control, and Betty lost their first and only try at a child, Craig gloried in his work, caught up in the challenge and the sweep of it, and never really strayed from the straight and narrow.

Actually, just once, he *did* try. It was on one of the last of the Apollos. Seems he knew someone in Fort Worth who knew someone in Havana who claimed that he had a client in South America who would be willing to pay a hundred grand for a one-pound moon rock. When Dunleavy approached one of America's soon-to-be-a-hero astronauts, he wound up with nothing better than a bloody nose and a cut under his left eye. It could have been far worse, but the uptight prick kept the whole thing very quiet so that the preflight medicos wouldn't zero in on the aching bones of his right hand and scrub him from the mission. But Betty found out about it through one of the wives, and made Craig sleep in the den for three weeks, until he finally came begging.

Herb Kleinfeld, amazingly enough, never laid eyes on Craig Dunleavy until the best of it was really all over for the both of them, when they were just two of about twenty well-groomed, hollow-eyed, early-middle-aged guys hanging around the personnel department of Oxidon Petroleum in downtown L.A. for four straight days, waiting not for an actual job but merely for the opportunity to be *interviewed,* for Christ's sake, just in case something should ever open up in, say, Alaska or Iran.

First they discovered that they both liked, of all damned things, peanut butter. Then it was George Shearing's quintet, the Cincinnati Reds, and citrus musk after-shave cologne. Then they found out they had been born two days apart and ten miles apart, had grown up in the same Orange County of California, had gone to blood-rival high schools, and that Herb had been as outstanding at tight end for his school as Craig had been on the debating team of his.

So the hell with Oxidon Petroleum, isn't there some place around here where we can go have a drink or something? And discover, finally, that Craig's Cape Kennedy and Houston years had been paralleled by Herb at the other end of the same space program, at the Jet Propulsion Laboratory in Pasadena and the Electronics Research Center in Cambridge, where he had fiddled in quiet anonymity with everything from analog-to-digital converters to large-scale integrated circuits for data-multiplexing telemetry, before the solar system turned weary, flat, stale, and unprofitable for the both of them and collapsed in on itself?

Inevitably the Dunleavys and Kleinfelds finally got together—a boozy three-hour dinner at Dale's Secret Harbor—and inevitably they went on from there to become a steady foursome, because the attraction was powerful and mutual in all directions, horizontally, vertically, and diagonally. Betty admired Harriet's tall, dark, brown-eyed strength. Harriet understood Betty's fine-boned, blond, blue-eyed vulnerability. And each man had good but lawful vibes going back and forth between himself and the other guy's lady. If there were any reservations at all, it was Harriet's private concern that her easygoing Herb was just a little too straight to see the con in some of Craig Dunleavy's glibness. Eventually, of course, she put the same blinders on, and became as emotionally sold on the big insanity as anyone else.

After the episode of the broken fan belt and the rainy afternoon at a bar in Hermosa Beach, Craig had no patience for mere talk any more. They had had enough of that. The time had come to take a deep breath and jump in. It was then—or never. And so they started.

Singly, or as couples, or all four together, they began to infiltrate the potential gathering places of the emotionally dispossessed, starting with the unemployment insurance offices in cities like Pasadena and Burbank and Glendale. They would sit in on the nightly poker games at Gardena, blend into the scene at the Swingles in Sherman Oaks and the Swap Shop in Tarzana, forgiving each other for the lustful pleasures that were a byproduct of their proselytizing. They would nurse their martinis and margaritas at all the right joints, and some that were wrong, as far south as Newport Beach, as far north as the weekends in San Francisco. They'd hit the encounter groups at Esalen on the way down, cover the introductory sales-pitch gatherings of EST, even spend a couple of nude sunny days and orgiastic nights of sexual freedom at the Sandstone Ranch in Topanga Canyon. And always, they would keep their eyes and ears open for the telltale signs of burnt-out lives and yearning desperation and failed hope that would not die. They learned to read the sad eyes above the suntanned smiles, and to hear the sound of weeping in the night beneath the loud laughter and the trembling hands that held too many highball glasses. They learned to use their own charm and physical appeal to seduce into closeness the ones who seemed compatible with them and their dream, the ones who seemed capable of going all the way with them, the really bold, the really lost ones, like themselves. And to those who were chosen, they cautiously spoon fed the plan on a very gentle gradient, so that it would go down well, or not at all. They made some mistakes, of course. It was a game they had never played before. But they didn't make many.

And when their repertoire started to run thin, Craig got out his little black book—Herb's was brown leather—and they reached all the way back into the earliest days when they were first starting out, when Craig was hiring Hughes rejects for assembly jobs and Herb was getting restless behind a counter at Standard. It was amazing how many of the guys they would have sworn would make it big were eating the rugs these days. Was there a curse on the land?

Within a half year, the four of them had grown to nineteen, and the use of code names was begun. By Christmas, they numbered twenty eight, feeling as comfortable in their new identities as they had felt uncomfortable in the old. The following May, when they met secretly as a group for the very first time, in several motels outside of Twentynine Palms, California, forty-two men and thirty-six women, most of them married to each other, all of them childless but not without sexuality, had become irrevocably committed to the plan. Craig and Betty and Herb and Harriet, of course, brought the total to eighty two. It was agreed that they would need another hundred or so like themselves to come in with them in order to make it all work. For this purpose, an informal committee was formed, to do the recruiting on a national scale, while Dunleavy and Kleinfeld would devote themselves mainly to matériel procurement and operational planning.

They met only two more times, once for a Labor Day weekend at Colorado Springs, where they pretended to be holding a kind of moral rearmament conference, and the second time, during Easter week in Baja California, where the group was ostensibly a deep-sea fishermen's get-together. At the latter meeting, with the roster of conspirators finalized at one hundred and seventy-four persons, with all weapons systems, forged documents, and cyanide devices accounted for, and with the supplies of doomsdealing chemite and pentolite and trinitrotoluene successfully cached in a silo in the vicinity of Bakersfield, California, it was unanimously voted to commence the operation in three months, on July 10, to be exact.

That would give them time to dispose of everything that was disposable, time to say their well-disguised final goodbyes, before they set out by plane and by train to take up passage on the S.S. *Marseille*. It was on July 10 that the 65,000-ton pride of the French Atlantic Line would sail from New York bound for Le Havre.

Strangely enough, working out the myriad details of the plan had not been the most difficult or time-consuming phase of the operation. Dunleavy's access to some of the more sophisticated computers in the land had made the impossible, at times, go ridiculously smoothly. And it was amazing, the kind of contacts you had that you'd never known you had. It was incredible, the easy flair for criminal ingenuity that lay so close to the surface of your civilized self-image. And the larger your numbers, the greater the odds that one of you would always have the hidden skill, or know someone who did, to meet each challenge that would suddenly present itself and threaten to destroy the dream. And of course firing their determination all the way, whetting their appetites and fueling their courage to the extreme, was the constant awareness of the staggering size of the treasure that would be theirs.

No, it was not in the planning or the preparation that the real problems had festered. Anything that could be computed or invented or blueprinted or photographed or memorized or Xeroxed or bought or crafted or stolen or rehearsed or hidden in luggage had been reasonably manageable. No, the truly formidable obstacle in the path of Craig Dunleavy and Herb Kleinfeld, in the path of the entire group, had been the human factor, the inescapable truth that there were limits beyond which, or rather *below* which, a number of them could not be easily made to go, particularly the ones who had already spent most of their years being decent and human.

No problem with the rifle association types, with the sporting bloods who had been snuffing out the lives of magnificent deer and other helpless creatures for years without ever feeling anything but good about it. For them, this would be merely another kind of hunting trip. As for guys like Lou Foyles and Wendell Cronin, their M-16s had strewn the Mekong Delta with so many corpses, there was nothing that was going to make *them* blink any more. But the softhearted were another matter. They had to be worked on, indoctrinated, re-educated. The word atrocity had to be redefined for them as meaning *necessity*. They had to catch the fever, and never lose it.

All in all, it had taken months of bitter tears and anguish, days and nights of pleading and cajoling, of verbal cruelty and gentle seduction, of shouts and whispers, of drugs and hypnosis, before the very last of the one hundred and seventy-four had been finally convinced, had given in at last and had solemnly agreed with all the others that the plan could never succeed, that they, the conspirators, could never attain both their dream and their permanent freedom, unless each and every one of them was willing to accept wholeheartedly the blood that would be forever on their hands.

So be it.

CHAPTER TWO

SHE HAD LEFT while the party was still going on, stealing away from her pier in the hazy sunshine, quietly leaving behind the foolishness and the noise and the mess of confetti and the unclean sky hidden by tall-standing glass and steel, and she had moved serenely down the Hudson River and out to sea where she could breathe again, and be alone again, her course set east for Nantucket Lightship. That night she would pick up Track Charlie and be on her way, on the comfortably familiar, glorious summer run of the North Atlantic, and in five days, God and the sea willing, if those who guided her and those she carried were kind to her and used her wisely and well, she would be back in her beloved France again.

On her bridge, the thick-set, stocky, uniformed Frenchman who stood gazing out at the gently swelling seas ahead of him felt uncommonly euphoric this day, and, indeed, why should he not? He was in fine health again. His ship was magnificent. He was in love with her. Undoubtedly she loved *him*. His staff and his crew were not only the finest, they were actually charming. The passengers he had watched hurrying up the gangplank had all seemed so handsome and carefree, just the kind to turn a routine crossing into a voyage of sheer delight. The French economy was booming. The franc was as good as—no—even better than gold. The Compagnie Française Atlantique sailed the seven seas with unprecedented command. And before long, his lovely lady would be joined by a sister ship, fresh from the yards at St.-Nazaire, the S.S. *Bordeaux.*

If Charles Girodt had failed to break open a bottle of Veuve Clicquot and join the presailing revelry on the Promenade Deck today, it was only because the Commandant had had no need for champagne. He was intoxicated enough as it was with a sense of his place high up on the curve of destiny. Had he not survived, and overcome, the worst that could happen to him?

Two years ago, a career that had seen Girodt rise with unprecedented swiftness from Lieutenant 2nd Class straight up through the maritime ranks to his present lofty position on the bridge of the *Marseille* had, without warning, been suddenly threatened by what his close friend and personal physician, Henri Cachon, could explain only by using the term male climacteric. The unaccountable swings from excessive joy to prolonged, unmotivated melancholy, the mysterious weeping spells and the frightening, unprovoked rages, had had to be handled quickly and with discretion, before they became noticed in the executive offices of the Compagnie Française.

Girodt had promptly requested of the Director General, and had been immediately granted, a six-month leave of absence to accompany his wife, Josette, to a private spa outside of Langenthal in Switzerland, ostensibly to be at her side while *she* fought her way out of a nervous breakdown. Henri Cachon had made frequent trips to the spa, administered a variety of chemicals to Girodt, including lithium salts, and within the allotted half-year period of time had him levelheaded again, on an even keel, as it were. Not just as good as new, the exultant Girodt had insisted on the flight back to Paris—*better.*

Certainly that was true today. Never had he sailed away from the port of New York in higher spirits than he was in right now. How could he know, or even suspect, that of the seven thousand nine hundred and sixty pieces of luggage in the cabins and staterooms and deluxe suites of his great ship, six hundred and twelve had secret compartments?

Unpacking them was the first thing they had done, the one hundred and seventy-four, in their far-flung accommodations throughout the length and breadth of the entire ship, portside and starboard, from stem to stern, on each and every deck, in First Class and Tourist, putting away carefully under lock and key their personal arsenals of handguns and automatic weapons and explosives, or if not that, then whatever had been assigned to them.

Then they had gone out to mix with the other passengers, and to indulge themselves at the bountiful buffet lunch in the great dining rooms. It was there that the tension and the excitement began slowly to build inside of them, knowing as they did, looking into each other's eyes and *knowing* where they would be and what they would be doing with each other so very soon, and why. Oh, they could hardly wait. It was so hard to wait until two o'clock. But that had been the agreement, the marvelous agreement.

They had decided that it would be a kind of thrilling, unforgettable commemoration of the *beginning,* of the new life that would be theirs, if they all, all of them, at one and the same time, in the privacy of their bedrooms, celebrated and luxuriated in the act that was the act of creating new life. At two o'clock in the afternoon, sated with food and beautifully loosened up by the wine and the champagne, they would all join in the one great shout of ecstasy that would signal their union and their determination to go forward with the dream, no matter what the challenges.

God, what a fantastic way to begin.

And afterward, spent and glowing and flushed with optimism, they used the warm lazy hours before dinnertime to wander through the ship, carefully, casually checking all the strategic locations, pleased with themselves that the steamship *Marseille* contained no unpleasant surprises. Everything seemed so familiar to them, so often had they been there in the photographs and diagrams and blueprints and, most importantly of all, in the giant scale model that they had so sadly and reluctantly been forced to destroy before leaving for New York. The communications room was *there,* the wheelhouse *there,* the bridge *there,* the engine room *there.* No need for them to go inside the forbidden places yet. They'd been there before. And they'd be there again, this time the real thing, soon enough, a matter of hours, that was all.

They met as planned in two loose, informal groups, in the vast reading lounges of First Class and Tourist, drifting in and out between the hours of five and six, scarcely noticed by those who were not one of them. They reviewed their assignments, compared their impressions, shared their observations, but mostly they chatted, quietly and amiably, the way passengers do who have just met for the first time, and if there was anything at all different about them, it would not have been sensed by a casual observer, because it was only in the way that they looked at each other, warmly and knowingly and perhaps a bit shyly, delightfully aware that each and every one of them had been loved that day at two in the afternoon.

And when they went off to their suites and cabins, to rest and relax and get ready for dinner and for the other beginning, the real beginning, there was not one of them who wasn't feeling that this had been one of the truly beautiful days, one of the best days in all their lives.

None of them would know this happiness ever again.

CHAPTER THREE

_____

THE LUXEMBOURG dining room, truly First Class, was awash with fine wines and high spirits. If he noticed any exceptions to the latter, Pierre Frontenac, the Chef de Réception, simply overlooked them, or looked _through_ such guests as Harold Columbine, and also William H. Berlin, M.D., and his wife, Mrs. Berlin, whose first name was Julie.

Mr. Columbine, a highly publicized, perennially best-selling American author of thick novels whose content was predominantly of a sexual nature, had several concerns as he sat, by his own request, at a table set for one. The concerns were: (1) that someone would find out who he was; (2) that no one would find out who he was; and (3) that among all the females in the Luxembourg dining room and in the six nightclubs and two discothèques and Christ knows how many bars in First Class and Tourist, he might possibly fail to find the one unattached, beautiful, fuckable woman he had been dreaming of for two months now, the only reason he was _on_ this boat instead of a jet, no matter _what_ bullshit about needing a rest he had given his editor, his publisher, his lawyer, his agent, his separated fourth wife, and the tired-of girl in New York he hoped would separate from *him* while he was off doing research in Spain.

Only his first night at sea, and already he was beginning to panic, already he found himself eyeing something at a nearby table that wasn't even alone. She was with a guy. He looked like a husband. They hardly talked to each other or looked at each other. And why would anybody not want to look at *her?* She was a little on the diminutive side, but Jesus, those large blue eyes, that face. He just knew that the rest of her had to be choice cut. Belting down his Gibson, he decided he'd like to get his hands on her *once,* just to make it an even once.

It appeared that Billy Berlin and Julie were not talking to each other. Actually, *she* was not speaking to *him,* except when it was absolutely necessary, and her coolness, unexplained, had chilled him into an uneasy silence of his own. Only two hours ago, she had discovered that her somewhat infantile, thirty-seven-year-old husband, a specialist in geriatric medicine, had, contrary to his promise to her, secretly taken aboard the ship and stashed away, *not* a pound of heroin or an ounce of coke or a kilo of grass, *not* one of the overripe sex-starved daughters of his patients—they were *always* in his office and *always* calling him at home, and who was kidding whom?—none of that, no, not her Billy boy. *He* had taken along and buried in the large suitcase under the socks and the underwear his goddamn *transceiver,* otherwise known to the nuts of the world as the Atlas-210, part of the extensive, expensive rat's maze of ham radio equipment in the den of their Bel Air home.

Once again, just as he had done on the trip to Alaska, and the winter holiday at Mauna Kea, and the two weeks that she had hoped would be heaven in Tahiti, he was obviously planning to ignore her in favor of a few dozen assorted ham friends all over the world on good old twenty meters. Only *this* time Julie was going to take drastic vengeance, the least of it being the turning in of the equipment to the Captain. Not legal on a French ship, your honor, the Captain. Violation of FCC regulations and the International Reciprocal Agreement or whatever between our two great nations, Captain, sir. She hadn't gone to all those ham parties that Billy had dragged her to for *nothing*. She had *listened*. What else was there to do but listen? And listen. And listen.

Phase Two of the retaliatory strike would positively wipe him

out. And maybe her too, but she intended to love every minute of
it. The mere contemplation of it was already giving her a wickedly
pleasurable tingle of lust, and *who,* she wondered, was that man
sitting all by himself who was staring at her that way, and as if she
didn't know, why was he doing it? She would find out before
bedtime.

If it was the last thing she did.

He blamed it on his excessive good nature, not that he was upset or
anything. A little bored, perhaps, but not upset. *C'est la vie.* In all
his years as the master of great ocean liners, he had never allowed
anyone to inveigle him into setting up a Captain's table on the first
night out, and yet that was exactly what he had allowed Peter
Broussard of the New York office to do. Inveigle him.

"In the old days we used to take seven or eight days to cross the
Atlantic, plenty of time for the slow buildup. But now, five days
and *poof,* it is over. So why not offer them Charles Girodt and
l'atmosphère Françat twenty-four hours earlier than usual? Remember, my dear Charles, we are now competing with jet-
propelled stewardesses in miniskirts woven from their discarded
bras, who move at twice the speed of sound."

"Rather than fight them, I think I would prefer to move with
them," Charles Girodt had replied, just before giving in.

Toying now with his *moules à la marinière* at this experimental
gathering, Girodt still retained far too much of the day's euphoria
to be annoyed by the prattle of the woman who sat to his right, a
plump, vapid chatterbox of about forty-two. Girodt took it all with
ease. For one thing, Peter Broussard's *other* experiment would
provide the Captain's table with a different set of guests for each
night at sea, and Girodt knew that the woman would soon be gone
from his life forever. Then, too, he knew that if she ever stopped
talking to him, he might have to hear what the others at his table
were saying, and that could be even worse.

So he let her go on, not realizing that, in a sense, she would soon
be changing his life forever.

She said her name was Helen Wabash, Mrs. Ralph Wabash, and
she was quite candid in telling him that she had practically *forced*
the Chief Steward to seat her at this table tonight. Not that her
husband didn't rate it. After all, he *had* been a vice president of the

California Chemical Bank and Trust Company once upon a time, before those wretched employees had put the bank in its grave. Unfortunately, Ralph couldn't make it to dinner tonight, too much of that heavenly buffet lunch . . .

"But I suppose what you're *really* wondering about, Captain," she said, when they got to the cherries jubilee, "is why I just about *invited* myself to your table tonight."

"To be exposed to my charms, I haven't the slightest doubt," Charles Girodt replied.

"Well, yes, of course, *that,* but not exactly," she said, without so much as a smile. "You see, there's something I just *have* to tell you, I simply must get it off my mind."

"Go on. Do it, Mrs. Wabash. And make it something delicious."

"Captain Girodt," she said, lowering her voice to a gossipy half-whisper, "will you promise not to laugh at me if I tell you something very, very foolish?"

"I will be the perfect gentleman. I promise."

"And you will never say *I* told you this."

He smiled. "Never."

"Oh dear, all right then. Well . . . I *overheard* something today. I have this nasty habit, Ralph despises me for it, this nasty habit of listening to what other people are saying, eavesdropping is what it really is . . ."

"My life would be so dull without it," Girodt sighed.

"Anyway," Helen Wabash went on, "this afternoon, doing my three times around the deck to work off some of this excess flesh, I stopped to catch my breath, and found myself under a cabin window that was slightly open. Well, I wasn't exactly *under* it. I moved over to *be* under it, because I heard voices. I can't help myself, Captain . . ."

"So few of us can, Mrs. Wabash."

"This man, this particular man I have in mind, then said something that shocked me so deeply, that I just *know* I never heard him say it. He said to someone, I don't know who, I only saw *him,* he said, 'The passengers must never know what we are planning, or they will fight back like an army, and lives will be lost.' That's what he said." She nodded grimly. " 'Lives will be lost.' I know it sounds silly, and hysterical, but that's what I heard him say."

The Captain looked at her without expression, aware that he was blinking rapidly, and rather more so than usual. Keeping his voice utterly calm, he said, "Did I understand you to say that you saw the gentleman?"

"That's right," she said eagerly. "I moved closer to the window and caught a glimpse of him and then walked away as quickly as possible. I was so upset. I do hope it teaches me not to *listen* to people."

He patted her hand and smiled reassuringly. "You did no harm, Mrs. Wabash, believe me. And I am sure that what you heard, or imagined you heard, meant absolutely nothing at all."

"Oh, I'm so glad to hear that, Captain. And I'm so relieved that I finally got the chance to tell you."

"I am too," he said.

He waited several moments, until the brandy that he had quickly downed had had a chance to take some effect, before he offered a casual query. "Do you think you might possibly describe the gentleman you overheard? Perhaps he is someone I have met."

"Oh, I can do better than that," said Helen Wabash. "There he is right over there, sitting at that corner table, with the dark hair and the horn-rimmed glasses and the nice suntan? You see him, with that attractive woman in pale yellow?"

Girodt peered across the room, waited for several waiters to move out of his line of sight, and gazed with studied casualness at the man who was Craig Dunleavy.

"Ah, yes." He nodded. "Yes. Definitely the dangerous type." He turned to her and chuckled. "So is the lovely lady." He chuckled again.

Helen Wabash chuckled.

Charles Girodt began to laugh.

Helen Wabash laughed even louder.

When dinner had ended and they rose from the table, Girodt was sure that he had appeared convincingly unconcerned. And Helen Wabash was just as sure that he would be doing something about it.

Which is what she told her husband Ralph and the others in the small group that met in Herb and Harriet Kleinfeld's stateroom a little later that night.

The request from the Commandant of the S.S. *Marseille* for a meeting with Craig Dunleavy came even earlier than they had expected, at 9:50 p.m.

The plan went into action immediately.

CHAPTER FOUR

———————

CHARLES GIRODT poured brandy for them both, set a small snifter on the table beside Dunleavy's chair, then took his own with him around the desk and sat down. Dunleavy busied himself lighting his pipe as the other man took a sip of the brandy and scrutinized him. Neither was really sparring silently, nor stalling for time. Girodt felt that the darkly handsome American seated before him was neither curious about nor troubled by the summons from the ship's master. Girodt had not yet classified him as an adversary, but he sensed that if he should turn out to be one, he could possibly be formidable. Dunleavy was neither nervous nor apprehensive, but within himself he was aware of the kind of stage fright that often spurs a performer on to giving the best that is in him. The talking, the dreaming, and the planning had been one thing. This was entirely different. For Dunleavy, this was the first of many moments of truth he knew he would be facing in the days to come. He did not intend to fail, for he knew that beyond failure lay nothing but death for all of them, death of the spirit and probably of the body, too.

"Mr. Dunleavy, I am embarrassed," Charles Girodt said. "A

member of my crew has reported to me that he overheard you saying something to the effect that there was some sort of plan you were contemplating which might be considered unfriendly to the passengers, and could possibly lead to violence and the loss of life. Forgive me. This is all quite ludicrous. Hearsay should be inadmissible even in a conversation such as this. However, as commander of this vessel, I felt that I should at least go through the formality of meeting you and having this brief chat with you, so that I might dismiss the matter and sleep with the easy conscience of a glorified sailor who has done his duty. I am sorry. You may laugh if you wish, and I will understand. But that is the sole reason for my asking you to come here at this awkward hour."

Dunleavy sucked on the pipe several times to keep it from going out. For a few moments, the only other sounds in the Captain's quarters were the soft whoosh of the air conditioning and the almost imperceptible creaking of the giant ship as it struggled with the sea. He took a bit of brandy, set the glass down beside him and looked at his host. "I and my colleagues have no intention of harming your passengers, Captain Girodt," he said in as level a voice as he could manage. "As far as we are concerned, there will be no unpleasantness, no violence whatsoever, just as long as we receive complete cooperation from *you,* Captain, and from every member of the staff and crew of the *Marseille,* and from the executives of the French Atlantic Line in Paris and New York and wherever else they may be."

Charles Girodt nodded slowly and mechanically, refusing to accept the message that his vital organs were sending him, that the life he had known and loved for fifty-four years had suddenly ended, to be followed now by something unknown and vaguely dreadful.

"I assure you, Mr. Dunleavy," he replied as pleasantly as possible, "that cooperation comes as naturally as breathing to those of us fortunate enough to be in the employ of the Compagnie Française. We are here to serve you. Whatever it will take to make this voyage an enjoyable one for you and your friends, you have only to ask for it."

"I take it then, Captain, that you would prefer we waste a little time here avoiding the inevitable truth. I'm perfectly agreeable to that," said Dunleavy, "if it will make things less painful for you.

You may not believe this, Captain Girodt, but I admire you and your kind immensely, and I want you to know that there is no personal animosity involved in what we intend to do."

Girodt found himself having increasing difficulty with the message from within. "Animosity," he said, trying to smile, and failing, "is the antithesis of the spirit we work so hard to engender on French Atlantic sailings. Animosity is for the unlucky souls on land. Would you like another spot of brandy, Mr. Dunleavy?"

"Really, Captain, why don't we get on with it?" Dunleavy could see the man's suffering. It was senseless to prolong it. Besides, he knew that, by now, the others had had sufficient time to do what had to be done.

Suddenly Girodt reached for one of the buzzers on his desk.

Just as quickly, Dunleavy said, "No, don't. I wouldn't."

Girodt withdrew his hand, and began to rub his face, as though he would wipe from it the expression of pain that was beginning to come to his features. "You mentioned 'cooperation,' Mr. Dunleavy. Perhaps you could be a little more explicit as to what you had in mind."

"I'd be very happy to, Captain." Craig Dunleavy got to his feet. He felt the need for space to move around in. "I suggest that you take notes on what I am about to tell you, so that there will be no misunderstandings." He pointed to the desk. "That pad should do the trick."

He waited while Girodt picked up a pen and flipped the pad open.

"Proceed, Mr. Dunleavy."

"I'll give you the short form first," Dunleavy said. "I and a group of colleagues—I will not tell you the number at this time, but it is sizeable and sufficient—have taken over your ship."

Charles Girodt tossed the pen on the desk and looked up at the American with an expression of annoyance and utter disbelief, trying to induce in himself the *conviction* of disbelief, as well. "Now, please," he said.

"I'm flattered by your attitude, Captain. It makes me feel that you consider what we have achieved, impossible."

"I have tried to be courteous, Mr. Dunleavy—"

"Just step to the porthole, Captain, and look out at the moon. Observe its position. Please. Do as I say."

Girodt stared at Dunleavy, then rose from his desk chair and went to the porthole.

"A half hour ago," said Dunleavy, "the moon was on the starboard side. Please observe it now on the portside."

"It means nothing," Girodt said with growing anger.

"My men," said Dunleavy quietly, "that is, those of us who are now in the wheelhouse and the chartroom, have arranged an alteration in the ship's course."

Without a word, Girodt moved swiftly to his desk, picked up one of several phones, pressed a button twice, and said, "This is the Commandant. Who is this?"

"First Officer Henri Ferret, sir," was the reply.

"Are there any unauthorized persons on the bridge right now?"

"Yes, Captain."

"How many?"

"Three, sir."

"I want them removed immediately."

"I'm afraid that will not be possible, Captain."

"Remove them, Ferret."

"They are armed, sir."

"All of them?"

"Affirmative."

"Have you changed the heading?"

"Yes, Captain."

"I gave no such order, Ferret."

"I know that, Captain."

"What is our new course?"

"Southeasterly, sir. One hundred forty-five degrees."

"Southeasterly . . ."

"Yes, Captain."

Girodt looked at the phone in his hand, then slammed it down on its cradle, uttering French obscenities he had not used in years. "Dunleavy," his voice grew hard, "I want you to remove those men from the bridge at once, and turn over their weapons to us immediately. There is still time to look upon this outrage as a practical joke, or something that was inspired by too much alcohol, and let it go at that. But any further tampering with the orderly running of this ship simply will not be countenanced. It is possible that you are unaware of the seriousness of the consequences."

"I'm sorry, Captain." Dunleavy shook his head wearily. "I just don't have the patience or the capacity for all this bullshit. First let me tell you that we have already seized all firearms on this ship, meaning you and your crew are defenseless, meaning it's idiotic for you to be standing there telling me what you will not countenance, meaning we have taken over. So will you sit down, Captain, and take up your pad and pen, Captain, and stop wasting time, because I have a lot to tell you. Go on, Captain. Don't make me take something out of my pocket and point it at you. I'd feel ridiculous."

Girodt's mouth tightened as he stared at the other man. Finally he turned, walked behind his desk, and sat down. "All right," he said coldly. "Give me the rest. Give me all of it. And then perhaps you will be good enough to get out of here, before I do something that you and I will both regret."

"Pad and pen, Captain. Save the threats for later."

"Get on with it," Girodt said.

Dunleavy relit his pipe, and paced as he talked. "The bridge, of course, is just one of the many vital centers that we have taken over. None has been overlooked. The communications room, for example, is now completely under our control. After I leave, I suggest you check on what I am telling you, just to satisfy your curiosity. All radio communications with your company stations and the home office in Paris will continue just as though nothing has happened. The same will apply to all contacts with ships at sea, coast guards, navies, marine radio, et cetera. It is absolutely mandatory, Captain, and I want you to put this down in capital letters, that no one, I repeat, no one in the world outside this ship must know that anything out of the ordinary is taking place on board the *Marseille*. Ship-to-shore telephone calls will be permitted, but our people assigned to monitor your switchboard will cut off any call that carries even a trace of unwanted suggestion. Also, teletype service to and from the ship must be carried on by your communications officers as usual. We want no passengers to wonder why they are not receiving stock market reports and baseball scores and other news of the world. Until such time as it suits our purpose, we want the passengers and the officials of the French Atlantic Line and all the rest of the world to believe that the *Marseille* is on course and on schedule. Am I clear up to this point, Captain Girodt?"

"Painfully so," said Girodt. "But it is all so pathetic and foolhardy and doomed to failure. I would have only to make sure that you did not get back to your stateroom alive, and it would all be over."

"You can kill me or any one of us, any six of us, any ten of us," said Dunleavy, "and there will be a dozen more immediately taking our place. You see, Captain, I have a distinct advantage over you. I know how many of us there are. You don't. I know *who* we are. You don't. We are spread out throughout this ship, anonymous, unspectacular passengers, all of us highly trained, heavily armed, and almost excessively motivated. I don't want you, or your crew, or any of the passengers, to make any fatal miscalculations as to the seriousness of our intentions. In fact, for the time being, you must say absolutely nothing to the passengers, and the crew must be so instructed. My people have in their wardrobes all the uniforms with which to disguise themselves as staff and crew when necessary. Nothing unusual need come to the attention of the passengers if you cooperate. What is important for you to keep in mind is that everyone on board this ship is to be considered a hostage to our success. Not only will we trade a life for a life if it should come to that, but we will summarily dispose of anyone who opposes us. Is that understood?"

"And if it is not understood, if I tell you that everything you have been saying has gone right over my head, what will you do, shoot me, Mr. Dunleavy, or perhaps hang me, for having insufficient intelligence to grasp the pretentious posturings of madmen? You and your people are dangerous, simple-minded children who are to be treated as such. It takes a very special kind of retarded mentality to believe that a ship as large and as distinctive as the *Marseille* can sail off course into the southern Atlantic without being seen and recognized by a dozen passing cruise ships and freighters and Lord knows how many aircraft and naval vessels."

Dunleavy smiled, but there was no warmth in it. "Forgive me for saying so, but your beloved *Marseille* is a spit in the ocean. Nevertheless, we still would have considered the slim chance of her being sighted as unacceptable to our plans, if we hadn't known that her sister ship, the *Bordeaux,* has been sent off into the South Atlantic during this week and the next for a secret trial run."

"You cannot know that," Girodt shouted, feeling suddenly betrayed by he knew not whom. "No one can know that. Not even I am supposed to know that."

"But you do," said Dunleavy with maddening calm. "And if you know it, why can't I know it? Why can't one of my people know someone in Nice whose brother is a member of the shakedown crew? And if I know it, I can assure you that any ship's officer in the entire Atlantic who is worth his salt must know it."

"Wrong. You are wrong," said Girodt.

"I would hate to think so," said Dunleavy, "after all the trouble we have gone to to *spread* this so-called secret, Captain."

Girodt refused to give him the satisfaction of a comment.

"But just to be doubly certain," Dunleavy added, "my men will be removing the illustrious name of the *Marseille* from the bows and between the funnels during the night. We haven't decided yet whether to repaint the funnels. There's something demeaning about that, as though we were in possession of a stolen car."

The anguish he felt at this mutilation of his ship was more than Girodt could conceal. He placed his head in his hands. "Why, why are you doing all this to us?"

"You will be given that information at the proper time," Dunleavy replied. "For the time being, it is sufficient for you to know that we are doing what we are doing in order to secure for ourselves a new life, far from the United States, in an extradition-proof country that will be delighted to have us. Are there any other questions, before I rejoin my wife and friends?"

"Yes," said Girodt in a weary voice, removing his hands from his face. "What shall I do if the passengers learn of this and we have mass hysteria on our hands?" Immediately he loathed himself for having asked this man anything.

"Tonight you must hold a series of meetings with every member of your staff and crew," Dunleavy said. "You must tell them my requirements and restrictions and the need for total secrecy, and, if you will pardon the word, *obedience*. Do that, and everything will go smoothly, and you and I won't find ourselves having to deal with the insanity of frightened people. That could be terribly messy, don't you agree, Captain?"

Charles Girodt was lost for a moment in a nightmarish vision of weeping women, screaming children and shouting men, alternately falling before firing squads or hurtling over the side into the sea. He came to with a start.

"Yes . . . yes . . ." He rose to his feet, intending to say, that will be all. But it came out, "Will that be all?"

Dunleavy smiled. "I hope not, Captain. I hope we have a pleasant, sunny day tomorrow. Good night."

He walked out, and Girodt stared after him, thinking, how dare the son of a bitch smile at me.

Then he pressed the button on his desk connecting him with his aide and said into the speakerphone: "Come in here at once."

They moved to the music of the Latin Quarter band, facing each other, looking into each other's eyes, their bodies undulating several feet apart. But before long, unlike the others on the dance floor of the discothèque, they moved irresistibly into each other's arms and locked their bodies tightly together. She clung to him as much to steady the dizziness of the three martinis in her head as to feel the rising hardness he was pressing into her.

"I'm so giddy I can hardly stand," Julie Berlin murmured. "D'you mind if I use your feet instead?"

"You should lie down," said Harold Columbine, brushing her ear with his lips, "and I know just the place."

He kissed her neck, and Julie wanted to tell him to be careful, someone might see them, but she didn't really want him to be careful, and besides, the only one who might see them together was Billy, and he was tight asleep in their stateroom up in First Class. It had been so easy to wait for him to go to sleep, and to leave an untimed note, just in case, saying she'd be in the reading room getting off some letters. Picking up Harold Columbine at the bar of the Montmartre Cafe, or maybe it was *he* who had picked *her* up, and following him to the relative safety of Tourist Class, had been almost as easy. Once she had had a couple of drinks and had gotten over the first shock of discovering who this man with the hungry eyes really was, she seemed to stop thinking about anything. She was all feeling, mostly erotic.

"My head is between my legs," she mused, half aloud, swaying to the music.

"Is that an observation or an invitation?" he asked.

"Mind your own business," she said, smiling to herself.

"All right," he said, stealing a glance at his wristwatch. Almost twelve-thirty. Time to make the move. Already his balls were aching from the hard-on in his jockey shorts. In all the years of his occasional prison breaks to freedom and the right to travel solo, he had never fallen into anything quite as quickly, smoothly, and easily as he had tonight with this slick little number. True, she wasn't stacked in a way that could have made it on the line at the Sands, but she was most definitely a looker, and she was married, she was safe, and she was asking for it. She might even, who knows, be a fantastic lay.

"Let's go to my room," he said, "and try on a nightcap for size."

The words slurred from her lips. "Harold, are you planning to put me in your next dirty best-seller?" Listen to me, she thought, pissed to the eyeballs. If Billy saw me now, or even heard me, he'd be appalled.

Fuck 'im.

"I'll make that decision," Harold Columbine was saying, "after you and I do a rough draft tonight."

"D'you like me, Harold? D'you like me a lot?"

"Well, I'll tell you, it's this way . . ." He took her hand from his shoulder, loosened his grip on her back, moved back a few inches and guided her hand down to where his body had been pressed to hers. She kept her hand there, squeezing ever so slightly.

"Oh my God," she said with admiration.

"Four-sixteen on the Upper Deck," he murmured. "You go first. I'll be there in ten minutes."

"Oh my God."

He pulled her hand away and shoved his stateroom key into it. "Go."

She kissed him with parted lips and broke away from him. He stood on the edge of the dimly lit dance floor, less to watch her slim hips weaving their way past tables to the exit than to give his erection time to acquire a low profile before he braved the journey himself. But for once in his middle-aged life, gravity was failing to make a dent in his lust. Her hand, that's what it was, he told himself. This one has more in her left hand than Ruth had in her whole body.

The dance number ended. He had to move off the floor. And though he stood out like a sore thumb (some thumb, eh kid?), he managed to make his way across the room and run the gauntlet unobserved. It was when he found himself in the brightly lighted corridor outside, only a few feet away from two overdressed ladies waiting for their husbands to emerge from the men's room, that he quickly decided to go in the wrong direction rather than walk his conspicuous self right past their eyes.

Less than five minutes later, realizing that he was hopelessly lost, and by now consumed with an overpowering desire to be in his stateroom biting the hand that had fed him, he chose to seek directions right then and there, no matter what, no matter that the door marked COMMUNICATIONS was also marked STAY OUT. And so abruptly did he barge in that the two men holding ugly handguns on the officers in the radio room had little chance to move the weapons out of view before he was upon them.

"Whoops . . . I'm sorry," he said with a sinking heart, knowing it was too late to be sorry even before he saw the expressions on their faces.

The great liner steamed southeastward through the moonlit sea, its many-thousand lights rivaling the jewel-encrusted sky above. The soft slow roll of the ship and the faint hypnotic vibration in its walls made it easy for Julie Berlin to stay deep in the dreams she was having on the double bed in Harold Columbine's stateroom. It was past three before the gin wore off and she awoke. She sprang from the bed, startled, turned on the lights, looked at her wristwatch and fought down instant panic. She glanced about.

"Harold?"

She looked in the bathroom. "Hello?"

Not in the parlor either.

She felt under her skirt. Pantyhose intact. She pulled them down a little, explored between her legs. Dry, clean, untouched. I'll be damned, she thought. Memory flooded back. The miserable bastard had given her his key just to get rid of her. In a flash of faulty vision, she saw him plucking another, more voluptuous woman from the dance floor, taking her to *her* cabin. Someone would pay for this . . .

Her head was splitting, her mouth dry and sour. She let herself out into the eye-stabbing lights of the corridor, mercifully deserted, and made her way back to her own suite. Billy was snoring softly where she had left him hours before. She peeled off her clothes, threw them into a closet, turned out the lights, crawled into bed and, before falling asleep, swore that she would get Billy for this tomorrow.

CHAPTER FIVE

IN A SMALL stucco building at Audierne on the west coast of France, Bernard Delade got up from his operating position, walked over to the windows and opened the Venetian blinds slightly so that he could look out. Squinting in the morning sun that hit his eyes, he let his gaze wander over the vast antenna farm that rose from the sprawling acreage almost to the edge of the cliffs overlooking the sea. He peered intently at the V-beam antenna that pointed west toward the first-stage checkpoints of the North Atlantic run of the ships of the Compagnie Française on the New York to Le Havre route. Both legs of the V-beam appeared to be perfectly normal. Closing the Venetian blinds, Delade went back to his radio position and sat down. The strange flutter, the low S-meter reading on the signals coming from the *Marseille* during its just-completed position report, had probably been due to one of the many unpredictable phenomena brought on these days by the degraded sun-spot cycle, Delade decided. There was no reason, as yet, for him to suspect that the *Marseille,* plunging through untroubled waters at well over thirty knots, had already moved out of the extremely narrow receiving and transmitting lobe of the highly directional V-beam array.

The position report which Delade now relayed to Paris—it had originated under duress from the communications room of the ship—was inaccurate by almost four hundred nautical miles.

That same morning, Filomena Mandrati, a short, buxom Milanese girl of twenty-six who was well into her second year as a chambermaid in Tourist Class, did something she never should have done and would never do again: she allowed herself to be coaxed into having a snack between meals. Filomena had been working hard at her diet, starving herself, denying herself, robbing herself of the joys of eating, all to make Enrico happy. Her sweet loving little busboy in the Vendôme dining room had her completely under his spell. Anything Enrico wanted, Filomena would do for him, and there were many secret places on the vast *Marseille* where they met late at night for just that purpose . . . to please Enrico.

"Come. You must taste it. I insist," Mrs. Gwendolyn Parker had said to Filomena, first placing the croissant on a little plate, then pouring an extra cup of hot tea.

The pretty blond lady from California had been so friendly to Filomena that it had been agonizingly difficult to say no, much as Filomena had tried.

"He will be angry, he will beat me," she had tried to make a joke of it.

"Enrico would beat you?"

"*Sì, sì.* He wants me to be as skinny like him, like a little stick."

She shouldn't have talked so much, but the American lady had been such a fine listener, sitting there daintily eating her breakfast, that it had been hard for Filomena to stop babbling. First she had told her about her mother and her father and her uncles and aunts and the five brothers and four sisters, and then she had told her how ashamed she was to be weighing one hundred and sixty-one pounds, and that had led to mentioning Enrico, and before she knew it she had found herself revealing how Enrico had been on the catwalk deep in the hull last night, and how he had seen what looked like a chain of explosives wired together, but he would never say a word to anyone because he had been down there to visit his secret supply of marijuana, which he kept hidden there, and she just knew that someday they would find out about him and then it would all be over for her and her dear Enrico. Oh, Enrico would be so angry if he knew what she had told to a perfect stranger.

His last name? Senestro. Enrico Senestro, Signora Parker.

"You will not report him? They will discharge him if they know he have the grass. He will go to jail."

"Don't worry, child, of course not." Gwendolyn Parker had smiled reassuringly. And that was when she had begun to insist that Filomena share some of her breakfast.

There was no hope now for the fat little Milanese girl. As much as she tried to busy herself, patting the bed pillows over and over, she knew that she would not have the strength to say no. It was even possible that, before she left here to straighten up the cabin next door, she would gobble up all three of the delicacies that remained on the silver tray.

"Here you are, Filomena." Gwendolyn Parker handed the little plate to her. "Just taste that, and then let me hear you say no." She withheld the cup of tea momentarily.

"Grazie."

Filomena stared at the crescent-shaped roll. She picked it up slowly, trying hard to appear disinterested, even as she was already anticipating the sweet, flaky, buttery taste of it. She looked at the American lady with a little smile of embarrassment, and then brought the croissant to her lips. Her mouth opened, and with a secret thrill of abandon, she took the tip of the croissant into it and caressed it with her tongue as her teeth came together and she bit a piece off.

The look that came instantly to her eyes was so filled with surprise and unbearable agony that Gwendolyn Parker had to turn away for the few seconds it took for the girl, in utter silence, to fall dead on the carpeted floor.

Gwendolyn Parker walked swiftly to the closed bathroom door and rapped on it. "George?"

The door opened and her husband emerged. He was a wispy-haired man of forty-eight with a small mustache and pale blue eyes. He quickly knelt beside the body on the floor, then rose and looked inquiringly at his wife. In a trembling voice, she started to tell him what he had to know, and continued as the two of them went to opposite sides of the bed and began to pull the top sheet out from under the covers.

"He accidentally stumbled on it last night. Senestro. Enrico Senestro. A busboy in our dining room . . ."

"Got it."

They brought the sheet over to the body and began to wind it into a shroud.

"She's the only one he's told so far."

"You better finish this," George Parker said. "I'll go take care of him."

He rose, went to the closet, took out his jacket and slipped it on. Before going to the door, he came over and kissed his wife on the forehead and patted her hair gently.

"Come on, Gwennie. Come on now . . ."

"Be careful," she said to him. "For God's sake, George, please . . ."

She waited until the door closed behind him. Then, as her hands continued to wind the sheet around the soft, full-breasted, still-warm body, she let herself go and began to sob.

Despite the explicitness of Craig Dunleavy's instructions the night before, Charles Girodt had decided against notifying his entire crew from top to bottom. There was no predicting how some of them would react, particularly some of the more temperamental types in the galleys and in the engine room. He could not yet bring himself to risk hysteria, emotional collapse, violence, and ultimately the immediate safety of his passengers. And so he had done what had seemed to him the most sensible thing to do. He had assembled in his quarters now those members of his staff who actually ran the ship and ran the crew.

He waited patiently while his Staff Captain, Andre Leboux, earnestly delivered the results of the morning lifeboat drill, using his customary verbal flourishes and dramatizations. While the passengers had been quite cooperative during the drill, Leboux reported, and had moved with pleasing alacrity, the readout on the Orion 98 computer in the wheelhouse showed an elapsed time—from first alarm to all lifeboats theoretically filled, in the water, and safely clear of the ship—of 13 minutes, 4.8 seconds, almost two minutes longer than the record time of 11 minutes, 9.3 seconds, set by the passengers and crew of the *Marseille* on a westward crossing the previous year.

Charles Girodt congratulated Leboux for a good performance, then promptly addressed himself to the others, and told them, as briefly but as thoroughly as possible, all he knew of the distasteful circumstances that had befallen the *Marseille*, realizing that some of the men probably knew as much as he did already, perhaps even more. Present, in addition to Staff Captain Leboux, and listening to it all with, he thought, admirable calm, were Chief Radio Officer Christain Specht, Chief Engineer Pierre Demangeon, Chief Purser Emile Vergnaud, Chief Medical Officer Yves Chabot, First Officer Henri Ferret, Second Officer Jacques Dulac, and Third Officer Lucien Plessier.

"I will welcome any questions, and any suggestions you may have," said the master of the *Marseille* when he had finished.

"Sir," the Chief Engineer was the first to speak, "suppose this Dunleavy is bluffing. How can we be certain that he and whoever else may be working with him will actually use force if we oppose him?"

"I can throw some light on that if I may," said Chief Radio Officer Specht.

"Please do," said Captain Girodt.

"Last night, one of the passengers, a gentleman from First Class named Columbine, stumbled into the communications room by mistake. My men have reported to me that he was struck a violent blow on the back of his skull and taken away. They seemed pessimistic about Mr. Columbine's immediate future. Also, I would like to add *this* to what Captain Girodt has told us: the efficiency and thoroughness with which these gangsters have taken over my department is astonishing. I daresay they know more about the equipment, the procedures, the frequencies used, than my own men do. We are not dealing with dilettantes. Let's not fool ourselves."

"Captain Girodt," Second Officer Jacques Dulac raised his hand briefly and received a nod. "There are well over fifteen hundred males among the crew and passengers. Why can't we seal off this group that threatens us, less than two hundred, you estimate? Why can't we corner them in one section of the ship and either lock them up or throw them overboard?"

"How are you going to identify them, Dulac?" countered Girodt. "They are passengers like all the rest. They never appear in groups of more than two or three. Sometimes they masquerade as members of the crew, in uniforms, wigs, spectacles, mustaches. If you can give me their names and their accommodations, I will try to answer your question."

"It is obvious then," said Jacques Dulac, "that the first priority for all of us is to devise some way of smoking them out."

There was a knock on the door.

"Come in," Girodt called out irritably.

Leon Carpentier, the Captain's aide, poked his head into the room, gulped at the sight of so much gold braid. "I'm sorry, sir," he stammered.

"What is it?"

"Several things, sir. A lady, sir, a passenger from First Class, a Mrs. Berlin, is waiting outside, and also—"

"I can't see anyone now, Carpentier. We'll get in touch with her . . ."

"Yes, I've already told her that—"

"Good. Then if you'll excuse us—"

"There's a phone call, sir. On that extension, sir. I told the gentleman you were unavailable, but he assured me that you would want to speak to him. Mr. Dunleavy, sir."

"Yes, thank you, that will be all, Carpentier." Girodt waited for the aide to withdraw, then, after a glance at the men gathered before him in the room, he picked up the phone. "Captain Girodt here."

"Good morning, Captain," said Craig Dunleavy.

"I find nothing good about it," said Girodt.

"My people," said Dunleavy, "have certain indications that you haven't yet followed my advice regarding the notification of your entire crew. I'm sure you were planning to get to it some time today, Captain, but just in case you weren't, I thought it only fair to let you know that we have selected, at random, ten of your lesser crew members, deckhands and cabinboys, I believe, to be disposed of in the event that you haven't followed my advice by two o'clock this afternoon. Understood, Captain?"

Girodt gripped the phone as though he would break it in two. "Yes. Yes. Understood."

"Also, I want you to know that none of us was happy about having to get rid of the little Italian girl and her boyfriend, Senestro. Please don't bother to look for them, because they are truly gone. I see no virtue in their deaths, unless you care to set them up as an example to the rest of your personnel . . ."

Girodt felt rage overtaking him. "I must hang up now," he said.

"*À bientôt,*" said Dunleavy.

Girodt put the phone back in the cradle and waited for his pounding heart to slow down before speaking. Finally, without looking at anyone, he said, "We are now dealing with murderers." The other men stared down at their hands, tightlipped. "Also, we have just been presented with an ultimatum," Girodt continued. "The entire crew must be given the whole story of the takeover by two o'clock. I leave it to each of you to see that the men and women underneath you are so informed. They must be made to understand that the passengers are to be kept in the dark. Plessier, you will contact the stewards."

"Yes, Captain," said the Third Officer.

"There is no need for me to go into the ugly details of this ultimatum, because we are going to do as we are told. Until I or any one of you discovers a reasonable alternative, that shall be our policy. At the same time, it is vital that we keep in mind the ultimate outcome: each and every one of these pigs will be either at the bottom of the ocean or standing before a firing squad in Paris when this is over. Remind me, please, that I said this to you. Now, is there anything else to be discussed?"

Yves Chabot, the ship's Chief Medical Officer, tried to let in a ray of hope. "I realize that, at this moment, with the exception of Craig Dunleavy and probably his wife, the identities of the conspirators are unknown to us. But if we should ever *gain* that knowledge, I would like to remind you that our hospital, which has facilities to save lives, is perfectly capable of using those facilities to *take* lives, too. My lethal medications and my hypodermic needles will be awaiting your ingenuity, gentlemen."

On that grim note, Charles Girodt ended the meeting.

But he was aware of a vague, disturbing aftertaste within himself. Had it been the commanding presence of Yves Chabot? Had he once again imagined that the probing gaze of his Chief Medical Officer had been directed at him too intently throughout the meeting, as though looking through him, into him, to see if he was measuring up under stress? Girodt had never told Yves Chabot, or anyone else on his staff, the truth behind his leave of absence. Why did he persist in reading suspicion in the doctor's eyes? He must stop this immediately. He must stop projecting his own secret fears about himself onto others.

Within fifteen minutes, the Captain found himself gazing across his desk at Julie Berlin, trying valiantly to keep his attention on her monologue, which was one long complaint about her husband. Girodt's mind kept wandering to the more urgent matters at hand. The effort to pull himself back into this room was indeed exhausting.

"Mrs. Berlin," he said, with weariness in his voice, "I do not mean to sound unsympathetic or uncooperative, but I cannot help thinking that you came here for a reason other than to inform me that your eight years of marriage have been less than idyllic. I have a married daughter in Avignon who is probably the same age as you, and one of the things I like least about her visits to Paris is her incessant quarreling with her husband, Paul. You remind me very much of my Marie. However, whereas I do nothing to help my daughter, I shall do everything I can to help you, provided, my dear Mrs. Berlin, that you do tell me exactly what it is you want."

"All right, I'm sorry. Perhaps I have been wandering all over the map." Wandering, hell, Julie, you've been crawling all over the place on your hands and knees. This uniformed gentleman isn't Billy, snoring through life, and he isn't wet-lipped Harold Columbine either, who didn't even have the decency to show up in the dining room for breakfast so she could vent a little spleen in his lecherous face. She'd get *him* later. "Plain and simple, it's this, Captain. Dr. Berlin, my husband, has smuggled something into our cabin which is illegal for him to use on this ship, and I want you to take it away from him right away, confiscate it, throw it overboard, anything, as long as you take it away from him before he gets a chance to use it."

Charles Girodt frowned. He really did not want to hear the rest of this. He could not stand any more surprises today. But he had to ask the question. "Smuggled what, Mrs. Berlin? I must take away from him *what,* Mrs. Berlin?"

"His Atlas-210," she said.

Girodt blinked. "His what?"

"His Atlas-210, the newest thing in amateur radio transceivers. This one happens to be fiendishly compact, weighs all of seven pounds. All my husband's ham radio friends own one. It's their favorite toy. They never make a move without their little Atlas-210s, the bloody bores. They talk to each other from their cars and they talk to each other from their boats. Sometimes I think the only way I can get Billy to talk to *me* is if *I* get an Atlas-210 myself. Would you believe that on our seventh wedding anniversary—"

"Excuse me," Girodt cut her short. "You say your husband was planning to use this equipment on the *Marseille?*"

"Oh, he'll deny it, you can be sure, just like he told me he wasn't going to take it along. But I know darned well that's his plan. I heard him making schedules with ham friends all over the East and West Coast, New York and California, that is. I heard him say that he was going to bootleg, that's the expression they use for illegal transmissions. You see, he couldn't get the French government to give him permission to operate on a French liner. He can do it on an American boat just by using his American ham call letters, and signing maritime mobile. But no dice on the *Marseille.* So you better take it away from him before he and I wind up in a French prison or something. I'll show you where he's got it hidden, and he never has to know that I ever even said hello to you. Okay, Captain?"

Charles Girodt felt the blood rushing through his veins. I must not get unduly excited, he told himself. "If I understand you correctly, this radio . . . this . . . this transceiver *sends* signals as well as receives them, Mrs. Berlin?"

"All over the world, if conditions are right," Julie said. "It's a transmitter and a receiver combined in one little box about nine inches wide and three inches high. When we were in Alaska on a ha-ha vacation, he used to talk to some idiot in the Virgin Islands every night, usually just as I was ready to go out to dinner. And in Moorea, while other people were scuba diving, *he* was talking to good old Vlad in Moscow like every single day. And what did they talk about? Their Atlas-210s. What else?"

Charles Girodt rose to his feet abruptly, as though shocked into action. "Mrs. Berlin . . ."

"Yes, Captain?" She rose too.

"I want you to promise me that you will say absolutely nothing about this visit, or its subject matter, to anyone on this ship, including your husband."

"But . . . but what have I done wrong?"

"You have done nothing wrong. It may turn out that you have done something that is very, very right. But I need time to handle this. I cannot discuss it now. You have my assurance that everything will work out to your satisfaction. May I have your promise, please, that you will say nothing for the time being?"

"I really don't understand, but . . . yes . . . all right. I promise. Okay?"

"Thank you." Girodt took her by the elbow, led her to the door. "Thank you, Mrs. Berlin."

"You're welcome." Julie shrugged, thoroughly bewildered. "I mean, it's fine with me."

"You will be hearing from me, Mrs. Berlin. Good day."

As soon as she had left, Girodt closed the door, moved to his desk, picked up the phone and dialed the communications room. Immediately after the phone was picked up at the other end, Girodt heard a telltale click.

"Hello?"

"Captain Girodt here. I wish to speak to the Chief Radio Officer."

"Moment." A pause, and then: "Christain Specht speaking."

"Christain, would you care to join me for a game of chess, or are you too busy now? I need something to take my mind off our current problems."

The pause at the other end was barely noticeable. "Very well, sir. I'd be delighted."

"Good. I await you." He heard Specht hang up. Then he heard the faint click again.

We will outsmart you bastards and destroy you, he told himself with a surge of conviction, as he placed the phone back in its cradle. He could feel the first faint stirrings of the manic onset, but he did not care. He would destroy Dunleavy personally, with his own two hands.

CHAPTER SIX

SITTING IN HIS OFFICE on the twenty-second floor of the glass-and-steel Tour Française in the new executive heart of Paris, never quite unmindful of the cruel fact that he was on the twenty-*second* floor of La Compagnie Française Atlantique and not on Françat's topmost twenty-*sixth* floor, Georges Sauvinage took several deep sucks on the fragrant cigar between his thick lips and decided that Fidel Castro was good for filling humidors if nothing else. An excess of food, which Sauvinage had placed in his mouth over the years to try to assuage his many dissatisfactions, had given his forty-year-old face and body the soft, gross contours of a practicing sensualist, which unfortunately he was not. He looked down now at the litter of unfinished business on his bleached oak desk, belched softly in fond farewell to the chocolate mousse with which he had terminated his lunch, and took up the first piece of paper his pudgy hand led him to. It was another telex.

Why did they bother him with this trivia? To Sauvinage everything was trivia. Nothing had importance. It was the only way the Assistant to the Director General of the French Atlantic Line had found to take the pain out of his own sense of unimportance. Long Havana cigars, Cardin suits, lunches at the Tour d'Argent, and an eight-cylinder, silver-gray Jensen Interceptor, none of which he could afford, somehow did not quite do the trick. It was also necessary for him to diminish everything that came across his desk as unworthy of his attention. He stared with disinterest at the sheet of paper in his hand, vaguely irritated by the jackhammer noises of the ever-rising new towers of La Défense, and the ever-increasing traffic on the Boulevard Circulaire far below. Some day he would defy destiny's gravity and rise four floors into an office with sealed windows and thick carpeting and original oil paintings, and, of course, a voluptuous young secretary with an overpowering interest in married men, especially fat ones.

The telex was from Bernard Delade at the Audierne installation. Sauvinage grumbled the moment he saw the signature. The little radio man was an obsequious bore with big feet and depressingly cheap clothing. Sauvinage had had to put up with him for an entire luncheon during the man's Christmas holiday in Paris. The message was:

HAVE INTERCEPTED REPORTS FROM SHIPS OF GREEK-AMERICAN, CUNARD WHITE STAR AND LIBERIA NATIONAL SIGHTING THE S.S. MARSEILLE SOUTHWARD BOUND VICINITY 36 N., 65 W., 1200 ZULU. INASMUCH AS THIS MUST HAVE BEEN THE S.S. BORDEAUX, AN UNDERSTAND-ABLE ERROR, IT PLACES THE BORDEAUX COMPLETELY OFF TRIAL RUN COURSE AS FORWARDED TO ME MONDAY LAST. PLEASE ADVISE NEW BORDEAUX PLANS. DELADE.

How the hell would *he* know what they were up to with the *Bordeaux*? Since when did they tell things to the Assistant to the Director?

Sauvinage chewed angrily on the wet cigar as he scribbled his reply on a white pad.

NO COMPREHENSIVE CHANGE IN BORDEAUX PLANS. TRIAL RUNS ARE AT CAPTAIN'S DISCRETION. SAUVINAGE.

He tore the page off and glanced at the message. At least it made sense without betraying his lack of information. He pressed a button on his desk, and when his secretary came in, he gave her the message to put on the telex. She was an aging, shapeless lump of a woman, and if Sauvinage hadn't let the mere sight of her immediately plunge him into new waves of self-pity, perhaps he might have been clear-headed enough to speculate, if only for a moment, that maybe the *Marseille,* off course, was indeed the *Marseille,* off course, and not the *Bordeaux.*

Couldn't she at least tint her hair and put that behind in a girdle?

The S.S. *Marseille,* its vivid orange and black funnels gleaming in the bright sunshine, glided swiftly through the soft swells of the Atlantic due north of Bermuda. The sea was becalmed by a gentle wind from the southwest, and visibility was good for at least twenty miles. Far off on the horizon, the skipper of a Norwegian freighter bound for Oslo swung his binoculars onto the giant passenger liner to the northwest, and the thought passed through his mind that the huge vessel seemed to have no visible identification, either on its hull or on its topmost deck. But then the Norwegian quickly dismissed the idea as ridiculous and, taking out a handkerchief, he began to clean the outer lenses of his glasses.

Beside the swimming pool on the Sun Deck of that nameless passenger liner, Harry Grabiner, his age-lined face and shriveling body thoroughly anointed with Coppertone oil, lay back on the chaise and tried to adjust his position so that he could more comfortably get down to the business of judging his own private beauty contest. Twice a day, on these transatlantic crossings, if the weather was kind enough to permit, Grabiner would systematically select Miss Marseille of the Morning, and Miss Marseille of the Afternoon, from among the bikini-clad females in and about the pool. They received no prize other than a cherished place in Grabiner's overworked hall of fantasies. In the eleven years that the wizened, balding president of Grabiner & Goldstein had been traveling back and forth between New York and Paris, he had crowned upward of seventy-five beauty queens ranging in age from fifteen to fifty. Of these he had, in the hall of fantasies, fornicated with perhaps seventy-four of them. (A platinum-streaked doll of about thirty-eight had kept vanishing from his mind every time he had tried her. Finally he had figured out that she reminded him of his wife's sister.) Such harmless little pleasures as these helped relieve the monotony of Grabiner's frequent trips to the Paris dress market, and he felt himself unaccountably frustrated now, as he realized that there was no way to watch the pool from his familiar, favorite vantage point without having the sun shine with unbearable directness into his watery blue eyes.

This has never happened to me before, he thought. I *own* this pool, and my clear shot at the lovelies. For eleven years the July sun has been at my back for the morning festivities, and nobody has asked Harry Grabiner if they could move the sun around in the sky.

He propped himself up on an elbow and summoned a waiter. "Bring me a Bloody Mary," he said.

"Yes, m'sieur."

"And listen, do you have any idea about this ship being off course or something?"

The waiter, whose name was Philippe, turned pale, but it did not show in the sunshine. "I beg your pardon?"

"The sun, the sun's in the wrong place," Grabiner muttered. "I wanna know if this boat is off course."

"Ah, *that,* yes, m'sieur. We are undergoing a routine course correction to compensate for a change in ocean currents." And he hurried away to fill the order. The Chief Steward had told them, at the briefing, that now and then a passenger would be querying them. But he had had no idea that the question when put to him, and his untruthful answer, would frighten him so.

Harry Grabiner, grumbling, lay back on the chaise and closed his scorched eyes. The hell with Miss Marseille of the Morning. He'd wait for the afternoon, and screw just one today.

Anthony Palazone, formerly with the McDonnell Douglas Corporation, Al Tomlinson, erstwhile safety engineer for Rockwell International, and Carmen Ferrante, one-time draftsman for Texas Instruments, entered the final watertight compartment on the starboard side of the bow at 11:50 a.m., gaining access first through a lateral tunnel and then through a manhole that put them squarely into the fuel and water-storage tanks that made up the double bottom of the ship along its entire length. Their faces were darkened with coal dust, their shirts and hands properly begrimed. Anyone seeing them here would have had no reason to doubt that they were crewmen. The plastic doom, the detonating caps, and the coils of wire were concealed in the pails they carried, hidden beneath dirty rags.

The dozen watertight chambers that lay behind them, toward the stern, had already been properly treated on the starboard side for eventual destruction. So artfully had Palazone implanted the lethal mixture of PETN and chemite, encased in the innocuous-looking, grayish-white putty, and so cleverly had Tomlinson painted the thin-gauge wire to match the pipes and walls and sills and tanks behind which the plastic explosive materials were fastened, that it is doubtful whether anyone (except a most unfortunate busboy) would have located the devastating network even if he had known of its existence. So far, Carmen Ferrante had had no reason even to reach for the revolver in his pocket. Not a soul had come their way, and when they finished this compartment, they would have the satisfaction of knowing they were exactly at the halfway mark. One down, and the entire portside to go.

"I just thought of one," said Anthony Palazone, molding a handful of pentolite as though he were modeling clay. "We give this stuff the juice and it doesn't go bang, it just goes poof."

"I got a better one," said Carmen Ferrante. "It goes bang, the plates fly to hell, two million tons of water pour in, but instead of sinking in less than seventy seconds like the computer says, the ship stays afloat."

"How come? That doesn't make sense." Tomlinson had a sharp knife in his teeth and the wirecutter in his right hand.

"Who said it makes sense?"

"I know why it stays afloat," said Palazone. "Because of all the Ping-Pong balls on the Verandah Deck."

"Very funny, Tony," said Tomlinson, not laughing. "You know what Dunleavy would do if this stuff didn't sink the *Marseille?*"

"Yeah, he'd shoot himself," said Palazone.

"Uh-unh," said Tomlinson. "He'd shoot the computer."

"That's even funnier," said Palazone. He took out a handkerchief and wiped some of the sweat from his forehead.

She couldn't *stand* the way everyone was having such a blatantly visible good time. It wasn't enough that they were shooting clay pigeons or splashing around in a swimming pool or driving golf balls into a net or walking briskly along the Promenade Deck. They *laughed* so damned much. They were so ostentatiously *happy,* it just infuriated her. As she walked along the deck, conspicuously alone, she had just enough sanity left to know that she was in one of those irrational states of hers, one foot in, one foot out.

I'm feeling guilty for turning Billy and his Atlas in to the Captain, and I *should* feel guilty. I'm feeling guilty for what I wanted to do with that Columbine man last night, and I shouldn't, because we didn't *do* anything. Also, I'm feeling guilty because I know I'm not happy, the way all these other voyagers are, and I'm *supposed* to be happy, because I graduated from Smith, and from three years on the Charles Eames couch of Dr. Albert DeGrooning. No, it was none of that. It was much more simple: she was uneasy, uneasy because she hadn't really believed Billy when he had told her to have lunch *without* him today because his stomach felt funny. Billy never lied to her. Broken promises, yes, but lies, never. And he had lied to her today. And she would go on feeling uneasy and uncomfortable and unhappy about it until she found out exactly why he had done something that was *not like him at all.*

It must have been somewhere between age two and age three (she hadn't known it was happening, so she couldn't exactly have recorded the date) that little Juliette Harrison decided it was dangerous to be alive. She didn't know there was any other way you could be, like dead, because she hadn't heard about people-death yet. All she knew was, being alive as a little girl on this earth, actually in and around a twelve-room house in Mamaroneck, New York, you could do almost anything, it didn't seem to matter what, and end up feeling either wonderful, or scared or sick or angry or hurt or confused or sad. And you could never predict the result ahead of time.

Like, you run up behind Daddy and you shriek BOO! And he turns around quickly with that big smile on his face, and he lifts you way up in the air and laughs as loudly as you do, and you feel so *good*. And then sometimes you do BOO! behind Mommy, or Aunt Jessie, and they jump and turn and give you that fierce look that makes you all cold inside and they say don't DO that, they're so *angry,* and you feel *awful.* And when you do BOO! to Amy, who's even smaller than you are, she hits your face so hard you cry. You have to be very careful who you do BOO! to. It can be dangerous.

Or you kiss and you hug with Mommy and Daddy because you love them so much, and they kiss you and hug you right back and you can't stand it, it feels so warm and tingly. And then you kiss and you hug with your friend Jamie, because you love Jamie too, and your mommy and Jamie's mommy start yelling at you both, yelling stop that, Julie, Jamie, you bad boy, Julie, come *over* here, and you get *sick,* you're so bewildered and ashamed. Yes, you have to be very careful when you kiss and you hug, very careful about *everything* if you happen to be alive. There are so many surprises . . .

But that's the way we all grow up, Julie.

I know that, Doctor.

Then what are you trying to tell me?

That I think I married him because he was safe, predictable and safe.

Whom would you have preferred, someone you couldn't count on, someone you were afraid of, someone dangerous?

Maybe. Who knows? It's possible. But how will I ever know? I'd be too afraid to find out. I'd never take a chance like that. *You* know that, don't you?

Yes.

Of course you do. If you said no, you *don't* know that, I'd fall in a heap, it would be so out of character for you. Why do you think I *picked* you? This town is lousy with analysts. I sampled a half dozen. But most of them scared me. But you don't. You're like Billy. I know what you're going to say even before you say it . . .

You could sit home and do this all by yourself then, and save fifty dollars an hour.

Even the jokes are the same.

Why have you been afraid to have a child?

What?

I said, why have you been afraid to have a child?

Who said—? What do you mean *I've* been afraid? Where do you come off assuming it's been *my* doing?

What are you feeling right now?

Angry, isn't that apparent?

What else?

I'm frightened.

You've been married quite a few years now. Why haven't you had a child?

Didn't you hear me? I said I'm frightened.

Look at me, Julie.

I'm looking at you. You scare the shit out of me.

I thought I was so safe and predictable.

I was wrong. You're not. You're just like everybody else.

Like who?

Everybody. *Nobody* can be trusted. Everyone's dangerous. I've always known it. Even you, you son of a bitch. How *dare* you tell me it's been *my* doing. Billy has been the one, always. It was predictable. I knew it even before we got married. He'd never want a child. He'd want to *be* the child . . .

You knew that?

Yes.

He told you that?

He didn't have to tell me, I knew it.

And you married him?

Yes.

So why haven't you wanted a child with him?

Who says I—? Well, I guess . . . because . . .

What?

Because I wanted to keep the back door open.

I don't follow you.

Yes, you do, goddamn it.

Why haven't you wanted a child with him?

Because I may want to get out of the marriage, isn't that *obvious,* for God's sake?

You mean, to get involved with someone dangerous and unpredictable and exciting?

Yes yes yes . . .

Well what's stopping you? Who's stopping you?

Me. I am.

Why?

Fear.

Of what?

I don't know.

Are you sure it's fear?

Yes. No, I'm not sure.

What else could it be?

I don't know.

What else could it be?

Billy.

Billy's stopping you?

Goddamn it, what's the *matter* with you today? You don't seem to understand anything I'm trying to tell you.

Like what?

Like Billy. That I love him. That *that's* what's stopping me.

Ah, now I get it.

About time.

Yes, of course. Because you love Billy, you'll never know what it would have been like to be married to the dangerous and exciting kind, so you're angry at Billy, at practically everything he does, his profession, his hobby, in bed, but as long as you don't have children there's always a chance that you can still get out of it and try that other fellow, except that you can't, because you love Billy. Now I get it.

Are you through?

Mm-hm.

Then tell me: what the hell is all *that* supposed to do for me?

I never said it was going to be easy, Julie.

And that had been several years and many thousands of dollars ago. She hadn't derived any shining certainties from it all. But she *had* learned to understand her doubts, and where they had come from. And she knew finally that she would always go on striving and searching, in her own circuitous way, until she made her life fall into its proper shape. She had thought that perhaps this trip might do it for her, that it might happen in Paris, or during a glorious week at St.-Jean-Cap-Ferrat, or on Rhodes or Corfu or Mykonos afterward. Maybe she would run through that open back door at last, or slam it shut forever.

Maybe it's happening *already,* she said to herself, as she strode along the deck of the *Marseille* now. She didn't know *what,* exactly, but God knows, *some*thing was happening to her. And *had* been happening ever since she and Billy had boarded this ship. She quickened her pace, eyes searching for anyone in a white jacket and a French Atlantic cap who might tell her the shortest route to Number 416 on the Upper Deck.

She hadn't noticed the key to Harold Columbine's cabin until just before lunch, when she had transferred the contents of last night's evening bag to today's purse. His absence from the dining room once again, the second in a row, had left her even more frustrated than had the mystery of Billy's transparent lie. Well, she would return the key in person. ("When it comes to sex, Harold Columbine, you sure *write* a good game.") Then she would confront her husband and demand to know why he had wanted to be alone in their suite for the hour and a half that it takes to get from the *oeuf en gelée* to the *crème caramel*.

Five minutes later, she was rapping softly on the door to 416. No one on this deck knew her. There was nothing to worry about. She rapped a little more vigorously now. Maybe he was one of those writers who bombed out with sleeping pills. No answer. She looked at her wristwatch. Almost two o'clock. This was ridiculous. She opened her handbag and found the key.

"May I help you, madame?"

She dropped the key back and looked up at the steward with a strained smile. "Not really," she said. "Unless you can tell me where I might find Mr. Columbine, the gentleman in four-sixteen."

The steward looked at her for a long time, as though he hadn't heard her. Finally he said: "Mr. Columbine has asked that he not be disturbed."

"Oh, I see." Why was it that she didn't quite believe him? "Thank you."

"Not at all, madame."

She watched him as he moved on. When he disappeared through the door to a companionway, she took the key from her handbag, glanced around and then inserted it in the lock. This is madness, she thought, as she opened the door slowly, calling out a warning "Harold? Are you there?" Inside the stateroom, she closed the door behind her and looked around. In the parlor there were no signs of life. She moved to the open door to the bedroom and peeked in. Empty. Coverlet on bed. And a crumpled piece of Kleenex. She walked over to the bed, picked up the tissue, saw the remnants of last night's lipstick. Everything in this room was exactly as she had left it, even the indentation on the coverlet where she had sprawled and passed out. She put the Kleenex in her bag, dropped the key on the bed, took a quick look in the empty bathroom, and left the cabin without being seen.

Back on the Promenade Deck, she found an empty deck chair and stretched out, trying to organize her thoughts. She felt that, somehow, she had a problem, but she wasn't sure exactly what it was. She knew that she would have to discuss it with *some*body, but the question was, with whom? Certainly not Billy.

Who has disappeared?

This famous novelist I almost slept with last night.

I didn't know you knew him.

I didn't, until I picked him up last night.

You were writing letters last night. I remember your telling me.

I wasn't writing letters, Billy. I was picking up Harold Colum-bine at the bar of the Montmartre Cafe, and then we went dancing down in Tourist, and then I went to his bedroom to wait for him and he didn't show up, and I just used his key to let myself into his cabin and—

Wait a minute. You almost *slept* with him last night?

Yes, Billy.

Okay, Julie. You get the house and the poodles. I get the Atlas.

No, certainly no discussion with Billy. But if not with Billy, with whom?

CHAPTER SEVEN

YES, DR. BERLIN, but what do you hams *talk* about? is
what they usually said to him, and he'd realize then that they'd never
understand, and he'd change the subject. But sometimes, though
rarely, he'd come across someone who really dug his hobby, and
then you couldn't get him *off*. He'd go on and on about the feeling
it gave him of being able to move himself through time and space,
annihilating distance, his mind, his body, his consciousness out
there roaming the planet like some cosmic spirit, and the sense of
power, benign power, not the evil kind, knowing that his voice was
rattling a loudspeaker in a far-off room in Bombay, or going out
through an open window in Johannesburg to someone walking by
on the street outside, or filling a room carved out of ice below the
frozen wastes at the South Pole.

The here and now, the physical and geographical limitations that
all beings were stuck with, would fall away from him as he im-
mersed himself in the action on twenty meters on a good night in
spring when the sun spots were dancing and the ionosphere was in a
reflective mood and the short path was open to Europe and the

Middle East and the Antarctic and Australia, and maybe Africa would come sneaking through the other way around, and later the Far East and Indonesia, you never knew what. He'd close his eyes, or gaze hypnotized at the speaker, and he'd listen to them and talk to them, voices in the night, his night, that is, with the moon shining into the den through the great beam antenna that rose from the lawn outside. And his long day at the office and at the hospital with the ones who were dying a little faster than the others, and his own free-floating anxieties and somatic symptoms, and the indefinable problem that was Julie and he would cease to exist for a while.

And while it was *his* night in California, it was tomorrow morning in Oslo and Hil was getting ready to shovel the snow from in front of the garage so he could go to work, and in Brisbane it was late tomorrow afternoon and Tommy had just gotten home from a rainy day at the lab, and Toshi in Kyoto had just finished tomorrow's dinner, and then later, Phil was talking to him from his car speeding through the Malaysian jungles to pick up Margaret at her French lesson in Penang, and Phil would lower the car window and let him hear the street noises of Penang even as he sat in his den in the house in Bel Air while the guy right next door was listening to the eleven o'clock news on Channel 2, for God's sake, and you ask me what do we talk about? We don't talk about a goddamn thing and it's terrific.

But he had secretly asked himself the same question, and others, many times, yes, many times, because, though he was not overly introspective, Billy Berlin *was* aware of certain incongruities (or were they really consistencies?) in his deep interest in amateur radio. He had been turned on to the hobby by a classmate during his second year at Pacific Palisades High School, a friend who had long since defected to high-fidelity stereo and quadraphonic sound, and had gone on, in the flush of adult prosperity, to filling his mansion in Trousdale Estates with enough ear-shattering music to make all forms of communication, except possibly touching, impossible.

The months of studying for the FCC license exam somehow didn't interfere with Billy's schoolwork at all, and he not only managed to get himself an Extra Class ticket, but graduated from Pali High with honors. His mother and father, who viewed his late night DX-ing with a kind of tight-lipped acceptance (once or twice allowing that it was better than his being out with some of the other boys his age getting stoned and smashing up either the Porsche or himself or both), they gave him a Collins KWM-1 transceiver as a graduation present, and he used that as his rig at Oregon State, operating out of his dorm with a little dipole antenna strung out of the window, when he wasn't buried in his books, or out learning how to get laid without mortification.

His first sizeable station was the one he accumulated when he moved back home to Pacific Palisades and entered the University of Southern California medical school. But med school turned out to be far too heavy to permit of fun and games on the ham radio bands, and his father had already started the long, malignant, downhill slide, and by the time Billy started his internship at Los Angeles County Hospital, amateur radio appeared to be slipping out of his life forever. When his mother decided to sell the big house and move to an apartment overlooking the ocean, Billy got rid of all the radio gear, and that was that, he thought.

Julie Harrison came into his life out of nowhere, a purely random accident. There he was, his residency completed, just another fledgling M.D. drifting in the Southern California sun, trying to decide whether to go into research at the U.S.C. gerontology center or set up a geriatrics practice of his own somewhere in the San Fernando Valley, when one night, *literally,* he looked across a crowded room and there *she* was, this lovely being, all of twenty-two.

It was in the living room of a house in Rustic Canyon, at a wine and cheese party a former girlfriend of his was giving to introduce everybody to her new fiancé. There was Julie, sitting in a corner, neglected by her blind date, a guy Billy didn't even know. She couldn't very well mingle, because she had just moved out to California from the East with her parents, and didn't know a soul.

We shall soon fix *that,* Billy said to her.

He had known from instant number one that he was going to marry her. Her beauty almost gave him respiratory arrest. Her petiteness of form divine made his own modest frame absolutely husky. And his male organ, on their third date during the week he met her, felt enormous inside of her. Also, though he wasn't aware of it at the time, her charming manner of personal discourse, which was a subtle blend of repartee and soft-edged insult, seemed to be perfect for his unique needs. Here was a girl you could communicate with, and still be kept at a distance. Here was someone you could be intimate with, but never get *too* close to.

It was almost like ham radio.

He borrowed enough money from his mother to set up his new bride in a modest house in Westwood, and *him* up in a not-so-modest suite of offices in Beverly Hills, and Dr. William Hoving Berlin, specialist in the practice of geriatric medicine, was on his way.

Julie provided the laughter, the parties, the weekends at Laguna Beach or Balboa or Palm Springs, and all the new friends they could handle. She was incredibly well-liked, by everyone, it was truly amazing. He was the native Californian and she was out of New York, and yet it was *she* who shaped the whole character and substance of their social life. He, in turn, provided the money—it came swiftly, as though he had struck oil in the backyards of the suntanned elderly—and gave them both a sense of purpose. He was not only a doctor, a most noble calling, but in a relatively new and exotic field that provided endlessly intriguing dinner-party conversation. Was there *anyone* who didn't want to know how not to grow old, or, having done that foolish thing, how to turn around and go back to being young again?

They were having such a good time together, they hardly seemed to notice that there was little said between them about, you know, having a family? Surely Yin and Yang—ridiculous names for French poodles—were only a rehearsal for the real thing, weren't they? Nor did they seem to notice that the lovemaking was getting just a little bit more infrequent, and a little bit less heartfelt, wasn't it? You bet it was, and they only *seemed* not to notice.

They noticed.

And looked the other way.

But they noticed.

And in their own way, each grew very quietly panicky inside, and did something.

Julie went to Albert DeGrooning.

Billy went to Henry Radio, just to browse.

And things were never quite the same after that.

Why had Billy chosen geriatrics and gerontology instead of orthopedics or pediatrics or cardiology? Simple. Julie could explain that to anyone, especially to him. She knew all the answers. And after they bought the larger house on Chalon Road in Bel Air, and

Billy unaccountably (to him if not to her) went back on the air again with a Tri-Ex tower and a Hy-Gain beam and a Henry 2K-4 driven by a Drake TR-4C transceiver, Julie could explain that too.

But she would give Billy the benefit of her insights only if she were angry at him, or overtired, or had had too much to drink at an unsuccessful party she had given, and after the guests had gone, during the shoes off, dress off, makeup off postmortems on their friends and mostly on him. Otherwise, he had to figure himself out all by himself, and who had time for that? He was much too busy.

About the only time periods available to Billy Berlin for introspection, for any kind of personal thinking, were during the twenty-minute drives from home to office to hospitals to sanitariums to office to home, and he always had his amateur radio two-meter FM mobile transceiver turned on in the car, so he could talk to the local guys in the Los Angeles area who hung out on the Henry repeater frequency. Once, he had kept the rig turned *off* for two whole days, trying to work out in his mind something fresh, a provocative theme for a piece he had been invited to write for the *Journal of the Institute*. A title had kept trying to push its way into his consciousness. He had resisted. Finally, it *forced* its way in.

"Home Is Where You Hang Your Head."

Immediately, he had turned the rig *on,* and always kept it on after that, if not to talk at least to listen.

He never did write the piece.

He was much too busy, he explained.

"You're always busy. What are you running away from? Is it me?"

"Don't be silly, honey. I was a busy, active person long before I ever met you, so what's it got to do with you?"

"Plenty."

"I happen to have a lot of patients who need me often, *very* often, because they're not exactly young and healthy, right?"

"Right."

"Maybe that's why I like my work so much and spend so much time at it, because I always feel needed . . ."

"You want me to tell you why you chose the geriatric field, Billy . . . ?"

"Not now, it's very late . . ."

"They're old and they're going to die anyway, most of them very soon, and they know it and you know it and their families know it, so nobody, including you, can ever say you *lost* a patient. You never really *lose* a patient, do you, Billy. It's a no-lose situation for you *going in,* and *that's* why you chose your little niche. It's not so much that *they* need *you.* You need *them* . . ."

"Maybe you're right, I wouldn't know, but what's the difference, as long as we're healthy?" He never had much trouble keeping the anger from showing. Julie wouldn't know what to do with it anyway. She'd fall apart, it would be so unexpected. Besides, anger was dumb, better off controlled. "I'll *think* about it sometime, all right?"

"When? When twenty meters goes dead, or the electricity fails? I suppose you're going to tell me that going back on the air when we moved into this house had nothing whatever to do with avoiding *me,* that you needed something to unwind with . . ."

"I gotta tell you, it *is* relaxing. It's fun, Julie, plain and simple fun. It doesn't have to be accounted for in terms of hidden significances. Sometimes a cigar is just a cigar, you know. Tell *that* to Dr. DeGrooning, but don't say I made it up because I didn't."

"Who did? Some Whiskey Able One in Boston? Or was it a Sugar Mike Five in Stockholm?"

"No. Sigmund Freud. He's the well-known Ocean Easy One from Vienna."

"Very funny. I'm going to sleep."

"Not a bad idea."

"Don't forget to turn the lights out after you turn off the receiver."

"Who said anything about my receiver?"

"*I* did, just now. G'night."

He had really been pissed off at her that night, without even showing it. But not half as pissed off at her as he was right now for the fact of her having told Captain Girodt about his hidden Atlas-210, and shoving *him* right smack into the middle of no man's land, with this relentless radio officer who would not get off his *back.* But he'd never show that anger to Julie. It would only drive them farther apart, and he loved her, and always would, despite everything, whatever the hell that everything was, he'd have to figure it out sometime.

"I am *no hero,* Mr. Specht," he fairly shouted at the man. "I have bad eyesight, flabby muscles, a trick knee and considerable

shit in my blood. You have *no right* to come to me with this . . .
this *suicide pact* . . ."

"We had no choice," said Christain Specht quietly.

At first Billy had thought it was one of Julie's practical jokes.
That was when the steward had come to him with a request from
the Captain that he remain waiting in his cabin, with no one else
present, with nothing to be said to anyone, including his wife, about
a meeting that would take place. And when the Chief Radio Officer
had arrived and locked the door, and had begun to spin the improb-
able details of the *Marseille* takeover, his first reaction had been
one of puzzled amusement, slowly giving way to curiosity. But that
was twenty minutes ago. Now, there was nothing left in him but the
defensive anger of a trapped coward.

"Suppose they discover what I'm doing? Then what?"

Christain Specht shrugged. "Your guess is as good as mine. How
many ways are there on board a ship at sea to put a man to death
with the least possible commotion? Pick one of them, and there's
your probable answer."

"Thank you," said Billy Berlin. "Thank you very much." He
paced back and forth in the small parlor of his suite, trying not to
look at the man. The utter calm of this radio officer, the faint,
sardonic smile that made light of everything, no matter how desperate, gave him a royal pain in the ass. "I mean, why the hell should I
risk my life because you guys don't know how to stay in command
of your own ship? The whole thing is just about as ridiculous as
anything I ever heard of."

"I agree with you, Dr. Berlin," said Specht. "Which brings us
again to the critical question . . . Are you or are you not willing
to make this attempt for us?"

"And don't try to make believe it *wasn't* my wife who told you
people about the radio, okay?"

Specht rose to his feet. "I'll go back to the Captain then and tell
him you feel it's personally too dangerous."

"Sit down a minute," Billy Berlin said with exasperation.

"Very well." The Chief Radio Officer resumed his seat.

"Why can't you or one of your men take my transceiver, hide it
in a pillowcase or something, and operate it in your *own* quarters, if
you can't in the radio room?"

"Well, for one thing," said Specht, "I and my men are totally unfamiliar with amateur radio techniques and procedures. We'd give ourselves away on the air immediately. But much more important than that, they are watching us, watching every move that we make. We'd be discovered in no time, whereas there's no reason for them to suspect *you,* as long as you keep your mouth shut and keep your equipment out of sight under lock and key if and when you're not here."

"What about Julie, my wife? She's a lovely girl, but she likes to blab, as you ought to know by now."

"Captain Girodt will personally handle the situation of your wife," replied Christain Specht. "Now—may I please have a formal yes or no from you, Doctor?"

"Goddamn it, the answer is yes and you know it, a reluctant, apprehensive, pessimistic yes." He ran a hand through his hair. "I've been in ham radio for over twenty years, and this is the first time I've ever regretted it." Which was only partly true.

Christain Specht had risen, and was already at the door.

"Where're you going?"

"To give the Captain the good news," said Specht. "While he is locating Mrs. Berlin and briefing her, I'll get up some kind of written résumé for you to study, giving you all the information you'll need. And I'll have my men get to work figuring out how to snake some thin coaxial cable through the electrical conduit and into here, so that we can hook you up to our auxiliary dipole."

"Without being seen, right? I mean, that *is* going to be the name of this game."

"We'll do our best, Doctor."

"You have to do better than that, Mr. Specht."

He unlocked the door, let the radio officer out, locked the door again and went to the closet where, obviously without much success, he had hidden his transceiver from Julie. Deep-seated fears, intimations of mortal danger, were nibbling away at his vitals, but they soon vanished in the rush of immediate problems that now faced him. He was going to go on the air from the *Marseille* and pretend that he was an American amateur radio station operating maritime mobile in the Atlantic on some fictitious ship. He was going to pray that no one in the communications room of the *Marseille,* listening on commercial maritime frequencies, would hear any spillover from his signals in the nearby amateur bands.

And most importantly of all, if and when he raised any amateur operators in the United States or elsewhere, he would have to know what to say to them that would bring help without alerting world-wide news organizations to his existence on the air.

He hefted in his hands the seven-pound, gray-and-black marvel of solid-state circuitry known as the Atlas-210 (actually, the 210x), gave it a little kiss on the top of its black vinyl-covered aluminum cabinet, and set it down on the table.

"Okay, baby," he breathed, "don't crap out on me now."

As the movie ended, the house lights slowly came up. The seven-hundred-seat theater had been only three quarters full for the matinee, and most of the passengers now making their way up the aisles felt vaguely guilty. Not only had they eaten far too much for lunch, but they had sat there in the dark for two hours knowing they had passed up fresh sea air, bright sunshine and exercise, in exchange for tasteless, meaningless trivia. Within a minute, the auditorium was practically deserted. In the first three rows of the center section, eighty-nine men and women who had arrived especially early to get those seats, remained standing where they had risen.

A tall, muscular, but graceful man with sandy, short-cropped hair left his aisle seat and went down front to face the group. He wore a white, short-sleeved shirt, blue denim slacks and blue sneakers. He seemed quite relaxed as he looked past the group before him to the rear of the theater to make sure no one else had remained behind. Then the man, who was Herb Kleinfeld, addressed his audience.

"Hi. Pretty boring, wasn't it?"

"I wouldn't know," called out a leathery-faced, suntanned blonde. "I slept through the whole damned thing."

"Smart girl, Francine," someone else called out.

"All right, just so that I know who's who and what's what here, will all members of Canyon Lodge Number Three raise their hands please." Eighty-nine persons raised their hands. "Very good," said Herb Kleinfeld, confident now that there were no interlopers. "I will now tell you what I plan to tell the other members of our lodge when I meet with them after dinner. First, Uncle Julian left Los Angeles yesterday via Air France, and is probably walking the streets of Paris this very moment. Second, Mr. Thompson, Mr.

Nesser and Mr. Teitelbaum today completed the first half of their legal brief, and are moving rapidly to a conclusion. And third, because the crew of this ship has been brought up to date by the Captain, you will have to choose very carefully the words you use in doing crossword puzzles in public places. Are there any questions?"

A portly, ruddy-cheeked man raised his hand again.

"Yes, John?"

"Herb," said the portly man, "is it out of order to ask whether there have been any casualties in Cambodia that we don't know about?"

"I don't think such a discussion would be of much use right now," said Kleinfeld.

"Right, Herb."

"Okay. That's it. See you at chow everybody." Kleinfeld walked quickly up the aisle and left through the rear lobby. The others dispersed through various exits, feeling pleased with the news that their contact had shifted from Los Angeles to Paris, and that half the *Marseille* was now successfully wired for doom. The warning to be on guard and keep their mouths shut was well taken. If they were the enemy within, it followed that they were surrounded by the enemy without.

Bernard Delade turned up the RF gain to maximum and switched to a broader crystal filter but it didn't help. He could hear the *Marseille* just below the static level, about Q3S2, and it wasn't good enough for reliable copy. He threw the switch to TRANSMIT, fingered the automatic paddle-key and notified FNRC to stand by a moment. He got up from his position, turned off the noisy air conditioner in the radio room, went back to the receiver, plugged in a pair of headphones, reached past the exciter to the coax switch on the wall and changed over from the V-beam antenna to the four-element rotatable Yagi. Then he clamped on the headphones and asked FNRC to give him about a minute of testing. He quickly retuned his transmitter to the new antenna and began to listen. The *Marseille* was a solid S7 now. As the ship's operator continued to send Vs, Delade happened to glance at the indicator dial of the beam rotator, and discovered that he had forgotten to turn the beam to the west. The big Yagi was still pointing south, where he had left it since yesterday's contacts with several French Atlantic cruise ships. He pressed the lever to the right to swing the beam around to the west, dead on the second-stage of the North Atlantic route of the *Marseille*. To his astonishment, the incoming signal peaked at 5 db over S9 as the beam passed through a position considerably *south* of west, and dropped off to a faint S3 when the beam reached the more northerly position. Quickly he rotated the beam back to the south, gave the *Marseille* a 5 over 9 report, and told them to go ahead with their transmission.

Second Radioman Marcel Fox glanced nervously at the two men watching him in the crowded communications room of the *Marseille,* and with faltering hand sent the message that falsely reported the ship's position at 43 degrees N., 58 degrees W. When he had finished, he handed the piece of paper back to the stranger who had given it to him. The stranger nodded to the man standing beside him, and then the two of them returned to their places near the door.

Bernard Delade put the position report on the telex to Paris, with copies to Le Havre, Southampton, and New York. And before signing off with FNRC, he swung the beam farther to the north again, and verified for himself the strange phenomenon of signal attenuation. As he puttered around in the radio room, guarding several channels on the speakers, Delade felt a resolve slowly building up within him to get on the land line with Paris to see what the front office thought about the situation. But his mood soured at the thought of having to confront that snot-nose Sauvinage on the telephone.

"My dear Bernard," Sauvinage would intone, "why do you bother me with questions about signal reports and beam antennas when you know perfectly well that I don't know the first thing about them?" Dear Bernard, my foot. "I am not a radio man. I am an executive. I am not interested to know where your antenna is pointing, so long as I know where the *Marseille* is pointing."

To hell with Paris. He'd call Lisbon and London to set up a triangulation on the *Marseille* signals with their radio direction-finders in the Azores and Bermuda. But not now. In the morning. Now he was going home for an early dinner. Just as soon as young Jean Patri, his assistant, came to relieve him.

In the ten minutes before Patri arrived, Bernard Delade changed his mind completely, and sent another telex to Paris, to Georges Sauvinage:

PECULIAR DIRECTIONAL CHARACTERISTICS OF S.S. MAR-
SEILLE RADIO SIGNALS LEADS ME RESPECTFULLY TO SUG-
GEST YOU CONTACT CAPTAIN GIRODT VIA SHIP-TO-SHORE
TELEPHONE TO VERIFY SHIP'S POSITION AND HEADING. IF
RECEPTION POOR TRY ROUTING CALL THROUGH AZORES.
DELADE.

Maybe that last sentence would get Sauvinage off his fat ass.

The great liner plunged south under the warming afternoon sun,
the huge dynoturbines driving her propellers to a straining, throbbing speed of thirty-three knots.

Deep within the hull of the vessel, a fresh team of amateur
demolition experts was at work strategically placing plastic death
along the portside plates. In the galley far above them, three dish-
washers from Lyon were neglecting their chores temporarily to
discuss, with much bravado, a plan they were hatching to take over
the rifles that still remained in use in the clay pigeon shooting
gallery topside, and thus armed, mow their captors down in cold
blood. When one of them, a man named Louis, asked who their
captors were and where they could be found, his companions stared
at him for a moment, and then all three put their hands back in the
dirty dishwater.

In a small, windowless cabin toward the stern on B-Deck, Harold
Columbine lay on the bed to which he was tied, listening to the not-
so-distant pounding of the ship's engines. His eyesight was still
blurred from the massive headache they had left him with the night
before, when they had almost brained him, but an imperceptible
smile curled at his full lips. It had taken him over fourteen hours,
but he had finally done it. He had figured out how he was going to
escape the two gray-wigged, dowdy-seeming matron types who sat
near the bed reading paperback novels, their Magnum pistols resting comfortably in their laps. He'd have to wait until later, though,
when they untied his wrists. Christ, what a bore. "Hey," he called
out sharply. The two women glanced up. "Which one of you chicks
would like to go down on me?" They looked at him for a moment,
and then resumed their reading.

CHAPTER EIGHT

_____

SHE IS WHAT the Captain described. Why did I walk past her?

Lucien Lanoux stopped, turned, and decided to go back to the pretty young lady who was reclining with eyes closed in the deck chair. Like all stewards, Lanoux was reluctant to disturb sleeping passengers, but he could not afford to make a mistake.

"Excuse me, please."

Julie Berlin opened her eyes. "Yes?"

"I'm sorry, but are you, perhaps, Madame Berlin?"

"I am, perhaps."

"I did not mean to wake you—"

"I wasn't asleep, just thinking," said Julie. "What's up, tea, coffee, hot chocolate, or a French lesson?"

The lanky steward glanced about, saw that no one was within earshot. "Captain Girodt has asked me to tell you this." Julie straightened up. "He wishes you to go to the ship's hospital right away to see the ship's doctor, whose name is Yves Chabot. I will take you to him."

"What's your name again?"

"Lucien, madame. Lucien Lanoux."

"Lucien, you tell the Captain I'm feeling perfectly fine. There's no need to see a doctor."

"But there is, madame. The Captain has ordered me to take you there. He said it is urgent. I am to walk a few steps ahead of you, and you are to follow me. Will that be all right?"

Julie shrugged. "Whatever you say, Lucien."

When they arrived at the hospital, the steward turned Julie over to an attractive, dark-eyed woman in a stylish white smock, and quickly departed.

"I'm Genvieve Bordoni, the head nurse," said the woman.

"How do you do," Julie said, thinking, she looks more like a Courrèges model.

"Please wait here, Mrs. Berlin." The nurse disappeared through the open doorway to the inner office, then reappeared a few seconds later. "This way, please."

Julie entered a cheerful room paneled in bleached oak and saw Yves Chabot standing before his desk, smiling.

"Thank you for coming, Mrs. Berlin. I am Dr. Chabot."

"Don't thank me," Julie said easily. "Consider it a command performance."

She shook his outstretched hand, feeling vaguely overwhelmed by the firmness of his handclasp and the intensity of his gaze. He's too handsome, she thought. He couldn't possibly be a good doctor.

"I will try to make this as brief as possible," said Chabot. "Would you step in here, please." He indicated the white, sterile examining room to the left of his desk.

"What is this?" said Julie.

"We will examine your sore throat."

"There's absolutely nothing wrong with me, Doctor."

"While I talk to you, Mrs. Berlin, and pass along a few words from Captain Girodt, it would be better that I appear to be examining you for some ailment should anyone happen to wander in here. Believe me, it is desirable."

"Why doesn't the Captain see me himself, instead of talking to me first through a steward and then through you? No offense, Doctor."

"If you will . . . in here?" He gestured toward the doorway.

With a little smile of bewilderment, Julie stepped into the exam ining room and sat down in the black leather chair that Chabot indicated. Immediately, the doctor inserted a thermometer in her protesting mouth, sat down on a high metal stool before her, took her right wrist in his hand to feel her pulse, and commenced to speak.

"The Captain would have told this to you personally, but he felt it would be extremely unwise to have a meeting with you right now. He is being watched, more or less constantly, and the last thing he wishes is that those who are watching him should wonder what business he might be having with *you*. It is about your husband, Mrs. Berlin . . ."

"I thought so," murmured Julie through the thermometer.

"The Captain has instructed me not to go into any fuller details than those I am about to give you, and I do hope that you will respect his wishes for the time being. Suffice it to say that there are certain passengers aboard the *Marseille* right now who are, shall we say, unfriendly to the interests of the Captain and his crew. We do not know, except in one or two instances, who these people are, or how many of them there are, but we do know that they have taken charge of various matters concerned with this voyage. We are unable to communicate freely with the company's offices on land, or with any maritime authorities, through normal radio or ship-to-shore channels, due to . . . your temperature is normal, Mrs. Berlin . . ." He had heard the door open in the outer office. Instantly, he held a finger to his lips demanding silence as he withdrew the thermometer. "Now if you will please open your mouth wide and say a-a-a-h . . ." He had taken a spatula to hold her tongue down, first tilting the spotlight to hit her throat.

"A-a-a-h . . ." Looking past the doctor, Julie could see the man with the wrap-around dark glasses coming into view in the doorway.

"Not bad," murmured Chabot, without turning. "Not bad at all. Just a tiny bit of redness which I'm sure will go away. Do you smoke, Mrs. Berlin?"

"Very seldom, Doctor. In fact, practically not at all."

"Well, that's one way of causing the medical profession to starve to death." He chuckled softly and turned away from her. "How do you do, sir? Is there something I can do for you?"

"No, that's all right. Just carry on," said the man in the dark glasses, standing in the doorway watching them. He spoke with a trace of Texas in his voice.

"I'll be through very shortly," said Chabot affably. "Would you like to wait outside?"

"You just go on doing what you were doing," the man said. "I may come back later, and then again, I may not."

"All right," said Chabot. He turned to Julie, who was now standing, and put his fingers on each side of her neck. "Please turn your head from side to side."

Julie obeyed, keeping her eyes on the man watching from the doorway.

"That's fine," said Chabot. "Be seated again, please."

"Wait a second." She pushed past the doctor and stopped in front of the man in the doorway. "You know something?" she said to him. "I don't feel very well, which is why I'm here, and it isn't making me feel any better to have a strange man *staring* at me while I'm being examined. So why don't you find the ship's social director and tell her you're looking for a little recreation. Okay, mister?"

The man's mouth broke into a cold smile that showed jagged yellow teeth. "Lady, you *are* sick," he said, and walked away from her.

Chabot waited until he heard the outer door close. Then he stepped past Julie into his office, looked about to make sure the man had actually gone, and returned to the examining room.

"Good girl," he said to Julie.

"Thanks. Was that one of them?"

"I wouldn't be at all surprised."

"He could use a good dentist, *and* a psychiatrist." Julie sank down in the black leather chair. "Now, you were saying . . . ?"

Chabot perched on the metal stool. "When you told Captain Girodt about your husband's radio . . . uh . . . the transmitter . . ."

"Transceiver," said Julie.

"Yes, the Captain immediately realized that this *transceiver* might be used as a secret means of communicating our plight to the outside world . . ."

"My God . . ."

". . . Our Chief Radio Officer, Christain Specht, met privately with your husband today . . ."

"While I was at lunch . . ." What a relief.

"Correct, and your husband has agreed to operate a clandestine amateur radio station from your stateroom."

"What have I done, me and my big mouth?" said Julie.

"Mrs. Berlin, you may just possibly become one of France's greatest heroines. But in order for that to happen, you will have to agree to do *everything* that we ask you to do, or rather, everything that we ask you *not* to do."

"If you let me order all the Grand Marnier soufflé I want, I'll do anything you say, Doctor." Maybe, she thought, if I don't take all this too seriously, it'll just blow away.

Yves Chabot liked her game. It made his task easier. "The first thing you must do is promise me, and yourself, that you will not breathe a word to *anyone* about the existence of that transceiver, much less your husband's using it secretly. And when I say not to anyone, I mean not to anyone. Captain Girodt and me you can trust. But there is no passenger on this ship who might not be one of our enemies. They even possess the various uniforms of the officers and men, and disguise themselves as one of us. The Captain and I and the rest of the staff will do everything we can to spread word that your husband is confined to his cabin with a bad case of the flu. We think that will cover his absence. If Dr. Berlin were to be found out, there is no telling what they would do to him."

"My little Billy boy?" she smiled ruefully. "Why would anyone want to hurt my little Billy boy? He's never done anything to anybody. He just holds the hands of very old ladies and very old men and leads them very gently and very kindly to their graves. And when he comes home at night after a hard day at the convalescent home or the sanitarium, he has a large glass of buttermilk and then he sits himself down in front of his great big receiver and his great big transmitter and calls CQ and QRZ and God knows what other fascinating letters of the alphabet till the wee hours of the morning, and he's so thoughtful and quiet when he slips into bed that he never never disturbs me, hardly ever at all. Do I sound awful? Yes I do sound awful. And I don't mean to sound awful. What's the matter with me, Doctor?"

"You're upset."

"I am?"

"Of course."

"Because of Billy?"

"Naturally."

"Because of what could happen to him?"

"Right."

"And because if I hadn't tattled to the Captain about the transceiver Billy wouldn't be *in* this mess?"

"Exactly."

"So what could happen to Billy, Doctor?"

"You want the truth, or a Grand Marnier soufflé?"

"Both," she said.

"Several of our crew have disappeared. We have good reason to believe they were murdered."

"Good God."

"One of them was a twenty-six-year-old girl."

"Oh . . ." Julie winced with horror.

Chabot patted her hand. "I'm sorry."

"I feel awful, terrible . . ."

The doctor rose, went to his office and returned with a small snifter, half full. Julie took the glass from him and stared at it.

"Brandy?"

He nodded. "Good for a sore throat."

She managed to down it all, making terrible faces. "What do I do next? Tell me what to do."

"Just this," said Chabot quietly. "Help your husband if he needs help. Leave him alone if he needs to be left alone. He is going to be very occupied, very harassed, perhaps a bit frightened . . ."

"I haven't been nice to him." Julie's lips quivered. "I feel like . . . like such a . . . what's the French word for a shit?"

He looked at her thoughtfully. "Shit-heel?"

She glanced up at him, and then they both burst into laughter.

"On that note," said Chabot, "I shall say goodbye to you."

Julie got to her feet.

He took her arm and steered her through his office. "We will be seeing much of each other, I'm sure."

"I hope so."

"Any time you need someone to talk to, or be frightened with . . ."

"Yes."

"And we may be using you to convey information to your husband, and from him to us."

"Tell me the truth," she said. "Is everything going to be all right?"

"Yes," he said. At the door to the waiting room he took her hand in his. "Goodbye," he said. "I will tell the Captain that you have been an admirable patient."

"Thank you, Doctor," she said.

She went out past the much-too-beautiful head nurse at the reception desk and headed for the elevator. She could feel the brandy working in her now, and it was a warm, pleasurable feeling. Either it was the brandy, or Dr. Yves Chabot.

"What happened?" Chabot asked Genvieve Bordoni after Julie had left.

"I tried, but he wouldn't listen to me," the head nurse said. "He just opened the door and went in."

"I don't suppose he gave any name."

"Nothing."

"All right. Get me the Commandant, please."

He went back into his office and sat down at the desk. Presently the buzzer sounded. He picked up the phone.

"Chabot here."

"Girodt."

"The patient has taken the medicine as prescribed."

"Thank you."

They both hung up.

Chabot rose and went to the examining room. The black leather chair was empty now, but a lovely fragrance still lingered in the small enclosure. Or was it just in his mind?

After a moment, he picked up a lavender and white aerosol can of air freshener and began to spray the room to remove the fragrance from his thoughts.

Bobo Crepin moved his tongue from side to side, then licked his lips, but could find no lingering aftertaste of *cassoulet* in his mouth. The trouble with his digestion was that it was too good. Two hours after lunch he had nothing to show for the meal except increasingly dim recollections. Bobo was fifty-nine. He had been a security guard on one or another French Atlantic steamship for twenty-two years, and never once had he had an occasion to draw his revolver from its holster. As he made his way through the gloom of the *Marseille*'s lowest level now, he found himself conjuring up all sorts of dinner fantasies, which in turn produced delicious pangs of hunger in his belly.

Would he choose *coq au vin* or would it be dover sole? Some *boeuf Bourguignon*, perhaps, with wild strawberries for dessert? He tasted a sampling of *blanquette de veau,* tried a morsel of *foie gras,* popped a few *pommes frites* into his mouth, was about to slice into the steak *au poivre,* when he heard sounds coming from a lateral tunnel to his right that caused him to leave the dinner table momentarily. The sounds consisted of a muffled hammering, and men's voices. With some annoyance, Bobo Crepin crept into the darkness of the lateral tunnel, snapped on his flashlight, and saw the open manhole cover. He leaned into the hole, saying nothing, and listened. He heard the muffled hammering stop, and then he fancied that he heard a man's voice saying, in English, "Take this and hold on to it," and another voice replying, "Roger."

Bobo Crepin drew back for a moment. At the morning briefing, he and all the other security forces had been instructed to ignore the unusual, and above all to provoke no trouble. After twenty-two years of service, Bobo found the order repugnant to his honor. He lowered his chunky body through the open manhole and carefully descended the iron ladder to the bottom. He was certain that he heard a voice say, "Quiet."

At the foot of the ladder, he called out, "Hello?" but received no reply. From far off, he heard the whine of the dynoturbines, and the occasional cracking sound of the hull plates. He began to move through the darkness, probing the gloom with the beam of his flashlight. In addition to the pangs of hunger within him, Bobo Crepin now felt a few twinges of fear. He made his way past several water-storage tanks, darted with surprising agility to his right and suddenly came upon the three men standing there with their backs pressed against the hull plates. Their faces were darkened with grime, their work clothes were soiled. They had several pails with rags, some coiled wire, and other materials which Bobo Crepin could not immediately make out. They were smiling at him good-naturedly.

"Hi, there," one of the men said. "You're just in time. We need some help." His French was very American.

Bobo moved a few steps closer. "Help? What do you mean help? I'm a security officer. What are you doing down here?"

"We're trying to fix this damned thing and we're having a lot of trouble," the second man said. "Do you mind giving us a hand? Here. Please." He stepped forward and thrust the coil of wire into the guard's left hand.

Bobo Crepin transferred the flashlight to the same hand to free his right hand for the revolver that he now groped for at his belt. "I want to know who you people are. Nobody is supposed to be here unless—"

"Here. Hang on to this, will you?" The first man wheeled sharply and thrust out at Bobo.

"I don't want—*oh*—"

The knife through his stomach killed Bobo Crepin's hunger pangs instantly.

CHAPTER NINE

WHEN SHE RETURNED to the cabin, Billy was waiting
for her. They had trouble meeting each other's eyes for a while. She
explained to him that she knew what was going on, and what was
about to happen in here. He told her he was sorry he had brought
the transceiver along on the trip, but that maybe it would turn out
to have been a lucky decision. Her voice, in reply, became edgy and
irritable. He looked so lost and childlike and alone, so unlike Yves
Chabot in so many ways. Suddenly she felt sorry for him, and for
herself, and then she realized that she was crying for the both of
them. They had become almost like strangers, and their new-found
knowledge of the plight of the *Marseille* was something else to hang
heavily between them.

"C'mon, honey." Billy took her face in his hands. "Nothing's
gonna happen. It's gonna be all right."

He started by kissing her wet cheeks, and then her lips, and soon
it seemed more comfortable to both of them to lie down on the bed
together, and to hold on to each other. Then they undressed each
other and got even more comfortable, and for the next hour and a

half, as the sun dipped lower in the western sky off the starboard
side of the ship, they moved together, coupling in slow, well-
remembered rhythms, but it was the nude, erect bodies of Yves
Chabot and Harold Columbine she was seeing behind her tightly
closed, fluttering eyelids as she came with savage intensity crying
"Billy, Billy . . ."

"I'm cold and I gotta take a leak," Harold Columbine said. "Now,
come on."

"Think about a scene from your latest book. That should warm
you up."

"Come on, beautiful, untie me and let me go to the john."

"I untied you when we fed you," the first woman said. "It's too
late now."

"That was only one arm. Please. There's no window in the toilet.
What've you got to worry about?"

"Let him go to the bathroom, Marge," the other woman said.
"I'm sick and tired of hearing him."

"You see? Now there's a broad who understands a man's bladder. Would you like to learn about my bladder, Marge?"

"Wash your mouth out while you're in there."

"Brrr, I'm shivering."

"Hold still if you want me to untie you."

"It's so goddamn cold in here. Would you please get my jacket
out of there?"

"What do you need your jacket for? You're going to the toilet."

"Please?"

"Get his damned jacket, Marybeth."

"Right."

"Look through the pockets first."

"You chicks have seen too many flicks," he said.

"Now just sit up."

"Will you stop pointing that thing at me?"

"Just sit."

"A wallet, a comb, a fountain pen, some change, some Life-
savers," the woman announced.

"All right. Here," the other woman said, handing him the jacket.

"Why is everyone so nice to me?" he said.

"And don't lock the door."

"You promise not to peek in?"

"Just go."

Inside the bathroom, he closed the door, raised the toilet seat and took a long leak, because he had to. Then he flushed the toilet, went to the sink and washed his hands. Examining himself in the mirror, he could find little to admire in the bloodshot eyes and stubbled cheeks. He looked like warmed-over shit. He took a white linen towel from the rack, and instead of drying his hands with it, he dropped the towel into the bowl to let it soak. Then he removed the fountain pen from the inside pocket of his jacket, and uncapped it.

After his fourth best-seller, and his first million, stashed away in twelve different savings and loans, he had decided that he was prime bait for kidnappers. Wiring the Westport house with alarm systems from attic to cellar took care of the home scene. But it was the sidewalks of New York, the midnight wanderings through muggers' paradise, that needed attention, too. Hence, the meetings with Mr. Moretti in a garage in East Orange, New Jersey, a treasure-trove of nasty little devices.

In the two years that he had owned the fountain pen, he had never, thank God, had occasion to use it. Only once had it gone off, and he had trouble resisting a laugh even now as he thought of it in this unsteady, slightly odorous bathroom. He and Walter Zeitlin had been seated in Himmelberg's office, literally on the verge of signing the contracts that would have given Himmelberg's publishing complex twenty-five percent of the soft-cover rights. Fortunately he had taken out the wrong pen and accidentally flicked the button. In the three hours it had taken the janitor's crew to clear Himmelberg House of gas, and make the place habitable again, Zeitlin, a canny agent who believed in signs and portents, had phoned Michaelson of B.&B., gotten him to reconsider, and had quickly closed a precedent-shattering five-book deal involving no percentage of soft cover to the publisher. This little fountain pen had made itself obsolete. To guard his net worth, Harold Columbine now needed a column of tanks and a Distant Early Warning System.

He took the soaking towel from the sink with his left hand, and with his right hand, which was holding the pen, he opened the bathroom door a little. "I feel much better," he announced in a loud voice as he pressed the button that ejected the cartridge into the bedroom. The small explosion and the women's outcries came simultaneously.

"Oh my God, what—?"

"Oh, oh, oh, oh, oh . . ."

Then they started the piteous choking and gasping.

He covered his face with the wet towel, got to his hands and knees, and crawled into the bedroom. Briefly he uncovered one eye, caught a quick glimpse of the two women tearing at their eyes as they stumbled about in the bluish-gray cloud that filled the room, their wigs awry, their guns lying on the floor where they had dropped them. Then, holding the towel tightly to his face, he made his way along the floor to the door, feeling himself beginning to choke.

"Help," gasped one of the women.

"Oh, I . . . oh, oh, I can't . . . *oh* . . ." cried the other.

He fumbled with the lock, pulled the door open and stumbled out into the corridor, shouting, "This way!" Inhaling deeply, he threw the wet towel at them and hurried away. He looked back only once, in time to see the two women sinking to the floor of the corridor, holding on to their contorted faces and making terrible sounds, as the first wisps of gas began to drift out of the poisoned cabin.

That'll teach them. Don't fuck around with the Mounties.

In the ship's hospital, as good a place as any to go with a lump on the noggin and a pretty goddamn hairy story, he got an unsurprised "Yes, we know all about it" from Dr. Yves Chartreuse, or whatever the hell his name was, and a provocative look from the head nurse, who really had *some* head. Also two aspirin. And later when he was let into his cabin by a steward and saw his key lying on the bed, he remembered Julie again, and that sweet little ass of hers.

If she had had any class, she would have waited for him.

Herb Kleinfeld picked up the phone in his cabin with a small twinge of trepidation and dialed Dunleavy's number. While he felt reasonably certain that the intraship phone system was safe, he still used it only sparingly.

Betty Dunleavy answered. "Yes?"

"Is he there?"

"Second."

While he waited, he gazed out through the porthole window. Clouds near the horizon were tinged with the colors of oncoming

CHAPTER NINE

evening, and the roll of the ship made them move in strange ways. Dunleavy came on.

"Yes?"

"Something's come up."

There was a pause. Then Dunleavy said, "Five minutes. The Verandah Deck lounge."

"Right." Kleinfeld hung up. Harriet was lying on the bed watching him. She wore nothing but a slip. He walked over to her, leaned down and kissed her on the lips. "Don't go away."

"Must you?"

"Yes."

"Shall I start dressing for dinner?"

"No, stay as you are. I'll be back."

She smiled up at him. He leaned over, raised her slip and kissed the sweetness down there. She gave a little gasp, holding on to the back of his head. He felt himself hardening and pulled away.

"Gotta go."

When he reached the cocktail lounge on the Verandah Deck, Dunleavy was already there, seated at a small table with his back to the wall, working on a martini. His tan had deepened, and he was dressed in a blue and white seersucker suit, pale blue sportshirt and sandals. Kleinfeld sat down at the adjacent table, parallel to him. When they spoke, they could hear each other, but no one else in the half-filled room would think they were together. After the waiter brought a Scotch on the rocks, Kleinfeld said, "Jerry and Lou are going to handle the wheelroom tonight. Lambert and Finney the bridge. Jackson and Wright in the radio room. Engine room, boiler room, generator room, I don't know who but it's all set."

"You said something's come up."

"Yes, that wasn't it. I just wanted to make sure you were up to date. The burials will be during the dinner hour. About nine p.m."

"You just made my day," said Dunleavy heavily.

"One other thing: Leonard Horner spotted a radio engineer up on one of the antenna masts about thirty minutes ago. He was attaching a wire to something or other, so Horner had him come down, and then he brought in Christain Specht, who explained that they needed the auxiliary antenna because the ship is getting so far off course that it's moving out of radio range. So Horner gave his okay."

"No sweat," said Dunleavy.

"Now . . ." Kleinfeld took a huge gulp of Scotch. "About Gwen Parker."

The other man's eyes narrowed. "What about her?"

"She's coming apart, Craig, totally and completely. George can't handle her. He came to my cabin. He's very worried about what she might do to our plans. She's never seen anyone die before. George feels it was a mistake to let her handle anything like poison."

"All right, it was a mistake. Tomorrow is another day."

"That's not what I'm trying to tell you, Craig . . ."

"Then say it."

"She doesn't want to go through with the deal. She doesn't want the rest of us to go through with it either. She may do something crazy. George doesn't know what to do, so he came to me."

"Go on."

"There is no go on. That's it."

Craig Dunleavy stared into his glass. His mouth was set in a hard, thin line. "How does George feel about Gwen, Herb?"

"I just told you, Craig."

"No, I mean . . . if I handled Gwen . . . how would George . . . feel?"

Kleinfeld looked at the other man for a moment, and then he looked away, down at what was left of his drink. "They've been married a lot of years," he said.

"What does that mean?"

"I think we'd have a problem on our hands with George. Emotionally. Especially after we get there. I don't think he'd ever get over it. I don't think he could live with it, if you want to know my honest feeling."

Dunleavy nodded. His expression was grim. "Have you told Harriet about this?"

"Not a word."

Dunleavy looked at him. "Don't." Then he finished his martini, put a few coins on the table, rose and walked away.

Kleinfeld sat there and played with his drink. He sat there even after the glass was empty. Harriet was waiting for him, but he'd be no good with her now. He was never any good when he felt sick to his stomach.

* * *

George Parker opened the cabin door a few inches and peered out. "Oh, I kind of thought it was you, Craig. Come in." He opened the door wider, and Dunleavy stepped inside, glancing about.

"Where is she?"

"In the bathroom." Parker locked the door, came over to him, running nervous fingers through the thinning hair that partially covered his freckled skull. "Listen, go easy, will you, Craig. I mean she's really hurting."

"I understand, George." He had spotted the letter lying on the table beside the bed. He went over to it, picked it up and skimmed it quickly. It was in Gwen Parker's handwriting, addressed to the Captain of the *Marseille*. It named names, told everything. Dunleavy tossed it back on the table and turned away. Parker was watching him.

"Aren't you going to tear it up?" Parker asked.

"What's the use? She'd write another one, wouldn't she?" When the man didn't answer, Dunleavy said, "Wouldn't she, George?"

"You've got a point," said Parker quietly, and looked away.

"Tell her I'm here, will you? And then, George, listen: I want you to leave us alone for about fifteen minutes. When you come back, if we're not here, be sure to wait for us."

"What are you going to do, Craig?" Parker's voice rose in an apprehensive whine.

"I'm going to have a little talk with her."

"But you *will* go easy now?"

"Of course I will, George."

Parker stepped to the bathroom door and rapped on it. "Honey, can you hear me?" He rapped again. "Honey?"

"What is it?" Her voice sounded drained, empty.

"Honey, Craig is here. Craig Dunleavy." There was no response. "Did you hear what I said?"

"Yes."

"Are you coming out?" He got no answer. "Craig would like to talk to you. Will you come out, honey?"

Finally she said, "All right."

Parker turned to Dunleavy. "Okay, now *please*, Craig." Then he went to the cabin door, unlocked it, and departed.

Presently the bathroom door opened, and Gwen Parker came out. Her face was pale and drawn, her uncombed blond hair loose about her shoulders. She was wearing a brief, filmy, pale yellow poolside robe that was tied at the waist and flared out to show her legs and thighs. The moment Dunleavy saw her thighs, he knew what he was going to do.

She couldn't look at him right away. "Where's George?"

"He'll be right back," said Dunleavy.

"Well . . . I guess you know . . ."

"Jesus, Gwen, I'm so sorry." The gentleness in his voice made her eyes go to his face. "I never intended *this* to happen to you."

"I've been to hell, Craig, and I can't seem to make it back, and I can't stand it there." She picked up the half-empty bottle of gin on the side table and poured some into a tumbler. "I mean, how much of this stuff can I pour into me without it doing anything for me?" She drank it all down, gasping at the shock to her throat, as he watched her carefully. "I want to be asleep, unconscious, dead, I want to go home." Her voice began to tremble. "I don't care how or why, I just want to go home. We're all going home, Craig, before it's too late, only it may be too late, and the more of this gin that I drink, the clearer I can see things, and what I'm seeing is, we're all going to call it off and go home."

"You may be right," Craig said quietly. "You may have a great big point there." She glanced at him quickly. "And I'm going to give it really serious thought tonight, if you'll give me that much time."

She tried to read his expression, then shook her head in pain. "Oh, please don't try to fool me, Craig. Please don't do that."

"Would I do that, honey, at a time like this?" He put an arm around her shoulder, picked up the bottle and poured more gin into the glass in her hand. "Finish that now, will you?"

She drained the glass again. "I'm beginning to feel better," she said, her speech slurring slightly. "Isn't that ridiculous? You say a couple of words to me . . . or maybe it's the gin . . ."

"Come on, we're going up to the Sun Deck."

"We are? What for?"

"I have to talk to you."

"How about right here?"

"I have to talk to you alone. George'll be right back."

"But, honey, look what I'm wearing."

"It's perfect."

"I don't even have a suit on underneath."

"It's fine. Come on."

"Where's my key?"

"You won't need it. Let's go."

In the corridor, he led her to the elevator, and she drew back. "Not the elevator. People. Let's use the stairway. I'm not dressed."

"I like the way you're not dressed," he said, and she glanced at him. He took her hand and helped her up the stairway. She was wearing high-platform shoes, and with the briefness of her robe, her legs seemed even longer than they were. At the landing, he did not let go of her hand even though she was walking quite steadily, considering the alcohol that was fogging her brain. Their palms settled comfortably against each other, and their fingers intertwined as they moved through the ship toward the stern.

"What're we going to talk about?" Gwen asked.

"I hope we're going in the right direction. Yes, I think we are."

"What're we going to talk about, Craig?"

"I have an idea, something that might make us all, particularly you and me, a lot happier while we're going through, well, all that we're going through right now. I wanted to get your reaction."

"I'll give it to you. You just ask me and I'll give it to you," said Gwen.

"Here we are. Right here. It's nice and quiet and we can talk all we want." He led her by the hand out onto the lower Sun Deck. By day, it was used by serious sunbathers. Now, deep in shadow, it was deserted. Beyond the rail, over a hundred feet below, the wake of the *Marseille* was a long trail of churning foam that seemed to be rushing away from them. "Look, not a soul here."

"And it's not even cold," she said.

He brought her over to the wall about a dozen feet away from the railing. She leaned her shoulders back against the wall to rest, and he came around to face her. "How you doing?"

"I don't know," she said. "Okay, I guess. I don't know. What's the diff? Mmm, this breeze feels good, doesn't it? So ask me something, Craig, go ahead and ask me."

"Gwennie, look at me."

"Okay, I'm looking."

"Do you remember the night we first met?"

"You mean the swappers club out in the Valley?"

"Right."

"Oh God, Craig, you were heaven, you were beautiful."

Betty had had George, and he had had Gwen, back in the days when they had been recruiting members for the group in any way that they could think of. Gwen Parker's orgasms had been like epileptic seizures in their violence.

"What would you say if we brought it back to the group again, starting tonight?" He saw her eyes focusing on his face. "Those who don't want to, don't. And those who want to, do . . ."

She was wide-eyed now. "Swap?"

"Swap."

"But, Craig, I thought—"

"I know, a year ago I said that that was out, it would interfere with what we were all trying to accomplish together. But I've changed my mind, Gwennie. I've just got to have it back. Do you know what I'm saying?"

She was breathing through parted lips now. "Yes, I think I do."

"I want you in bed beside me every night, all night long."

"Oh, Craig . . . oh, honey . . . if I weren't so goddamn drunk . . ." She looked into his eyes, searching for the past.

He moved in closer, put his left hand behind her head and brought their mouths together. With his right hand he went through the folds of her robe to her nakedness and found her vulva. Their tongues met, and she pushed against his hand. She began to moan softly, then broke the embrace, breathing heavily. "You've got to stop this . . . We'll be seen . . ."

"Nobody here. And what if there was. Come here, you."

She stepped into his arms, put her hands on his head and slowly kissed him with her open mouth. He held her soft buttocks in his hands and brought her tight against him. She murmured into his open mouth, and he could taste her gin. "What'll we do about George and Betty?"

"Don't worry," he said, "I'll talk to them. I'll handle that."

"You like to handle things, don't you," she murmured. "Oh . . . you better stop handling things, honey . . . you better stop . . ."

"I like this robe . . . I really do . . . I like the way it opens here . . ."

"Ah . . . Jesus . . . we better go back . . . Craig, honey, George'll be waiting. We better . . . oh my God . . ."

Her wetness was moving in his grasp, and her moaning was in his ears.

"Yes," he whispered. "Now . . . yes, now . . ."

"Oh God, I'm so drunk . . . so dizzy . . . Oh, beautiful," she groaned. "Oh, beautiful . . ."

"Move over here," he murmured, leading her by his free hand to the railing. "Sit up on this so I can—"

"Oh, honey, Jesus, don't take it away . . ."

"I'll help you. Up. That's good. That's perfect . . ."

"It's so . . . God, I'm afraid to look down . . . Oh yes, keep it there . . . Keep it there . . . Oh, you beautiful . . ."

"Hold on tight to the back of my neck. Hold on to me . . ."

"Oh, baby . . . Oh, honey . . . Oh, beautiful . . ." Her legs began to spread out wide as she sat on the rail holding on to him. "Oh, Craig . . . Oh, Craig . . ." Her mouth was opening and her eyelids were fluttering and he could feel the first deep warning contractions inside of her. "Oh, Craig . . . Oh, Craig . . ."

He moved very close within her widespread legs. "Find me and put it in," he said urgently. "Help me." Suddenly he withdrew his hand.

"Oh . . . where did you . . . oh, I'm . . . I'm going to . . . oh Jesus, i'm coming . . . Craig, I'm—"

"Help me, quickly," he cried. "Put it in."

"Ohhh . . ." she shouted. "Ohhh . . ." Convulsively her legs clutched his body and her hands came off his neck with an urgent need that knew no caution and thrust down with frantic, futile groping to find him, to fill her pulsating emptiness, but he was not there and never had been and it did not matter because nothing could stop her now, and the sound of her coming was an uncontrollable shriek in his ears as he quickly reached back, seized her ankles, pulled them apart, pushed them upward and forward and sent her tumbling backward, heels over head, into the awful void behind her, and then suddenly her head shattered against the jutting steel of the hull below, whacking the downward wail of her orgasm into instant silence. Her body bounced off and fell into the rushing sea and quickly sank from his view.

He used the men's room of the Brittany Lounge to wash his hands, carefully avoiding his own eyes in the mirror above the sink. Then he went out to the bar, ordered a double martini and hung on to it, waiting for the tremor in his hands to subside. The thin, watery-eyed man on the stool next to him had had too much. His loud voice was assaulting the bartender, who was trapped in a frozen smile.

"I been around much too long, Roland, I don't fool so easy, not on the North Atlantic run, no sirree, boy. We are away off course by a million miles, and they can gimme the bullshit about ocean currents and course correction all they want around here but I ain't buyin', fella. They don't kid Harry Grabiner, because Harry Grabiner happens to be *me,* and you know who *I* am, Roland. I am the guy who is now tellin' you he don't want any ice in the next one, eef you pliz, mon-sewer." He shoved his glass at the bartender, and looked at Dunleavy. "What's the matter with *you,* buddy boy, got the shakeroonies?"

"I wasn't aware of anything being the matter," said Dunleavy.

"Didn't you ever hear of a ship bein' off course? Does that shock ya, does that grab ya, does that get ya right here?" He gripped Dunleavy's thigh.

"Get your hand off me," said Dunleavy evenly.

The man searched his face, looking for the smile. "What's that?"

"I said get your hand off me, or I'll beat the living shit out of you."

"Oh boy, oh boy," the man laughed raucously, but he removed his hand. "You're worse than this friggin' ship, y'know that? You are farther off course than this whole friggin' frog boat."

Dunleavy got off the stool and walked away from the man. Actually, the more pricks like that he ran into on the *Marseille,* the better it was for him . . . the windbags, the assholes, the spoilers of life. Their deaths would not be mourned by many.

When Dunleavy buzzed, George Parker opened the door. For a moment, the man looked puzzled. Dunleavy went in past him. Parker glanced out into the corridor, then closed the door and turned. "Where is she?"

"I took her down to see Betty," said Dunleavy. He went over to the table where the letter was, and saw the cabin key in the ashtray next to it.

"Well, how did it go?" Parker asked. "I came right back, but you were both gone. What happened? Is she all right?"

"Everything went fine." Dunleavy put the key and the letter in his pocket as he turned. "She's going to be all right, George."

"I mean now. How is she now?" The apprehensive eyes wouldn't leave Dunleavy's face for a moment.

"She's much better."

"Are you sure?"

"You don't believe me, why don't you call her?" He indicated the phone. "Go on, call her."

Parker shook his head. "No, that's all right. But I have to know what went on, what she's going to do . . ."

"She's not going to do anything, George. It's all taken care of. Now you and I, we're going to have to have a little talk."

"How in the world did you swing it, Craig?"

"Not here, George. We go for a little walk, okay? I need it badly."

"A walk?"

"*And* a little talk. On the Sun Deck. All right?"

Parker shrugged. "If you say so."

Dunleavy opened the cabin door and waited.

Parker said, "Will I need a sweater?"

"No," Dunleavy said. "Where you're going I don't think you'll need anything."

He let Parker go out first, so he could size him up from the rear. Then he took him by the arm and they started for the Sun Deck.

He figured him to be about a hundred and forty-two.

CHAPTER TEN

————————

MISS RUTHANNE HARTWELL of Modesto, California, placed and successfully completed a ship-to-shore telephone call from a phone booth in the Verandah Deck lounge of the S.S. *Marseille* to a Mr. James Heck, proprietor of a saloon called Heck's Bad Boy on Lexington Avenue in New York City. During the brief conversation, duly monitored in the communications room out of interest rather than necessity, Miss Hartwell informed her boyfriend that she was feeling fine and having lots of fun. Immediately after she hung up, James Heck took a handful of quarters from the cash register, left his saloon, went outside to a telephone booth, placed a station-to-station call to a number in Phoenix, Arizona, and told the man who answered, who identified himself as Stanley, that all was okay with Ruthie. The man named Stanley hung up, and promptly made an overseas phone call to Paris, France, to an establishment on the rue des Beaux-Arts which specialized in the art and handicraft of Southeast Asia. Waiting for the phone call ever since his arrival in Paris that day, after the polar flight from

Los Angeles, was the man named Julian Wunderlicht. The message from Phoenix was brief and to the point. It consisted of three words: We are ready.

CHAPTER ELEVEN

————————————

AS HE SAT now at a small sidewalk table at the Brasserie
Lipp, nursing his glass of Perrier water and gazing idly at the traffic
of slender, long-haired girls and trim, well-tanned young men who
moved slowly by in the summer evening dusk, Julian Wunderlicht
resolved that he would not let any transient twinges of apprehension spoil his pleasure at being in Paris again, at being able to sit
here on the Boulevard St.-Germain, among people who appeared to
be devoted solely to the joys of eating and drinking and making
love in public and outdoing each other with uniquely attractive
costumes. True, it had been in nobody's plans, not Dunleavy's, not
Kleinfeld's, certainly not his, that the Director General would be
away from his desk for the week, away in Antibes to comfort a wife
whose mother had just passed away. No one could have prepared
for that. But he was simply not going to let it worry him now. There
was no reason to believe that the Assistant to the Director General,
this man Sauvinage they had switched him to, could not accept
instructions and relay them to a board of directors just as promptly
and forcefully as his superior.

By nature Wunderlicht was an optimist. He had undertaken an assignment, therefore it would be carried out. He had ordered Georges Sauvinage to meet him here. Georges Sauvinage would arrive. A good head had carried Julian Wunderlicht through a lot worse than an accidental change in plans. He was a handsome man of forty-eight with graying blond hair and a pleasing German accent that he had somehow never managed to lose in the years spent at Lockheed Missiles & Space after being brought over to the United States from Stuttgart as the *wunderkind* of solid-state propulsion. The months of standing on long lines at the unemployment insurance office, after the cutbacks and shutdowns, and the year of ignominy as a used car salesman in Lancaster, had not dimmed his quick smile or his sanguine outlook. If they took away the work you were trained for, the work you did so well, you found something else to do, and you did that well, too. In this case, the work had found *him*.

When Craig Dunleavy had come wandering into the used car lot for the first time that memorable afternoon in May, Dunleavy had truly seemed to have nothing more on his mind than the possibility of unloading six vehicles belonging to friends of his, with delivery to be withheld until July 8. Wunderlicht had been his usual cooperative and pleasantly conversational self, and why not? That's what he was being paid for. The very next day, Herb Kleinfeld had appeared with a similar inquiry, this one for four cars, with the same unusual delivery date. And so Wunderlicht was hardly surprised when the two men showed up together as a team a few days later, and asked him if he'd like to have lunch with them.

He was never sure exactly which of the anecdotes he had told them about his past, or what qualities of personality and character he had unwittingly revealed, had appealed to them so much. Over cocktails, they had seemed decidedly unamused at his recounting of the sweet uses of his sexual prowess to coax a Cadillac Seville out of a wealthy La Jolla widow fifteen years older than he was. In fact, they showed interest and pleasure only when he told them that he had finally had to *sell* the damned car in order to pay for his expensive clothing and his vintage wines, to which, unfortunately, he was addicted. Technical skills aside, he had tossed very little else into the air other than his many temperamental scrapes with the authorities at Lockheed, his blissful years of bachelorhood with its colorful female entanglements, and of course his current disdain for his role as a peddler of soiled motor vehicles.

Whatever it was that he had said, or *not* said (there was little crap about remorse or ethics in Wunderlicht's vocabulary), the proposal that Craig Dunleavy and Herb Kleinfeld had cautiously begun to put to him over the shrimp cocktail, and fully revealed to him by the time the coffee arrived, was startling to say the least, a proposal which he was sure they would not have made to just any used car salesman they happened to chance upon. And though the assignment would be unlike anything he had ever undertaken in his whole life, he had had total confidence in his ability to handle it. If he had felt otherwise, he never would have accepted the twenty-five thousand dollars that was finally agreed upon.

Looking up now from his sidewalk table at the Brasserie Lipp, Wunderlicht saw the pudgy man with the rumpled suit and the oily black hair crossing the boulevard toward him, and knew immediately that it had to be Georges Sauvinage. His appearance so closely matched the weariness and disappointment with self that his voice had conveyed on the telephone, that Wunderlicht would have recognized him even if he had not been carrying the folded newspaper under his left arm as agreed upon. Wunderlicht rose to his feet, beckoning to him, and Sauvinage came over to the table.

"Wunderlicht?" He was damp with sweat, and clearly irritated.

"That's right. Please sit down, Mr. Sauvinage." Wunderlicht's French was good, thanks to five years at the Sorbonne during the formative years, but his accent was sufficient to leave little doubt that he had been born and raised in Germany. They would be searching the lists looking for all Germanic foreigners who had recently arrived at French ports of entry, and would pay scant attention to an American from California, particularly one whose forged passport bore the name James Taggart. "Come have a drink," he said, pulling back a chair for his reluctant guest.

"I am late for dinner, as you can well imagine," muttered Sauvinage, easing his overweight body into the chair. To the waiter he said, "A Calva, please." Then he glanced at his wristwatch and looked at his host. "I have exactly ten minutes, Wunderlicht, not a minute more, in which to hear from you, a total stranger, the information which will prove so 'vital' to my future with the Compagnie Française, but which, unfortunately, is far too 'sensitive' even to be hinted at on the telephone. If you are an insurance salesman, Wunderlicht, or a freelance journalist—"

"We have seized one of your ships."

"—or someone looking for a complimentary voyage to Tahiti on one of our winter cruises—"

"Sauvinage."

"—I beg you to spare me now, because I cannot live with my wife's sullen expression when I walk in past the deadline for duck à l'orange."

"We have seized the *Marseille*," said Wunderlicht.

"Oh, for heaven's sake," said the Frenchman with weary impatience. "Is this the kind of—?"

"I suggest you listen to every word," Wunderlicht broke in. "If there is something you don't understand, please tell me and I will repeat it. As soon as I finish, I will place a certain telephone call for you. You will then be able to verify, to your own satisfaction, what I am about to tell you." The Frenchman was twisting around in his chair, looking about. "I might add that it would be suicidal, right now, for you even to *think* of the police."

"Then to prevent my untimely death," Sauvinage snapped angrily, "suppose you get on with it."

Wunderlicht took a sip of his Perrier water, and with maddening calm he began to tell the Frenchman how the *Marseille* had been taken over. Strollers on the Boulevard St.-Germain who glanced down at the two men in passing might have thought that the blond German was telling the dark-haired Frenchman how he had just taken his wife away from him, for the Frenchman wore a pained and sullen expression, and he did not look at the other man at all, but merely gazed across the boulevard with blank, unseeing eyes. When the waiter brought his Calvados, he finished it in one great gulp, but it did nothing to relieve the dread that was growing in his stomach. This man had to be lying. The whole thing was a gigantic hoax. Someone was trying to play a nasty trick on him. If only he could stop recalling those messages from that radioman, Delade. He should have paid more attention to them. There might still have been time to do something. He would be accused of gross negligence.

"You are lying," he suddenly blurted out.

"Let me finish," the other man said evenly. "Then we will make the phone call."

"I am already late for dinner. This is terrible." Sauvinage wiped his sweating face with a handkerchief.

"Your dinner, Mr. Sauvinage, early or late, is a trivial matter compared to the responsibility I am now going to lay in your lap, namely, the saving of three thousand lives."

Sauvinage winced, shaking his head in pain. "Now stop this. You have gone far enough. I want you to stop this . . ."

"The group I represent has not seized the *Marseille* for the sport of it, or to prove it can be done, like climbing Mount Everest. Unless their demands are met—"

"I don't want to hear anything about demands. How dare you talk to me about demands." The man's voice shook with fear.

"Please, Mr. Sauvinage."

"I have had *enough* of this," he cried.

"Unless their demands are met, the *Marseille,* its passengers and its crew will be sunk without a trace," said Wunderlicht evenly.

Sauvinage tried to say something. His mouth moved, but no words came out. His face seemed to be going to pieces.

Slowly, Wunderlicht repeated, "Sunk . . . without . . . a trace." He wet his lips with a sip of Perrier water and glanced at the other man, who had slumped in his chair. "Perhaps you would like another brandy?"

The Frenchman's voice was flat and empty. "Give me your demands, you son of a bitch. Then I will have you thrown in jail."

Wunderlicht smiled. "Certain colleagues of mine on the other side of the boulevard are watching us through Bausch and Lomb's best lenses. They would take unpleasant action, if you did." He saw the Frenchman's quick frightened glance to the other side of the crowded street, and was pleased with his little lie. He allowed the tone of his voice to become more imperative. Sauvinage had delayed him long enough. "Now, these are the terms that you will deliver to the Director General and to the board of directors of your company, but to no one else. Any revelation of the *Marseille* matter either to the news media or to the authorities of any government will lead to instant and total disaster in the Atlantic. Is that completely understood?"

"I hear you—"

"Good."

"—But if you expect me to guarantee the silence of people over whom I have no control, you are a bigger ass than I think you are."

"It is up to you, Mr. Sauvinage. All I can guarantee to you is the consequences, if you fail."

"Goddamn it, will you tell me what you *want*."

Wunderlicht's features hardened. "There are approximately two thousand passengers on the *Marseille*. We feel it is eminently reasonable to consider the life of each of them to be worth five thousand dollars in ransom."

Sauvinage blinked several times. "Ten million dollars?" He tried a bravura laugh, but it came out weak and unconvincing.

"We will throw in the lives of one thousand crew members, including the Captain and his staff, without charge," said Wunderlicht, without smiling.

"Your generosity is overwhelming," said Sauvinage bitterly.

"Now, as to the ship itself—"

"Ah, yes."

"To avoid the total destruction of the *Marseille,* to guarantee its immediate passing, undamaged, into the hands of the Captain and his crew, an additional ransom payment of twenty-five million dollars is to be made. The total, therefore, is thirty-five million."

The Frenchman stared at Wunderlicht. Wunderlicht stared right back. "Are you through?" Sauvinage said, with contempt in his voice.

"Listen to me carefully," said Wunderlicht. "The money is to be placed, in the form of gold ingots, in the passenger cabin of a 747 jet aircraft to be provided by you. The aircraft containing the gold is to be parked at the extreme northern end of the field at Charles de Gaulle Airport, beyond runway 800, and is to be left standing there, fueled for a flight of nine thousand miles and ready for takeoff, with no one inside the plane or within one thousand yards outside on the field, except for a minimum ground crew necessary to start up the engines, and they are not to appear until notified by the control tower. We will provide the pilots, and after its use, the plane will be recoverable by its owner. When the plane bearing the gold arrives safely and securely at its destination, the *Marseille* will be contacted. The ship, its passengers, and its crew will be released immediately, in an orderly fashion that will permit my people to take leave of the ship for their own private journey. If the plane bearing thirty-five million dollars in gold bullion fails, for any reason whatsoever, to reach its destination safely and securely, nothing on earth, or on the sea, can prevent a catastrophe." Wunderlicht glanced off to his right, pointing. "You will observe, now, the time on the clock in the tower of the church of St.-Germain-des-Pres." Sauvinage turned his head reluctantly and looked off at the clock. "You and your colleagues have exactly forty-eight hours in which to meet our demands."

The Frenchman glanced at him sharply. "It is impossible," he said.

"There will be no extension, Sauvinage. Forty-eight hours." He met the Frenchman's stare. "And now we will call the commandant of the *Marseille* by ship-to-shore telephone to verify the situation on board. Two or three discreet questions will have to suffice." Wunderlicht stood up. "Come with me, please."

"This whole thing is—"

"Come. It's getting late." Wunderlicht walked away from the table to the curb and crossed the street to the taxi station, as the Frenchman slowly got to his feet. Wunderlicht opened the door of the lead cab, signaled with his right hand to his nonexistent colleagues across the boulevard, and gestured to Sauvinage to join him. Then he told the driver to take them to the Hotel George V.

During the ride, he spoke only once to the Frenchman, who sat beside him in gloomy silence. "Undoubtedly the Compagnie Française and various agencies of the law will be tempted to try to locate the *Marseille,* even though you have been warned of the consequences, even though the ship is a mere speck in the vastness of the Atlantic. So again I must remind you that the radar equipment aboard the *Marseille* is in the hands of my people. If any vessel should come within fifty miles of the *Marseille* on an onward course, the lives of fifty passengers will be forfeited. And if any aircraft should overfly the ship in a suspicious manner, the same number of lives will be sacrificed. It pains me to make such statements, but I am following the instructions of desperate men."

Sauvinage looked briefly at Wunderlicht, then turned away to gaze out of the cab window with dull, unseeing eyes. He thought of all the little things that used to make him unhappy, before this night, and he longed for just one of them.

At the George V, Wunderlicht steered Sauvinage across the crowded lobby to a leather sofa near the entrance to the telephone room. Then he himself went up to the window behind which the three operators sat, and arranged for the placement of the call to the S.S. *Marseille* by way of marine radio.

"What is your name and room number, please?" inquired the woman at the switchboard.

"I am paying for it in cash," replied Wunderlicht.

"And you are the calling party?"

"The Compagnie Française," said Wunderlicht. "The Compagnie Française Atlantique is calling the commandant, Charles Girodt. G-I-R-O-D-T."

"Charles Girodt."

"And would you please connect the call to both telephone booths out here? There are two of us."

The woman looked up. "I don't know about that, m'sieur."

Wunderlicht gave her a smile. "I would deeply appreciate it, young lady."

The woman shrugged. "Very well."

"Thank you."

Wunderlicht went to the sofa and sat down beside Sauvinage. He took out a pack of cigarettes and offered one to the Frenchman, who shook his head sullenly. He lit one for himself and exhaled slowly. He felt surprisingly relaxed, almost fulfilled. True, this evening's work was not the kind of work he had been trained for, but doing anything well was, in its own way, satisfying, so much more satisfying than haggling over fifty dollars with some greedy buyer of a used Chevrolet pickup truck under the hot California sun. He gazed about the lobby, noting with pleasure the profusion of modish, desirable women. In Paris, they seemed to grow even more attractive as they passed forty. He began to speculate, with supreme confidence, on the lovely liaisons he would be having when he made his way back to this enchanting city after everything had blown over and his trail had been forever lost. A fantasized idyll on the thick living room carpet of a penthouse apartment on the Ile St.-Louis was interrupted by the voice of the switchboard operator calling him.

Wunderlicht went quickly to the phone booth on the right, gesturing Sauvinage into the booth beside it. Both men picked up their telephones and heard the hollow, metallic crackling on the line. A voice at the other end said: "This is the *Marseille*. Go ahead, Paris."

Wunderlicht heard Sauvinage first. "Hello? Hello? Is this the Commandant, M'sieur Girodt?"

Another voice came in through the static. "Charles Girodt here. Go ahead."

"Sir, this is Georges Sauvinage of Françat. I am Assistant to the Director General."

"Yes, I am aware of you, Sauvinage. Will you please speak louder. The connection is poor."

The Frenchman's voice rose. "Sir, this call is being monitored."

"I am being monitored too," said Charles Girodt.

"I am calling to tell you that I have just been given complete details of the situation that now prevails. I have been instructed to call you to verify the matter, sir."

"Instructed by whom, Sauvinage?"

"By one of their representatives, who is here right beside me . . ."

Wunderlicht broke in. "Finish it, please," he said tersely.

"Commandant, sir," said Sauvinage, "just tell me this: Is control in other hands?"

"That is correct, other hands," said Girodt.

"Completely?" asked Sauvinage.

"Totally," replied Girodt.

"Don't worry," Sauvinage cried. "God bless you, sir."

"Thank you," said the captain of the *Marseille*. "Goodbye."

Wunderlicht heard Sauvinage hang up, and then he heard the first voice at the other end come back on. "This is the *Marseille*. We are ready."

"This is Uncle Julian," said Wunderlicht. "Do you know me?"

"Yes, Wunderlicht, we do."

Wunderlicht looked at his wristwatch and said, "The deadline will be, I repeat, the deadline will be exactly forty-seven hours and twenty-one minutes, forty-seven hours and twenty-one minutes from . . . *now*."

"We have that, Uncle Julian. Thank you, and until we meet again, good night."

Wunderlicht hung up and went outside to pay for the call. Sauvinage was still sitting in his booth when Wunderlicht came away from the telephone operator's window. He rapped on the door of the booth, and the Frenchman opened it.

"Are you satisfied with what you heard?" asked Wunderlicht.

Sauvinage did not look at him. "Yes," he said.

"I will call you at your office at twelve noon tomorrow, just to inquire after your health."

"I don't suppose there is any place we can reach you?" the Frenchman said, tentatively.

"I don't suppose so," said Wunderlicht.

"Then excuse me." Sauvinage abruptly slammed the door of the booth in his face.

Wunderlicht smiled and walked away. Let the poor bastard win the final pot of the evening. It was such a small one at that. He inhaled deeply of rich female perfume as he moved through the lobby to the entrance, wondering which call Sauvinage would be making first, the one to the Director General with the grieving wife in Antibes, or the one to the angry wife with the overcooked duck à l'orange.

Outside, a slight breeze had come up, and the night was fragrant. He turned to his left and started for the Champs-Élysées. He would take a leisurely stroll, surrounded by the delightful people of Paris, and then he would give himself over to a superb and endless dinner at some expensive restaurant. He would order a cold bottle of Clos Sainte-Odile, and a heady Château La-Mission-Haut-Brion '59, and top it all off with a bottle of Dom Pérignon, and then he would look across the room and . . . and then . . .

Suddenly a pang of deep loneliness clutched at his heart. He began to walk faster.

CHAPTER TWELVE

THE NEW SENSE of urgency in the communications room was palpable. The place crackled with a tension that was equal to the crashes of atmospheric static coming from the loudspeakers. Charles Girodt stood waiting for Christain Specht to arrive, feeling a dull ache at the base of his skull. The Chief Radio Officer had been summoned by the two strangers who had carefully supervised Girdot's phone conversation with Paris. After that conversation, the strangers had explained to Girodt, without emotion, the same terms that had been laid down by Julian Wunderlicht in Paris.

Girodt had not been surprised. He had recently lost much of his ability to be surprised by any actions involving humans. It had taken effort, though, to conceal his heart-sinking dismay at the threat that fifty innocent lives would be the penalty for each infraction of their instructions. He thought of the young doctor, Berlin, and his appealing wife, Julie, and his palms began to sweat. Had he had the moral right to place their lives, and the lives of so many others, in jeopardy by requesting that a clandestine radio station be set up on the *Marseille?* Nowhere in the codes and manuals of the sea was there anything that gave him the right to play God.

For an instant, a vision of the lovely peaceful view from his bedroom window at the spa in Langenthal flashed through his mind. Josette was beside him, and Henri Cachon, too, soothing him. Quickly he erased the picture and turned as Christain Specht entered the communications room. The Chief Radio Officer glanced at Girodt, then at the two men who moved toward him. Apprehension flickered in his eyes. Girodt quickly stepped forward, saying, "Allow me," and turned to Specht. "The Compagnie Française has been contacted in Paris with a set of demands. I will give you and the rest of my staff all the details. But first, these gentlemen apparently have some business with you."

The younger of the two strangers, a pasty-faced man with rapidly blinking eyes, addressed the Chief Radio Officer. "Mr. Specht, starting immediately, there is to be a total radio blackout of the *Marseille* until further notice. That means ship-to-shore, teletype, navy, coast guard, marine radio, company radio, all bands, all frequencies. No transmissions whatsoever outside of radar scanning. However, all frequencies must be monitored on a twenty-four-hour basis, inasmuch as we expect to receive certain occasional communications. We have already instructed those of your men on duty now. I will count on you to notify the rest of your men."

Specht stared at him for a moment. "Very well." Then he glanced briefly at Girodt, and Girodt knew that he had just thought of Dr. William Berlin.

"May we be alone now?" Girodt inquired of the strangers. "There is much to be handled."

The pasty-faced man nodded to his companion, and the two men departed.

Christain Specht spoke quietly to his superior. "The antenna is connected. As soon as we decide what it is we want him to do, he is ready to go on the air."

"I think I have already decided," said Charles Girodt.

At nine o'clock that night, ship's time, near an opening deep in the stern just above water level, two passengers disguised in the garb of the kitchen detail assisted in the disposal of kitchen waste and other refuse into the sea. Regular crew members did not bother to object to the presence of their unwanted assistants, knowing full well that they had no power to resist them.

Eggshells, melon rinds, beef bones, half-eaten rolls and orange peels skimmed onto the churning wake of the *Marseille* and disappeared into the darkness. The sheet-swathed bodies which the two disguised passengers had wheeled up to the opening in a canvas-enclosed towel truck soon joined the other refuse, and sank below the surface immediately upon hitting the water.

Before taking Betty to a late dinner, Craig Dunleavy phoned several acquaintances in their cabins to tell them that Uncle Julian was feeling fine in Paris, and please spread the news. He told no one, not yet, that Gwen and George Parker had dropped out of the bridge game permanently. Meanwhile, Herb Kleinfeld relayed the glad tidings to *his* shipboard friends, before escorting Harriet to the Vendôme Room for a lobster and champagne dinner. His stomach was in fine shape again. Apparently many of the passengers were feeling good that night, for there was an inordinate amount of champagne consumed in the dining rooms of the *Marseille,* in Tourist as well as in First Class. The sommeliers, comparing notes, attributed it to the unusually warm air and sunshine they had had all day.

"I feel it would be foolhardy for us to sneer at their terms," said Captain Girodt to the staff group he had assembled in his quarters. "Let us proceed on the assumption that they mean what they say, and let us also assume the worst; namely, that the Compagnie Française will be unwilling, or unable, to raise the thirty-five million dollars. The question becomes then, what can we do to overthrow this phantom group of individuals in less than forty-eight hours, without visiting bloodshed onto the decks of the *Marseille?*"

"Are you worried about the blood of passengers and crew?" asked Second Officer Dulac. "Or of the phantoms?"

"God forgive me," answered Girodt, "but the blood of the phantoms must be considered spillable. Now, let us go around the table, starting with Dr. Chabot."

"If we knew who they were," said the Chief Medical Officer, "and I mean to the last man or woman, why then I would seek some means, exclusive of the firearms we do not have, some means of wiping them out simultaneously. A tall order, I grant you. With your permission, Commandant, I would like to prepare an inventory of all drugs and chemicals in our hospital, hopefully for transmission to someone on land who has a more brilliant and creative imagination than I seem to have at the moment."

"An excellent idea," said Charles Girodt. "Please do it." He turned his head. "Now what about you, Leboux?"

The Staff Captain cleared his throat. "I am a broken record, repeating the same unpopular tune. I think we should make a full disclosure to the passengers of every detail of their predicament, and rely on their mass motivation to find and eliminate the rotten apples among them. I admit, I have no idea how they can find out which are the rotten ones."

"I have deep respect for your opinions, Andre," said Girodt, "and I may be terribly wrong in disagreeing with them, but I still believe we will create more hysteria than we can handle, and more killings than we can stomach, if we throw this open to the passengers. In my opinion, we are doing them a great service by letting them relax and enjoy themselves, oblivious to the danger they are in. If and when there appears to be a clear and urgent need to destroy their illusions, why then, of course, we will do it."

"I will try to get my broken record unstuck," said Andre Leboux.

"Emile Vergnaud?"

"Yes, Captain," said the Chief Purser. "Why was the busboy, Senestro, killed?"

"We have no idea, Vergnaud. He confided to no one before he died."

"What about the maid, Filomena?"

"We know nothing about her either," said Girodt, "other than the possibility that she and poor Senestro may have been sleeping with each other."

"The last time she was seen alive by any of my staff, she was working in the cabin of a Mr. and Mrs. Parker, two Americans."

"I suggest you question them, Vergnaud, though I doubt that you will learn anything significant."

"Very well, Captain."

"Anything else? Any other suggestions?" Girodt glanced around the table. "Mr. Specht? Demangeon? Ferret? Dulac? Plessier?"

The Chief Engineer, Pierre Demangeon, spoke up. "Sir, am I correct in assuming that we are not to reveal the new developments regarding ransom, et cetera, to the crew?"

"Correct," said Girodt. "With the exception, of course, of Mr. Specht's radio men, who must be alerted. The crew has, I must say, been behaving admirably under the present circumstances. Either because they have been well instructed by you gentlemen, or because of fear, or simply out of lack of imagination, they appear to be going about their duties as though nothing extraordinary is happening to the *Marseille*."

"Forgive me, Captain," said the Chief Engineer, "but I do not want you to sleep too peacefully tonight. I must tell you that *my* men, down below, were extremely upset at the disappearance and probable death of the security guard, Bobo Crepin. I would hazard a guess that if, somehow, a large supply of weapons should suddenly materialize in our midst, your well-behaved crew would quickly become a secret army of one thousand guerrillas with blood in their eyes."

"Then thank God there are no weapons on the horizon." Girodt was momentarily shaken by the Chief Engineer's remarks. He rose to his feet. "All right, gentlemen. Thank you. Dr. Chabot. Mr. Specht. A word with you, please."

When the other men had departed, Girodt addressed himself to the Chief Medical Officer and the Chief Radio Officer. "Nothing I have just heard here has changed my own previous decision. The executive branch of the Compagnie Française is holding a complete passenger information list for this sailing. I don't know how it is to be done, or who will do it, and I know I am asking the impossible, but I know it must be done, and done with impossible speed. From that information list of two thousand passengers, we must somehow uncover the names of those on board this ship who are our secret enemies, and then find the means to do away with them. Gentlemen, you have a radio station. I have just given you its immediate mission. And now, if you will excuse me, I am going to dinner."

Girodt was pleased with the way he had conducted himself, despite the ache in his skull.

Sitting behind his own desk twenty minutes later, Dr. Yves Chabot buzzed Genvieve Bordoni and asked her to summon Mrs. Berlin to his office immediately. He wished to give her the results of the throat culture examination.

"Throat culture?" The head nurse sounded puzzled. "Do you happen to have it, Doctor?"

"No," said Chabot.

"Well, I'm afraid I don't have it either," she said.

"I am well aware of that," said Chabot. "And Miss Bordoni, I know it's late, but I do want you to remain at your desk until I'm through with Mrs. Berlin. I want absolutely no interruptions while she is here."

"I will try," said Genvieve Bordoni.

A short time thereafter, Julie Berlin visited the ship's hospital, and then returned to her cabin to convey the results of her medical examination to her husband, who sat propped up in bed eating dinner. To any itinerant steward, waiter, or busboy who might wander in, he presented the easily readable picture of an indisposed passenger, confined to his bed and his closed-circuit TV.

When Julie had finished her twice-repeated, carefully spelled out set of instructions, Billy Berlin swallowed the grapefruit section in his mouth and said, "If they want to believe in miracles, that's fine with me. I'll do my best. But, Jesus, they haven't the faintest idea how tough this is going to be."

"There must be some way I can help, isn't there?" asked Julie.

"Yeah," said Billy. "Number one, I want you out of here."

"No, I'm staying right here with you," she protested. "If I don't do something, I'll go out of my mind worrying."

The young doctor sat up straight in bed. "Honey, now don't argue with me, because this is one you're not going to win. It's *danger* time in this cabin. If anything should happen, like maybe I get caught red-handed with the microphone stuck down my throat, I am not going to have *you* involved. I want you to go put your face on, and something else that's equally pretty, and get the hell out of here and have yourself a terrific dinner and whatever *else* the French Atlantic Line has to offer other than sea pirates. If I need you, I'll know how to find you. But don't call me, I'll call you."

"You say the sweetest things."

"That's why you married me."

"I knew there must've been a reason."

"All right. Screw."

"You said that was number one," said Julie. "What was number two?"

"Nothing specific really," said Billy. "But, look, you say you want to do something to keep your sanity . . ."

"Absolutely."

"Well, I'm sure the Captain wouldn't exactly *object* if you found some way of ferreting out, right here on board the *Marseille,* what I'm supposed to pull out of the goddamn thin air."

Julie nodded slowly. "I like that." Her eyes narrowed. "Yes, I think I like that . . ."

"Now listen, I don't mean exposing yourself to any kind of serious trouble, do you understand?"

She smiled at him and leaned down over the bed and tasted grapefruit on his lips. "Don't worry about Mata Hari," she murmured.

"Yeah? *She* wound up dead," he said.

Julie patted the look of concern from his face and started for the closet, turning things over rapidly in her mind.

She'd put on her Estée Lauder Eyes in Persian Sea, and those long fake lashes she'd been dying to try for months now, and the new Joseph Magnins with the incredible spiked heels, and the filmy black chiffon Vicky Tiel from Giorgio's that showed everything and then some, and she'd just follow her shadowed blue eyes and her not bad little nose and, if she managed to forget the bra, anything *else* she had (which was not inconsiderable) that could point the way, and she'd see where they led her . . . and if it was to trouble, well, there were all kinds of trouble, good trouble and bad trouble, and maybe if she was lucky tonight, she would not be alone when she got into either one of them.

A certain ink-stained wretch was no longer among the missing, and he'd have to show his face *sometime.*

CHAPTER THIRTEEN

HAROLD COLUMBINE, shaky on the inside but resplendent on the outside in a Dorso tuxedo, black patent-leather Guccis, and a black velvet tie, walked slowly down the great staircase of the Luxembourg dining room, as always, prepared not to be at all surprised should the entire room rise to its feet with a shattering burst of applause. His queasy stomach and rubbery legs told him that he should have taken to his bed. But years of creating intrepid and indefatigable male protagonists for his worldwide reading public had had a permanent effect on his psyche. He had become incapable of any behavior alien to the mythic creatures of his dreams. He wanted to talk like them, think like them, fuck like them, and possibly even die like them. What was important to Harold Columbine, even more so than what the critics said about his books, was what the press said about his lifestyle. He wanted above all to be permanently Number One on the Best Heller List.

He started uncertainly toward his table (it seemed like years since he had seen it), studiously avoiding the effusive welcoming crap of the maître d'. When, out of the corner of his somewhat bloodshot eye, he saw Julie Berlin seated alone at her appointed table, his fertile novelist's brain instantaneously dashed off a scene in which he, the guilty party, walked right by her table, ignoring her now and forever more, the character known as Harold Columbine muttering lightly to himself, "Fuck 'er." But in the next instant, taking a cue from this rough first draft, his fertile brain immediately rewrote the line to read, "I'd still like to," and put the character into a new scene, which the author decided to accept as final. He walked over to her table, to brazen it out.

"Hello, sweetie. How's my doll?"

Julie looked up at him and smiled brightly. "Oh, hello there, Harold. So nice to see you."

He stood there staring down at her. What the fuck was all that sweetness and light about? "Where is your *hus*-band?" he asked, for a filler.

"Not feeling well," said Julie. "Nothing terminal. Just the flu. He had dinner in our stateroom, and turned me loose for the evening."

"Now that's what I call an understanding husband. May I join you?"

"I'm surprised you'd want to," Julie said. She had already decided how she'd handle him.

"Listen, I just came in," he said, sitting down beside her. "Have I missed something important? I seem to be somewhere out in Stupidsville."

Julie smiled. "What's troubling you, Harold?"

"Well, for one thing, don't I owe you some sort of apology, or explanation, for last night?"

Julie patted his hand. "I thought your behavior was perfectly understandable, considering the circumstances."

"Really?"

"Sure. I did a little cock teasing . . . and got results."

He blushed. Jesus Christ, blue pencil that blush. Harold Columbine doesn't blush. But that gorgeous childlike face of hers with those wide-eyed baby blues . . . "You continue to astonish me," he said.

"All right," she said.

"About last night . . ." he started.

"Here's what happened," she broke in. "As soon as I left you, I got cold feet, quickly went back where I belonged and promptly fell into a much-needed coma. I can imagine the agony you must have endured when you got to your stateroom and found your bed empty. However, to quote my husband, a medical authority on all sorts of matters, no man ever died from a case of blue balls."

He blushed again, and eyed her carefully. "You mean, you didn't go to my cabin?"

"Only to drop the key on your bed."

"I didn't, as we say, stand you up?"

"No, Harold, you didn't," Julie said.

He looked at her steadily and she held his gaze until the waiter came and took his order. Then he lit a cigarette and gazed at her again. "Y'know, you're a pretty fantastic broad."

She looked at him with great innocence. "What did I do?"

"You forgot, or decided to forget, or hoped I wouldn't notice, the mound of half-smoked, lipstick-coated cigarette butts in the ashtray next to my bed."

Julie grimaced. "Damn."

"Most people go out of their *way* to find reasons to call me a shit, and they don't have to go very far," he said. "You, on the other hand, *you* make like it was the other way around, to protect me. Now don't go making a nice guy out of me, baby. You'll destroy me."

"I'll be careful, I promise."

"So why'd you do it?"

Julie shrugged. "Hell hath no fury like a man accused. And I think I may need you."

"Me?"

"Yes. It has to do with why you were no-show last night."

"Listen, if I told you what happened, you wouldn't believe me, believe me."

Julie looked at him with a little smile. "Harold, I'd believe you even if you told me someone hit you over the head and knocked you unconscious and you were held prisoner all night by two armed, middle-aged ladies."

He stared at her for a long time, shaking his head in awe.

"It's not that mysterious," she said finally. "We have the same doctor. On this ship, he's the only thermometer in town."

"Ah," he nodded. "Ah."

They waited until the waiter had set the hearts of artichoke before him and moved away. Then Julie spoke in a more serious tone. "I have an idea. Tell me how it sits with you."

"Okay."

"You and I may be the only two passengers on this ship who know that something terribly wrong is going on . . ."

"All I know is what I felt on the back of my skull, and what the doctor told me. I only suspect the rest," Harold Columbine said.

"I intend to bring you as completely up to date as *I* am," said Julie. "But only if you really want to take the responsibility of knowing."

"Just out of curiosity, what are the consequences?"

"A slight case of getting killed," said Julie.

"Hell, I've been there and back," he said.

"It'd be just the two of us, Harold."

"What about your husband?"

"He's aware, but for reasons I'll go into some other time, he has to be ruled out. We'd be a secret army of two."

"I'm practically a marked man, sweetie, you know that, don't you? I escaped from these people. I don't know who they are, but I did escape from them. They'll be looking for me."

"And we'll be looking for *them*," Julie replied. "At least *you* more than anyone else have a logical reason to be snooping around."

"But won't that put you in danger, being associated with me?"

"Without going into details, I already *am* somewhat in danger, Harold."

He nodded, and busied himself for a few moments with his artichoke hearts. "So what's the general plan?"

"Simple. I'm the young wife on the loose while her husband is confined to his cabin, and you're the notorious lech out for his usual score. Type casting."

"I don't know whether to feel flattered or insulted," he said.

"Sleep on it," Julie said. "It'll come to you."

"All right, so much for the cover story," he said. "Now, exactly what are we going to be doing?"

"Without getting anyone killed, including us, you and I are going to try to uncover the identities of every passenger who is really a secret member of this . . . *Marseille* Mafia. And we have less than two days to do it."

"Jesus, where are we supposed to start? I mean, what do we do for openers?"

"You're the writer," said Julie. "You're the one with the best-selling ideas, not me."

"Yeah, but I only write things I know something about, like two people deciding the fate of the world for the next thousand years while in bed, copulating."

"Use your imagination. Make believe it's for your publisher. Think of those paperback rights, Harold, and get hot."

He looked at her with undisguised admiration. "You're a bitch, you know that? A sexy little bitch. Mind if I kiss you?"

"Excellent idea," she said, glancing around the dining room. "Very good for our public image." She pouted her lips and leaned forward, and he gave her a nice long one, and she hated herself for liking it.

"Mmm. You smell of alcohol," she murmured.

"That's not alcohol," he said. "It's the bump on my head. Witch hazel."

"Poor baby," she said, with a trace of sarcasm.

"Say," he brightened suddenly. "Maybe that's not a bad place to start."

"Where?"

"The two guys in the radio room. I got a quick look at their faces before I got clipped on the bean. And then there's Marybeth and Marge, the two broads who tied me to a bed for the hell of it. I couldn't forget their faces if I wanted to, and believe me, I want to. They're probably still in their cabins, seeing the world through rose-colored eyes." He paused, momentarily distracted. "Honey, will you please tell those tits of yours to stop staring at me?"

Julie gave him a cool smile. "Why is it that the crudest, most vulgar, grossest, most foul-mouthed, most dirty-minded, most un-principled, most bestial men are always the biggest prigs?"

Harold Columbine tried to smile it off, but his facial muscles weren't up to the strain. "Sweetheart," he said, "you and I know that you're going to pay for that remark dearly before this crazy voyage is over, but right now, let's not even think about it. Okay?"

"Anything you say, love." Julie gave him a friendly smile and patted his hand. All her life she had said things she immediately wished she hadn't said. Why should Harold Columbine be the first and only man to escape her sharp tongue? "I just had a thought," she said.

"You're ten minutes overdue."

"Earlier today when I was in the ship's hospital getting briefed by Dr. Chabot, a man wandered in and acted rather weird. I had a strong feeling that he was one of them. Tall, lean, Texas drawl, and the kind of ugly yellow jagged teeth that'll do until yellow bantam comes along."

"Good. Now what else can we throw into the pot?"

"Only what everyone else seems to know," said Julie. "The ringleader of the group is a passenger named Craig Dunleavy, who keeps a low profile, but surfaces now and then at crucial moments to threaten the Captain. I guess whoever we can manage to see him with would be, at the very least, open to suspicion."

The novelist started drumming the table with his fingers, shaking his head slowly from side to side. "The trouble is . . ." he said. "I mean, of all the troubles, the big trouble is that they'll know it's us doing the sniffing around the minute we take our first sniff. *They're* the ones who go into disguises, who put on uniforms and aprons and jackets and smocks and gold braid and God knows what else, to keep their ears close to what's going on around them. I wouldn't be surprised if I just gave my dinner order to one of them. But us, we're out there naked." He glanced at her cleavage and smiled broadly. "Especially you."

Julie frowned at him. "Tell me," she said, "am I imagining it, or aren't we sometimes behaving as though this were all just fun and games instead of the horror it really is?"

"Simple self-preservation, sweetie. If you and I stopped to consider the chances that we or anyone else have of coming out of this alive, we'd just plain cave in. So let's not. That's it. Cut. And meanwhile, back at the ranch, one of America's foremost writers, sitting beside the girl of his dreams, fought desperately against his overpowering lust, and waited for a bright idea to materialize."

"I think I've got one," said Julie suddenly. "Listen. There's a masked ball at midnight tonight. I've seen posters all over the ship. We could put on costumes and masks and mix with whoever we wanted and wander about the ship at will like a couple of lost partygoers, and nobody would know it's us."

"That idea is so good," he said, "that I deeply resent your thinking of it first. Now what do we do for costumes?"

Julie was looking off. "Here comes, perhaps, the answer to a lot of our questions, right now."

Harold Columbine followed her gaze and saw Yves Chabot approaching. When he reached the table, the doctor said, "May I?" His expression was grave.

"Please do," said Julie.

He sat down and told them flatly that two passengers were missing and presumed dead . . . murdered. A couple by the name of George and Gwendolyn Parker.

Harold Columbine and Julie looked at each other.

Yves Chabot ordered a brandy.

None of them felt very much like talking for a while.

The soil of France lay under a dank and oppressive blanket of humid air at this particular one-twenty-five in the morning. To most who were not already asleep, the fetid atmosphere was just something to put up with. To three men, however, it was an excessive burden to their already preoccupied souls. All three were suffering from the same malady . . . the inability to wipe from their minds two conflicting mental-image pictures: (a) thirty-five million dollars worth of gold bars being neatly stacked, and (b) a sixty-five-thousand-ton ocean liner blowing up and sinking swiftly.

Georges Sauvinage, wearing only his Lanvin undershorts, sat sweating at the kitchen table of his stuffy flat in the 15th Arrondissement and drank cognac heavily from the tumbler in his grasp, wondering why he still sat up when his wife had already fallen asleep in the bedroom, taking her rage at his tightlipped secrecy to bed with her. He had already shut off the telephone bell. He had already set the alarm for six. Why could he not put his weary body to bed and allow himself the oblivion he deserved?

The cognac had long since numbed the pain of his call to the Director General in Antibes, and the humiliation of not even being believed until he had sworn on the graves of both his parents. Alcohol had already healed his heart of the melancholy he had suffered, sitting there alone in his office in the silent building to which he had been ordered, with the body odor of those ugly charwomen in his nostrils, making his intrusive calls to each of the nakedly disrespectful members of the board, who had treated his message that the Director General was convening an urgent, special meeting of the board at seven in the morning as though it were an obscene phone call.

Then, having to sit at his secretary's typewriter, in his secretary's office, tapping out with his own manicured fingers the report on the plight of the *Marseille* and Wunderlicht's demands . . . having to make the copies himself on that infernal Xerox machine, all the time being forced to listen to the filthy exchanges of those two witches with their vacuum cleaners. His secretary. He had finally risen in the company to be as high as his lump of a secretary.

Agh, but those sicknesses of the soul had already died under the fermented grape. He was sweating in the kitchen now, gulping more cognac, only because he thought it might make two conflicting mental-image pictures disappear from his brain. Would they never go?

It was the same question that was plaguing Max Dechambre hundreds of miles to the south, as the Director General of the Compagnie Française Atlantique sat uncomfortably in the back seat of the black, chauffeur-driven Citroën that was racing him northward through the darkness on the outskirts of Valence. Too well had his chauffeur understood his request for speed. With a little luck, the car would fail to negotiate a curve and he would be free forever of the problems that Georges Sauvinage had dumped in his lap. But one couldn't count on the chauffeur.

Dechambre was a dapper, diminutive man of fifty-four with sharp features that were not softened by his small black goatee or its matching mustache. His gray eyes, behind gold-rimmed spectacles, peered through the darkness at the sleeping countryside rushing by, and found no solace out there, either. For so many years he had trained his defenses on the enemy in the sky, he was finding it awkward now to focus on the sea. Françat had no urgent problems on the water, now that a permanent ceiling on the price of oil had been achieved, and the development of the Corell-Flambert dynoturbine had reduced the need by sixty percent. All *their* problems were up there above forty thousand feet, where the jet engines had continued to suck passengers out of broad staterooms into narrow seats, where the DC-9s had fattened into 747s, and the Concorde had shot by, screaming ominously of dealing the final blow to sea travel with its new-found routes to the United States and South America.

In his head, the *Marseille* exploded, and his heart ached. He ran it through again. The *Marseille* sailed on serenely, and his heart sank as he thought of the cost. How could he continue to tread lightly on eggshells with the board of directors, and dance his ever-so-careful steps with the Minister of Transportation, keeping the inner circles of French finance and government glowing with optimism, when his neat and narrow size-7 shoes would now be weighted down by tons of gold bricks?

Pay up or die.

Pay up *and* die.

He loosened his tie and opened his collar, strangling on alternatives, not even hearing the blue-flashing police car that was rapidly overtaking the speeding Citroën from the rear.

Nor was the man in Paris who had created these problems doing much better. Lying naked on his back on a soiled bed in a foul-smelling room of the Hotel Lefolle off the Place Pigalle, Julian Wunderlicht, who had dreamt of far, far better things for himself tonight, was telling the blond-wigged whore who was trying in vain to get him hard that he was sorry, nothing personal, he had too much on his mind. When she asked him what, and he told her a ship, she became so insulted, she took his money and threw his American jockey shorts in his German face.

Far off to the southwest, three time zones away, the steamship *Marseille* inexorably plowed the swelling seas under a canopy of cold blue stars, carrying within it men and women of far-ranging and diversified interests. Most were intent on nothing more complicated than a night of sheer pleasure, as though there were not much longer to live. Some, who had eaten far too much of a wonderful dinner, had the immediate goal of smooth digestion. Some were busy forcing others, through the pointing of weapons, to do their bidding. Others, in gold braid, were holding brief meetings to determine what to do should mass hysteria break out. It can safely be said that, of the three thousand souls on board the *Marseille,* there was only one who had the rather odd but single-minded purpose of conversing on short-wave radio with a television writer and producer in Beverly Hills, California, by the name of Brian Joy.

CHAPTER FOURTEEN

H E T H O U G H T he would go out of his goddamned mind, waiting for that waiter to come back to the cabin and remove the dinner tray.

Finally, the man showed up and left.

Immediately, Billy Berlin sprang out of bed, hung the DO NOT DISTURB sign on the outside of the door, locked and double-bolted the door from the inside, removed the Atlas transceiver and its small portable power supply from their temporary hiding place under the bed, and set them down on the table. From behind one of the floor-length drapes he uncoiled the coaxial antenna lead-in cable that Christain Specht's men had cleverly snaked through the electrical conduit using an outside entry point safely removed from the cabin. He attached the coax connector to the antenna post on the rear of the transceiver, plugged the power cable into its receptacle, the A.C. cord of the supply into the wall socket, set the Shure 404-C hand-held microphone temporarily on the table, sat down on the edge of the bed, tuned the VFO of the transmitter section of the Atlas to a point just below the lower edge of the twenty-meter amateur phone band, turned on the power switch on the front panel, throwing a test carrier on the air, and breathed a short, irreverent prayer.

"All right, goddamn it," he muttered. "Get lucky."

He fastened his eyes on the output meter and held his breath and slowly advanced the microphone gain control, and then he heard a loud sigh of relief escape from his lips as he saw the needle swing to the right and almost hit the pin. He grinned. The Atlas was loading into the ship's auxiliary antenna like a veritable dream. He would have at least a hundred and twenty watts of forward power going into an antenna that was four wavelengths long at a tremendous height with the whole damned Atlantic Ocean as a reflector.

"Not bad," he exulted to himself. "Not bad at all."

He backed off slightly on the mike gain to minimize the possibility of splatter and the attracting of unwanted attention, then rotated the power switch to the straight-up RECEIVE position that would permit press-to-talk operation, and was ready, now, to listen.

He clamped the earphones on his head, shoved the jack into the rear panel, turned up the R.F. gain and the audio gain on the receiver section, seized the main tuning knob, and tiptoed past 14,200 kilohertz up into the band. The crash of summer static brought an involuntary grimace to his face. But a smile that he was completely unaware of soon wreathed the grimace. The band was alive, it was jumping with signals.

For the next few minutes, Billy Berlin was like a child again. He had never listened to an Atlas-210 from this vantage point in the Atlantic, and he couldn't resist sampling the goodies . . . Brazil, Morocco, Zambia, Sierra Leone, the Canary Islands, Sweden, St. Helena . . . hams like himself on single sideband radiophone, speaking in the international language of amateur radio the world over, English. And then he remembered that there was work to be done, and he began to listen carefully for the United States. He heard a few stations, but they were very weak, and mostly southern or East Coast stuff. It was still a little early for California, or a little late, you never knew. He fine-tuned around 14,220, where Brian Joy usually hung out, and heard nothing but static.

He had long ago decided that Brian Joy was the only ham he knew whom he could trust to work with him in the kind of deadly secrecy that would be needed now. All the others, the whole Southern California DX gang, were washerwomen at heart, backfence gossips who could hold only one secret: the amount of illegal power they were running. That was *his* opinion anyway, even if no one else agreed with him. Brian Joy was his one big exception. He could *talk* to Briney, about *anything,* not just about resistors and diodes and two-meter scanners and what kind of signal report he had gotten from that guy in New Delhi. More important right now, he happened to know that Brian Joy possessed a copy of *The Anatomy of a War.*

Once he had hit upon the idea of using a code, Billy Berlin had worked over *his* copy of the book for several hours, and then again, hastily, after Julie had relayed the Captain's "mission" to him. It would be the codebook that would prevent any of the other hams who might be listening in from understanding what they were hearing. Then, too, if the conspirators manning the receivers in the communications room of the *Marseille* should, God forbid, accidentally tune across the amateur bands, they'd hear *something* going on, but they wouldn't know what they were hearing.

He decided that, to all intents and purposes, and to any ears that might hear him, friend or foe, he was operating in the southern Atlantic aboard the mythical freighter, the *Flying Unicorn,* of Panamanian registry. If they heard him in the nearby communications room, they would hopefully surmise, from the shattering loudness of his signals, that the *Flying Unicorn* must be just beyond the horizon. At least that was his plan—a plan and a hope and a prayer.

Nursing the tuning dial carefully across the low edge of the band again, he muttered fiercely, "Come on, Brian, where the hell are you?"

He knew full well it was the cocktail hour in that far off Beverly Hills English Tudor house, time for Brian Joy to get up from his typewriter even if he were in the middle of a curtain line, time for him to start putting a dent in the batch of margaritas he'd have laid into the refrigerator as the afternoon waned. Now he and Maggie, handsome, warm-hearted Maggie, one of the few wives who really *liked* her husband's hobby, would be moving into the den and settling down to do their thing. Hers was needlepoint. His was sipping margaritas nonstop, slowly getting beautifully oiled while sitting in front of his equipment-strewn desk, listening to the twenty-meter band. Occasionally he'd communicate with another ham, but mostly he listened, listened and chatted with Maggie. And sometimes they'd eat their dinner in the den, with the receiver on, ready for action. It was all quite cozy. Brian Joy was one of the few active members of the Writers Guild of America, West, whose wife always knew where he was . . . either in front of a typewriter, or in front of a receiver.

But where the hell was he now?

Without even so much as a prayer, Billy Berlin brought the microphone to his mouth, pressed the mike button, and started to call him.

"W6LS, W6 Lima Sierra, calling W6 Lima Sierra . . . This is W6VC, W6 Victor Charlie maritime mobile Region Two. Are you around, Brian?"

He listened, waiting, hearing nothing but an OA4 in Peru calling CQ near the frequency. He repeated the call again, aware that his voice was shaking, that the hand holding the microphone was trembling too. Every word he sent out on the air from this cabin was an invitation to his own death if anyone in the communications room should discover the origin of these transmissions.

Again no reply. He glanced at his wristwatch. Jesus, suppose he never did reach Brian at all? He decided to put out a general call.

"CQ stateside, CQ stateside, CQ stateside, from W6 Victor Charlie maritime mobile Region Two." He repeated the call for thirty seconds, then listened. A fish was tugging on the line. He pressed the earphones tightly to his head.

"W6 Victor Charlie, W6 Victor Charlie maritime mobile. This is WA5JIK, Willie Alpha Five Japan India Kilowatt, WA5JIK calling and standing by."

Billy could feel the adrenalin flowing as he pressed the mike button. "WA5JIK from W6VC mm 2. Good evening, and thank you for the call. You are readability five, signal strength six here in the southern Atlantic, Q5, S6. Not too strong but in the clear. The handle is Bill, Baker Ida Love Love, and I'm running about a hundred watts into a dipole and receiving you on an Atlas-210 aboard the freighter *Flying Unicorn*. How do you copy me? WA5JIK. W6VC mm 2. Go ahead."

"Roger Roger. W6 Victor Charlie maritime mobile. This is WA5JIK coming right back. Good evening and thanks for the report there, Bill, ol' buddy. You're not too strong yourself. I'll give you a Q5, S5. Five and five here in Roaring Springs, in the boundless state of Texas, where the girls are almost as pretty as the cattle." His drawl was soft and pleasing to the ear. "The handle here is Jake, as in everything's Jake. I'm running two KW P.E.P. into a home brew linear, the receiver is a Kenwood TS-820, and the antenna is a three-element cubical quad up about seventy feet. So whatcha doin' out there on a freighter, Bill, and where ya bound for? W6VC mm 2, WA5JIK."

No ham likes to be rude, but there was no time now for the answering of questions or the observance of the amenities. "Okay, Jake," Billy replied, omitting call letters. "Copied everything a hundred percent. Listen, Jake, I wonder if I could ask you to do me a big favor? Break."

Back came the drawl. "Will if I can, won't if I can't. Go ahead, ol' buddy."

"Jake, you better get out a pencil and paper. Here goes. I want you to please make a collect call, that's a collect call, to Beverly Hills, California. The number: area code 213-472-3397. To Brian Joy, as in pride and joy. He's W6LS, that's London Sugar. There's more. How copy?"

"Roger Dodger, Bill. Keep going."

"Please tell W6LS to meet me on 14,220 right away. If we fail to connect, tell him to look for me every hour on the hour. It's very important. There's more. Over."

"A hundred percent copy, Bill. Go ahead."

"Tell him that if and when we make contact, he is not to say anything other than specific replies to my questions. I repeat, he is not to say anything other than specific replies to my questions. Do you have that, Jake? Over."

"Roger Roger. Only specific replies to your questions. Anything more, or is that it, ol' buddy?"

"Just one more thing. Tell him to head his beam slightly south of east. That's it, Jake. I'll stand by on the frequency."

"Hold the fort, Bill. W6 Victor Charlie maritime mobile. WA5JIK temporarily clear."

"This is W6VC maritime mobile Region Two running traffic with WA5JIK in Roaring Springs, Texas. A clear channel will be appreciated."

He waited, listening. A few weak South Americans started calling him. There was always someone calling you when you asked for a clear channel. He ignored them, and they soon gave up. Presently, he heard the smooth Texas drawl again.

"W6VC from WA5JIK. Are you still there, Bill?"

"Roger Roger, Jake. You're Q5, go ahead."

"Okay, ol' buddy, I spoke to your friend, Brian, a real funny guy, by the way, and he said he'd be callin' ya on 14,220 in a coupla minutes. He said he hadda kick the sandbox first. Hi hi. I'd sure like to stick around, Bill, but the XYL is hollerin' for me to sit down to supper, so if you'll forgive me, I'm gonna say my 73s now and throw the big switch. Real happy to help ya out. Thanks for the QSO. Hope to see ya down the log. W6VC maritime mobile, this is WA5JIK pullin' the cork. So long, ol' buddy."

Billy Berlin went right back to him with profuse and rapidly delivered thanks, and just as he was signing off, he heard what sounded like a knocking on the cabin door, and his heart sank. He whipped off the earphones. But it was just the sea, suddenly gathering new force, pounding against the sides of the *Marseille*. Quickly he put the earphones back on his head and started tuning carefully for the foghorn voice of Brian Joy.

The anticipatory excitement he felt now might have been cruelly diminished had he known of the troubles a sixty-year-old maiden lady by the name of Aimee Costigan was experiencing in her cabin several accommodations away. The herringbone patterns that had been intermittently superimposing themselves for the past ten minutes on her closed-circuit TV viewing of a new Paul Newman film were making her increasingly irritable. She felt that Newman's features were somewhat robbed of their beauty by such interference, and when the actor took off his shirt in one scene and revealed a herringbone chest, Miss Costigan picked up the phone and complained angrily to the ship's switchboard operator, who advised her to dial the communications room.

Ah . . . Jesus . . . was there anything more soul-satisfying than a long overdue leak?

Brian Joy, tall and lean with short-cropped hair and an aquiline nose, stood in the mosaic-tiled bathroom of his Beverly Hills home, looking down into the toilet bowl and idly rerunning the phone call from Texas through the computer in his head. Billy and Julie were supposed to be on the S.S. *Marseille,* weren't they? They'd been boring Maggie and him about the trip for almost two months. So what the hell was this business about a freighter called the *Flying Unicorn*, or was it the *Flying Eunuch?* Either way, it made no sense. Unless . . . Holy Christ . . . unless the dumb son of a bitch was bootlegging. Sure, hadn't the French Atlantic Line *and* the French government nixed Billy's attempts to get permission to operate maritime mobile aboard the *Marseille?* That would account for the strange restriction the guy in Texas had relayed to him . . . don't say nuthin' unless you're asked.

He shook off the last few drops and zipped up his fly. What a dirty, rotten thing of Billy to do to his best friend, telling him to keep his mouth shut and listen, especially when his best friend was one of those cats who could stop breathing far more easily than he could stop talking. Perhaps if he gargled with paregoric? He flushed the toilet, opened the bathroom door, and went inside to the den.

Maggie was sprawled comfortably in the big leather chair, working on a needlepoint pincushion. She was a large-boned, ample-bosomed redhead with warm green eyes and a very soft voice. Only her husband, and about fourteen of her closest women friends, with whom she lunched, shopped, and gossiped five days a week, would have suspected that, with regard to sexual intercourse, she was exclusively interested only in being on top. A waiter at The Bistro in Beverly Hills never did quite get over the day he set a plate of cherrystone clams before a soft-voiced lady just as she was saying to the other three women at the table: "I just *love* to ride his cock to heaven." Early in their marriage, Brian had forbidden her to call it a Joy stick.

She glanced over at him as he sat down at the desk before his radio equipment. "In case you get him," she said, "tell him to tell Julie that the Marksons are splitting up."

"I'm not allowed to tell him anything unless he asks me," said her husband, whose voice at times was not dissimilar to a growl. "I told you the rules."

"Also, Nancy Minor had a hysterectomy."

He gave her the look she had learned to interpret as a loving punch in the mouth, then picked up the chrome-plated D-104 microphone that was plugged into his already-warmed-up Signal One transceiver, which he used to drive the final, and began to call W6VC maritime mobile on 14,220 kilohertz. The huge Henry 3K-A linear amplifier standing on the floor near the desk hummed and vibrated with each word as its two 3-500Z grounded grid triodes poured slightly over a kilowatt of peak envelope power into the four-element Telrex beam antenna atop the eighty-foot aluminum tower behind the house. Then, he listened.

Loud and clear from the speaker on the desk came the answering voice of Billy Berlin, quavering with nervous excitement, filling the room with decibels and causing Maggie Joy to pause in her needlework. "W6 Lazy Susan, W6 Lazy Susan, this is W6 Victor Charlie maritime mobile Region Two aboard the freighter *Flying Unicorn*. You've got a terrific signal, Briney. Twenty over nine. How do you read me, and did you receive my explicit instructions? Go ahead."

"He sounds strange," said Maggie.

"Hold it," her husband said to her. He pressed the mike button. "Okay, Billy. I read you surprisingly well, considering the low power. You're peaking S9 with some QSB and a lot of QRM, natch. The answer is yes, I got the instructions. Go."

"Are you alone, Briney? Are you alone?"

He glanced at Maggie and shrugged. "Roger Roger. Alone."

"Briney, do not mention the title. I repeat: do not mention the title. Do you recall the book we gave you for your birthday two weeks ago? Break."

He glanced quickly at Maggie. She said, *"The Anatomy of a War."*

He pressed the mike button. "Affirmative. Affirmative."

"Do you have it there now?"

"Hold on a minute," he said to Billy Berlin, six thousand miles away. And to Maggie, in the den, he said, "What the hell did I do with it?"

"It's upstairs, I think, beside the bed."

"Do me a favor, and hurry, will ya?"

"You two nuts." She put her needlepoint aside and got up from the chair. He looked at her plump behind as she left the room and felt himself getting ideas.

"W6 Victor Charlie maritime mobile, this is W6 Lima Sierra. Stand by, Billy, stand by. I'm looking around. I'll have it in a minute. Okay?"

"Roger. W6LS. W6VC mm 2 standing by on the frequency."

Brian Joy heard a faint voice in the loudspeaker saying, "Break."

"No breakers, please," he replied.

"Sorry," said the voice.

He picked up the sterling silver pitcher that was meant for finer things, and poured another margarita over the melting ice cubes in his highball glass. He was savoring the sharpness on his tongue and the fire in his belly when Maggie walked back in with the book.

"Drink one more of those and *you'll* be maritime mobile too," she said easily.

"Fun-*nee.*" He took the book from her and made a grab for her crotch, but she was too fast for him. "Hey, Billy," he said into the microphone, "Maggie says if I have one more margarita, I'll have to sign maritime mobile."

"Are you alone, Briney?" the voice in the loudspeaker was frantic. "I repeat: are you alone?"

Oh, shit. "Yes," he lied. "Yes, Billy." He glanced at Maggie, settling into her leather chair again. "And I have the book right here on the desk. W6VC from W6LS. Go ahead."

"What's the *matter* with him?" said Maggie.

"Shhh."

"Yourself."

The loudspeaker was overriding them. "W6 Lima Sierra from W6 Victor Charlie maritime mobile Region Two aboard the freighter *Flying Unicorn*. Briney, get a pencil and plenty of paper, and take down what I give you in the order that I give it to you. I repeat: in the order that I give it to you. And please break me if you need a repeat on anything. Are you ready?"

Let's see, a yellow pad . . . *and* a pencil. "Yes. Ready. Fire away."

Long afterward, he would look back on this moment and recall, with amazement, that he had actually been thinking there was something slightly amusing about his friend's little game.

The voice that came back to him now from the loudspeaker suddenly took on an inner strength of its own, commanding his pencil to its function with precise and forceful enunciation. "Page two, twelfth word from the top," began Billy Berlin from the far-off southern Atlantic. "Page forty, a hundred and sixth word from the top. Page forty-two, second word. Page forty-two, third word. Page eight, twentieth word. Underline it. Page eight, twentieth word again. Underline it again. Page nineteen, last word on page. Page twenty-one, tenth word from top. Page one, sixth word. Page one, seventh word. Page seventy-nine, forty-first word. Page one, eleventh word. Period. Briney, how're you doing? Break."

"A hundred percent solid copy. Is there more? Go ahead."

Yes, there *was* more, much more. But after seven more words, Billy Berlin said, "Briney, there's a long way to go, and I don't want to continue this until I know for sure that you understand how to work out the system. So take your notes and open the book, and I'll stand by until you're finished. Gimme a Roger on that."

"Roger Roger, Billy. It's gonna take me some time now, so don't go away."

"Don't worry. W6 Lazy Susan, this is W6 Victor Charlie maritime mobile standing by on the frequency."

Brian Joy turned down the audio gain on the receiver, took up his copy of *The Anatomy of a War* and opened it, first to page two, then to page forty, then to page forty-two, and back to page eight, and right on through to the last page number in his notes, swiftly but carefully counting down on each page to the indicated word, and transcribing the words in pencil in their proper sequence on a blank sheet of his logbook. He could feel his heart beginning to hammer a little as the words gradually filled out the opening sentences of the message. He groped for the margarita glass on his desk and took a gasping draught as he stared down at the words he had printed:

OUR COMMUNICATIONS MUST BE TOTAL TOTAL SECRET
EXCEPT AS I INSTRUCT YOU. THREE THOUSAND LIVES AT
STAKE INCLUDING MINE.

He could feel Maggie's eyes watching him. "What is it?" she said.

He shook his head, wishing she were out of the room. "I don't know yet."

He turned up the audio gain, picked up the microphone, pressed the button, and told Billy Berlin, "Message understood." He was aware of the heaviness in his voice.

"I'm ready to continue," came back the voice of his friend. "How copy?"

"You're up and down a bit, but still peaking S9. Billy, hold on a minute, will you?" He released the mike button and looked at Maggie. "Hon, this may take a while. Why don't you start whipping up dinner?"

She met his gaze silently for several moments, then rose to her feet and said, "How do you feel about salad tonight?"

"I think I can skip it."

"Me too," she said, heading for the kitchen.

He knew that she knew he was asking her to leave. Not acknowledging it was her act of kindness that would make it easier for them to get close again later.

He picked up the glass again, drank until it was empty, and then into the microphone he said, "W6VC maritime mobile from W6LS. I'm ready for your transmission now. Go ahead, please."

His fingers tightened on the pencil, and his hand began to take its bidding once again from the voice that now emanated from the loudspeaker. This page, that word, this page, that word, this page, that word, taking it all down on his yellow pad as fast as it came into the room from the distant ship at sea. Some words, Billy obviously had been unable to find in *The Anatomy of a War*. And so it would be "Page eleven, first letter of first word, first letter of sixth word, first of fourteenth, first of twenty-first, first of fifth, first of nineteenth, first of third, first of third, first of fifth" in order to spell out just one word, M-A-R-S-E-I-L-L-E.

As he took everything down, Brian Joy tried to force from his mind what his years of experience around the short-wave bands was naggingly telling him: the twenty meter band was slowly and subtly changing. Billy Berlin's signals were beginning to take sickening dives into the noise level as the paths of propagation in the ionosphere began to shift with the darkness that was moving swiftly across the United States toward California. His lips tightened with determination, and he gripped the pencil even harder as he listened and wrote, as though he would will the band to stay alive until this contact came to its intended end. It took no spectacular powers of perception or intuition for him to realize that this, of the thousands of contacts he had logged over the years, would be the extraordinary one.

His shirt was damp, and his fingers had an arthritic bent by the time Billy Berlin finally came to the endless end and turned it over to him.

He struggled to keep the fatigue from his voice as he picked up the microphone and said, "I've got it all, Billy."

"Terrific," came the eager reply. "I'll stand by, Briney, while you work on it."

"I hate to tell you this, Billy, but your signals are beginning to go way down. I'm going to have to move real fast, so hold on."

"Roger Roger. Go ahead. W6LS. W6VC maritime mobile standing by on the frequency."

An angry voice broke in, speaking with a heavy New York accent. "Hey, what'sa matter with you guys? Don'tcha know it's a violation of FCC regulations to use anything but plain language to communicate with?"

"A clear channel will be appreciated," was Billy Berlin's only reply.

"You guys make me wanna throw up," said the voice.

"Why don't you shut up?" chimed in still another voice on the frequency, this one obviously from the South.

"Why don't you go take a flyin' frig at the moon?" said the New Yorker.

"Talk about FCC regulations," said the Southerner. "What are your call letters, sir?"

"Up ya bunny with a harpoon," said the New Yorker. "I am now leavin' this frequency to the assholes."

"A real gentleman," said the Southerner.

"This is W6VC maritime mobile Region Two," said Billy Berlin. "A clear frequency will be appreciated."

Brian Joy had heard none of this. He had turned down the receiver, quickly poured himself another margarita and downed it fast. Never, he thought, had he needed one more. But within minutes, as he used his scribbled notes and his copy of *The Anatomy of a War* to find the right words to set down sequentially on his logbook sheet, he began to realize, as dismay sneaked up on him, that that last quick margarita had not been the one that would prove to have been needed more than any other.

He read, now, the words he had printed, the words that had been so laboriously sent to him from far away, and for one brief, foolish moment he tried to tell himself that it was all a joke, and was immediately overwhelmed by the harrowing truth. Sick at heart, he read it all again.

OUR COMMUNICATIONS MUST BE <u>TOTAL</u> <u>TOTAL</u> SECRET
EXCEPT AS I INSTRUCT YOU. THREE THOUSAND LIVES AT
STAKE INCLUDING MINE. THE MARSEILLE HAS BEEN
SEIZED FOR RANSOM BY LARGE GROUP OF HEAVILY ARMED
WELL DISGUISED PASSENGERS, IDENTITIES AND CABIN
NUMBERS UNKNOWN. SHIP IS BEING SAILED OFF COURSE

TO THE SOUTH TO PARTS UNKNOWN. ALL ON BOARD ARE
HOSTAGES. I AM SECRET AND ONLY MEANS OF COM-
MUNICATION WITH OUTSIDE WORLD FOR CAPTAIN AND
STAFF. WILL BE KILLED IF DISCOVERED. SEVERAL
VIOLENT DEATHS ALREADY. URGENT YOU IMMEDIATELY
ADVISE TOPMOST OFFICIALS OF FRENCH ATLANTIC LINE
IN PARIS OF EXISTENCE OF THIS SECRET MEANS OF COM-
MUNICATION WITH SHIP, BUT ADVISE ABSOLUTELY NO-
BODY ELSE. PARIS AWARE OF TAKEOVER. HAVE THEM
GIVE YOU FULL DETAILS OF ENEMY TERMS AND DEAD-
LINE. HERE IS URGENT URGENT TOP PRIORITY REQUIRE-
MENT OF CAPTAIN. WITHIN 36 HOURS, 40 AT MOST, USING
EXISTING CONFIDENTIAL PASSENGER INFORMATION LIST
OF FRENCH ATLANTIC, LAND FORCES MUST DETERMINE
DEFINITE OR PROBABLE IDENTITY AND CABIN NUMBER OF
EACH AND EVERY PASSENGER MOST LIKELY TO BE MEM-
BER OF WELL DISGUISED ENEMY GROUP IN ORDER TO EN-
ABLE CAPTAIN AND STAFF TO TAKE SUDDEN OVERWHELM-
ING ACTION. ALSO, HAVING LOST ALL WEAPONS,
URGENTLY REQUEST SUGGESTIONS AS TO METHODS OF
FOOLPROOF LIQUIDATION. HOSPITAL MEDICAL SUPPLY
LIST BEING PREPARED. ENEMY GROUP BELIEVED TO CON-
SIST OF ANYWHERE FROM 50 TO 200 MEN AND WOMEN,
PROBABLY ALL BETWEEN 35 AND 50 YEARS, PROBABLY
ALL WHITE AMERICANS. LEADER IS AMERICAN WHO CALLS
HIMSELF CRAIG DUNLEAVY. FIRST NAMES OF TWO WOMEN
IN GROUP MARYBETH AND MARGE. CAPTAIN FEELS GROUP
IS WELL EDUCATED AND PROBABLY NOT PROFESSIONAL
CRIMINALS. IMMEDIATELY AFTER THIS MESSAGE ENDS, I
WILL MAKE DISGUISED SUGGESTIONS TO YOU NAMING
AGENCIES WHICH MIGHT HELP YOU AND OR PARIS TO GAIN
DESPERATELY NEEDED INFORMATION AND INSTRUCTIONS
FOR US. NO OTHER ACTION MUST BE TAKEN OR DEATH TO
HOSTAGES. ENEMY HERE MONITORING MANY RADIO
CHANNELS INCLUDING WORLD NEWS BROADCASTS. LAND
FORCES MUST USE EXTREME CAUTION AND SECRECY.
PRAY TO GOD FOR US. THE END.

The end. Brian Joy bowed his head. Suddenly his mind boggled.
His heart vanished. His will deserted him. He was going to faint. He

was going to die. "It's too much," he whined softly, shaking his head. "It's too much . . . I can't . . ." And then, just as suddenly, he straightened in his chair and muttered fiercely, "Shut up, you miserable fuckup, shut your goddamned mouth," and, wiping the few disgusting tears from his cheeks, he turned up the receiver, and spoke into the microphone.

"W6 Victor Charlie maritime mobile from W6 Lima Sierra. Are you still there?"

Weak but readable, naked with eagerness. "Yes, yes, go ahead."

He pumped confidence into his voice. "Okay, Billy. Everything received and perfectly understood. I repeat, perfectly understood. Don't worry about a thing. And speaking of bad jokes, you said you were going to try to come up with a few ideas for my new television series while you were away. I still need new locales, new backgrounds, fresh subject matter. Do you have any suggestions? Go."

"W6LS from W6VC maritime mobile Region Two aboard the *Flying Unicorn*. Briney, I've been racking my so-called brain for that show of yours, and this is about all I've been able to come up with." Brian Joy took up the pencil, to take notes for Paris. "I don't recall ever seeing on TV anything at all dealing with the world's largest, most sophisticated computer. It's either with the CIA or at M.I.T. Then, how about an episode involving the think tank at the Remo Corporation in California? Also, even though this is not exactly fresh, I think there's still plenty of drama left in the FBI, the French Sûreté Nationale, Scotland Yard, Interpol, and the Office of Naval Intelligence. What do you think? Go ahead."

"Not bad, Billy, not bad. I've taken it all down. Now let me give it some thought. Can you set up a schedule with me right away? The band is falling apart rapidly. Go ahead."

"All right, Briney, let's listen on this frequency every hour on the hour, give or take some sack time, in case either of us needs to communicate. That's 14,220 every hour on the hour. Gimme a Roger on that."

"Roger Roger Roger," he found himself almost shouting. "You're disappearing fast, Billy. 73s. Take it easy. Have fun. Keep smiling. Talk to you soon. W6VC maritime mobile. W6LS signing clear after a very pleasant QSO."

He had to wince at that last bullshit of his, and he heard Billy, way down in the mud, giving *his* final. And then, like a swarm of bees, onto the frequency came the hum and buzz and chatter of the hundreds of ham operators who had been eavesdropping on their (he hoped to God) mystifying conversation, all of them calling Billy now for no better reason than to say hello to a seldom heard maritime mobile in the Atlantic. But they called in vain. He was probably already in the bathroom, enjoying his hard-earned diarrhea.

Brian Joy turned down the gain on the receiver, shut off the overheated amplifier, and rose from his desk chair, his stiffening joints snapping like popcorn. He picked up the logbook containing the fateful message and took it with him through the living room and the dining room into the kitchen. There were some secrets that you didn't try to live with alone. Maggie was at the stove, gazing down with approval at her veal scaloppine drenched in Marsala wine. She glanced at him as he approached.

"You don't look well," she said.

"I wonder why," he said, holding out the open logbook.

She kept her eyes on his as she wiped her hands clean with a cloth and took the logbook from him. He watched her as she read the message from Billy. It could have been an old recipe. Getting upset was something she did only when she wanted to. Finally she looked up at him and handed the logbook back.

"Should I bother doing the maybe-it's-all-a-put-on number?" she asked.

He shook his head. "I already tried that on myself. It worked only for about a millisecond. You heard his voice."

She nodded slowly. "Did he mention Julie at all?"

"Not once. But I'm sure she's all right."

"Sure. With a husband like that to protect her . . ."

"Don't be a bitch."

"He's a schmuck and you know it."

"A prick maybe, but a schmuck, no."

"It's all his fault, you know."

"His?"

"Sure," she said. "They wouldn't *be* on that boat if he wasn't afraid to fly."

They looked at each other for a moment, and then, simultaneously, they started to chuckle. Presently, guilt quieted them.

"How come you decided to let me in on the secret?" she asked.

"Why should *I* have all the fun," he replied gloomily.

She regarded him for a moment. "What are we doing standing here in the kitchen?"

"I don't know what *you're* doing, I'm thinking. He never told me exactly who to call in Paris. I'm trying to figure out where I begin."

"How about beginning with my beautiful veal scaloppine?"

"I may never eat again," he said.

"Maybe if I put some in your sterling silver pitcher, you'll get it into you by mistake."

"You're liable to get something into *you* by mistake, if you don't watch out."

"I think I'd like that," she said, putting a hand on his waist.

"Don't touch me," he said. "I'm trying to think."

"I've got it all figured out," she said, unzipping him with her other hand. "First you're going to call Joe to tell him to call the network and say that you've got a flu bug and won't be able to deliver the first draft tomorrow as promised. (Hello, there.) Then you have to make a few dozen calls to find out who to call in Paris and how to get their numbers, and then you're going to phone them in Paris, whoever they are (oh, my . . .) and read the message to them, and then they're going to start giving you a lot of instructions, and after that, you're going to get very, very busy and you may or may not have time for one hour of sleep for the next who knows how many days (nice . . .), and you're going to forget to eat and forget not to drink and you're gradually going to feel worse and worse and worse, and finally you'll up and die of starvation and acute alcoholism and too many contacts with Billy Berlin. So, inasmuch as all this is absolutely, positively going to happen, I see no chance of your ever, ever having one more moment of pleasure in what little is left of your lifetime, unless you have it right now, before you start doing *anything*."

He looked at her, trying to stand still. "I think what you mean," he said, "is that I should go upstairs and get ready to use the phone next to the bed."

"What's wrong with right here in the kitchen?" she said.

He looked down at the floor and frowned. "Isn't it kind of hard and dirty?"

She smiled and said, "I certainly do hope so," as she helped him down.

* * *

"I'm am very sorry, madame," said Ferdinand Bellet, the radio officer in charge of closed-circuit television. "If it is not there for me to see, there is nothing I can do about it."

"But it *was* there, all over Paul Newman."

"My dear Mrs. Costigan—"

"It's *Miss* Costigan. And if it happens again, I want another TV. I'm calling you people until it's fixed."

"Please do that, mademoiselle. Please do."

He left quickly, followed by the man who had accompanied him, a man who had watched and listened with silent interest, a man whose hair and mustache didn't quite match.

CHAPTER FIFTEEN

———————

THE DIN WAS INCREDIBLE. It was New Year's Eve in the middle of July in the middle of the Atlantic. The air in the Cabaret Afrique was redolent with perfume and champagne and gin and the musk of what would surely happen when they disrobed each other of masks and costumes in the privacy of their cabins later on.

"And whose little girl are *you?*" the stranger in sheriff's guise wanted to know, above the music and the shouting.

"I may be little but I'm no girl. I'm a woooooman. I'm Madame du Barry, can't you tell? I mean, how many silver-wigged ladies *are* there? Or can't you see through those slits?"

"Those slits happen to be my eyes, which are beginnin' to cross. Either this ship's capsizin' or I'm drunker'n I thought I was."

"It's all right, I'm holding on to you, podner. It's an old-fashioned style of dancing but it does keep us off the floor. What did you say your name wasn't?"

"I didn't say. But for *you,* I'll tell ya . . . it isn't Kenny Mc-Cracken."

"Hi ya, Kenny."

"So whose little girl are you?"

"I already told you. I'm du Barry. Joe du Barry's little girl." Julie made her lips smile below the black mask that covered her eyes.

"You're so gahdam cute I could cry," sighed the stranger named Kenny McCracken.

"It's just the costume. By the way, where's Craig?"

"Craig who?"

"What do you mean, Craig who? I can't recognize a soul around here with these flashing lights and masks and stuff. Could he be that one, the one with the top hat and the blue pajamas? Over there, look."

"I'm tellin' ya, du Barry, I don't know who the hell you're talkin' about."

"Well, if you're no friend of Craig's, then I just might as well say toodle-ooo and mosey along."

"Aw, c'mon, don't leave me *alone* here . . ."

" 'Bye."

She pushed her way through the squirming bodies on the dance floor to the white-masked Nijinsky in the black leotards standing on the edge of the floor watching.

"Strike three. Nothing." She leaned on him for support. "How did *you* do?"

"Without distinction," Harold Columbine said. "Unless you want me to boast about an invitation I just got from Lady Godiva over there."

"The one in the flesh-colored body stocking?"

"Uh-huh."

"What was the invite?"

"A masked ball for two in a small cabin on C-Deck."

"Could be worse."

"Look closer. Lady Godiva is a guy."

She exploded in a short burst of laughter. "Oh, Harold . . ."

"You should have heard our A cups clashing away."

"What do you say we if-at-first-you-don't-succeed?"

"One more," he said. "Then I've had it."

"Party pooper. This time *you* cut in on someone. I'm going to play the tables."

"See ya."

They went their separate ways, eyes roaming, bodies hanging loose, lips smiling, as though the game they were playing was just a game. It was the only way you could play it without getting sweaty palms and a trembling voice and giving yourself away. She saw him hook up with a lanky young redhead in a Twenties flapper getup, and was glad for him. Definitely not a guy.

She wove her way slowly through the maze of tables, watching male heads turn, eyes looking up through voyeurs' little helpers to once her over hungrily. Right on, Miss Shanneli, she smiled inwardly, thanking the ship's hostess for insisting on this costume. She thought about Billy for a brief moment, keeping his lonely, dangerous vigil in the cabin, and when she felt anxiety for him rising within her, she quickly turned him off and came back to Le Bal Fantasque, back to the Cabaret Afrique, where the band was now playing a bossa nova arrangement of "Fly Me to the Moon."

The two couples at the table directly ahead seemed to be having some sort of trouble. One of the men, a pirate, was halfway to his feet shouting, "Fly *yourself* to the moon . . ." and waving his wooden sword, and one of the girls, a Barbie doll, was trying to pull him back down into his chair, saying, "Now stop it . . . please . . . *Charlie* . . ." And the man was crying to nobody in particular, "I don't wanna *hear* that song, ya hear me? Don't wanna *hear* it . . ." and fell back into his seat, shaking his head slowly.

A gut feeling. Why not try? They *were* Americans.

Julie stopped, looked down, and said, "Move over, Charles, will you." It was a quiet command that said she not only knew him but owned him. The others glanced up at her, momentarily startled, as she took an empty chair from the next table, pulled it over and sat down. She looked at the staring masks with offhand intimacy. "How ya doin'?"

The second girl at the table, a black-haired harlequin, said, "Fine. Just fine."

A little carefully, Julie thought. But then, wouldn't they naturally be wondering: do we *know* her?

The other man—Groucho Marx?—said, "The important thing is, how're *you* doing?"

"I'd be doing a lot better if Craig were here," Julie said. Why waste time? Get it over with.

The sudden silence turned her heart to stone.

"Who's got a cigarette?" she asked quickly.

"Here," said Groucho, tossing a pack of Pall Malls to her, and reaching across to light her with his Zippo.

She blew smoke at the unhappy pirate beside her. "Come on, Charles, it's not as bad as all that."

He turned on her with fierce drunken anger. "I don't *like* that fucking song, and don't call me Charles."

"Charlie!" shrieked the Barbie doll.

"Shut up, Frances," he sneered.

"Knock it off, you two," Groucho said easily.

"I need more Scotch," said Charlie.

"You don't need more anything," the harlequin said.

"All right, Betty," said Groucho, warning her, obviously his wife.

"Fran, maybe *you* can tell me," Julie took another drag on the Pall Mall. "You're all so goddamn unhappy sitting here, what're you doing it for? Who wants to go with me for a walk out on deck? Betty?"

The harlequin shook her head. "Eric says no."

"That's *Eric?*" said Julie. "I thought it was Harpo Marx."

"Not Harpo," the man said, with weary impatience. "Groucho, for chrissake."

"Well, I never would've known," said Julie in a mocking voice. "It not only doesn't look like Eric, it doesn't look like Groucho. Fantastic disguise."

"Y'know something, Shirley, you're beginning to gimme a pain in the ass."

Julie realized that Charlie, the pirate, was addressing *her*.

"Well, now that really would bother me, Charles, if I happened to be Shirley . . ."

"I told you," Frances whispered too loudly to the other girl.

"Speak up," Julie said. "No whispering."

"Betty thought you were Shirley, too," the Barbie doll said, "but I *told* her Charlotte."

"God," Julie managed to laugh heartily. "This is so funny."

"I'm glad *you* think so," grumbled Charlie.

"You're not Charlotte?" said the Barbie doll.

"If I am, I'm sleeping with the wrong guy."

"Well, I'll be . . ."

"Quite a costume," the eyes of Eric peered at her through Groucho. "Who *are* you?"

She met his gaze through her mask. "Madame du Barry."

"Who are you?" he asked again. "Come on, now."

She laughed teasingly. "I won't tell, because nobody at this table will tell me why you're all acting so blah when you should be joyous and carefree. Am I wrong? Is something being kept from me? Isn't everything working out just peachy?"

"We're all just a little sore, that's all," the Barbie doll shrugged. "And a little drunkee too . . . because we weren't picked for tonight."

"Don't include me," said Eric.

"Well, was I picked?" said Julie. "Am *I* sore?" she asked, quite reasonably.

"That's what I keep telling them," said Eric. "If it takes a dozen for a particular action, you pick a dozen, you don't use everybody, just to keep them from feeling left out. But *these* two here . . ." indicating the women, "have such an *itch* to run their little lily-whites over anything with *diamonds*—"

"*And* rubies *and* emeralds," said Frances yummily.

"—that they can't wait, like everybody else. They can't *bear* to be down *here* at two a.m. instead of up there, not helping or anything, just drooling."

Julie's wristwatch said 1:35.

"You're a cold fish, do you know that, Eric?" Betty said.

He turned on her. "It's a dumb idea anyway. Craig knows it and Herb knows it, and they're only allowing it because some people, who shall go nameless, have a hard-on for jewels. What's the stuff gonna be worth, a few hundred grand? Chicken shit."

"You gotta admit it would be nice to be there and see those faces," Charlie the pirate sighed with longing. " 'Specially the puss on that Purser when he realizes what's happening."

"Oh, there he is, gotta go, he's looking for me." Julie jumped to her feet. "See y'all."

"Who?" the women chorused.

"My stupid husband," she called back, hurrying away.

She thought she heard the man named Eric calling after her, "You didn't even tell us who . . ." But it was lost in the music and the shrill chatter.

Eric and Charlie and Betty and Frances and Shirley and Charlotte . . . Six down and twelve more to go in the Purser's office.

When she reached Nijinsky in the black leotards, still dancing with the lanky flapper, she jabbed him twice, said very loudly, "Outside the entrance in two minutes," and kept on going. Nijinsky watched her go, then pirouetted toward the swinging doors, hearing the bossa nova ending behind him as he followed her out.

On the Cabaret bandstand, a man dressed as a Swiss yodeler began to struggle with the leader, wrestling him for the bullet-shaped microphone. A few people laughed, thinking it was a gag. The Swiss Yodeler won, and held the microphone aloft in victory. Some people cheered and applauded. The band leader stepped back, looking on, straining to smile. The Yodeler whipped off his mask and said into the microphone, "Ladies and gents, I'm Harry Grabiner . . ." But there was instant jeering.

"Put on your mask. No cheating . . ."

"Boo . . . boo . . . boo . . ."

"Ladies and gents . . ."

"You look better with your mask on . . ."

"Listen to me . . ." shouted Grabiner.

"Put it back on, take *yourself* off . . ."

"I'm Harry Grabiner and . . ."

"Siddown, Harry."

"And I think you should know that this ship ain't no way going where it's supposed to . . ."

"You're drunk, Harry. Siddown before you *fall* down . . ."

"They're fooling you," Grabiner cried hoarsely into the microphone. "They're taking you someplace else, listen to me. We are so far off—"

But his voice was drowned out by the jeers and catcalls, and then the band leader wrested the microphone from his grasp, and the music started up again, and Grabiner walked slowly, shaken, toward one of the exits, as everyone started to dance again.

Two of the celebrants got up from their table and caught up with Grabiner on the deck just outside the Cabaret.

"We heard what you said, Mr. Grabiner," the first man said, "and frankly we're kind of intrigued."

"Well, thank you, gentlemen," Grabiner's face lit up. "I was beginning to feel like the village idiot."

"If you don't mind," the second man said, "we'd like to hear more about this."

"Mind?"

"Something sure as hell *is* going on around here . . ."

"You're goddamned right," Grabiner said. "Those dummies in there . . ."

"Where can we talk?" the first man asked.

"Anyplace is okay by me. One of the bars?"

"If I have to look at one more drink tonight," the second man said.

"It's fine out here on deck as far as I'm concerned," the first man said. "Nice and warm."

"That's just my point," Grabiner said with eagerness. "I'm just an old dress manufacturer from New York. I wouldn't know what *you* two gentlemen do even if you took your masks off. But I don't have to be an ancient mariner or a navigator to know that you don't get warm air like this in the North Atlantic, and that's where we're *not* . . . we are *not* in the North Atlantic."

"Shall we wait till we lose some of these people?" the second man asked. Several costumed groups of twos and fours were straggling by on the otherwise deserted deck, enjoying the senseless hilarity of too much champagne and nothing to worry about.

"Let 'em hear me," Grabiner said. "That's what I want. Let them all wake up."

"We're with *you*," the first man said, looking around, as they strolled on along the slightly rolling deck.

"Weren't you in the Brittany Lounge bar tonight, wasn't that you?" the second man inquired.

"Me?" Grabiner asked.

"Yeah, wasn't that you, just before dinner, at the bar, telling someone about how we're off course?"

"Oh, yeah, yeah, were you there?" Grabiner seemed delighted.

"No, I heard about it from someone, I don't know who, maybe the bartender. I thought maybe that was you. I guess it was."

"That was me all right," Grabiner said proudly.

"I'm getting pooped," the first man said.

"Take off your mask, you'll breathe easier," Grabiner said.

"That makes sense," the first man said.

"Everything I say makes sense," Grabiner said, grinning.

"He's absolutely right," the second man said. They both took off their masks and stuffed them into their pockets.

"Hey, now it's easy," Grabiner said, smiling, looking from one face to the other. "You look even more like a pirate, and you, young fella, you still look like . . . like . . ."

"Groucho Marx?"

"Yeah, that's what I was gonna say, Groucho Marx. Enough

schleppin' for now. Why don't we sit down here and schmoose? Okay?"

"Look at those stars, and the moon on the water. It's too much," the first man said. "It makes you want to say hello to God."

"How about these deck chairs here?" Grabiner asked.

"How would you like to say hello to God?" the first man asked him, kneeling down as though to adjust his shoelaces.

"Anytime," laughed Grabiner.

"Are you ticklish?" the second man asked, coming up behind Grabiner.

"Hey," Grabiner laughed.

The first man had seized his ankles and the other man had put his hands under his arms, and together they had lofted him playfully into the air.

"There he is up there. Hello, God."

"Hey," Grabiner laughed. "Fellas . . ."

"Whee . . ." said the first man.

"Whee . . ." said the second man, holding him now by the wrists.

"Watch out," the old man laughed, as they swung him back and forth like a curved clothesline of skiprope. "I ain't up to this, guys." He was gasping a little. "I mean, what the hell are you—?"

"Whee . . ." said the first man, laughing.

"Put me down, please."

A young couple in costume were stumbling along the deck toward them, giggling loudly, grabbing at each other like children.

"Upsadaisy," called out the second man, laughing boisterously, as they swung Grabiner's comically struggling body in ever widening arcs.

"Stop them," Grabiner cried feebly as the giggling couple came closer. "Please, I'm getting sick, stop them . . ."

"Shame on all you naughty boys," the girl called out merrily.

"Please . . . this is not . . . wait . . ."

"Upsadaisy . . ."

"Go to bed, you'll miss tomorrow," the laughing girl sang out as she and her escort continued away, still giggling.

"Wait . . ." Grabiner cried.

"One . . ." called out the first man.

No, it can't be, the old man moaned to the swinging stars.

"Two . . ." called out the second man.

Please, God . . .

"Three."

It can't be, it—

"Wheeeeee . . ."

Oh oh God oh Momma oh oh oh soaring outward oh and down oh no oh no through the dizzying darkness oh God into the black and icy grave oh no the bursting heart crying out oh no through the open soundless mouth God please as he drank himself quickly to death.

CHAPTER SIXTEEN

HE KNEW A GUY at CBS down on Fairfax in Hollywood who knew a guy in CBS News in New York who could be reached on the tie-line up to midnight. But the guy in New York, a senior vice president named Leonard Ball, wasn't due back at his apartment at the Park East, they said, until eleven, which was eight o'clock, California time, so Brian agreed to have the veal scaloppine in the meantime and it wasn't bad. And then his friend down on Fairfax located Leonard Ball having dinner at Twenty-One and told Brian to call him there right away. Brian had trouble with the switchboard at Twenty-One, but they finally put him through to Ball's table, and he told him who he was and what he needed, and Ball said he had a close friend with the U.S. embassy in Paris who he was certain could get the information for him, but it was four ayem over there, for chrissake. Yeah, but I need it now, Brian told him. Wait a minute, the CBS guy said from his table at Twenty-One. There's this girl I know at the Paris *Herald Trib*. She writes all night and sleeps all day. Marvelous chick, marvelous writer, knows everybody and everything. Yeah, but how do I reach her? Let me try her,

said Ball. I happen to have her home number in Paris. Happen to?
said Brian. Now look, said Ball. Cut it. Gimme your number and
I'll have her call you. When? Now. From Paris? Right. You're
kidding, said Brian. Yeah, I'm kidding, said CBS. So gimme your
number. Brian gave it to him and hung up and waited around,
listening to twenty meters and hearing nothing, and then when the
phone rang and the operator said it was Paris calling, he said to
Maggie, I'll be goddamned, and then this terrific voice from a few
light years away said, Is this Mr. Joy? And he said, It certainly is.
And she said, This is Lisa Briande of the *Herald Tribune.* Lenny
says you need me. Do I ever, Lisa, you're a dream, he said. You
can call me Brian. Just tell me what you want, Mr. Joy, she said.
I'm right in the middle. So he told her. And in less than a minute
from that little black book of hers he had the names and the
telephone numbers he needed. He thanked her a hell of a lot and
hung up and told Maggie, Isn't she terrific?

The number one guy, Dechambre, lived in Neuilly and for no
good reason it took the overseas operator in Denver almost twenty
minutes before she got someone there to answer the phone, an
angry-voiced French lady who sounded just like anyone sounds
when the phone rings in the middle of the night. He listened to the
long screeching hassle with the Paris operator, who finally trans-
lated to him that Monsieur Dechambre was at another number, at
Antibes, on the Côte d'Azur. Get me that other number please, he
told the Paris operator. But it is twenty-five minutes past four in the
morning, monsieur. Get me that number, he said, and waited,
wiping the sweat from his sweating sterling silver pitcher. The
woman who finally answered at the Antibes number at least could
speak English, and he heard her telling the operator that Monsieur
Dechambre had left by motorcar for Paris and would get there by
daybreak. Ask her if she knows what time he will be in his office in
the morning, he screamed at the operator. Ask her what time the
French Atlantic Line opens for business. I cannot do that, monsieur, said the operator. Ask her, goddamn it. Brian, shouted Maggie. Eight o'clock, said the operator and terminated the connection.
Eight o'clock, he said to Maggie. That's almost four goddamn more
hours. If you don't stop drinking, she said. You'll what, he said.

He got the overseas operator again, a different one, of course,
and he gave her the number of the number two guy, Georges
Sauvinage, and it took about fifteen minutes to get that number to

ring, and after ringing for five minutes without an answer, Brian said to Maggie, Nobody in Paris ever goes home where they belong, and she said, They probably know you're going to call, and he said, Fuck you, and thanked the Paris operator for all her trouble and hung up and, pouring another drink for himself, said, Shit.

Then the phone rang and it was this terrific voice again, saying, This is Lisa Briande again. I hope I'm not disturbing you. And he said, There's no one I'd rather be disturbed by. And she said, I thought maybe you ought to know that I just found out through the *Trib* desk that Max Dechambre, the Director General whose number I gave you before, was picked up by the police outside of Valence several hours ago. Picked up? shouted Brian. For what? Speeding, she said. Why are you getting so excited? I'm not excited, he said. Anyway, she said, my people tell me he told the police he was speeding in order to make it to Paris in time for a very special meeting at the Compagnie Française at seven o'clock this morning. Seven o'clock? he said. That's right, she said. That's very interesting, he said. It certainly is, she said. And very sweet of you, he said, to call me again. Who pays your phone bills? Why Lenny, of course, she said. Good old Lenny, he said. Do you know him well? she asked. Oh very, he said. Then maybe you won't mind doing a big favor for a very good friend of good old Lenny's, she said. Anytime, he said. Maybe, she said, you'll tell me exactly what is going on, and why this very special seven o'clock meeting at the Tour Française. If it's a big story I'd hate to miss it. Wouldn't you hate me to miss it, Mr. Joy? Of course I would, Lisa honey. Then are you going to tell me what it's all about? she asked. Of course I am, Lisa, but you're not going to believe it, he said. Tell me, she said. All right, he said. They have just found out, he said, the French Atlantic Line has just found out that last night, in the kitchen of the First Class dining room of the S.S. *Marseille,* on the current run from New York to Le Havre, the chef discovered a herring in the *ile flottante*. Thank you, Mr. Joy, she said. You are in your own unique way a genuinely limp prick. And she hung up on him.

Why are you so horrible? Maggie said.

I wasn't so horrible in the kitchen, he said.

How do *you* know? she said.

I know, he said.

CHAPTER SEVENTEEN

"I DON'T FEEL SO GOOD."

"Now what?"

"I'm a little nauseous. I don't think the Harry Grabiner agreed with me."

"You never should have touched it. Your eyes are always bigger than your stomach. You never know what's good for you, and you never listen to me, so I don't want to hear you complaining all night about your damned indigestion. Why can't you learn to be sensible and stick to simple things like silver blues and lemon eyes and dorsals?"

"I know. I know. It's just that whenever I see a Harry Grabiner I can't seem to resist. Maybe it's because I happen to *like* Harry Grabiner, even if it doesn't agree with me."

"Well, go ahead and eat all the Harry Grabiner you want, just as long as I don't have to be listening to you complaining about it afterwards . . . Where are you going?"

"I'm going up and take some sandbugs and herring to settle my stomach."

"Taking something. Always taking something. If you would listen to—"

"Would you two cut it out already. If you think you're being funny, you're just being disgusting, that's all."

"You're just sore, Frances, you're a sorehead . . ."

"Leave her alone, Charlie."

"You mind your own goddamn business."

"Hey, don't you talk to my wife that way."

"Well, she's just sore, that's all, 'cause she's down here instead of up there. She thinks she's missing something. Say, let's get a waiter over here. I feel like some Harry Grabiner. How about you, Eric?"

"I'd like to but I can't, Charlie. It's not on my Weight Watchers."

"You two are *sick.*"

CHAPTER EIGHTEEN

————

THEY WATCHED AND WAITED, just out of sight, and then finally, at five minutes to two, they saw them beginning to appear, a few of them singles, like the man in the clown costume with an expensive digital wristwatch and a fat wad of fifties to get rid of, and the dumpy woman with the heavy legs wearing the guise of Ophelia, struggling to get the incongruous earrings free of her fleshy lobes as she waddled up to the desk . . .

(*"Let's get out of here." "Will you shut, Harold." "Idiot woman." "Miserable coward."*)

Mostly they were coming in pairs, couples, Mommy and Daddy, honey and sweetie, wifey and hubby, their masks slightly askew, their gauze and silk and cotton and taffeta and all the foolish props sagging pathetically under the perspiration and the weariness. God, what a fun night, wasn't it, Ralph? Wasn't it just the darlin'est, most ever-lovin', livin' end?

A dozen of them now, all told, twelve of them to be dealt with by Claude Cabachoux as he smiled at them and beamed at them and nodded understandingly, listening to their abominable accents and enduring their gross valuables making contact with his hands on the short journey from the desk to the safety deposit boxes and the vault behind him. How many years he had worn that smile and thought, how fortunate I am that I do not want what they have, or want to be what they are? The Purser indeed *was* a fortunate man, for how many are there who can honor and cherish the safety of so much treasure, week after week, crossing after crossing, without once feeling, why *them,* why *these* people, when my beloved Christine and my beautiful grandson have nothing?

The area in front of his office was alive with late-night foolishness now, and he tried to accommodate everyone, opening their boxes and scribbling out receipts with patience and good humor. But they were Americans, and they were intoxicated, all of them, and really quite rude, and he could feel improper anger rising within him. The Commandant would not be proud of him.

"All right, Claude, you can go to bed now," the tall, red-faced man was saying to him from behind the mask.

"No, no, please, that is quite all right. That is why I am here . . . to serve." He smiled and nodded with practiced charm.

"Lemme say it again, Claude," the red-faced man leaned across the desk. "Get your ass out of here."

"Oh, Sandy, be nice," one of the women said reprovingly.

"I wanna see old Claude get his French ass moving right now."

Claude Cabachoux laughed with magnificent appreciation. He always saved his best laughter for the ones, like these, who showed up toward the end of the night, after the ball was over, the ones who made bigger fools of themselves than they really were. They needed his laughter almost as badly as he did, for without it, the morning after and the days that remained would be too painful.

"You had a good time, all of you, yes?" he asked, smiling.

"What's that one in the back?" another man asked him, pointing.

The Purser glanced back, then turned to the man, who was dressed as some sort of janitor, or convict. "That is the vault where the finest ooh-la-la is kept," he chortled.

"No kidding? And what the hell is the finest ooh-la-la?"

"The jewelry that is real, m'sieur. And the currency of very large denominations."

"Oh, that's nice," the man said. He looked around at the others and said, "Isn't that nice?" And then he turned back to the desk and held out his hand and said, "Gimme gimme."

"Pardon, m'sieur?" Cabachoux's face was still smiling.

"I said gimme." The fingers were beckoning.

"Ah." Cabachoux nodded, still smiling, but his sickening heart had begun to understand everything.

"The keys. The keys." The fingers snapped impatiently. "The works. Everything." The man waved his hands about with expansive good humor and the women tittered.

"No," said Cabachoux quietly.

"He said no," the man said.

"No," Cabachoux cried, stunned at the revolver he felt in his hand. He had no sense of having snatched it from its hiding place under the counter, from behind the secret panel they had all overlooked, and it felt horrible and cold to the touch as he pointed it, backing away. "No. All of you. No."

A heavy-set masked matador put a hand on the arm of the janitor and said, "Wait a second, Carl," and to Cabachoux, "Now come on, fella, don't make it difficult, all right?"

"You are pigs," Cabachoux's lips trembled and the revolver wavered in his shaking hand. "Let the Commandant and the others pussyfoot with you, but not me. You will all die before this is over, and some of you now."

The janitor grabbed the counter to pull himself up and over, and the matador seized his leg to stop him, and Cabachoux took a frightened step backward, and then the girl in the silver wig whom nobody had noticed rushed forward out of the group—had she been in the foyer or right there?—and quickly shouted, "Hold it. We don't *need* it this way. Just let me . . ." It happened too quickly for startled glances to get exchanged, or for keyed up minds to shift gears into logical thinking.

"Let me handle this," the girl in the du Barry costume said, starting over the top of the counter with remarkable grace.

"Get back," warned Cabachoux, wavering.

"Dear mister Purser," she moved to him, smiling. "Darling mister Purser man, please don't make us hurt you, please?" as she eased the gun from his yielding hands, and Nijinsky's sinking heart started beating again as he drifted in among them, unnoticed in the tension of the moment. The crazy bitch, he thought. How am I ever going to get her to stop getting us killed just because she isn't getting enough fucking? And then, of course, he thought of the answer.

"All right now," Julie said to the others, her heart hammering with fear, "let's not be shitty about this." She heard their confused murmurs of assent behind her as she put an arm around the now weeping Purser and led him to a chair and sat him down.

"Give me all the keys," she said gently. "All of them."

"Yes," he said softly, weeping. "Yes."

And he gave her the key ring and she turned and said, "Catch?" And the heavy-set matador cupped his hands and said, "Here." And she tossed the keys to him, shouting, "Everybody make yourselves useful."

And then they ignored her in the sudden rush to swing the counter open and go through.

"My God," she murmured to no one in particular, Nijinsky already being off with the rest of them at the vault and the boxes. Where had all those fabric carryalls come from suddenly, dazzling-hued sacks that could hold a man's fortune? From their skirts? Their hats? Their handbags? It was incredible. Room enough and more to haul away the *world*.

"Can I help you, honey?" she asked one of the women.

"You've done enough, dahlin'," said the nameless one. "You were just super."

" 'Twasn't nothin'," Julie shrugged.

"Say," the other one said, "where's ya whatchamacallit?"

"What?"

"You know . . ." She held up her cotton gunnysack.

"Oh," Julie laughed. "Would you believe it? I forgot it at the last minute. So did my guy."

The woman peered at her for a moment through her mask. "Well, you were just super, so what's the diff?"

"Please don't say anything to Craig, will you, honey?"

"Ah will. Ah most certainly will. Ahm gonna say, Craig, darlin', wait'll ya hear what our little Charlotte did tonight. She was absolutely super-dooper." She giggled, pleased with herself.

"You're a dear." Julie gave her a peck on the cheek and hurried toward the rear where she found Harold.

"I'm Charlotte," she murmured. "I don't know who *you* are, but you're mine."

"I'm sick," he sighed, watching the frantic action. "I thought I had all the money there *was* in this world."

They both stared in wonder at the sparkling diamonds and emer-

alds and ruby treasures being swept into the carryalls with hysterical laughter, at the stiff, stacked, fat, solid, positively sexy bundles
of banknotes of God knows how many different treasuries, dollars
mostly, and francs and pounds and marks and guilders, beautiful to
behold in the swiftly moving hands of the vault-snatchers, their
mouths emitting lustful, guttural grunts of pleasure.

One could hardly hear Claude Cabachoux sobbing, so loud was
the sound of their laughter and the cries of greed and wonder. One
scarcely noticed du Barry and Nijinsky, doing whatever little they
could to help out, picking up a necklace here, retrieving a fallen
pear-shaped diamond pendant there.

"Thank you, Charlotte."

"Always a pleasure, dear."

"You were terrific."

"Aren't we all?"

"No, you really were."

"I'll remind you of that in the morning."

"Isn't this exciting?"

"If you happen to like money," Nijinsky butted in, hating to be
left out.

Who would think to count heads and find two extra at a glorious
time like this? They were the Masked Marvels, that's who they all
were, and tomorrow they would be the heroes and heroines of the
whole damned group. And wasn't it just fantastic, how right-on
Craig had been about the need to post a guard outside against any
late-straggling passengers who might wander onto the scene at the
worst possible moment?

Sorry, madame, we are closed now. Sorry, monsieur, you will
have to keep that in your cabin until morning, said the man with
the lousy French accent in the well-fitting Purser's uniform outside
the entrance. Yes, yes, I know, but unfortunately you are too late.
Good night and sleep well and may pleasant dreams be with you.

Moving them on with his unctuous tones, sending them off to
their beds with grumbling frustration and the lingering memory of
his unpleasant smile.

She hadn't noticed him at all, earlier, and paid little attention to
him when he came inside and announced to everyone that it was
time, as he put it, to end cycle. *And let's make it sweet and fast, my
friends.* He was just a tall, goateed man wearing steel-rimmed
glasses, a gold-braided hat and a uniform of the ship's staff, using

his puffed-up, authoritarian voice to make himself heard and obeyed by all the demented children. They took up their sacks full of goodies and prepared to leave, chattering like magpies, calling out little mocking farewells and thank-yous to the forlorn figure who still sat on the stool, his head bowed in shame.

The tall, uniformed man went over to him and said, "Listen to me, Mr. Cabachoux. There's only one story you and your staff are going to tell the passengers in the morning. A safety feature has backfired. The locks have jammed. Nothing can be opened, to put in or take out. But you're working on it. Did you hear me, Mr. Cabachoux?"

The Purser looked up at him for a moment, then turned his head away and nodded slowly.

The tall man turned and said, "Lock 'em up, Benjy."

"Anchors away," replied the heavy-set matador, and went to the safety deposit boxes and the vault and secured them.

"It's bedtime, folks," said the tall man.

"If you say so, Don," sang out the janitor type.

And everyone started to move out, Julie and Harold staying in the center of the group, using their hands to support the sacks of those in front of them, anything to be helpful, to be useful, to be visibly, observably helpful and useful, all the while grooving new lyrics to add to the old ones . . . Ralph and Sandy and Carl and Benjy and Don . . .

She was only a few feet from the entrance, from the doorway to safety, when he stopped her. Well, he didn't *stop* her exactly, but the way he planted his uniformed body, and the way he peered at her through the steel-rimmed spectacles, and the tone of voice he used that was a little too hard for the innocuous words, sent warning signals to her body and advised it to stop.

"What's the hurry? There's no place to go, is there?"

"I don't know about *you,* Don, but *I* am *très fatigué.*" She tossed it off lightly.

"Well, stick around for a moment anyway," he said.

"Gee, I don't really think—" she started to say.

But he said, "You don't have to think. Just stay here." He was calling good nights to the others, who were disappearing now, and she was looking to Harold, who was staring at her dumbstruck, and she started to tell him, "If that headache gets worse you really ought to see the ship's doctor," but the man in the uniform turned around suddenly and gestured to the Nijinsky character to get moving, which he did, reluctantly, and then the man said to her, "They were having such a goddamn beauty of a time, they've worked so hard for jollies like this, I just didn't have the heart to dump shit on it and spoil it for them." He had taken her arm, and was leading her gently to the exit. "Let 'em go to sleep happy, I said to myself. Old Donny boy'll handle it all by his lonesome, like they were children that needed protecting. Christ, I must be sentimental or something. Would you figure me as being sentimental?"

Her mouth felt unaccountably dry. "I wouldn't even *try* to figure you out, Don."

"Anh, I'm a cinch." He was moving her along the corridor now, actually not too far from her cabin. "I'm as simple as ABC," he said. "Easy as apple pie. I'm just one of those plain, homespun American bastards who never forgets a beautiful pair when he sees them . . ."

"I should hope not." Her heart was fainting.

"Also, I never forget any bitch's voice that talks down to me, either." The sudden hatred was frightening.

She looked at him and he smiled at her coldly, and that was when she saw the jagged yellow teeth and knew that she was probably going to die.

"And how's the sore throat? All better?" He chuckled, pleased with himself.

Her sickening fear made her furious. "You're so fucking clever, aren't you . . ."

"*And* suspicious, *and* nosey, *and* persistent . . ."

"Won't that smart ass of yours shrivel with shock when I take off this mask and turn out to be somebody else."

The movement of his hand whipping out the instrument was so quick that she caught only a flash of the dagger-shaped blade before it slashed at the back of her head and the mask fell from her face to the floor of the corridor.

"Jesus," he shrieked softly. "Why it's Mrs. Berlin, the doctor's wife. Jesus, and I thought it was Lady Macbeth. What brings you to these parts, Mrs. Berlin, at this awful hour of the night? Why aren't you in bed with your hubby, the doctor, in little one-sixty-four Première?"

"Fuck off," she said.

"Oh no," he said. "I will take you there. I will escort you to your place of repose and see that no harm befalls you on the way. I ain't gonna make the same mistake with you my friends made with your male ballerina sidekick, Columbine, locking him up and talk talk talking about how maybe we better not dispose of him because he is too goddamn well-known on this ship. Can't blame anyone a bit for using their wits to escape if you're cheese-brained enough to give 'em the chance. Now, we don't wanna do nothin' like that with you, do we, lady . . . ?"

He must have seen the man and woman coming toward them along the narrow corridor at the same time as she did, but it didn't seem to concern him at all. He didn't even try to prevent her from calling out to them, "Will you please help me? This man is trying to harm me. Please help me. Please?"

The couple were shy and truly embarrassed by the strange woman in the odd costume being helped to her cabin by the distinguished officer in the fine uniform. "She'll be all right in the morning," he said to them, smiling, and they hurried on, feeling a bit sorry for him.

Julie thought of screaming after them, screaming for help down the vast corridors of emptiness on this sleeping ship, but his tightened grip on her arm and the stiletto in his other hand seemed to be vetoing the idea. Each step they took brought them closer to her cabin, closer to Billy. Oh God, was he asleep, with his radio tucked away out of sight, or was he—?

"Listen to me," she blurted out, summoning up ridiculous command. "I want us to go to *your* cabin, right now, and then *we* are going to have a *talk* . . ."

"Are we now?" he said.

"Don't give me any arguments, Don, or whatever your name is, let's just *do* it. I promise you it'll be important to you."

He just laughed at her, and she couldn't blame him. "I don't know what you've been doing with your life, lady, but you sure as hell oughta be an actress. I mean I was watching you tonight and you put on one helluva performance. I gotta give you that. Only the curtain is *down* now, so stop trying. Forget it. That's where the expression comes from. That's what this is all about, little lady. For you . . . tonight . . . it's curtains."

They were coming to her door. Jesus God, they were coming to one-sixty-four. There was nothing she could do. Good Christ . . . nothing . . .

"Come on, Don," she murmured, "why don't we go to your place?"

"Now look—"

She put her hand on his crotch. "Why don't you let me give you some of my nice sore throat?"

Her head suddenly exploded in a white-hot flame as his open hand smashed across her face, and his snarl was lost in her anguished outcry as he slapped her hard, again and again, then stepped back, breathing hard, soiling her with obscenities, and the tears were coming to her hard-bright eyes. Oh, mister, you shouldn't have done that—shaking her throbbing head, clearing the dizziness— Oh, *that* you never should have done. That was a mistake . . .

"Now open the door," he was saying very quietly, very calmly, "and don't say one wrong fucking word or I'll cut your heart out and stuff it in your cunt."

She managed to get her key out and turn it in the lock but it didn't do any good because of the double bolts on the inside, and then they both heard Billy's muffled, cautious, "Who is it?"

"Not one fucking word."

"It's me. Julie."

The bolts clicked. The chains rattled. The door opened. The lights snapped on. He was in yellow pajamas, the Atlas-210 glowing behind him beside the rumpled bed. His eyes were blinking, only half awake, his face scowling. "Where the hell have you been? I got—"

"Shut up." She moved quickly inside, away from the stiletto. "Don't say a word and turn that goddamn stupid radio off . . ."

"I managed to get through to—"

"Shut up, we don't need any baseball scores at a time like this." She flicked off the gray-and-black box.

"Oh, hi, I didn't—" seeing the familiar uniform.

"Hello there, Doctor," said the entering man.

"Don't say a word. He's not—"

"Delivered the whole message," Billy yawned.

"He's one of them," she cried.

"Hours ago," Billy said to the ship's officer who was locking the door.

"Baseball scores and American jazz," her voice rose desperately. "We spend a fortune on this trip and all he wants to do is listen to

American news broadcasts."

"Get your clothes on, Dr. Kildare," said the tall man softly, his flickering glance taking in everything, the transceiver on the table, the microphone on the bed, scribbled sheets of yellow paper.

"Wait a minute," Billy said, blinking at Julie.

"Fuck it, what's the use?" she groaned, sinking into a chair.

Billy turned to the man. "Look, aren't you—?"

"My sister's kid used to fool around with this ham radio thing when he was in high school." The man was studying the yellow sheet of paper in his hand. "Never could get him to do his homework." He glanced up at Billy, held out the piece of paper. "You sent this out? You sent this to someone?"

Billy took the sheet from him and tossed it aside. "Who the hell *are* you?"

"You sent that to someone?"

"Julie . . . ?"

"Who do you *think* he is? He's one of *them*. I *told* you. You didn't listen. You're always so . . . so . . . oh God, I'm sorry. I'm sorry. It's all my—"

"Aw, come on, let's not be *that* sorry, little lady," the tall man's voice turned bitter. "We're not *lepers,* y'know, we're just unusual specimens from another planet, that's all. So cut the shit." He turned on Billy. "Now, you gonna take those pajamas off and put some clothes on like I asked?"

"What for?" Billy demanded, staring at him white-faced.

"Because we're going to a little meeting, that's what for. Because I don't wanna be seen walking around this ship with you in your pajamas. Is that good enough for you?"

"What sort of a meeting?"

"You and me and your wifey here, Sarah Bernhardt, are gonna explain to some of my friends—"

"My wife stays right here."

"—exactly what's been going on . . ."

"She has nothing to do with this."

". . . and then my friends and I decide what to do about you two individuals, which is also known in some parts as killing two birds with one stone."

"This is *my* radio setup," Billy said. "My wife had nothing to do with it."

"And the Captain had nothing to do with it, either," the tall man said harshly.

"That's right," said Billy.

The jagged yellow teeth came into view, and through the soft creaking of the ship and the distant, muffled boom of water against steel, Julie suddenly heard the click of a blade opening somewhere behind the blue uniform.

"Wait a minute." She leaped to her feet, twisting to her right, and tore open the wardrobe door, the violence of her movements momentarily distracting both men. And then she pulled at the first clothing that her hands met and, turning, hurled the suit into Billy's face, crying, "Put that on, goddamn it, and let's *go* with the man."

Billy looked down uncertainly at the clothing in his hands.

"Go ahead," she moved swiftly into the bathroom, calling out, "I wouldn't miss this meeting for the world."

"You heard her." The man in the uniform stared at Billy, and watched him as he tossed the suit on the bed and began to unbutton his pajama top.

"For a little guy," the man said, "you make an awful lot of trouble."

Billy didn't look right at him. He was staring past the man's left shoulder, his eyes straining to look blank and unstartled. He reached down to the bed, picked up the jacket and trousers and shoved them at the man, saying, "Hold these . . ."

The man glanced down.

Billy said, "Hold them . . ."

The man's hands reached for the garments reflexively before his brain could formulate a good reason not to, and it was in the middle of his preoccupation with that formulation that he heard the panicky grunt of expending energy behind him, too late, as the hair dryer smashed into the right side of his skull behind the ear with a shattering explosion of metal and bone.

"Kill him," screamed Julie, raising the dryer again, but the metal was hopelessly twisted and useless and she dropped it to the floor crying, "Kill him. Hurry . . ."

Slowly the powerful stunned body, mouth moaning softly, sagged downward, hands groping blindly and finding emptiness.

"Jesus," Billy whispered, staring.

"Kill him," Julie moaned.

The cracked head hit the floor with a sickening thud and the steel-rimmed spectacles flew away.

"Do something," Julie cried hoarsely.

The open mouth groaned, drooling.

"My God," said Billy, staring down.

"Kill him," she cried, crashing her foot into the fallen hulk. The head . . . the back . . . the jaw . . .

"Stop it," Billy grabbed her.

"Let me . . ." she struggled. "Let me . . ." Hurled back on the bed. "Goddamn you . . ."

"Stop it," Billy shouted, panting.

"Look . . ." she cried, seeing the clawing hands climbing up the bedspread like great brown crabs, dragging the groaning body slowly up . . . up . . .

She sprang from the bed and seized the stool and Billy's tackle was too loose and she sent him stumbling back . . .

"Wait . . ."

Arriving at the filthy upstaring eyes of the powerful wounded undying unkillable. "*You* . . ." she sobbed, raising the stool high up over the frightening hulk that was rising on one elbow, knife in its claw, jagged mouth twisted in a grimace of pain. "*You* . . ." she screamed and smashed down with terrifying force, again and again . . . *you* . . . *you* . . . *you* . . . *you* . . . blood and bone and wood and splinters and nothing left to smash. "*You* . . ." she sobbed, smashing the unmoving crimson clay . . .

"Julie . . ."

"Oh oh oh, hold me, help me . . ." Shivering with horror.

"God . . . Julie . . ."

"Help me . . . help me . . ." Fainting with exhaustion.

"Julie . . ."

He got his bag and gave her an intravenous, and when she was mercifully unconscious, he got dressed and went out and awakened Yves Chabot, and they got some powerful cleaning fluid from the galley, and while they waited for the open veins of the corpse to empty out into the bathtub, they cleaned the carpeting thoroughly. At a little after four, unseen by anyone as far as they knew, they managed to get the body to the ship's hospital, where Chabot locked it away in his enormous freezer.

Then Billy Berlin went to bed. He was very tired.

BOOK TWO

COUNTERPLAN

"Lord, Lord! methought, what pain it was to drown:
What dreadful noise of waters in mine ears!
What ugly sights of death within mine eyes!
Methought I saw a thousand fearful wracks;
A thousand men that fishes gnaw upon."

WILLIAM SHAKESPEARE

CHAPTER NINETEEN

MAX DECHAMBRE WAS FURIOUS. He had all he could
do to keep from leaping to his feet, slamming his notes down on the
boardroom table and shouting right to their faces, "How dare you
look at me that way. How dare you use that tone of voice when you
address me. I am the *victim,* not the villain. *I* did not do this to you.
I did not perpetrate this foul act against Françat. It was done *to* me,
and to you, by *others*. I only report it to you. I am only the bearer
of bad tidings. How dare you look at me that way, you contemptible stuffed-shirt bastards."

But Dechambre had not risen to be Director General by accident. He had not achieved his eminence without certain admirable
and indispensable qualities of character. And not the least of these
was his remarkable ability to control his professional rages and
furies until such time as, feeling it had no bearing on his career, he
could unleash them on his wife.

He took another sip of the acrid black coffee before him,
squinted at the pale early morning sunlight slanting across the

rooftops of the city into the boardroom of the Tour Française, and waited for the anger in him to move aside and clear the way for his nimble, quick-shifting mind. Setting down his coffee cup, he smiled at the faces of the directors, and decided what to do to them.

"My dear gentlemen, much as I dislike not having my own way, I am nevertheless grateful to you. This is not the first time your collective wisdom has shown itself to be the perfect balance for my sometimes impetuous boldness, though I am sure you will agree that there have been many occasions on which my impetuosity has served the company in good stead." He paused, but not one of them so much as nodded. "Call it naïveté, call it wishful thinking, call it the Casino-at-Monte-Carlo instinct that lurks inside of me, but I truly did feel it would be a worthwhile gamble, I truly did feel that thirty-five million of gold bullion is so immense in sheer bulk as to be virtually unconcealable, and therefore totally and quickly recoverable. I actually did, for a few moments last night and this morning, believe in the possibility that the S.S. *Marseille* might indeed be destroyed, and that three thousand people might indeed die, as threatened. Even as a child, I used to frighten easily." He waited for a friendly chuckle and got only the sound of their restless stirring. "And there, gentlemen, you have the total basis for my original, and obviously unpopular suggestion that we temporarily consign the assets of Françat to the government in exchange for an immediate transfer of treasury gold to a waiting plane at Charles de Gaulle. It was as simple as that: pay off the filthy bastards with thirty-five million of French gold, get back our ship and our people, then recover the gold, and take back our consigned assets. It felt so reasonable to me that—"

A door had opened.

He frowned. *"No,* Mrs. Grillet . . ."

She stood in the doorway, trembling. "Forgive me for interrupting, sir . . ." Heads turned impatiently.

"*N*o, Mrs. Grillet . . ."

"It may be imp—"

"*Please.*"

His secretary withdrew. Dechambre smiled again. "I was on the point of saying, your cooler, wiser heads have prevailed, and I am proud of you, my friends. Stern moral fiber such as yours is all too rare in this day and age. There are too many who would look the other way when evil stares at them, too many who would go to bed with anything wearing a skirt . . ."

Anton Stenger said, "What has this got to do—?"

"I commend you all for your moral stance, and your dedication to the shareholders whom you represent. I agree with you that your primary concern should be the fiscal health of the Compagnie Française, and I also agree with your beautifully stated belief that it would be a sickening act of the worst kind of immorality to give in to the demands of vicious pirates, to give them the money of decent people. *That,* I know, more than anything else, offends you . . ."

"Max, please . . ." cried Henri Blondeau wearily.

"At this moment, which is twenty minutes before eight," he went on, "there is no doubt in my mind that it will be the unanimous vote of this board to flatly reject the demands as set forth in Mr. Sauvinage's expertly prepared memorandum, and turn the matter over to the proper authorities . . ."

"May we get this over with, please?" said Fernand Ducroux testily. "Some of us have not had breakfast."

"It would be easy, too easy, to talk of three thousand lives hanging in the balance, and other such melodramatic nonsense," continued Dechambre, "and thus forget completely our duties and responsibilities to the solvency of this company, and to the morality that does not traffic with thieves. If three thousand souls expire in this tragedy, and mind you, I do not for a minute imply they will—but if three thousand citizens of this planet sink under the waves, choking to death, they will be dying in the cause of the decency and honor which you are espousing here this morning. Françat does not do business with pirates. A fool and his gold are soon parted, the saying goes. But that saying does not go here, not at the Compagnie Française Atlantique . . ."

"This whole speech is irrelevant," muttered Roger Munerot under his breath.

"Thanks to you, gentlemen of the board, our assets shall remain intact, and God will look out, you may be sure, for those out there in the Atlantic who look to the tricolors of France for their protection . . ."

"How long do we—?" tried Alain Bonjalet.

"I want to apologize to each and every one of you for having summoned you from your beds at so unseemly an hour, but I thought this was important enough to warrant your immediate safeguarding the future of this company . . ."

"Let's vote, for God's sake," cried out Jacques Faucheron, cracking.

"And now, just before we formalize the proceedings, may I have a show of all your hands to indicate your solemn oath that you will tell no living soul of the plight of the *Marseille* until such time as I authorize it."

Hands went up.

"Roland, your *right* hand, please," said Dechambre.

"My right hand went to sleep ten minutes ago," said Barrière.

"Thank you, gentlemen," said Dechambre. "And now may I offer a simple suggestion in the hope of avoiding the hour or two of discussion—"

"Oh my God . . ."

"—that will inevitably follow if we make formal motions and follow formal procedures to arrive at the formal predictable outcome of this meeting. Inasmuch as it is self-evident that I, your Director General, am clearly aware of your deep feelings in this entire situation, I ask for another show of hands giving me your immediate authorization, a mandate as it were, to handle the *Marseille* matter as swiftly as possible in the best interests of the company." He paused, waiting. "Unless you feel that several hours of discussion . . ."

All hands went up.

"Thank you, gentlemen. This meeting is adjourned." He got to his feet quickly. "I wish you all a good day."

And he hastened from the room before they realized what he had done to them.

Their wishes be damned. His own personal integrity be damned. He knew now, and it pleased him immensely, that there was nothing he would not do to save the *Marseille* and all the helpless souls on board.

Striding along the corridor, he glanced at his watch. In four hours, the man named Julian Wunderlicht would be calling Sauvinage. It would be good to be able to make Mr. Wunderlicht a happy, contented man. It would save the need for further phone calls. Suspense was necessary in the theater and the cinema, but Dechambre had little use for it in his corporate life. Now that he knew what he wanted to accomplish, he would do it as swiftly as possible and, who knows, he might even be enjoying the frog's legs at Chez L'Ami Louis today without a care in the world.

Entering his office, he saw his secretary standing beside his desk, waiting for him with an apprehensive expression. She was a slight, fine-boned woman of forty-eight with gray hair, milky white skin and large, mournful brown eyes. "Get me the Minister of Transportation immediately," he said to her. "If it is too early, try him at home."

"Yes, Monsieur Dechambre."

Sitting down at his desk, he saw that she had not moved. "I know, Mrs. Grillet, you wish to apologize. But I do not wish you to apologize. If there is anything I hate to hear from those who believe they are doing the right thing, it is apologies." He looked up at her and smiled. "I like you in navy blue. Please wear it more often."

"Thank you, Monsieur Dechambre." Her eyes were moist with gratitude. "I must learn not to overreact to hysterical phone calls. The crackpots get to me far too easily."

"Turn them over to Sauvinage," he said, barely listening.

"This one wanted only you, m'sieur," she said, starting away.

"Which one?" he asked idly.

She stopped at the door and turned. "The American. The one who kept calling from California . . ."

"Americans like to waste their dollars on long distance calls . . ." He took up a pen to rough out what he would say at the Palace.

"He said his name was Mr. Brian Joy . . ."

She was interfering with his concentration. "Brian Joy. The name means less than nothing to me. Sorry . . ." He hoped she would leave.

But she didn't. She was now actually inching her way closer to his desk, damn it. "He was unwilling to give me any information about himself. He said he was calling on a matter of extreme urgency, which is why I—"

He dropped the pen on the desk. "Everything these days is urgent, Mrs. Grillet." He controlled his exasperation. "My speaking to the Minister of Transportation is urgent, because I want something from him. My speaking to the President of France is urgent, too—"

"Monsieur le Président?"

"—because I will be wanting something from him, too. So if this

California fellow tells you it is urgent, Mrs. Grillet, you can be sure he wants something, too. Everybody wants something, and that is why we have Sauvinage. Now, if you please . . ."

"He said it was too grave a matter to discuss with anyone but you, Monsieur Dechambre . . ."

"Well, naturally . . ." He picked up the pen again and stared down at the memo pad.

"I told him that you could not be reached, that you were in an important meeting, and he said he knew all about the important meeting . . ."

"Thank you, Mrs. Grillet." He frowned, disturbed at the confusion she was causing in his mind.

"He said that he knew you had motored from Antibes to Paris last night and were arrested for speeding, all because of your need to attend this meeting . . ."

California, she had said. This man had called from . . . "What did you say his name was?"

"Joy," she said. "Brian Joy."

"Never heard of him," he shook his head, to make him go away.

"He said that the urgent matter he wished to discuss with you was probably identical with the urgent matter being discussed at your meeting . . ."

Dechambre began to feel an unaccountable tingling up and down his back.

"Inasmuch as I had no idea, and still have no idea what the meeting—"

"What else did he say?"

"He was very cautious, Monsieur Dechambre . . ."

"Tell me what he said." His tone startled her.

"Well, the second time he called, when he became quite angry . . ."

"Yes?"

". . . even a bit rude with me for not putting him through to you . . ."

"Go on . . ."

". . . he wanted me to walk into the meeting just like that . . ."

"Yes?"

". . . and say to you very privately, that there was a man on the phone . . ."

"Yes?"

". . . a friend, not an enemy, but a friend, who has the means to save the three thousand . . ."

"Who has *what?*"

"Who has the means to save the three thousand. I didn't know whether he meant francs or dollars because he was getting so excitable—"

"Mrs. Grillet." Suddenly he was on his feet. "Why in the name of heaven did you not walk into that meeting and *interrupt* me?"

"But Monsieur Dechambre . . ." She looked at him, stunned.

"Where is this man?" he demanded.

"In Beverly Hills, California," she said in a trembling voice.

"Do you have his number?"

"Yes."

"Get him."

"But, m'sieur . . ."

"Get him immediately."

"But what about the Minister of Transportation?"

"Don't confuse the issue with questions," he shot back. "Do as I say."

"Yes, Monsieur Dechambre."

"And Mrs. Grillet?"

"Yes, Monsieur Dechambre?"

"I don't know what I would do without you. Don't ever forget that."

"Oh, m'sieur, oh, m'sieur . . ."

"For heaven's sake, don't start crying."

She hurried out to her office. He pressed a button on his desk. The voice of Georges Sauvinage came from the little brown box on the desk.

"Yes, m'sieur?"

He leaned toward the box. "Are you alone, Sauvinage?"

"Yes, m'sieur."

"Take notes, please."

"Ready."

"Get through to Creasy immediately. Do not stop until you get through."

"The Minister himself, or will one of his aides do?"

"Creasy personally. No one else."

"Yes."

"He owes Françat many favors. I will wipe all of them out in return for this one. Make that crystal clear to him"

"Yes."

"He must, positively must, arrange that I see the President by eleven this morning."

"The President, m'sieur?"

"Yes, Sauvinage, the President. A twenty-minute audience will suffice."

"What reason may I give?"

"None, Sauvinage. You have no idea why I wish this meeting. If pressed, you may speculate that it has to do with rumors of a shocking scandal at the highest levels of the government."

"Yes, m'sieur."

"If you get nowhere with Creasy, you may have to say to him, 'The Director General sends you greetings from Suzanne and her friends.' "

"Suzanne who, m'sieur?"

"Sauvinage, please do as I say."

"Yes, m'sieur."

"Do you have that personal message?"

"If I get no results with the Minister of Transportation regarding an audience with the President of the French Republic, I am to say, 'The Director General sends you greetings from Suzanne and her friends.' "

"Excellent, Sauvinage."

"Thank you, m'sieur."

"Next. I want you to leak a cover story to the news media to account for this morning's extraordinary board meeting, and all other signs of unusual activity in and around the Tour Française during the next day or two. This means the wire services, morning and afternoon papers, television and radio. Use some of your contacts at *France-Soir* and the *Herald Tribune* and those bums at the bar of the California. Also those two faggots who hang out at La Coupole. I leave it to your discretion, but see that it gets out fast. Tell everyone it is confidential and in the grave, and must not be used or told to a soul. That will ensure complete disclosure."

"I understand, m'sieur, but what is the story?"

"The terrible news which the Director General and his board of directors are trying to keep from the public is this: the secret trial run of the new S.S. *Bordeaux* in the southern Atlantic has turned up grave deficiencies in the construction of the vessel. We here at the Compagnie Française are attempting with much desperation to work out a way of putting a good face on it for world consumption, not only for the stockholders but also for the maritime honor of France. Does that make sense to you, Sauvinage?"

"It is so convincing, Monsieur Dechambre, that I almost believe it myself."

"Good. Get moving. My phone is ringing."

He picked it up. It was Mrs. Grillet. She had the man from California on the line. Was Monsieur Dechambre ready to take the call?

He was.

CHAPTER TWENTY

———————

Beverly Hills, California—1:04 A.M. Brian Joy, lulled by twenty-one fluid ounces of tequila, seven fluid ounces of triple-sec liqueur, and a deep trust in the overseas telephonic voice of Max Dechambre, lay curled in sleep, his body snuggled against the warm back and soft behind of his wife, Maggie.

New York, New York—4:04 A.M. Leonard Ball, sleeping lightly in his Park East bedroom, emitted a sudden snore that almost woke him, then turned over restlessly on the waterbed and felt his right elbow jab someone's soft shoulder. A muffled feminine voice said, "Jesus," but the CBS vice president was not sufficiently close to the waking state to recognize the voice, other than to know that it was not his wife. Presently he began to snore again.

Latitude 26°N., Longitude 57°W.—6:04 A.M. Harold Columbine, still dressed as a male ballet dancer but with his mask off, lay sprawled on top of the coverlet of his bed, dreaming heavily. It was the fourth REM sleep cycle he had entered into since lying back to wait for a possible visit from his accomplice of the evening, to compare notes with her on the night's adventure. He had been confident that it would not take her long to shake the tall guy in the phony uniform, but he had, without realizing it, fallen soundly asleep after waiting only six minutes.

One deck below, Julie Berlin lay motionless in a deeply drugged, dreamless sleep, while on the edge of the bed, her husband sat in yellow pajamas and gray headphones, listening for a voice that wasn't there.

Two hundred feet forward and one deck below, the woman who had come to know herself as Louise Campbell, wife of Don Campbell of Houston, Texas, stirred in her sleep and thrust out an arm to feel for her husband's presence. But her hand felt only emptiness on the other side of the bed, and her partially narcoticized brain worked out the explanation that he was probably still in one of those all-night meetings with Craig and the others. But as she sank more deeply into sleep again, a terrible uneasiness crept into her soul and poisoned her dreams.

Paris, France—10:04 A.M. Julian Wunderlicht, standing in La Salle des États on the first floor of the Louvre, looked at the Mona Lisa, and smiled.

CHAPTER TWENTY-ONE

S E V E R A L M I L E S to the west of the Louvre, Lisa Briande of the *International Herald Tribune* shifted down into third, then into second, then back into third, and then back into fourth.

"Merde," she said.

A few moments later she uttered her second-favorite word, "Fuck."

But no one heard her. She was alone in the car.

She kept a safe distance behind the black Citroën, cursing the disgusting morning traffic that was slowly ruining Paris. She might have played it safer and stayed closer, but she had no wish to give Max Dechambre something to think about. He seemed to be having enough to think about as it was, if the expression on his face when he had emerged from the building and clambered into the car had been a true indicator. Trouble. Classification: *big*.

Not that he would have attached much significance to the un-washed red midget of a Peugeot that was following him. But if, by mischance, she were to draw abreast of him at a red light, it was conceivable that he might recognize her and add two and two.

They had met several times over the past few years, once at a gala cocktail party given by the Compagnie Française at the Ritz to introduce the press to Charles Girodt, the new Commandant of the *Marseille,* another time at the ceremonies celebrating the opening of the shiny new Tour Française. Oh, there had been other occasions—she was much too tired to recall them all—and on all of them he had gazed upon her and attended her and conversed with her in a way that had been quite clearly above and beyond the call of duty of a Director General trying to please the press. Her colleagues had been bitchily envious. She had felt flattered, and unjournalistically sexy.

Right now, maneuvering her Peugeot through the angry monoxide snarl along the Champs-Élysées, she was numb with sleepiness. Her pale green eyes strained to stay open and hold in view the quarry up ahead. It was hours past her unique bedtime, and she did not know whether to thank or to hate that smart-ass bastard in California who had inadvertently put her on to a possible story, and had thereby ruined her sleep schedule.

She decided to hate him.

He could have made it so easy for her. He could have told her whatever he knew. He could have told her what was really going on at Français, why he had had the need to reach top officials of the company in the middle of the night, what he knew of the special meeting of the board so early in the morning. If he had only done that, like a true friend of Leonard Ball's, it would not have been necessary for her to park outside the Tour at six forty-five in the morning like some minion of the Sûreté, merely to see who was coming and going. And it would not have been necessary for her to be following Max Dechambre now, at five past ten, through the choked streets of Paris, on the mere off-chance that she might learn something.

You are really getting desperate, Lisa old girl. The closer you get to thirty, the more desperate you become. What you will do to get a story that is probably not even there is pitiful. Really pitiful.

That son of a bitch, Brian Joy.

When she had come to Paris after the four years at Bennington and the two at Columbia, and had landed the job with the *Trib,* she had been young enough and foolish enough to believe all the party talk, all the hyperbolic assurances of the backscratchers. It would be so simple. Mary Blume's days as the reigning queen (beautiful, talented reigning queen) were definitely numbered. Lisa Briande would have the column, the space, the interviews, the byline, within a year, two at the most. How could she miss, they all told her, with that face, those eyes, that hair, those legs, that body, and that gorgeous mind? Lisa, just be kind and don't squeeze too hard, Leonard Ball had said on one of his weekend flights, because, believe me, darling, you've got Paris by the *cochon*s.

Dear Lenny, he was so used to Madison Avenue, he hadn't realized. Paris didn't *have* cochons. Paris wasn't a *man*. Paris was a *bitch*. And the bitch had Lisa by the claws. The beautiful bodies at Castel's and La Coupole and Regine's seldom included hers these nights. *She* was too busy trying, not to take over, but just to *hold* on. The soft throaty voice and the long flaxen hair got you so far—like one inch on the bottom of page twelve—and no farther. Let the combos play and the champagne flow. *She* spent many of her nights now in her little flat hunched over a typewriter, trying to write the book that would topple the Eiffel Tower, or the letter-from-Paris that would send Janet Flanner leaping into the Seine. And when that wasn't working, she'd prowl the streets and bars and bistros, looking for the story that would enable her, at last, to squeeze and squeeze hard, to have Paris by the old clit.

Well, maybe this wasn't it, she told herself, pushing the Peugeot along, but what the hell, it was the only game in town this morning, and they were past the Rond Point now, and the black Citroën was swinging left onto the Avenue Matignon, and then turning right and entering the rue du Faubourg St.-Honoré, leading her past the boutique windows she no longer could afford to glance at.

With my luck, she thought wearily, he's on his way to do some shopping, to buy a gift. And for his wife, probably. Not even for his mistress.

Suddenly her foot was braking the Peugeot, slowing it down. Up ahead, the Citroën had lost speed for no apparent reason. It was coming to a stop on the left-hand side of the street, right in front of the elegant window display of Louis Feraud. She brought the Peugeot to a halt. So he *was* going to buy something chic and feminine, after all. Then she noticed the bustle of activity to the right of the Citroën, across the street from it. The beautiful guards in their beautiful uniforms. The ones who guarded the entrance to the courtyard of the Élysée Palace, the residence and executive headquarters of the presidency of France. The guards appeared to be lowering the covered chain that protected the entrance. Yes, they actually were lowering the chain. And now the black Citroën was moving again. It was executing a slow rightward arc.

Lisa Briande felt herself coming awake as though she had just been injected.

The Citroën was going through the archway and disappearing from her view. Quickly she drove forward, drew abreast of the guards, came to a stop, peered past them across the graveled courtyard, and saw Max Dechambre stepping out of his car before the entrance to the palace. He glanced about for a moment, perhaps to get his bearings, perhaps to see if he was being observed from the street. And then he hurried up the marble steps and through the large glass door that opened for him, and disappeared inside the residence of the President of the French Republic.

Lisa Briande put the Peugeot in gear and drove off, her green eyes shining through the mists of oncoming exhaustion. Across the Seine on the rue Récamier, her bed awaited her and she sped toward it eagerly. She would allow herself four hours of sleep, not a minute more, but it would be a good sleep, filled with hope. And then, as the rest of Paris rose from the luncheon table, she would arise from her bed, have her orange juice and black coffee, and get ready for what now promised to be the beginning of a great adventure. In fact—she smiled to herself as the car approached the Pont de la Concorde—she had a feeling it had already begun.

Seated behind the great desk that dominated the small but possibly most important room in all of France, Aristide Bonnard continued reading, with agonizing slowness and a slight movement of his lips, the four-page document that Max Dechambre had finally placed before him, the Georges Sauvinage summary of the entire *Marseille* situation.

The formalities of greeting had been easy for both men. Dechambre had known the President as far back as the early days when the young Deputy Commissioner of the Interior under General Gallois had begun his climb to eminence. But once the formalities were over, it had been awkward, painfully awkward for both men. Not often, perhaps never, had a President of the French Republic been told by a private citizen that the purpose of his visit could not be revealed until the President had solemnly agreed that he would divulge the matter to no one, nor take any official action whatsoever, unless requested by his visitor.

So startling had been Dechambre's demand that Bonnard had, at first, been slightly amused by the Director General's presumptuous air. Then had come the duel of cautious words, with power matched against stubborn will. In the end, rather than lose an old friend by asking him to leave, Bonnard had capitulated. And if he had been anything less than the President of France, he probably would not have been able to do it so good-naturedly.

Dechambre sat watching him now, in one of the two high-backed chairs facing the desk, his eyes fastened on the familiar, rugged features that hovered over the Sauvinage report. He waited for some sign of inner shock, of dismay, of anger, of outrage. But Aristide Bonnard, once a man of volatile emotions, had learned the value of the poker face, paying for it with the reputation for having chilled red wine in his veins. He read on with unchanging countenance.

Dechambre's gaze wandered to the tall windows, to the sun-dappled leaves of the heavily wooded gardens outside. The chirping of birds and the soft distant hum of traffic on the Champs-Élysées were the only sounds intruding on his thoughts. His left hand moved unobtrusively to the inside pocket of his jacket and felt the folded sheet of paper there. Guilt stabbed at him, and was quickly banished.

The startling radio message from Commandant Girodt, which the strangely earnest Californian, Brian Joy, had forced him to take down in his own hand after insisting that Mrs. Grillet hang up on the other extension, had excited him on first reading. But instinctively, after thanking the American and assuring him of swift action and further communication, he had folded the lengthy handwritten message and carefully put it away in the pocket where it now rested. Instinctively, he had made no copies and told no one of its contents, not Sauvinage, not the President of France. Only he and the American in California, whose dedication to secrecy surpassed even his own, knew of its existence.

At sea, Charles Girodt was in command and must be obeyed. But on land, it was the Director General. And he would countenance no foolhardy attempts to overthrow the pirates. The radio message, with its accompanying suggestions for the calling in of the

Sûreté Nationale, the FBI, and Scotland Yard, was an invitation to international leaks, worldwide publicity, swift reprisals, the sacrifice of lives, and the loss of the *Marseille,* too. Compliance with all terms was what Julian Wunderlicht had demanded, and compliance was what he would get. Two of the terms, total secrecy and non-intervention, rested securely in Dechambre's breast pocket. The other terms rested within the power of the man seated behind the desk, and would have to be won from him.

Suddenly Dechambre was jolted from his revery by the voice of Aristide Bonnard. "Deplorable . . . deplorable." Dechambre turned quickly and saw that the President had finished reading. "Tragic and deplorable," Bonnard repeated, looking across the desk at the Director General with smoldering steel-gray eyes. "I understand better now your passion for secrecy, though I still do not approve of it."

Dechambre met his gaze. "Yes, Monsieur le Président."

"I assume you have not informed the Minister of Transportation," said the President coolly. "Otherwise, he would most certainly have told me of this grave situation."

"Other than my assistant, Sauvinage," replied the Director General, "and seven members of the board of directors of the Compagnie Française, you and I alone in France know of these facts."

"Have you not forgotten one other?"

Dechambre's heart leaped. Brian Joy? How could—?

"This Wunderlicht fellow," said Bonnard.

Dechambre flushed with relief. "Perhaps I would *like* to forget him, Monsieur le Président."

Aristide Bonnard did not smile. He rose slowly from behind the desk and moved to the windows, looking out at his beloved gardens.

"Tell me, my friend, so that we do not waste time. Have you come to the palace merely to inform me what you plan to do about this frightful matter, or have you come here to ask me to tell you what must be done?"

Dechambre did not respond immediately. He framed his words carefully before replying. "If you are asking me whether I have made a decision, the answer is yes, I have, most emphatically, Monsieur le Président. However, that does not mean that I would not welcome any wisdom that the President would be kind enough to give me."

He watched the figure at the window and saw only its back. The face was still averted.

"Tell me your decision, Dechambre."

"I will be brief," said the Director General.

"Please," said the President.

"Five hundred and twelve passengers and nine hundred and ten crew members out there in the Atlantic are citizens of France. Their country cannot afford to let them die." He paused.

"Continue," said the President.

"Over fifteen hundred passengers are Americans, looking to the tricolors flying from the mast for their safety and protection. France cannot afford to let them die."

"I am waiting," said the President.

"The S.S. *Marseille* represents the pride and the glory of our great nation's maritime prowess wherever it sails. France cannot afford to lose that pride and glory."

Aristide Bonnard turned sharply, and the expression on his face was not clearly discernible in the back lighting of the windows. "You have been telling me what France cannot afford, Dechambre. But perhaps what you are really telling me is what the Compagnie Française Atlantique cannot afford."

"I beg to differ with you, Monsieur le Président." Dechambre got to his feet, feeling the need to rise to Bonnard's height, if not his power. "What Françat cannot afford is quite different," he said. "Françat cannot afford the bankruptcy into which it would be immediately plunged if it attempted to raise thirty-five million dollars in gold. Françat cannot afford the financial ruin that would overtake it if the heirs of three thousand departed souls rightfully sued the Compagnie Française for gross negligence at sea. In sad truth, Monsieur le Président, Françat cannot even afford the loss in prestige and public confidence and future revenues that would ensue if word were to get out that you and I had even *considered* not paying the ransom."

Aristide Bonnard stared at him for a long time. "I believe that what I have just heard, Dechambre, is your decision."

Dechambre looked into the steel-gray eyes. "That is correct, Monsieur le Président."

"Despite the absence of thirty-five million dollars in your company's vaults."

"That is correct, Monsieur le Président."

"And you have ruled out the advisability of calling in the Sûreté and Interpol and other such agencies in France and the United States."

"Yes, Monsieur le Président."

Aristide Bonnard walked over to his desk and sat down again. Dechambre remained standing, facing him. The President looked up. "What kind of man is it, Dechambre, who would make a decision for which he cannot pay?"

"In this case, I sincerely believe, a wise man, Monsieur le Président."

Bonnard's face took on a thoughtful expression. "And suppose I were to tell you that I cannot do it, that the answer is no?"

The Director General shrugged. "You are the President, Monsieur le Président. Your word is final. That is the great power, and the terrible vulnerability, of the Presidency. I am sure I do not have to tell you that."

"Vulnerability?" Bonnard eyed him with suspicion.

"World opinion is treacherous, inaccurate, and lazy," explained Dechambre, beginning to pace as he talked. "World opinion personalizes governments, reduces nations to one man, one figurehead, the *leader*. China was not China, it was the Chairman. Cuba is not Cuba, it is Castro. The United States is the President. Jordan is King Hussein. France is Bonnard. Will the world press say that the French *government* or that *France* turned its back on the pleas of three thousand lost souls? No, it will be *Bonnard* who did it. Just as the world press has for years unfairly accused de Gaulle and Pompidou and now Bonnard of being greedy for gold, when all along it has simply been a policy of the Minister of Finance to acquire gold rather than paper currencies. So perverse and unpredictable is the press, Monsieur le Président, that if you were to say *yes* to me, I would not be at all surprised if the headlines chose to ignore you personally, and instead shouted to the world that *France* has put the lie to years of false charges by demonstrating that three thousand lives are more precious to it than thirty-five million dollars of gold stockpiled in its treasury. It would be magnificent for France, but so unfair to you, Monsieur le Président."

Aristide Bonnard looked at Dechambre and shook his head slowly, a reluctant smile coming to his stern face. "Dechambre, you must never enter the government, promise me that. I cherish too much my reputation as the craftiest politician in Western Europe."

"You flatter me, Monsieur le Président," said the Director General. "I am merely a humble businessman, a glorified shopkeeper trying to save the store."

"Oh, yes, Dechambre. Oh, yes."

The President rose to his feet behind the desk. It was the signal that the meeting was over.

Dechambre leaned over and picked up the Sauvinage document from the desk, speaking hurriedly. "Am I correct, Monsieur le Président, in assuming that when the call comes from Julian Wunderlicht at noon, we are empowered to tell him that the terms are met?"

"When have you *not* been correct this morning, Dechambre?" said the President. "I shall call the Caissier General personally and commence the arrangements for the transfer of the bullion tomorrow afternoon."

"May I say by one o'clock?"

"Very well. One o'clock."

"And the plane?"

"The Minister of Transportation will be ordered to charter a 747 from Air France and have it at Charles de Gaulle Airport, fully fueled and ready to receive its cargo. No explanations will be given."

Dechambre was fairly giddy. "I am more grateful to you than I can ever express, Monsieur le Président."

"May France prevail. Go with God, Dechambre. And keep me informed."

"Good day, Monsieur le Président."

"*Au revoir,* old friend. Oh, would it be possible for me to keep that copy of the report?"

"Certainly, Monsieur le Président. Certainly." Dechambre handed over the document he had removed from the desk. "Again, good day."

When his visitor had departed, the President summoned his aide, M. Dupal, and said to him, "I must talk in the most protected manner possible to the President of the United States. I must be connected with him immediately. If necessary, his aides may be told that the call is of a most urgent nature, and concerns the discovery of imminent nuclear peril in the Middle East situation. Is that clear?"

"Yes, Monsieur le Président. But it is now ten minutes before five in the morning in Washington."

"Immediately, Dupal."

When his aide had closed the door, the President of France called his wife at their private summer residence in St.-Germain-en-Laye, using the special white telephone. In a voice that was gentle, yet overwhelmingly irresistible, he instructed her to cancel her plans for the day and instead, invite to her home for a twelve-thirty luncheon, Jean-Claude Raffin. Madame Bonnard's committee, suggested the President, had demanded that she meet secretly with Raffin today, and if he failed to accept the invitation, she was to call the President back at once.

The wife of the President knew better than to ask even one question. She sent her husband a sweet kiss over the telephone, and hung up.

It was perfectly logical, decided Aristide Bonnard, should anyone on the surface of the earth choose to examine such things, that the chairwoman of the committee investigating the rise of cocaine addiction among the pre-adolescents of France would be having a private luncheon in her manor house at St.-Germain-en-Laye today with the Director General of the French Sûreté Nationale.

As logical, actually, as would be the headache that would come to the cranium of the President of the French Republic later that morning, causing him to return to his quiet bedroom in St.-Germain-en-Laye for a brief nap shortly after midday.

CHAPTER TWENTY-TWO

———————

"MR. PRESIDENT . . . Mr. President . . . Mr. President . . ."

"Hm? Hm? Huh? What? Oh. What time is—? Goddamn it, Monty, will you look at the time."

"I'm sorry, Mr. President. I know."

"Am I *ever* going to be allowed *one solid night?* Just one . . . fucking . . . night?"

"It's Aristide Bonnard, sir."

"What happened? Did he die?"

"He's on the blue line, sir. Urgent."

"*Now* what, for chrissake? Another revaluation of the franc? Tell him to order his Minister of Finance to purchase one billion American dollars, and *then* I'll talk to him."

"Mr. President, sir, he's on the line, waiting."

"Would it be all right with you, Monty, and would the President of France be too terribly upset, if the President of the United States took a leak first?"

"By all means, sir. Go right ahead."

"Well, thank you, Monty . . . Ah . . . oh . . . whew . . . ah . . . Where are you going?"

"The blue line is right there, sir. President Bonnard has given explicit instructions that he will talk to you only if you are alone at the time, and no one is monitoring the call. I'll be outside."

"You'll be outside and *I'll* be a son of a bitch. Just wait until we narrow the trade deficit. Give me six straight months of surplus in the balance of payments and Western Europe will come crawling to us, do you hear me, *crawling,* between halves at a Redskins game, with Washington leading twenty-eight zip at the half."

"The blue line, sir?"

"Get the hell out of here, Monty."

"Yes, Mr. President."

"Hello? Hello? Aristide? How are you, my dear friend? It is so good to hear your voice again. Yes, all alone. No, she has her own bedroom now, Aristide. She felt that her sleeping interfered with my phone conversations, ha-ha. And how is Madame Bonnard? Well, please give her my most affectionate best wishes. No, Aristide, you did not awaken me. Not at all, not at all. Here at the White House these days, we rise at five in the morning to launch an early attack on the affairs of state. No, Aristide, on the *affairs* of state. No, not an early attack on— (Oh, shit) *An early attack on the affairs of state.* Right. Right. Right. What? No. No, Aristide. I have no idea why you're calling. What? I don't understand. What do you mean? With all due respect, Aristide, are you being absolutely serious now? Well, how can I do that? Yes, but how can I give you my solemn oath when I don't even know what it is I'm swearing not to divulge? But, Aristide, just because *you* did, does that mean *I* have to follow suit? Follow suit, follow suit, as in playing bridge. Wait a minute. Let me get this straight. Are you saying that you will be forced to end this conversation unless I agree to—? I see. I see. I see. Well, of *course* I'm curious. Look, why don't you put it to me another way, Aristide? Give me something I can live with. Well, why don't you just say to me that what you are about to tell me is for my ears only? That's right. For my ears only. How does *that* strike you? Good. Fine. We're in business then. All right, I won't say a word, I'll just listen. Oh? How long is it? Four pages single-spaced or double-spaced? In that case, maybe I better sit down. All right, Aristide, I'm ready. Fire away . . . Mm-hm . . . Mm-hm . . . Uh-huh . . . What? . . . Jesus . . . My

God . . . Oh my . . . No . . . Christ Almighty . . . I can't believe
. . . This is . . . This is . . . Too much . . . Bastards . . . Terrible . . . Terrible . . . Unbelievable . . . Pricks . . . Yes, I'm
here, I'm here. Is that it? I'm too shocked. I don't know *what* to say,
not just yet, anyway. Yes. Yes, of course I heard it. Fifteen hundred and something Americans. Uh-huh. Uh-huh. May I ask you
how you intend to handle this appalling situation? Oh, you are. Oh,
really. Well, then, aside from *telling nobody,* what is it you'd like
me to do, Aristide? I see. Oh, I see. I see. Yes, but how could I ever
do that? I mean, even if I were to *agree* with you that ten million
would be an equitable share of the burden for the United States,
there is no way I can snap my fingers and change the official policy
of this nation, which is dead set against the payment of ransom *to*
anyone *for* anyone or *anything,* on land or sea or in the air. And
even if that were not national policy, I do not carry a key to Fort
Knox on my automobile key chain, Aristide. The Congress does.
Not the President. I know, but I'm sorry, Aristide, truly sorry. The
answer is no. I'm sorry. However, please let me have some time to
recover from the shock and to digest all this, and then I will be in a
better position to get back to you. To *advise* you, Aristide. Well,
sometimes advice can be helpful. I'm sure you would not have
called me if you didn't think so yourself. I know. Yes, I know. I'm
perfectly aware of the number. One thousand five hundred and
fourteen American citizens. Let me do some thinking now and I
will get back to you. Well, I'll call you anyway. No, you don't have
to worry about that. In one ear and *not* out the other. No, not even
to her. Now please try to cheer up, my dear friend. With God's
help, it will all work out. I won't, don't worry. Goodbye now,
Aristide. Thanks for calling. *Au revoir* . . . Monty? . . . Monty?
. . . *Monty* . . ."

"Yes, Mr. President."

"Close the door."

"Yes, Mr. President?"

"Aside from you, who knows about the call from Bonnard?"

"Absolutely nobody was listening, sir. It was—"

"Who knows he *called?* Not what he said."

"Alice Lentworth on the switchboard, sir. And Wilma. She woke
up when I got the call. That's it."

"Talk to Lentworth *and* your wife. It never *happened.*"

"Got it, sir."

"As for Mrs. Yours Truly, I don't like her to know I get awakened this early. She worries too much about my health. Therefore, she will not hear about this call. Correct?"

"Right-on, Mr. President."

"Now, who am I scheduled to spill coffee on this morning?"

"Senators Jackson and Wheeling are rolling down from the Hill, sir."

"Oh, Christ, and I really *owe* them, too. Well, cancel them."

"But, Mr. President.

"Goddamn it, Monty."

"Yes, Mr. President."

"And have the following here for breakfast at seven: Nolan, Holmes, Fahnsworth, Kemmel, Haig, and Knox."

"Nolan, Holmes, Fahnsworth, Kemmel, Haig, and Knox. Yes, sir. And if the press corps should ask any questions about that?"

"Well, it's like this. The Redskins are going to be hotter than ever this year. So, we decided to get together over bacon and eggs to work out the White House season tickets situation *early,* who gets in on it, who doesn't . . . Goddamn it, don't give me that look. Would you rather tell them the *truth,* that Bonnard's thirty-two-year-old daughter has run off with a nineteen-year-old pot-smoking guitar player from Nashville she met in front of the American Express in Paris?"

"Jesus, no, Mr. President. But . . ."

"Then make one up yourself. You get paid a lot of money around here. Just ask yourself the question, why would the President of the United States be having breakfast with the Joint Chiefs and the heads of the CIA, the FBI, and the Office of Naval Intelligence? And then answer it. It's as simple as that. Now get moving."

"Uh . . . yes, Mr. President."

CHAPTER TWENTY-THREE

GEORGES SAUVINAGE TRIED not to look at the telephone on his desk. It was enough that his visitor, the Director General, kept his eyes fixed on it from the vantage point of his chair across the room. It was two minutes past noon, and the phone had not rung since 11:35, when Marie Latouche, one of the switchboard operators, had called him for further information. She and the other girls had now received a total of thirty-seven calls over the last two and a half hours from Parisians who wished to report to the Compagnie Française that they were unable to get through by telephone to the *Marseille*. Did Monsieur Sauvinage have a new estimate on the resumption of service? Tell them shortly, he had snapped, hanging up quickly.

He glanced down with sour expression at the sheaf of telex messages from the Audierne installation. They were all variations on the same monotonous theme by Bernard Delade: HAVE LOST ALL RADIO CONTACT WITH S.S. MARSEILLE. PLEASE ADVISE. His replies had been no less monotonous. TEMPORARY EQUIPMENT FAILURE BEING REPAIRED. RELAX.

Sauvinage's mood was poor, and he saw little hope of immediate improvement. Though his personal report had been a feature of the board meeting, and the Director General had commended him for it before the others, he had recognized a bone when it was thrown to him. Dechambre had not let him open his mouth at the meeting, nor had he taken him into his confidence regarding the visit to the Élysée Palace. A messenger boy, that's what he was, with one meager, dirty assignment for the day, to disseminate foolish lies to the press about the S.S. *Bordeaux*. He had been embarrassed by the knowing smiles on the faces of those to whom he had spread the manure this morning. Even through the telephone he had seen those smiles.

"Where in hell *is* he?" Max Dechambre's voice rasped irritably.

"His watch may be slow," said Sauvinage, without looking at him. What depressed the assistant most was the physical presence of the Director General in his office. It served to remind him that not once before had his superior ever favored him with a visit. And he was here now not for Sauvinage but for Wunderlicht.

Suddenly the ringing telephone shattered the silence.

Dechambre came out of his chair. A buzzer sounded. Sauvinage picked up the phone. His secretary said that a man wished to speak to him, but would not give his name.

"Put him on," said Sauvinage. "Then go off the line please. And hold all calls."

Quickly he turned on the cassette tape recorder which was connected to the telephone through a suction cup device. He pressed down on the red RECORD button and waited. Presently he heard the hated voice.

"Good morning, Sauvinage," said Julian Wunderlicht in his cheerful but imperfect French.

"Good *afternoon*," replied Sauvinage. "It is five minutes past noon."

"Thank you," said Wunderlicht. "I did not know that one of the many services provided by the Compagnie Française is the correct time."

"The Director General is standing beside me," said Sauvinage. "He has come to Paris specifically to handle the situation. He wants to talk to you now."

"Why are you in such a rush to be through with me, Sauvinage? Was I unkind to you last night?"

"Perhaps you did not hear what—"

"I heard you very well. And what I understand is that you yourself have no great desire to converse with me. Maybe you would like me to hang up the phone—"

"No, please," cried Sauvinage. "Don't do that." He felt the sweat under his arms. If only Dechambre would not stand over him impatiently. He strained to hear Wunderlicht.

"Actually, my fine fat friend, I am trying to give your police sufficient time to trace this call, so that they can come here and seize me . . ."

"There are no—"

". . . That way, I will know with certainty that you mean to betray us."

"There are *no police*." Sauvinage's voice went shrill. "The Director General of Françat wishes to speak to you now. May I put him on, Wunderlicht?"

"If you insist," said Wunderlicht. "This is goodbye, then, Sauvinage."

"Wait a minute, hold on." Sauvinage quickly thrust the instrument into his superior's hand.

"This is Max Dechambre," announced the Director General.

"And this is Julian Wunderlicht," said the voice at the other end. "May I offer my profound condolences to you on the recent loss of your mother-in-law? We should all be so lucky."

"I am herewith officially notifying you, Wunderlicht, that all your terms will be met," said the Director General brusquely. "The gold, the plane, everything, by tomorrow at one p.m."

There was a moment of silence at the other end.

"If you were I, Dechambre, would you believe that statement?"

"Listen to me." Dechambre gripped the phone tightly. "Everything will be exactly as you demanded. I swear to it. Do you understand? You have it all."

"I have *nothing*," said Julian Wunderlicht. "Words are only something to stick up your ass, not put in the bank. There are several pairs of eyes watching Charles de Gaulle Airport. When they see what they are waiting to see, *then,* and only then, will I, as you put it, have it all. You, sir, have a little less than thirty-two hours. Use them wisely. Until tomorrow at the same time?"

"Wunderlicht? . . . Hello? . . . He has hung up." Dechambre handed the phone to his assistant, who restored it to its cradle. "The insolent son of a bitch."

Sauvinage snapped off the recorder, wondering whether his superior had lied to the German, or whether he actually did have some secret plan to meet the terms, despite the contrary wishes of the board. But he was feeling too low to think it through. Wunderlicht had treated him like shit. Everyone treated him like shit. He *was* shit.

Dechambre looked down at the mournful face of his assistant. He might need the man's good will someday soon. Also, his silence.

"Come," he said to him briskly. "We go to lunch. I know a good place to take you, where they will not sneer if we have double martinis first."

Sauvinage examined the bone that had just been thrown to him. He felt like a dog. And so he picked it up.

"I could use several," he said, rising.

It would be the first time his superior had ever lunched with him.

Julian Wunderlicht went outside to the Avenue George V, still smiling to himself, and walked next door to the Hotel Prince de Galles. He crossed the lobby to the elevator, ascended to the sixth floor, traversed the hallway to a door near the end, and sounded the buzzer three times. The door was opened by a heavy-set man in his early sixties with short-cropped gray hair and a florid complexion. He was wearing white boxer shorts and a white ribbed undershirt, and held playing cards in his left hand.

"Well?" he said to Wunderlicht, in German.

Wunderlicht went past him into the small parlor of the suite, and met the questioning gaze of the other man in the room, a hairless, pink-domed European of fifty-seven, dressed in shapeless brown trousers and bare above the waist. He was seated at a small table on which there were some playing cards, loose piles of German marks, an overflowing ashtray, several drinking glasses, and a half-empty bottle of Wolfschmidt gin.

Wunderlicht waited until the man in the underwear had closed the door and come back to the table to sit down again and resume the card game. Then Wunderlicht leaned over, picked up the gin bottle and held it ceremoniously in the air.

"From now on," he said, "no more of this stuff. It looks to me like you two are going to be doing some flying very soon."

The card players glanced up at him and saw the twinkle in his eye.

The man with the hairless pink dome let out a whoop of laughter and threw his cards into the air.

The man with the gray hair said, with great solemnity, "But we cannot fly. Lufthansa says we are not fit to fly." Then his weather-beaten face crinkled into a broad grin. He held out his hand, and Wunderlicht placed the gin bottle in it. The man poured some gin into the two glasses. "Also Lufthansa says we are negligent, and a menace to life and property. Sorry, Wunderlicht." He and the hairless man laughed themselves into a coughing spell, then drank to each other's health and resumed their card game.

Wunderlicht went inside to the bathroom and started the water in the tub. It would be his second bath today. He had a terrible, embarrassing itch. And he wondered if it could be from last night.

Faulty bridgework?

She had set the alarm for two-thirty, but when a passing police car siren on the rue de Sèvres pierced through her ear plugs and woke her at quarter to one, she came out of sleep long enough to remember why she had allotted herself only four hours today, and like *that* she was scrambling out of bed, walking naked into the bathroom, removing the ear plugs and popping two Ritalin tablets into her mouth. They would keep her going until midnight if necessary.

The orange juice was too cold. The coffee was too hot. And when she phoned the paper, practically everyone was already at the Beaujolais getting stuffed on *tripoux* except Jimi Brocke, copy boy by avocation, hairdresser-in-training by profession. He would do anything for Lisa Briande. Anything, provided she never asked him to go to bed with her. He absolutely adored the girl.

What was new and exciting? Nothing, really. Who was doing what to whom? Zilch. Paris in July. *You* know. And what are *you* doing up at this hour of the day, you gorgeous thing? A smart-ass, all right, but smart.

"Then tell me what's *boring*," Lisa said as she lit a cigarillo. "Come on, Jimi, you don't wriggle your hips at Le Berri Bar for *nothing*. What's *not* new? What's *un*exciting?"

"Well, lemme see now, Lisa with an 's.' Mary the Blume is pissed off at your favorite novelist, Harold Columbine, because he never called her from the incoming *Marseille,* as promised, to confirm the interview on the sixteenth, and *she* can't reach *him* 'cause the *phones* have been out or something on the *Marseille* for the past like *sixteen hours,* and if it isn't gonna *be* with Columbine, she's got a shot at Norman Mailer, except she can't do them *both* and she doesn't know if it's yes or no with Harold the Horemonger. That's spelled with an 'h' for alliterative purposes. Am I being sufficiently boring, adored one?"

"It'll do until the real thing comes along. Keep going, lover."

"Jimmy Baldwin and Tom Curtiss are secretly collaborating on a cookbook for expatriates. Millicent Murphy, who obviously is fucking *someone* in the Élysée Palace, told Hennessey's secretary that ze Prézident of ze French République went home to St.-Germain-en-Laye feeling ill less than an hour ago. Alzo, an eighty-year-old native of Paris immolated himself today on the sidewalk in front of a new apartment building in the Sixteenth Arrondissement as a protest against the rape of beautiful Paris. Poured a bottle of Remy Martin over himself and lit a match . . ."

"You're getting too exciting, Jimi," said Lisa. "I can't take it. Tell me, by any chance has anything at all even remotely connected with French Atlantic come the way of your hot little ears?"

"French Atlantic . . . French Atlantic . . . Well, I already told you about the *Marseille,* the no-phone-service bit. And then, of course . . . No, I *didn't* tell you about this, did I? Now how'dja *know,* Lisa? You oughta be on a noosepaper, kid . . ."

"What is it?"

"Well, Wide Ass Walter came in, late as usual, all charged up 'cause he had himself a goodie. Picked it up off a friendly bartender at Le Fronton, I think, or a toilet seat, I forget which. Top secret, hush-hush, stop the presses, he cried, waving his foolscap in the air . . ."

"Cut the shit and give it to me," said Lisa.

"He wrote it up real lush and front pagey. French Atlantic officials trying to conceal shocking malfunctions and dysfunctions and nonfunctions in new sister ship of the *Marseille,* to wit, the S.S. *Bordeaux,* not to be confused with the wine country of the same vintage, now shaking down on a trial run in the southern Atlantic. In other words—all of them Wide Ass Walter's—the *Bordeaux* is a disaster and French Atlantic is trying to cover up . . ."

"Keep going," she said, feeling suddenly hollow with disappointment. So that was what it was all about . . . "Sounds like Walter finally got himself one."

"Yeah, that he did. He got himself one, all right," Jimi Brocke chortled. "Hennessey reads his story and says, Walter, I don't believe it. Whaddaya mean? cried Walter the Wide One. I checked it out with the number two guy at Françat, Georges Sauvinage, aide to the Director General. He almost *died,* demanded to know where I got it, said yes, it was true, but it would be an act of treason if we ran it, said the company would sue the *Trib* for malicious slander and all that kind of bullshit. That's funny, says Hennessey. *You* tell me it's true. Françat *admits* it's true. But I *still* don't believe it. Howdaya like *that,* Walter? I *don't* like it, says Wide Ass. In fact, I don't understand it. You understand, Lisa love, I am only *approximating* the verbiage . . ."

"You're doing beautifully, Jimjam . . ."

"Anyway . . . *Walter,* says Hennessey, I have been taking advantage of you. In fact, I have taken advantage of French Atlantic, too, and I'm proud of it, says Hennessey. Do you think for one minute that the *Tribune* is going to sit back and wait for the *Bordeaux* to arrive back at Saint-Nazaire, and wait for those fellows in the penthouse of the Tour Française to announce the results of the trial run to one and all? Not on your ass, Walter. There happens to be a very unablebodied seaman aboard the *Bordeaux,* and *we put* him there. You might call him our seasick seagoing correspondent, Walter. And when the *Bordeaux* lays over the other night at Tenerife in the Canary Islands, our man called *this* man, *Hennessey,* and gave him the very secret, very official facts and figures on the trial run. Namely, the *Bordeaux* has surpassed every single specification it was designed to meet. It is superior to the *Marseille* in every single aspect of performance . . . speed, maneuverability, steadiness, *everything.* Françat knows *nothing* about this yet, because the *Bordeaux* is maintaining radio silence until it gets home. But *we* know it, and the *Trib* is going to sit on it until the day before the *Bordeaux* arrives. How nice it will be, because it's so rare, to have an exclusive that also happens to be *good* news, too. So now you know, Walter, why I don't believe your story. You have been took, Walter. But why, asks Wide Ass, why would this Sauvinage Assistant Director General fellow admit *my* version was the truth and make such a brouhaha about keeping it from getting out? What am I, a mind-reader? asks Hennessey. But I will lay you eight to five, says Hennessey, that he was pulling the old reverse leak play, hoping you'd file the story and hoping we'd run it, to draw attention away from some *other* troubles they're having over there. It's too much for me, cries Wide Ass, tearing his story into shreds. Walter, says Hennessey, why don't you try to find out *why* they're leaking this phony? No thanks, says Walter. I've had enough of this *mal de merde*. From now on, *I fly*. And out he goes, no doubt to get shit-faced at your favorite saloon. Are you still there, my glamorous globulin?"

"Laugh? I thought you'd never finish." She tried to sound disinterested. "Listen, hon, you've been a living dull. Remind me to do something nice to you when I see you later."

"If you as much as *look* at me down there, I'll scream."

"See ya, Jimjam." She hung up and tamped out her cigarillo. Her mind was racing, and it wasn't all due to the Ritalin. Some of it had to do with a mess of unassembled, nonsense-making, unrelated, highly intriguing tidbits of information.

She flipped through her black leather directory, found a number and dialed it. They put her through, and she wound up with Georges Sauvinage's secretary.

He was out to lunch with the Director General.

What restaurant?

We are not permitted to give out that information. May I tell him who called please?

We are not permitted to give out that information.

She called Françat again, this time asked for the Director General, and said to the secretary who answered, "To whom am I speaking, please?"

"This is Mrs. Grillet, executive secretary to the Director General."

"Mrs. Grillet, I am Madame Yvonne Longeville, aide to Marshal Pierre Duquesne at the Élysée Palace."

"Yes, madame."

"Just before the Director General departed the palace this morning, it was arranged that President Bonnard would be placing a telephone call at one o'clock directly to Monsieur Dechambre at the restaurant where the Director General would be having lunch. Marshal Duquesne has regrettably misplaced the slip of paper on which Monsieur Dechambre wrote the name of the restaurant, and the Marshall would appreciate it very much if you would keep this unfortunate oversight completely confidential. May I ask you to do that, Mrs. Grillet?"

"Why, certainly, Madame Longeville. Certainly. And the restaurant is the Relais de Porquerolles."

"Of course. In the rue de l'Éperon."

"Would you like the telephone number?"

"Yes, please."

"Six two one, one seven, one two."

"Mrs. Grillet, you have been most kind and most helpful. Thank you so much."

"You're very welcome, madame."

She knew the maître d', and called him immediately.

"My lovely Miss Briande. Why have we not seen you? It has been too long."

"Claude, be an angel. Max Dechambre and another gentleman are there . . ."

"Yes, yes, I am looking right at them."

"Don't say a word, but I have to know how far along they are, beginning, middle, or demi-tasse?"

"Ah, but that is an easy one, Miss Briande. They have been destroying their taste buds with martinis, and the vichyssoise still waits in the wings. And that, of course, is only the beginning."

"Can you keep things running rather slowly, Claude?"

"For you, my darling, I will keep them here until the thirty-first. We close in August."

"And what about a small table, say in three quarters of an hour, as close to them as possible?"

"You will be seated in their laps."

"Love you, Claude."

She hung up, moved quickly to the shower, and tingled with excitement under the hot spray. She had never realized before what a terrific, absolutely smashingly deceitful liar and conniver she was.

CHAPTER TWENTY-FOUR

BEING NOTICED JUST HAPPENED. It was never something she *did*. Hearts stopped, genitals stirred, and women died when she walked into the Relais de Porquerolles. Her long blond hair was freshly laundered, her heels were Paris high-rise, her flowery gauze frock was three inches above her dimpled knees, and she had absolutely nothing on underneath but her pointed nipples, the remnants of a St.-Trop tan, and the soft golden fuzz that you could sense was there where it ought to be.

Getting invited to their table was nothing at all, thank you, Claude, and just *about* in their laps, too. She sat sandwiched between the two of them, the self-assured arrogant one and the harried, hangdog one, and listened raptly, attentively, *interestedly*, to their martinied maunderings, until finally she decided to disarm them with her own small talk and the clouds of atomized, irresistible Via Lanvin. Dechambre was easy. The other one was like lead, dark and heavy and unmoving. Over pears *flambé*, she decided it was time to move him.

She placed her hand, which was under the table, ever so gently on Dechambre's thigh. He did not look at her. Instead, he turned to Sauvinage and said thickly, "I hate to disturb you, but would you mind making a quick call to your office?"

"I hardly think anything could be—"

"Please?" said Dechambre.

Sauvinage eased his body from the table and walked away.

Lisa moved closer to Dechambre and her hand slid farther up. "Can you get rid of him?" she asked.

Dechambre looked at her with feverish eyes, the alcohol of cocktails and wine firing his senses. "Miss Briande, really, I am confused. I don't know exactly what—"

"Not Miss Briande. *Lisa*. For God's sake, Max, we're not children. Don't toy with me. Every time we meet . . . *every* . . . *time* . . . you *play* with me, you get me all excited and then you walk away as though nothing had happened. Why do you do this to me?"

He flushed with pleasure. "I swear to you, my dear, I had no idea. I am truly astonished."

"Get rid of him, Max. Please. We're alone now. Doesn't it feel marvelous?"

"Yes, yes . . ." My God, what was happening?

"Let's keep it that way and see where it leads to. The afternoon is young, and you're a busy man, but I know what I'd like to do with that busy man if he'd let me."

He gazed into her green eyes and was stunned at the swiftness and enormity of the erection he could feel growing and growing as though it would never stop. Suddenly it met her caressing hand, and he knew then that nothing in the world could stop him from wanting to be naked in bed with her, right now. To hell with everything, Wunderlicht, the *Marseille,* the President of France, everything. God, what he would do to her. "Lisa." He pressed his lips furtively to her hair and almost came. "He'll be back," he said hoarsely. "Where can—? Do you have any suggestions?" He knew so little about these things.

"Get rid of him," she said.

They moved apart. Sauvinage was approaching. When he arrived at the table, he announced, "There was nothing, only a call from some woman who—"

"Don't sit," Dechambre said quickly. "I want you there, at the office, just in case. You can take my car and send it back."

Sauvinage stood, hesitating, looking from Dechambre to the girl, and back to his superior.

"Very well," he said. Then, "Good afternoon, Miss Briande."

"*Ciao,*" she said, giving him a smile.

He walked away, feeling like shit again.

Dechambre moved closer and looked at Lisa. "There," he said.

"Well done," she said, her hand wandering beneath the table again.

"Nothing worthwhile is ever easy," he said, staring at her moist lips.

"You need relaxation, Max."

"Oh, yes," he said to her.

"Relief from all this tension . . ."

"Yes, Lisa."

"You're like a finely drawn instrument that is ready to pop."

"You couldn't have put it more accurately," he said.

She brought her hand above the table and placed it over his hand. "It's this *thing* that you're in the middle of, Max." She worded it very carefully. "I want you to know that I know exactly what you're going through, and I'm going to do everything I can to help. So far, I'm the only one on the paper who knows, and I'm going to try to keep it that way."

Dechambre would have removed his hand from under hers, but that would have been too obvious. He did not want her to know that every nerve-ending in his body had gone on alert, lights flashing, alarm bells clanging in his brain. As fast as it had come, his erection was going now, and he was too busy with other matters even to mourn the loss.

"Bad news has a way of finding ears," he said, "no matter how many doors we lock, no matter how many lips we seal." He toyed with the dregs at the bottom of his demi-tasse. "The shipyards at St.-Nazaire will make her a thing of perfection, you can be sure of that. I can remember the trial run of the *Ile de France,* also a disappointment, yet she went on to become as sleek and as swift and as big a winner as the finest filly ever to run at Longchamp. True, it is a worrisome time, but I am totally optimistic."

Beautiful, she thought. Even the tone of his voice, false cheer through genuine concern.

"Darling Max," she said. "I don't blame you for not trusting me. I'm a newspaperwoman and you know it. Take away the dress, the high heels, and the eyelashes and what have you got . . . ?"

"An instrument ready to pop," he smiled, hoping to change the subject.

"The new breed," she said. "The investigative journalist. Meaning one who wants to know only what she's not supposed to know. So I really don't blame you for trying the *Bordeaux* story on me, Max, even though it hurts a little, it really does, that you can't trust me as a friend. I *am* Lisa, Max. Not just the *Herald Tribune*."

He carefully drew his hand away, feigning the need for a sip of water. "Are you going to be hurt if I say I don't know what you are talking about?"

"No," she said, "I promise not to be hurt, no matter *what* you do. I sympathize with you, Max, and as I said before, I want to help."

He eyed her shrewdly. "Thank you, my dear. Now, what shall we do with this young afternoon? A walk through the Bois, a drive in the country, or something even more intriguing . . . such as a little Courvoisier to round things off until my car returns?"

"Courvoisier. Perfect." She lit a cigarillo while Dechambre waved the waiter over and ordered two brandies. They were practically alone in the restaurant now. Even Claude was nowhere to be seen. "By the way." She exhaled. "I didn't say a word to Walter MacMillan when he checked the *Bordeaux* thing with your gloomy friend Sauvinage this morning."

"I know nothing about that," said Dechambre, irritated that they were back where he didn't want them to be.

"If Françat wants the *Trib* to wear falsies on its front page, and the *Trib* is careless enough to do it, I say let 'em both be happy." She turned to him. "You know, you really do owe me *some* points, Max, even if it's just one teeny weeny point, for not breaking the *real* story."

He smiled at her coldly, and his tone was slightly mocking. "Now, I imagine this is the place where I'm supposed to say, what do you *mean*, 'the real story'? What do you *mean,* the *Bordeaux* disappointment is a falsie on the front page? Is that what comes next, Lisa? Give me the cue. You're the writer, the '*investigative*' writer. Give me the script."

It was time, she decided. Time to take the rubber tip off her dueling sword and make stabs in the dark, thrusting right and left.

"Max, Max." She shook her head slowly, her green eyes made sad for him. "Don't you think I *know* why you were arrested for speeding last night near Valence . . . ?"

He watched her with blank expression.

"Don't you think I *know* why you called an emergency meeting of the board for seven o'clock this morning . . . ?"

His eyes did not waver, but she was beginning to frighten him.

". . . Why you met with Aristide Bonnard at the Élysée Palace this morning . . . ? What you brought to him . . . ? What you came away with . . . ?"

Dechambre blinked once, but held himself together with a grip of steel. "My dear girl, did you think I was going to sit by and allow the shocking results of the *Bordeaux* trial run to mushroom into a national scandal? I hardly think I was overreacting, to hurry to Paris, to meet with the directors, to give the bad news to the President of France. I think I acted wisely under the circumstances."

"You *have* no bad news about the *Bordeaux* to give to the President of France." *Stab*, Lisa, *stab*. "Her radio silence doesn't end until she gets home. You have *no results at all.*"

She saw his face go pale.

"Max," she clutched his arm. "Don't you think I *know* why there is no phone service to the *Marseille?*"

She felt his arm tighten suddenly.

"The *Marseille?*" He tried to clear the tremor from his voice. "What . . . what has that got to do with . . . with the *Bordeaux?*"

Blood. My God. Blood. Oozing from the stab. All over his face. In his eyes. She could see it. Blood and fear.

"Don't you think I *know,*" she said, lunging at the heart, "what Brian Joy told you over the telephone?"

He began to die, before her very eyes, pierced through the heart.

"Brian . . . Joy . . . ?"

"Yes, Max. Brian Joy."

"Impossible." He shook his head dazedly. "I told no one, not even Sauvinage. I did not even show it to the President, or tell him about it. Even *he* does not know. Lisa, how did you—? Please, I have to know. It must be stopped. Tell me."

"It was Brian," she said quietly. "He told me everything."

He stared at her with stunned expression. "No . . . Never . . . He would never . . ."

"*Everything,*" she said. "Do you hear what I'm saying? *Everything.* We were lovers, for almost four years, in New York, and here in Paris. There is nothing that he doesn't tell me, even to this day."

"But *this?* How could he?" The confusion was too much for him. "To a newspaperwoman? A reporter?"

"He trusts me, Max, even if you don't . . ."

"The way he made me swear . . ." he said to himself.

"He trusts me, and you don't, but I don't blame you for having lied to me," she said.

"I had to," he said, still trying to understand. The man had been so cautious. Not even Mrs. Grillet could listen in, and use her shorthand.

"Well, there's no need for you to lie to me any longer."

"I had to," he said again, feeling shamed and humiliated before this beautiful girl.

The waiter came and set brandy before them, but neither was interested.

Lisa watched him, sensed his vulnerability, the weakened defenses. "Max," she said, "why didn't you show it to the President?"

It, she wondered. What was *it?*

He looked at her with guilt in his eyes. "Lisa, promise me that you won't tell him."

Tell whom?

"The President left the palace after you saw him," she said. "He returned home to St.-Germain-en-Laye not feeling well."

"Not feeling well?" There was too much concern in his voice. "Are you sure of this?"

"Yes."

"Can you find out how serious it is?"

"If you want me to, of course I can." She toyed with the brandy snifter, twirling it with her fingers. "Max, why didn't you show it to him?"

"Are you going to tell Brian Joy? You won't," he pleaded, "will you?"

"Max, I want to *know.* Now *tell* me, why didn't you show it to the President? *Why?*"

"Because Bonnard would never have agreed to pay the ransom if I had let him read it," he blurted out, and her heartbeat quickened. "A piece of paper with false hope written on it is all the excuse the President needs to lock the treasury vaults and say no to me. So now, the gold *will* be handed over to the pirates, the *Marseille will* be saved, three thousand lives *will* be saved. In my heart I did the right thing. Maybe Charles Girodt wouldn't understand that. Or your friend, Brian Joy. I did the right thing . . ."

He wished she would agree with him, say, "Yes, Max, you did, you did . . ." But no . . .

"What have you done with it?" she asked.

"With what?"

"The piece of paper . . . with false hope written on it . . ."

"It's here, right here." He jabbed at his chest where the breast pocket was. "The only copy. I should burn it." His voice was weary. "Why haven't I burned it?"

"Yes, why haven't you?" she asked.

He shook his head slowly. "I don't know."

"Give it to me," she said firmly.

He glanced at her with surprise.

She picked up her cigarette lighter, flipped on the flame and held out her hand. "Give it to me, Max."

He hesitated, unsure, but her gaze was powerful and demanding. He reached into his pocket and handed the folded sheet of paper to her, averting his eyes as though he could not bear to face the neglected appeal for assistance.

Quickly she unfolded it with one hand, holding the lighter with the other. Dechambre's neat handwriting faced her, right side up. "Are you sure it's all right with you?" she asked, eyes racing across the words of Billy Berlin, heart leaping through sentences that stunned her.

"Yes," he said, not looking at her. "Yes."

"Give me the ashtray." That would take time. Time for more words, shocking words. My God, she thought, reading. Holy Mother of God.

He pushed the ashtray in front of her.

She brought the flame to the upper right-hand corner of the sheet of paper and let it spread slowly downward, consuming in its path the pleas for help from the captain of a ship that was truly lost at sea, her darting eyes imprinting the desperate words in her memory just before they turned to ashes: . . . *use extreme caution and secrecy. Pray to God for us. The end.* She turned what was left of the sheet upside down, dropped it into the ashtray, and watched it curl up and die.

"*Finis,*" she said quietly.

And yet, only the beginning.

She turned to Dechambre and covered his hand with hers.

He looked at her, and was surprised by the softness in her eyes.

"Shall we go?" she said.

"My car has not returned yet," he replied.

"Good," she said. "We don't want a chauffeur with us, anyway. We'll take a cab."

"Where to?" He was puzzled.

"Would you mind very much dropping me off at my flat?"

"Of course not," he said, still slightly puzzled.

"I would ask you to come up," she said, "but I know how terribly busy you must be."

"Yes," he said, a little less puzzled.

"But I would so much like you to see my place, Max. Perhaps just for a little while?"

He hesitated, no longer puzzled.

"We'll talk about it in the cab," she said. "Won't we."

Looking into her eyes, he felt her happening to him again. Quickly he summoned the waiter for the check.

It seemed only right, she thought. Here in this restaurant, she had really screwed the man. In her bedroom, turnabout would be fair play. Besides, there were details still to be drawn out, and the soft hand that held his hand now would work delicate miracles on him, and draw cries of pleasure from his lips, and afterward, whatever else she wanted, and nothing more urgently than immediate possession of the passenger information list.

And besides all that, she was perfectly aware of the other truth, that at times like this, when she felt flushed with a sense of her own powers, heady with the excitement of triumphs won and more to come, she hungered for a stiff live prick inside of her, and it didn't matter all that much *who* was on the other end of it.

They didn't talk very much about anything during the cab ride home. They were too busy with each other.

CHAPTER TWENTY-FIVE

Latitude 23° N., Longitude 55° W.—11:32 A.M. There was no rain yet, but the cloud cover at seven thousand feet was ominously dark, and visibility from the bridge of the S.S. *Marseille,* pitching and rolling in moderately heavy seas, was less than five miles. Though most of the passengers either grumbled about bad luck, or just generally slipped slightly down-tone, because somehow whatever you did just wasn't as much *fun* when the sun wasn't shining and you couldn't see a blue sky or the horizon, Craig Dunleavy was pleased. He could feel just a little more secure, knowing that the ship could scarcely be sighted from the sea or the air under prevailing conditions, and the barometer had indicated even worse to come. He wondered briefly whether they would be lucky enough to have this kind of lowered visibility when they finally made the rendezvous with the *Angela Gloria,* and sailed off, hopefully, not into the sunset but into concealing shrouds of mist.

Right now, he had more immediate concerns on his mind. He was on his way to a meeting in the Promenade Deck lounge with the tight little handful among them whom he and Herb had been more or less kowtowing to, feeling that they would need their special ruthlessness if the going ever really got brutal. He and Herb privately referred to them as the Hot Heads, a misnomer actually, because they were led by their viscera rather than by their heads. Don Campbell had been one of them, impatient, quick to anger, eager for unnecessary blood. And now that Don was missing and presumed dead, the Hot Heads wanted Harold Columbine's life in reprisal.

Craig's argument that the elimination of a widely known celebrity aboard the ship would be a premature and dangerously provocative act hadn't made a dent in their determination. Lou Foyles and Wendell Cronin had turned Craig's logic around ass-backwards and argued that Columbine's death was just the kind of PR they needed. Preventative retaliation, Lou had called it. Appropriate remedy is what Wendell Cronin had called the obvious choice of Louise Campbell to carry it out.

If Craig failed now to talk them out of the entire idea, perhaps he could at least get them to reconsider the choice of Louise. In her present condition, she could get all crazy-eyed and rageful and hysterical, and possibly blow the whole goddamned thing, and much more besides.

In one-sixty-four on the Première Deck, Dr. Yves Chabot, sitting on the edge of the bed, listened to Julie's heart, checked her pulse and her blood pressure, and told her to get out of bed and get dressed and have a hearty lunch, because she was doomed to live.

Billy Berlin, standing there watching, his receiver turned way down, said to Julie, "Didn't I tell you?"

"Doctors' wives never trust their husbands," Chabot said to him, smiling. "If you haven't learned that yet, take it from one who has." He got to his feet.

Julie looked up at him. "You wouldn't have some kind of pill for forgetting, would you?"

"You Americans and your pills." He shook his head. "It is better that you *remember* last night, so that you can be on guard *today*. These people will be on the prowl, you can be sure of that, trying to discover who *was* she, who was that lady?"

"That was no lady, that was my wife," said Billy, scowling with apprehension.

"I'll wear low heels and dark glasses and no panties," Julie said.

"And nothing else," said Chabot. "Perfect. No one will even look at you."

She managed a wan smile.

Chabot turned to Billy. "What shall I tell the Commandant?"

"It's six-thirty a.m. in California. My guy is probably still asleep. As soon as I get to him, *if* I do, I'll give him . . ." He peered at the slip of paper on the table. "Eric . . . Charlie . . . Betty . . . Frances . . . Shirley . . . Charlotte—"

"All *right. Okay,*" Julie interrupted sharply. "He gets the point."

Billy glanced at her, then back to Chabot. "And naturally I'll find out whether he has anything to tell *us.*"

"Good. I will be getting the inventory of medical supplies to you shortly." Chabot went to the door, unlocked it and turned to look at Julie. "Listen, young lady, if you don't cheer up, you're going to have to pay for it by having tea with me this afternoon."

"You've got yourself a date," Julie said. "How's about fourish?"

Chabot looked to Billy for approval. "Doctor?"

"Be my guest," said Billy. "The Rover Boy will remain at his post."

Yves Chabot nodded, and left the cabin to seek the Commandant.

Perhaps in having tea with the lovely American girl, he would not be able to cheer *her* up, but maybe it would help *him* to forget the frozen, bloodless corpse in the hospital refrigerator.

Betty Dunleavy and Harriet Kleinfeld, co-chairing the meeting in the game room, both agreed that they were getting nowhere. How were they going to find an unidentified female passenger if they couldn't even decide whom she looked like? Charlie MacGregor said Shirley Lewis. So they put the mask on Shirley, and Charlie backed down. But Betty Scheirer said, yes, like Shirley, well, *sort* of. Then Frances MacGregor and Eric Scheirer said, let's look at Charlotte Segar again, with the mask on, and then off. Nope. Not Charlotte. It must have been the lighting last night. But Carl Swenson said, *I* think she looked like Charlotte. Maybe *I'm* crazy. Then Harriet Kleinfeld got a bright idea, and it was so obvious they couldn't understand how they had overlooked it. Why don't we ask Olga Shanneli? The ship's hostess had provided quite a few of the costumes for the ball. She ought to be able to tell them whether she had or hadn't helped someone out with a Madame du Barry getup last night. And if she had, and they were lucky, she might even know the *name* of the bitch.

Harold Columbine walked briskly along the Promenade Deck, breathing deeply, feeling the blood course healthily through his veins, his legs spread apart slightly in shrewd adjustment to the circular pitch and roll of the ship. He was wearing the billowy-sleeved black cotton shirt from Rome, the off-white polyester slacks from Beverly Hills, the white wet Gucci loafers from New York, and a white silk scarf that a grateful lady in Cannes had sent to his suite at the Carlton after a glorious night of fressing.

His body felt good today, and his head, too. The sleep had been long and deep, but he knew it was more than that. It was last night. Being with Julie Berlin. Conspirators together. Risking their lives together. Playing himself and doing it well, *being* himself, *living* himself, instead of writing himself into the lives of others who did not even exist except on paper. He wished she were there beside him now, cutting him to ribbons with her withering disrespect. But her phone had been off the hook when he had called several times during the morning. He was walking alone now, enjoying the challenge of the rising violence of the sea, breathing deeply and thinking of what it would be like to be with her.

She was good for him, and made him forget all the others, the ones who used to be careful not to bump their heads getting in under the kneehole desk, while he was on the phone, yet, talking to one of his ex-wives, yet. The legend that was Harold Columbine. The man, his yacht, his Silver Shadow and his girls, the best that money could buy.

He was good for *her,* too. He could tell. The little girl-wife of the boy-husband doctor became a woman when she was with him. Right then and there, he decided he would begin to take her away. This would be the day when, looking back, it would be said that Harold Columbine had started to make it happen, had started on the course that would see him eventually lying between her legs, coming endlessly, married to her forever. Yes, this would be an important day in the life of Harold Columbine, a milestone, a date to remember when they did his biography.

He continued on along the Promenade Deck, striding swiftly,

enjoying the sound of his inhale and exhale, going past the windows of the lounge where, inside, the Hot Heads were refusing to change their minds about anything, *including* Louise Campbell. She *deserved* the privilege, they were insisting. It was appropriate, it was only *right* that she should be the one to do it.

Washington, D.C.—9:32 A.M. J. Elton Knox, Chief of the Office of Naval Intelligence, having gone directly to his desk after the extraordinarily lengthy breakfast at the White House, advised the President, when the latter came on the line, that two nuclear submarines of the United States Navy were within seven hundred and nine hundred nautical miles, respectively, of the very broad area of the southern Atlantic where the S.S. *Marseille* might possibly be. The President asked whether it would be feasible to airlift a man, or men, to either of these submarines, and drop them by parachute into the ocean so that they could be taken aboard the underseas craft.

J. Elton Knox replied that, in his opinion, that could be done.

Would it be within the realm of probability, inquired the President, that a submarine could approach the S.S. *Marseille* undetected, and put this special team in the water alongside the ship in motion, in such a way that the team could board the ship without being discovered?

That would be within the realm of possibility and somewhat marginal probability, the ONI chief advised, provided that it was done under cover of darkness. However, more importantly, the actual position of the S.S. *Marseille* would have to be determined before any such undertaking could even be attempted.

How, asked the President, can this position be obtained?

Inasmuch as overflights and sea approaches are, as I understand it, forbidden right now, the ONI chief replied, visual sightings are highly unlikely and would be purely fortuitous. However, if we could pick up any radio signals from the *Marseille,* we could determine her position rather quickly.

Then that accounts for her present radio silence, the President said.

Yes, said the ONI chief, we need radio signals from the *Marseille,* and they know it. However, Mr. President, I believe you are unaware of a more transcending factor, if you will forgive me for saying so.

What would that be, John? the President inquired.

Our ongoing problems in NATO right now could not withstand the stress of the French government discovering the American government once again breaking its word at the highest level.

Who says so? inquired the President.

The Office of Naval Intelligence says so, replied J. Elton Knox.

Thank you very much, said the President. I appreciate your conveying this opinion to me privately.

You're very welcome, Mr. President.

You can rest assured that I will immediately advise the others at our breakfast to drop the whole matter, said the President.

I have already done so, Mr. President, said J. Elton Knox.

Oh, replied the President.

New York, N.Y.—9:32 A.M.   Leonard Ball, comfortably settled behind his desk at CBS News on West 57th Street, took the call from Peter Hackenbush, one of his CBS correspondents in Paris. Would Ball be interested in considering about three minutes on the satellite from Hackenbush, for the Walter Cronkite *Evening News,* regarding an unconfirmed but fairly reliable report that the new French Atlantic ship, the S.S. *Bordeaux,* had had a secret trial run in the southern Atlantic and had come up smelling like a sixty-five-thousand-ton lemon, a potential national disaster for France?

"Peter, see if you can't nail it down so that it's a hundred percent. It sounds like a helluva story, but Walter will never go for it unless we can get confirmation. Get back to me in the next few hours if you can, Peter, and I'll call *you* if I can dig anything up at this end."

Hanging up, he thought, French Atlantic . . . Paris . . . the French Atlantic Line . . . last night at Twenty-One. The phone call. Tony Salmagandi's friend, what was his name? Brian Joy. Urgently needing the telephone numbers of French Atlantic officials in Paris. Could there possibly be a connection?

"Honey, get me Tony Salmagandi in Hollywood, will you? Call his home, wake him up, ask him for the telephone number of Brian Joy, that's J-O-Y. Tell him I threw it away at Twenty-One last night. No, wait a minute. First try Los Angeles information for Joy's number. L.A., Hollywood, Beverly Hills, Bel Air, Brentwood areas. I don't know which."

He glanced briefly at *Daily Variety,* opened some of his mail, mostly bills. The one from La Grenouille was staggering. He'd have to give up either eating, or drinking. He couldn't afford both. Within three minutes, his buzzer sounded, and he took up the phone.

"Mr. Joy is on the line, Mr. Ball."

"Thank you, honey. Brian? Leonard Ball."

"Who?"

"You know how to hurt a guy, don't you. Leonard Ball. CBS News, New York."

"Jesus Christ, Leonard, haven't you heard about time zones? It's six-thirty-seven a.m. out here. (It's for me, Mag, go back to sleep.)"

"Well, I heard you Hollywood types stay up all night smoking chicks and balling pot."

"You're lost in the wasteland, Leonard. What's up, besides *me* at an ungodly hour?"

"Brian, tell me, did Lisa Briande ever reach you from Paris?"

"Yes, she certainly did, and I want to thank you very much."

"Anytime. Listen—"

"What's the story on her, Leonard?"

"Nothing unusual. Her father is chairman of the board of Mc-Clelland Steel, her mother owns half of St. Louis, Missouri, and Lisa won't take a dime from either of them or leave Paris and go home and get married until she's topped them both. Listen, tell me, Brian, did she give you what you wanted?"

"Yes, Leonard. I already said thank you."

"And did you reach those French Atlantic officials in Paris you were in such a sweat to get to? . . . Hello?"

"I'm here."

"Did you hear me?"

"Yes, I heard you."

"Well . . . did you reach them?"

"Why do you ask, Leonard?"

"I'll give it to you straight, Brian, but only because you're a friend of Tony Salmagandi's. Otherwise it's bullshit time on Channel Two . . ."

"Give it to me any way you want, but give it to me. I wanna go back to sleep."

"Brian, I heard all about the disaster that's happened to that French Atlantic ship—"

"You *what?*"

"—and before I let Cronkite or anyone else go on the air with it, I thought I'd touch base with you, to see how much you might know . . ."

"Ball . . . for Christ's sake . . . Jesus . . . how could you have heard?"

"Brian, why do you think we have a staff of thirty-two in our Paris bureau, to report on *skirt lengths?*"

"Listen to me, Ball, goddamn it, you're not going to put that story out on national TV. There are three thousand lives hanging in the balance, two thousand passengers and the whole fucking crew of the *Marseille* . . ."

"What the hell are you talking about?"

"Will you believe me, Ball? Will you trust me? The pricks who have seized that ship will execute passengers as hostages the minute their radios pick up any indications that *anyone,* you, me, *or* French Atlantic, have revealed what's happening out there . . ."

"(Honey, get on the line, quick, and take this down.) Wait a minute, Brian, simmer down. I'm not arguing with you. I just want you to understand the position I'm in, that CBS News is in, and then maybe you can help me figure out what to do under the circumstances."

"Let me save you the time. I *know* the position you're in. I also happen to know the position the captain of the *Marseille* is in. Don't ask me how I know, because I can't tell you. I'm sworn to secrecy . . ."

"I respect that, Brian. Go ahead, continue."

"I don't know *you,* Leonard, and you don't know *me.* Right?"

"Right."

"So we have to take each other on a little faith here . . ."

"Absolutely."

"You're going to have to believe me when I tell you that *very secret moves* are in the works to save the *Marseille* and her three thousand people, but if they were to suspect—"

"Whaddaya mean, *they?*"

"The group that's taken over the ship. If they hear on their radios that the *whole world* apparently knows about the takeover, they'd have to start suspecting that *someone* violated the agreement that total secrecy would be maintained until the ransom was paid.

That's one of their terms, Leonard. With the *Marseille* transmitters and ship-to-shore phones completely silenced, they feel safe that nobody on land except the French Atlantic Line in Paris, with a gun at its head, knows what's going on out there. We've got to *keep* it that way, Leonard. *You've* got to. CBS News has got to. Until the ship is freed and everyone is safe."

"Do you realize what kind of a story you're asking us to sit on?"

"You're goddamn right I do. And I know what kind of story there'd be if you *don't* sit on it, with the entire responsibility for the result all yours and CBS's. Run that one up on the flagpole, Leonard, and color the flag black crepe."

"May I ask you something, Brian?"

"Go ahead."

"Just what the hell is *your* position in all this?"

"Officially? No position."

"Well, what do you *do,* if you'll forgive me for not knowing?"

"I'm a television writer and producer, and I *don't* forgive you for not knowing."

"CBS?"

"No. ABC."

"You can't win 'em all."

"Fuck you *and* Nielsen. The pendulum has swung."

"I still fail to see your connection with all this."

"And you're going to *continue* to fail to see, 'cause I ain't gonna tell ya, not until the *Marseille* is free. Then I'll tell you, and *not* ABC, because I owe you a favor, Leonard. You hooked me up with that Briande girl in Paris last night, and she really helped. Tell me, is she as delicious as she sounds on the overseas?"

"None of your goddamn business, Joy. I've told you enough about her. Just stay there in Hollywood—"

"Beverly Hills."

"Beverly Hills, and screw your own kind."

"Listen, I gotta take a leak. Can I go now?"

"Yeah, I suppose so."

"And you're not going to do anything with the *Marseille* story, right? At least not yet."

"Nothing, goddamn it. You've made me feel so guilty for even *knowing* it, that I'm sorry I ever heard about it in the first place."

"Well, you and your staff of thirty-two in Paris."

"I didn't hear about it from *them*. What I heard about from them is why I called you, Brian baby."

"What do you mean?"

"I was calling you only to check on a story I got out of Paris about the disastrous trial run of the new French Atlantic ship, the *Bordeaux* . . ."

"Huh? . . . Oh . . . *Oh, shit* . . ."

"Can I help it if you come back at me from out in left field with this fantastic thing about the *Marseille?*"

"*Shit . . . Shit . . .*"

"G'bye, keed."

"You—"

"Talk to ya." He hung up and flipped the intercom on. "Did you get all that?"

"Yes, Mr. Ball. I'll type it up now."

"No, bring the notes in here. I'll hold on to them."

"All right."

"And, honey, forget what you heard, huh?"

"Naturally, Mr. Ball."

The phone was ringing.

"If that's him calling back, I just stepped out."

It was Harley Sarineen, the CBS White House correspondent.

"Morning, Har. What gives?"

"Not a helluva lot, Leonard. The President had a two-hour breakfast this morning . . ."

"He was always a slow eater."

". . . with the Joint Chiefs."

"The Joint Chiefs."

". . . and Clark Kemmel of the CIA . . ."

"The CIA."

". . . and Everett Haig of the FBI . . ."

"The FBI."

". . . and J. Elton Knox of the ONI."

"The Office of Naval Intelligence?"

"Uh-huh."

"The Office of Naval Intelligence."

"Monty claims they were conferring on the allocation of White House tickets for the Washington Redskins home games."

"Jesus, that reminds me, I'm not set for the Giants yet."

"*You* don't believe that explanation, do you, Leonard?"

"To tell you the truth, Har, no, I don't."

"I was wondering whether you might have heard something up there, or had some idea why the President would have broken a breakfast date with Henry Jackson and Keith Wheeling, who are sore as a boil, to spend two hours with the Joint Chiefs, the FBI, the CIA, and the ONI."

"Harley, I haven't the foggiest."

He hung up, and his secretary came in with three pages she had ripped from her steno pad. Her name was Thelma Stutz, and she was discomfitingly beautiful. He took the pages from her and stuffed them in his top desk drawer, saying, "Honey, check on my season tickets for the Giants, will you?"

"Right."

"And get me a small table at Twenty-One for one o'clock."

"Right."

"Then call Cronkite and tell him to cancel whatever he's got on and meet me there."

He heard nothing, and glanced up at her. Her smooth mocha face with its wide-set brown eyes was expressionless. It was the same look she gave him whenever she caught his eyes taking liberties with her body.

"Well?"

"Now, Mr. Ball . . ."

"What is it, goddamn it?"

"Mr. Ball . . ."

"Don't Mr. Ball *me* or I'll Mr. Ball *you.*" Hell, Walter would probably refuse to go near it anyway. Him and his fucking integrity. "I know what you're thinking and you happen to be all wrong."

"That's good," she said.

"In fact, you can forget the lunch reservation. I'll eat at my desk today. Alone."

"Very well, Mr. Ball." She turned and started away, and he punished her by denying himself the sight of her lovely ass and her long dark legs.

But what if Walter *had* gone for it? What if he could have conned him into it with a lot of bullshit about the people's right to know? Just for a moment he allowed himself the luxury of seeing Wallenrod, sick-faced and defeated, walking out of NBC in disgrace, and then he began to hate himself for realizing that he'd never have the stomach to do a thing like that to Brian Joy, whom he had never even met, or to three thousand people he didn't even know.

If anyone around here ever found out how gutless I really am, he told himself, I'd be out on my keister.

Going back to bed again hadn't helped Brian Joy. All he'd come up with were a few lousy half-awake dreams but no real unconsciousness. Listening on twenty meters hadn't helped either. There had been no sign of Billy Berlin in the low dull hiss of early morning band conditions. He sat on the toilet now, reading but not laughing at something funny about the Dodgers in Jim Murray's column, trying not to think of the possible consequences of his stupidity with Leonard Ball, hoping a decent bowel movement would improve his mood. The sudden rapping on the bathroom door didn't help at all.

"I'm busy," he called out.

"Telephone," Maggie said through the door.

"Who is it?"

"Your girlfriend . . ."

"Oh, Christ . . ."

"Your new French girlfriend in Paris."

"In a minute."

"And listen, I wish you'd answer your own phone calls from now on."

"Well, if you had let me put an extension in the bathroom like I wanted . . ."

"I'll tell her you'll be with her as soon as you finish reading the newspaper, okay?"

"Shit."

Which is exactly the word he used a few minutes later when Lisa Briande finished delivering her smashing blows to his solar plexus. *Pow!* She knew the whole damned story about the *Marseille. Pow!* Max Dechambre had decided to bury the radio message from the ship and was not going to do a goddamn thing to help Captain Girodt and his staff overcome their captors. *Pow!* Dechambre, instead, was nurturing high hopes of raising the ransom money under conditions which gave Lisa grave misgivings.

"Shit," Brian Joy shouted into the crackling telephone over the six thousand miles of distance that separated them. "I've wasted precious time trusting that son of a bitch."

"He thinks he's doing the right thing," Lisa Briande said. "Anyway, I thought it important for you to know what is and *isn't* going on over here in Paris."

"Is that why you called me?" he said with unreasoning bitterness. "You know, your thoughtfulness baffles me. I mean, you've *got* the whole story now. Why are you being so nice to me?"

"Do you really think I'd use it under these circumstances?"

"Sure I think you would. You're a newspaperwoman. And from what you've told me, you seem to know your way around real real good."

"You're even more unpleasant than usual today, Mr. Joy. What's wrong with you?"

"You can call me Brian. This phone call is what's wrong with me. I'm underslept is what's wrong with me. Also by mistake I let the goddamn cat out of the bag this morning with your friend, Leonard Ball."

"You didn't."

"All right, I didn't."

"What's he going to do with it?" She sounded genuinely concerned.

"He *said* he'd sit on it, but how do I know I can trust him? After all, *I'm* not the one who sleeps with him, you know."

"Why don't you buy yourself a new mouth, Mr. Joy?"

"Why don't you call me Brian?"

"I'm going to hang up now."

"It's your dime."

"But before I do, I think you ought to know why I have serious doubts about Max Dechambre's plan. You see, he's convinced himself that Aristide Bonnard—that's the President of France—"

"Thanks."

"—that Bonnard is going to cough up thirty-five million dollars of government gold to pay the ransom, when in actuality what I think Bonnard is really intending to do is double-cross Dechambre with another kind of game, and a dangerous one, too . . ."

"How would you know all this?"

"Educated guesswork, for one thing. And you'd be amazed at the bits and pieces of seemingly unrelated trivia that flow into the *Trib* every day. Like Bonnard faking a headache today to meet secretly at his summer home in St.-Germain-en-Laye with Jean-Claude Raffin—"

"Who's he?"

"Only the Director General of the Sûreté Nationale."

"Uh-huh."

"Like Raffin then speeding back to his office and pulling in the top men of every criminal detection branch in this overly branched government of ours . . ."

"Give me the bottom line, will you," Brian Joy said with impatience.

"Obviously they're planning some kind of hostile action against the conspirators, probably those here in Paris, which could lead to a bloodbath on the *Marseille,* while Dechambre naïvely sits by thinking his secret is intact and his ship and those three thousand lives are going to be saved with France's gold."

"Jesus," Brian Joy groaned. "And the Captain and my friend Billy Berlin naïvely sit by waiting for *me* to relay information that's never going to come." His voice grew harsh with anger. "Well, I've *got* a message for the Captain: All your enemies are not on shipboard."

"That's more or less the real reason why I decided to call you, Brian," said Lisa Briande, with more kindness than she had yet shown.

"What the hell are we going to do?" he said.

"We?" said the girl in Paris. *"You."*

"Me?"

"Yes. I've done what *I* can for now, not that I'll stop trying. But I've given you fair warning, the bad news. It's up to you now to get your hands on that passenger information list."

"What are you talking about? Isn't Dechambre sitting on that list in Paris?"

"He says not. The only copy is in the New York office of French Atlantic. I wormed *that* out of him this afternoon. It contains all the confidential information they managed to gather on each passenger, usually without the passenger even knowing it . . ."

"All right. *So?"*

"You've got to get that list out of the New York office without their knowing what's happening, and then you've got to get *some*-body, *some* geniuses over there in the States who can keep their mouths shut to break the list down quickly and figure out which ones on that ship have to be wiped out."

"And just how am I supposed to pull this off?"

"I'm in Paris, Brian."

"And I'm in Beverly Hills."

"But Leonard Ball is in New York," Lisa Briande said.

"Leonard Ball?" he cried.

"You say he already knows everything."

"He doesn't know about Billy's secret transceiver. Christ, that's all we'd need . . ."

"He hasn't betrayed you *yet,* has he? And I don't think he will. And I should know Leonard pretty well, shouldn't I?"

"Look—"

"After all, you're not the one who sleeps with him, you know."

"Look, I'm sorry about that. Okay?"

"I know that. You were jealous, that's all."

"I still am."

"Take a couple of aspirin."

"I thought you said you were going to hang up."

"My three minutes aren't up. Are you going to call him?"

"Lisa?"

"What?"

"What made you decide not to break the story in your paper?"

"I'm not sure. Maybe it's because I'd like to be able to sail to New York on the *Marseille* next summer."

"I'd like to meet you there," he said.

"Tell me, are you going to call Leonard Ball or not?"

"Yes. Did you hear what I said?"

"I'm going to hang up now," she said.

"Wait a minute. First promise me that you'll stay close to Dechambre and do anything you can to help make his lousy ransom plan go *right* instead of wrong. Okay?"

"I thought he was such a son of a bitch."

"He *is.* But suppose I strike out over here? *Somebody's* got to save the *Marseille,* or we'll never meet in New York."

"G'bye," she said, and hung up.

CHAPTER TWENTY-SIX

Paris—5:45 P.M. He heard them coming into his gray-walled office, clearing their throats behind him, but he did not turn immediately. He stood at the window, staring vacantly at the rich green chestnut trees bursting with reddish flowers, and allowed himself to feel hatred for the man whose official portrait hung a few feet away. Sucking on his sour, unlit pipe, Jean-Claude Raffin could taste the resentment in his mouth. His shoulders were heavy with unwanted secrets, his body stiff and awkward under the straitjacket in which he had been bound by Aristide Bonnard. It was both insolent and ignorant of the President to expect the Sûreté to find the man calling himself Julian Wunderlicht within twelve hours, without permitting either the Director General or his five branch chiefs to reveal to any of their men the true nature of the desperate search.

"You may tell them that you have picked up reports of an impending Air France hijacking," Bonnard had intoned, "and that is all."

Raffin's protests had been met with an upraised hand. The presidential honor was at stake. Aristide Bonnard could not afford the kind of leaks that would reveal the obvious hollowness of his sacred word. And incidentally—just incidentally—would not this veil of secrecy perhaps help in keeping Wunderlicht from finding out that he was being lied to, unwittingly, by that officious little manipulator over at Françat, M. Dechambre?

Raffin turned away from the window now, and moved to the chair behind his antique desk, nodding to the men who had seated themselves in a semicircle before him, their dark rumpled suits blending poorly with the green velvet upholstery of the armchairs. Their eyes did not quite meet his, as if they blamed *him* for this threat to the pride and performance of what they knew to be the finest police force in the world. You did not give an agent in the field a simple order. You let him share the mission, you fired him up with its importance. You made him feel it was worth the exhaustion, the boredom, the sleeplessness, the violent death.

"I cannot speak for your hearts or your minds, gentlemen," said Raffin, forcing a smile as he looked across the desk, "but I can tell you this: your faces have already given up."

The men chuckled politely.

"Let's take this in order," the Director General began. He looked to his left at the pudgy, perspiring features of Felix Lafon, head of the Police Judiciaire. "Felix?"

Lafon cleared his throat, glanced down at some papers in his damp hands. "Fifteen districts accounted for, two partially covered; results: zero. Gendarmerie Nationale reports many complaints in the field about the vagueness of the description . . ."

"I grant you that this fellow Georges Sauvinage who wrote the Françat report is no poet," said Raffin, "but that will be a poor excuse for our failing to put some German flesh on his words."

"Agreed," said the director of the PJ. "Nevertheless, as of this moment, until one of my colleagues here hopefully contradicts me, there is no Julian Wunderlicht presently within the borders of France. For what it's worth, however, Commissaire Blondin of the Brigade Criminelle suggested that I throw the following into the pot. As you know, his men have always made expert use of the whores of Paris, most of it nonsexual . . ."

There were a few smiles.

"Among the more than two hundred prostitutes covered this afternoon, a streetwalker by the name of Yvette Goutay vaguely recalled picking up a middle-aged man near the Arc de Triomphe last night who spoke with either a Danish or a German accent and somewhat fit the description given by Sauvinage. Moreover, the girl seemed to think she heard him exclaiming something unintelligible about a boat or a ship during what I understand to have been the throes of his passion."

"I am trying to work up a passion myself for this sort of information," said Raffin, "but it doesn't seem to be happening to me. I take it you are having the girl watched should the man come back for additional throes?"

"I rather doubt that he will," replied Felix Lafon. "It seems the whore threw him out of her bedroom for insulting behavior."

"Now I ask you," said Raffin, "does that sound like the type of man who goes about demanding thirty-five million dollars in gold and expecting to get it?"

"Exactly what I told Commissaire Blondin," said the head of the Police Judiciaire.

The Director General shook his head slowly and looked to Victor Cabanal, the iron-gray, craggy-featured chief of the Bureau de Sécurité Publique. "And what delicacies does the BSP have on its tray?"

"Not so much as a crumb, my dear Raffin," replied Cabanal. "We still maintain our previous position that the S.S. *Marseille,* though subsidized by the French government, is not technically *owned* by it. Therefore, strictly speaking—"

"Oh, come now, Cabanal," Raffin's voice rose. "Must we speak strictly in here today?"

"I am not saying that the BSP refuses to help, Jean-Claude. I am simply reminding everyone present that we are not a private security agency. I have no authority to protect, either directly or indirectly, that which does not belong to the state."

Raffin stared at the man tight-lipped for several moments, then directed his gaze to the thin, aquiline features of Maurice Devillaine, who dabbed incessantly at his nose with a wad of Kleenex. The aging head of the Corps Républicain de Sécurité seemed far more concerned with the drip of his allergic sinuses than with the proceedings in this stuffy room. Without even looking at the Director General he said, "Give us some live bodies to work on, Raffin, and the CRS will exterminate them like mosquitoes in a swamp. Until then, I urge you to see that the French Navy and Air Force are pulled into this thing before it is too late."

Raffin's face grew red. "Goddamn it, Devillaine, you know perfectly well that my hands have been tied."

Maurice Devillaine merely shrugged, and blew liquid from his nose.

"Magnificent," Raffin muttered to no one in particular. From outside, the distant sounds of traffic on the rue des Saussaies intruded on the silence. "So far we have the valuable memoirs of one overly sensitive streetwalker, hot off the pavements of the Champs-Élysées, and nothing more. Superb, gentlemen."

André Simon, second from the end, stirred nervously and glanced at the older man on his left. "Perhaps you should go first, Brunel," he said under his breath.

"No, after you," said the other quickly.

Raffin turned to the dark-haired, mustached young chief of the central records office. "All right, let's have it, Simon."

"Very well, sir." The newly appointed director of the Renseignments Généreaux had not yet learned how to be philosophical about defeat. The nonchalance in his voice struck the others as painfully hollow and transparent. "It should come as no surprise to anyone here, it certainly didn't to me, that no one called Julian Wunderlicht has ever previously appeared in our archives as having come to the attention of the French police. Whoever he is, the man is now obviously using an assumed name. And would he not have to be something of an idiot, gentlemen, for us to expect to find that assumed name on one single disembarkation card, or on one hotel registry card either inside or outside of Paris? Well, he isn't an idiot, and we haven't found a trace of him. Of the ten thousand odd German nationals who have recently arrived in the vicinity of Paris, not one of them has been foolish enough to call himself Julian Wunderlicht."

He took out a pack of cigarettes and worked one into his mouth.

"Is that it?" asked Jean-Claude Raffin.

"Precisely," said André Simon, lighting his cigarette.

The Director General tossed his pipe onto the desk with a clatter, spilling black ashes all over its ancient top. His glance quickly went to the mournful eyes and sagging mouth of Hector Brunel, chief of the Direction de la Surveillance du Territoire, and he knew, without asking, that this meeting, perhaps the entire mission, was as good as ended. He liked the old man, and hated to prod him now with useless, painful questions, and so he hesitated, and in the hesitation the phone on his desk suddenly sounded its nasty ring.

"Excuse me, Hector," he said to the man from the DST, and picked up the phone. "Madame Duval, I thought I told you—"

"I'm sorry, m'sieur," interrupted the voice of his secretary. "Colonel Schriener of Interpol. He said it was urgent so I—"

"Put him on."

He waited, avoiding the gaze of the other men in the room, who watched him without expression. Then Schreiner came at him through the receiver in his high-pitched voice.

"Claude? Arsène here. You are not alone, so I will do most of the talking."

"As usual, Schreiner."

"Ah. *Touché.* Now. Regarding your interest in finding a suitable flight crew for the 747 aircraft which Madame le Président's charitable group plans to charter for the trip to Tokyo . . ." The high-pitched voice paused. "You know, of course, what I am really talking about . . ."

"Of course," said Raffin flatly. The man's distrust of telephone lines was a joke around Interpol.

"My staff has looked into the matter with more haste than I would ordinarily prefer, so I cannot vouch for total accuracy . . ."

"I understand, Schreiner," said the Director General, drumming impatiently on the desk top with his fingertips.

He heard the other man clearing his throat and rustling some papers at the other end.

"Of the approximately thirty-two carriers of the world using the 747, only five were able to name flight officers trained to fly them who are not presently employed and on active duty . . ."

"Five," said Raffin.

"Correct," said Arsene Schreiner.

"Continue," said Raffin.

"Swissair reports three men, one of them the victim of a multiple-fracture skiing accident, another, terminally ill of cancer of the rectum, and the third, awaiting surgery for cataracts on both eyes. Japan Air Lines named one man, unfortunately electrocuted at home while installing an American television set. Sabena listed three, all of them presently hospitalized, two with cardiac conditions and one with bleeding ulcers. As for Alitalia, they admit to two former 747 pilots, but both of them are now serving terms in a penitentiary outside of Genoa. They would not say for what. If you asked me to bet on it—"

"All right, that's *four* carriers," interrupted Raffin.

"Ah, yes." There was more rustling of papers. "That leaves us with these two pilots here . . . These damned bifocals. I'll never get used to them . . . Let me see, let me see. Here we are. Both of them discharged for negligence, endangering the safety of lives and property and, would you believe it, for alcoholism?"

Raffin felt his body straightening up. "What airline?"

"Lufthansa," said the Interpol man, and cackled with triumph.

"Jesus Christ . . ." Raffin reached for pencil and paper with fumbling fingers.

"Their names," continued Schreiner.

"Yes."

"Klaus Freuling, of Stuttgart . . ."

"Yes."

"And Wilhelm Gritzen, of Munich . . ."

"Yes."

"And by the most curious of coincidences, they both departed their native cities and checked into the same hotel suite yesterday. Is that not something, Raffin?"

"Where, damn it, where?"

"Right here in Paris at the Prince de Galles."

"For God's sake, Schreiner, why the devil didn't you tell me this in the first place?"

The other man's sadistic cackle became a squeal of delight. "Shall I come over there, or would you prefer to come here?"

"Stay where you are," Raffin fairly shouted, and slammed down the receiver. The other men in the room stared at him expectantly. "Gentlemen," he announced. "In honor of the occasion, we will take the big German Mercedes and talk as we drive."

He rose to his feet and started around the desk, moving rather swiftly for a man in a straitjacket.

Purple clouds had moved in over the declining sun, robbing the Tour Française of its sparkle and bringing an unseasonable chill to the early evening air. As she entered the deserted lobby and hurried to the elevator, Lisa found herself wondering what the weather was like out at sea, and the thought momentarily depressed her. On the ride up to the twenty-sixth floor in the empty lift, she took a quick reading of her emotional temperature and decided that she was simply quite normally fatigued from insufficient sleep and more than sufficient lovemaking.

She had come three times under Max Dechambre's long struggle to fall off the cliff, and while she had needed and luxuriated in it, there was a price to be paid for everything, Ritalin or no Ritalin. What she was determined not to do was overpay, by adding emotional involvement as a tip. By the time she emerged from the elevator into the softly lit red-white-and-blue of the Compagnie Française, she felt in command of herself again, and, hopefully, of Max Dechambre, too.

The bony-faced night receptionist with the oversized glasses looked up at her and said, "Yes?"

"That's quite all right, dear," Lisa said with brisk authority, and walked right past her down the carpeted corridor.

"But, mademoiselle—"

Lisa pushed open the door lettered DIRECTOR GENERAL and surprised Edith Grillet in the act of examining her sagging face in the mirror on the wall, something she did only in the strictest privacy.

"Good evening," Lisa said cheerily.

Mrs. Grillet apologized with a wan smile. "My hair falls to nothing by the end of the day."

"Would you tell him Lisa Briande of the *Tribune* is here please?" Someday, she thought, I may tell you that I am also Madame Yvonne Longeville of the Élysée Palace, but not right now.

"Oh, I'm sorry," the older woman said, going to her desk. "Monsieur Dechambre is preparing to leave now."

"Just say Lisa Briande. All right?"

"I'm afraid it is too late, Miss Briande."

"Not at all. Announce me. Yes?"

"But is he expecting you?"

"Tell you what," Lisa smiled. "I'll surprise him." She walked past the gray-haired woman to the closed door beyond the desk and went inside.

He turned from the bar, startled.

"Hello, my darling tiger," she whispered.

Too quickly the empty brandy glass came away from his lips. His eyes widened. "Lisa . . ." He did not smile.

"I had to, I wanted to," she said closing the door and going to him.

"This brandy . . ." He put the glass down. "It's like fire . . ."

"You're a man of many secret vices," she murmured, "all of them delightful." And she kissed his mouth slowly, tasting the Remy Martin on his tongue with her own.

The sound of the buzzer on his desk made him pull away. He went to the phone and picked it up. "Yes? . . . No, it's quite all right. You can go home, Mrs. Grillet . . . Absolutely not. I want you to go now . . . Good night." He hung up and turned to Lisa, working a smile onto his face. "I never dreamt there would be still more of you today. I am giddy with gratitude and surprise." But his eyes were dull behind the gold-rimmed glasses.

"Max, what's wrong?" she asked him quietly.

"Wrong?"

"You. What is it?"

He stared at her. "May I offer you something?"

She shook her head. "Was it me? Did I disappoint you this afternoon?"

"Don't say that." His voice shook. "My God, when I think of the wonder of it, of *you*, I haven't been able to stop reliving it, over and over, and I don't want to stop . . ."

"Is that why the drinking?" she asked. "Truthfully."

He sat down slowly behind the desk. "Of course not."

"Then what is it?"

He looked up at her, and took too long before he answered her. "My wife has just returned unexpectedly from Antibes. Perhaps I had been secretly dreaming of a few more days of freedom, nights, actually, with you . . ."

She met his gaze, and sensed that he was lying. "Max, Max, listen to me . . ." She went around the desk and stood behind him, kneading his shoulders with her hands. "I assured you I would help you through the agony of the *Marseille* in any way that I could, and it seems to me that I've proven myself beyond the call of duty by sitting on a story that could *make* me, Max—"

"You *know* how I appreciate that," he protested.

"Then show it, why don't you?"

"How?"

"By sharing everything with me, not holding back."

"How many times . . . ?" He rose abruptly, breaking from her hands. "I told you this afternoon, *New York* has the passenger information list."

"I know that."

"Then what is it you want of me?"

"Everything that happens with the *Marseille*, Max, *when* it happens."

"For the love of Christ . . ." He turned away. "I can't get you out of my mind, and I can't get you out of my hair."

"That's right," she said, with fierce exultation. "And that's the way it's going to be."

He turned, looked at her with haunted eyes and nodded grimly. "All right, Lisa. If that's what you want." He picked up a sheet of paper from the desk and handed it to her. "I did not want to do this to you." His voice was heavy. "I felt that I was the only one who deserved to cry in this office today."

She looked down at the piece of paper that had been torn from a teletype machine, hearing him say, "High-speed telex . . . direct from the ship . . . a short burst, and then silence . . ."

She read the printed words with sinking heart.

> FOLLOWING PASSENGERS AND CREW EXECUTED FOR IN-
> TERFERENCE. MR. & MRS. G. PARKER, H. GRABINER,
> D. CAMPBELL, B. CREPIN, F. MANDRATI, E. SENESTRO.
> LET THIS BE A WARNING TO ANY AUTHORITIES WHO
> WOULD THINK OF DISOBEYING OUR INSTRUCTIONS.

The blood drained from her face. Fear gripped her, and she felt she was going to be sick. This wasn't the way it was supposed to be. Not death. Didn't they know it was just a game, an exciting game of transatlantic phone calls and marvelous intrigue and love in the afternoon to get close to the source? Everyone knew nothing would *happen*. Reality flooded in on her, leaving her chilled and confused.

"Oh God, Max, this is terrible . . ." She went to him and leaned her head against his chest. "I'm sorry. I'm so sorry."

He patted her shoulder. "Nothing I have done has caused this to happen," he told himself in a mournful voice. "And nothing I have not done could have prevented it."

"Maybe it's a fake," she said, without conviction.

"Anything is possible," he replied. "This whole thing could be somebody's nightmare from which we will all suddenly awake. But

I checked the manifest discreetly with New York. The names are authentic and so, I'm afraid, is the message."

She smelled defeat in his voice, and suddenly she would have none of it. She could feel her lips tightening with determination. There was too little time left to wallow in fear and confusion. Just because Max Dechambre's way of fighting this war was not her way, or the way of her new-found comrade-in-arms in far-off Beverly Hills, that was no excuse for allowing Dechambre to be quietly betrayed, and lose the war for them all. She stepped back from his protective, encircling arms and looked at him.

"Max, you must send this telex to President Bonnard immediately."

Dechambre made an impatient gesture. "No. Never. I will do nothing that might inflame his emotions and make him change his mind. He is my only hope."

Her voice grew insistent. "I think perhaps you'd better, Max."

He peered at her through his spectacles with narrowing eyes. "Why do you say that?"

"Can't you just do it, and not ask questions?"

"Why Bonnard?" he demanded.

"Because . . . maybe . . ." She was not sure how to put it. "Because maybe it will strengthen his resolve to keep his word, to keep his promise to you." She had to believe that that was so.

"I have no doubts about his word or his promise," Dechambre insisted, much too loudly. His eyes searched her face. "Should I have?"

She saw the look of desperation on his face and decided that it would be dangerous to undo him completely. "No, Max," she said.

But he was not satisfied. He moved toward her, saying, "He's told you something, hasn't he?"

"What?" Her bewilderment was genuine.

"Your lover, that man in California, Brian Joy . . ."

She managed to smile. "My poor tiger is fishing, and without bait, or a rod, and where there is no water." She kissed him lightly on the lips. "You're jealous, Max. I love it. Now do as I say, before I get angry and take you right here on the floor." She kissed him again with parted lips.

Dechambre's genitals stirred faintly, distracting him, then fell back, limp. Suddenly he found himself without the will to oppose her, or displease her. "Perhaps you are right, Lisa," he said quietly. "It cannot hurt our cause, and maybe it will help." But he could not banish the strange uneasiness that gnawed at him.

As he moved to the desk to speak into the intercom, Lisa glanced down at the fateful telex and began to memorize the names. It might help Brian Joy if he had a few names to eliminate from the list of possible conspirators, once Leonard Ball, please God, did his thing in New York. She'd call Brian again in California, if she could ever get around to it. The first thing she was going to do now was try to smoke out Jean-Claude Raffin at the Sûreté.

Suddenly she heard the dispirited voice coming from the little brown box on Dechambre's desk. "Yes, m'sieur?"

"Is your girl still there, Sauvinage?" inquired Max Dechambre.

"Yes, m'sieur."

"Send her up here in five minutes please. Not sooner."

"Very well," said the voice of Georges Sauvinage.

"I am sending down to you a sealed envelope marked urgent and personal. It is for President Bonnard."

"Yes, m'sieur."

"On your way home I want you to take it yourself to the Élysée Palace and see that it is handed personally to the President as soon as possible, wherever he is. Is that understood?"

"Perfectly, m'sieur."

"Good night, Sauvinage. And don't shut your phone off tonight."

"I wasn't planning to."

"And be careful with the envelope."

"Yes, m'sieur."

"Good night."

"Good night, M'sieur Dechambre."

The Director General sat lost in thought for a moment, stroking the hairs of his goatee. Then he turned his gray eyes on Lisa and rose to his feet. "You see? I do as you say."

She smiled. "I accept the awesome responsibility."

He came around the desk and took her hands in his. "I hope you know, my dear, that the only reason we are not having dinner together tonight is the unexpected return of my wife from the Côte d'Azur."

"No, Max, there's another reason," she said. "*I* have work to do tonight." She pecked his lips. "Good night, darling. Call me if you need me . . . and even if you don't."

He watched the glide of her moving hips as she walked to the door. After the glorious exhaustion in her bed this afternoon, he had no appetite for sex tonight. He was glad his wife had come home.

Miraculously recovered from his noonday headache and seated now at the dinner table in the green and white dining room of his summer residence at St.-Germain-en-Laye, Aristide Bonnard plucked a shiny fresh strawberry from the bowl in front of him, dipped it in the mound of Chantilly cream on his plate, and inserted the beautiful combination in his mouth, smiling across the table with lascivious pleasure at his wife, Althea.

Now he heard the front doorbell ring. Then, urgent conversation could be heard at the door. And presently, René Dumont, the Bonnards' aging manservant, entered the dining room bearing an envelope from a palace courier. Wiping cream from his fingers, the President took the envelope and tore it open, confident that it would contain news from Jean-Claude Raffin, some kind of news— he knew not what—that would herald the dissolution of the nagging *Marseille* problem.

When Aristide Bonnard's eyes fell, instead, on the fateful telex and its message of death from Max Dechambre, a violent spasm of pain seized his intestines.

"Anything serious, my darling?" asked Madame Bonnard gently.

"Not really. Not really." The President rose from the table, signaling to the servant to leave, and walked to the sideboard where he picked up the telephone and stared down at the telex, thinking, good Christ, this is terrible.

"Get me Raffin at the Sûreté," he said into the phone. Perhaps he had gone too far, taken too much of a risk in meeting with the Director General and turning him loose. If things were to go wrong now, the pigeons would come home to roost and leave their droppings all over the Élysée Palace.

A voice came back to him on the phone and explained that M. Raffin had left his office for the evening on urgent matters and could not be reached. Would Monsieur le Président like them to keep trying?

"Never mind," said Aristide Bonnard. "Cancel the call."

It was just as well, he decided suddenly. To hell with the threats of those pirates on the *Marseille*. There would be no change of heart or of plans. The Sûreté would prevail. France would prevail. By the time the President reached the dinner table again, he had torn the telex into many small pieces and was stuffing them into his pocket.

He sat down, looked down at his heart's delight in the bowl, and then across the table at his wife. "The *fraises* are so endearingly luscious, I cannot bear to stop," he said. "What shall I do?"

"Don't stop, my sweetheart," she replied. "I love to watch you when you are happy."

Bonnard dipped a berry in the whipped cream and placed it on his tongue. "My compliments to your grocer," he murmured, sucking the fruit. "And to the beautiful creature who selected the basket."

Althea Bonnard smiled with lowering eyes, and the President knew that they would be going to bed early this night. But he would keep the telephone lines open for the good news that would surely come. Madame Bonnard did not mind such interruptions. She had long ago assured her husband that she found interruptions particularly exciting.

CHAPTER TWENTY-SEVEN

New York—2:10 P.M. Peter Broussard was really an awfully nice guy, and a handsome son of a bitch, too. Ball hated to do it to him. Broussard had smoothed many a summer sailing to Paris on the *Marseille* for CBS executives who regretted they had but one wife to send to another country. Ball hated to do it to him, but the end, he told himself, justified the meanness. And besides, what the hell choice did he have anyway? Brian Joy, a muted hysteric if ever he heard one, had somehow managed to make him feel that the entire responsibility for saving the *Marseille* was his now, and he goddamn well better come through. Or else. Or else what? Or else Lisa would never speak to him again? Or else three thousand people would never speak to *anyone* again?

I never should have taken that call at Twenty-One last night, and I never should have called Paris, he told himself. Every time I get involved with Lisa, no matter how indirectly, it's trouble in River City.

The last time—that incredible weekend in Cannes—Amanda

had caught him in a barefaced lie, and it had taken almost a year for their marriage to get back to being held together by a slender thread. And now, here he was right smack in the middle of more chicanery, nonsexual, to be sure, but inspired by Lisa Briande, nevertheless. He wondered what those minimum-security prisons were like, where you played tennis and wrote your memoirs while you did your one-to-three years.

He put the cigarette lighter back in his pocket, exhaled a stream of sincere smoke into the air, and continued to lie like hell to Peter Broussard, who sat behind the desk watching him, with fingertips pressed together as though in prayer.

"I wish I could say it was *my* idea instead of the Old Man's," Leonard Ball said, "because it's such a damned good one. But about all I come up with these days are beauties like an examination of the effect of compact cars on the declining incidence of backseat venereal disease." He chuckled, but the man behind the desk just looked at him without smiling.

"How soon would you want to put your camera crew aboard?" Broussard inquired.

"Frankly, I'd like to fly our guys over right away and have them meet the *Marseille* and do their coverage on the return trip to New York. Salant believes in striking while the Old Man is hot."

"What about Cunard and the *QE 2?* What about the Italian Line?" the Public Relations Director asked.

"Oh, they'll probably squawk all over the place, and get on my ass *and* Mike's. We're used to that," Leonard Ball replied. "I don't think we've ever done a single *Sixty Minutes* without someone bitching and complaining: what about me, what about us?"

Peter Broussard eyed him, his expression still contemplative. "Mind you, Leonard," he said, "I'm not questioning anyone's judgment over at CBS, particularly when this could be such a juicy promotional plum for French Atlantic. But will it not strike some people as rather odd that *Sixty Minutes* does (how do you call it?) a big number on the resurgence of transatlantic sea travel, when everyone in maritime circles knows that what we have been given is not really *new life* but merely a stay of execution?"

"Peter, we are in show business journalism, pure and simple." Leonard Ball spoke with great earnestness. "We are not pretending to be social or economic theorists. What is true for today, or even seems to be true, is good enough for us to hang our hats on, if it smells like a provocative show. You people and the French treasury have just built the S.S. *Bordeaux*. That's a gargantuan vote of confidence for sea travel. And the *Marseille* is still the glamour-puss she always was. So right now I couldn't care less that maybe French Altantic will be an *airline* in five years, or that maybe *Sixty Minutes and* CBS will be down the toilet in less. I say we should get moving on this right away. What do *you* say?"

Broussard reflected for a moment, then held his hands up in mock surrender. "You're too much for me, I give up."

"Good." Leonard Ball rose to his feet and sauntered to the windows, as though the traffic far below on Fifth Avenue were more important to him than what he was about to say. "Now the first thing I do, with your help, of course, is leave here with some research material for my writers to get started on."

"What did you have in mind?" he heard Broussard ask.

He fixed his attention on a slow-moving bus that was caught in the congestion of the avenue. "We'd need a good overall view," he said. "A cross-section of the *kinds* of people who prefer ocean voyages to the jet stream these days." The bus fought its way to the outside and broke free. "Your passenger information list for the current sailing of the *Marseille* to Le Havre would be just perfect, Peter."

He turned away from the bus, not needing it any longer. Broussard was shaking his head.

"That's out, Leonard, completely."

"Out?"

"Confidential. We don't release that information list to anyone, not even within the company."

Leonard Ball blinked several times and started back to the desk. "*I* know that, Peter." He casually tamped out his cigarette in the ashtray. "I wouldn't dream of asking you to turn it over to me. I just want to be able to glance at it, right here in your office, so that I can background my own head into shape and sound like I know what the hell I'm talking about when I start pulling this thing together." He gave a chuckle of reassurance. "Hell, I wouldn't know *who* sails on the *Marseille* these days, Nellie Glutz from Jersey City or Gore Vidal."

"Both," said Peter Broussard.

"So be a nice girl then and go get the Pentagon Papers out of your bomb-proof vault, or wherever the hell you keep them, and I'll

sit myself down right here and glom the whole thing once over
lightly while you file your fingernails. Or bite them, I don't care."

"Damn it, Leonard, I really shouldn't . . ."

"Listen, when CBS finally cools me, as it does to all men, I want
to be able to go right over to Cunard–White Star and say: How
would you like to hire a guy who's memorized all of French Atlantic's atomic secrets . . . in five minutes?"

Peter Broussard shook his head in awe. "You're *more* than too
much. You're impossible." He leaned forward, pressed the intercom
button. "Hélène?"

"Oui, M'sieur Broussard?"

Nice, Leonard Ball thought. Nice.

"Bring the latest PIL in, will you?"

"Pour le Marseille?"

"Right."

"Tout de suite."

Ball wandered across the office to the half-open door at the other
end, casually glanced in. "We're on to a good one here, Peter." He
was right. The conference room *did* have an outer door to the
corridor. He turned. "I can feel the creative hard-on already."

"Just be sure you don't give *us* the screwing," said Broussard.

Ball exploded in a cackle that was genuine. The irony was just
too goddamn much. Then Hélène walked in with a rustle of silken
thighs, trailing clouds of Je Reviens and carrying in her right hand
a large manila folder bulging with a sheaf of legal-size white sheets
of paper. She gave Ball a sudden flash of her violet eyes and shining
teeth that left him hurting with longing for Lisa Briande.

Oh God, he thought, somehow, out of all of this, I've got to wind
up in Paris again.

He'd never learn.

The girl placed the folder on the desk. *"Voilà."*

"You can leave it, dear," Broussard said, looking up at her in a
way that filled Ball with envy.

She walked past him on the way out, meeting his gaze head on,
lips parted slightly, until she was sure she had killed him. He stared
after her, breathing her wake in deeply.

"Leonard? . . ."

She disappeared from view.

"Leonard? . . ."

He left Paris, and turned. "Hmm?"

"We have here the S.S. *Marseille,* New York to Le Havre, July 10." The Public Relations Director held the manila container in his hands with pride on his face. "They talk of *l'atmosphère Françat* on our ships as if it were some ephemeral ambiance created by magic." He shook his head. "Words, Leonard. We do it with words on paper. *Reportage.* Right here. A mass of personal tidbits is what makes it possible, gathered together with patience, diligence, and a fine French flair for snooping and gossip."

Ball stared down at the prize in front of him and thought, how incredible, that this man should know everything there is to know about the *Marseille* and its passengers except the simple fact that they were sailing toward their possible doom in the southern Atlantic . . .

He glanced at his wristwatch.

. . . in a little over twenty-four hours.

Brian Joy was waiting. Captain Charles Girodt and his staff were waiting. What they were waiting for, what exactly would come out of this sheaf of papers and what they would do with it, he did not fully understand. All he knew for certain was that the next move in this strangest of games was his by acclamation. And so he leaned forward and took the proffered manila folder from the outstretched hands of Peter Broussard, turned his back on him and walked right past the waiting club chair toward the half-open door to the conference room, announcing with inarguable intention, "I'll do my browsing in here where we won't be in each other's hair."

"No, no, that's all right," Broussard said quickly. "You can stay right—"

"If I have any questions I'll poke my head back in." He glanced back. "Carry on, Peter."

And before the man could say another word, Ball was inside the conference room and closing the door behind him. He waited a moment, listening for trouble, heard none, then went to the door on the other side of the table and opened it a crack. The corridor was empty. He stepped outside, walked quietly down the hall to the door marked EXIT and went through.

Thelma Stutz was waiting on the stairway landing, her wide brown eyes betraying nervousness. She quickly dropped her cigarette, stepped on it and came forward, opening a black leather briefcase. "I thought you'd never—"

"You worry too much," he said. He took the sheaf of papers out of the manila folder and stuffed them into her briefcase, saying, "One copy for now. Nobody near the machine but you. Take Forty-ninth Street west. Have the cab wait. Go down Eleventh and take Forty-eighth on the way back. I'll be in the men's room—"

"The men's room?"

"Give me seven knocks on the door . . . shave-and-a-haircut . . . shampoo. Okay?"

"God, Mr. Ball, this is—"

"Shocking, I know. Now beat it, honey."

He watched her start down the staircase. Then he opened the door and went back to the hallway with the empty manila folder in his hand. He walked quickly to the men's room and entered.

The washroom was deserted. There were three stalls, all unoccupied. He went into the one nearest the door, locked himself in, opened the manila folder and placed it on the white tile floor where it could be seen from outside the stall. Then he took off his jacket, hung it on the door hook, undid his belt, unzipped his fly and bared himself to the cold toilet seat, keeping his legs slightly forward as he sat down so that his shoes and lowered trousers could also be seen beneath the stall door. For the first time, he became aware of the quickened beat of his heart and the dampness of his shirt.

He reached up into his jacket pocket. found his cigarettes and lit one. After a few deep drags he felt the first distant early warning signals of his intestinal tract, telling him he'd be able to force a movement if it really became necessary. Peter Broussard, he was sure, was the fastidious kind who would be too embarrassed to bear witness to the indelicate noises of a friend.

The outside door banged open and he heard the loud voices of two men entering. Their footsteps took them to the urinals, then briefly to the sinks, and then they were leaving, and the washroom was silent again. He sat there on the warming seat, conjuring up visions of Thelma Stutz bending over the xerox machine. He glanced at his wristwatch and helped her into a waiting cab a few miles away. Then he heard the washroom door opening again, quietly. Footsteps entered and quickly came to a stop. He sensed eyes looking down, and heard Peter Broussard's tentative query, "Leonard?"

"Who's that? Is that you, Peter?"

"Yes, I . . . uh . . . I didn't know where—"

"This stuff is fascinating. Absolutely fascinating. I'm having a ball with it."

"Well, I'm . . . I'm glad . . . I didn't—"

"Were you looking for me, Peter?"

"Uh . . . not exactly. I just happened to buzz you to see if there was anything you wanted and when you didn't answer—"

"Jesus, I'm sorry, Peter. I guess I should have told you when I decided to go to the john."

"No, that's all right."

"Now you know everything. I'm a water-closet queen. In fact I've caught some of my best ideas off toilet seats." He heard Broussard's unappreciative chuckle, but no indication that the man was going to leave. "Excuse me, Peter. I feel an idea coming on." He bore down hard on his sphincter muscles, straining, pressing, flirting with a double hernia, and got almost immediate results.

Broussard coughed loudly and said, "I'll be at my desk if you need me, Leonard," and fled.

Immediately, Ball began to get ready. He was immaculate and clean and waiting just inside the washroom door when the soft rapping of Thelma Stutz finally sounded. He opened the door slightly.

"How'd it go?"

"No problems." His secretary sounded breathless.

"Good girl. Gimme." He stuck his hand through the opening and took the leather briefcase from her. He pulled back, closed the door, quickly transferred the passenger information list to the manila folder and emerged from the washroom.

"I'll try and make it fast," he said, giving her the briefcase. "Hold the cab."

"Are you okay, Mr. Ball?"

"I don't know. Did you ever spend a week in a men's room?" He waved her away and moved down the hall to the conference room door. It was locked.

"Damn."

He had forgotten to release the button.

He went around to the French Atlantic entrance, breezed by the receptionist, explaining, "I'm Leonard Ball of CBS, returning this to Mr. Broussard," and went through the next door into a cloud of Je Reviens.

"Ah, M'sieur Ball . . ." The violet eyes looked up at him with surprise and a certain amount of pleasure.

"Hélène, honey, thank him and tell him I had to run, will you?"

"Oui, m'sieur."

"And this belongs to you." He dropped the folder on her desk and started to turn away but never made it. Instead, he heard a voice saying, "Now how about you belonging to me?" And was surprised to realize that it was his own. "I *must* have lunch with you tomorrow. Give me a fast yes or *oui*."

She smiled slowly. "*Oui*."

"Your place or mine?"

"*Qu'est-ce que c'est que* your place?"

"The Park East."

"Parks I adore," she sighed. "Especially Le Bois de Boulogne."

"One-ish?"

"*Mais non*." She pouted with a smile. "Twelve to two."

He swayed a little, steadied himself, and walked away quickly from the smile and the accent that he knew were going to drive him delirious.

On the way down in the elevator he tried to figure out exactly when it was that he must have decided to leave the conference room door locked. But by the time he reached the waiting cab and climbed in beside Thelma Stutz, he conceded that it had been just plain dumb luck.

They talked their way across town in the speeding taxi, Ball doing most of it, his secretary trying to get it all down on the steno pad in her lap. "You'll be calling Tony Salmagandi on the Coast while I'm setting up the Flash Studio. Go direct, no tie-line on this. He's to be in the videotape room ten minutes after you hang up. The material coming through will be headed S.S. *Titanic* . . ."

She glanced at him. "*Titanic?*"

He pointed impatiently at the steno pad. "Highly confidential background material for a special to be written on the Coast by Brian Joy . . ."

"I get it."

"Tony is to watch it come through on the monitor, and as soon as the feed is complete, have it piped to his office. He's to have a still photographer waiting there with plenty of film and a closeup lens . . ."

"Waiting in his office?"

"Correct. To photograph each page of the material off the screen and transfer it to ten-by-fifteen glossies, one copy only. How many pages?"

"I counted a hundred and sixty," Thelma Stutz said, as the taxi careened into Tenth Avenue.

"Tell Tony that, plus one for a title page."

"Right."

"As soon as the negatives go to the quick lab, he's to call Brian Joy and have him start down to Fairfax to pick up the material, including the negatives. Underline that. And when Tony has the positive prints in hand and he's certain they're legible, he's to have the videotape sent to his office and erased. Any questions?"

"Yes, Mr. Ball."

"Shoot."

"When you're out looking for a job, may I look with you?"

He smiled into her warm brown eyes, and it pleased him to realize that, if he had had the time, he would have been perfectly capable of spending the next few minutes thinking about being unfaithful to a French girl he hadn't even laid yet. Anything that reinforced his low opinion of his own character always pleased him. But he had too much else to think about right now, so he just patted his secretary's hand reassuringly and started fishing in his pocket for money to pay the cab driver.

In his office, he picked up the phone and dialed Air Control, then pulled open his desk drawer and took out the Xeroxed pages. Good, clean black and white, sharp definition, better than the originals.

"Marty, this is Leonard Ball."

"Oh, hi, Mr. Ball."

"Is the network still down?"

"Yep, for another thirty-five, check, thirty-seven minutes."

"Anything going on in the Flash Studio?"

"Too damn much, sir. Right now there's a talent audition, a screen test, being sent to California, highest priority. The V.P. of Programming needs a casting decision by five p.m. Pacific Daylight. Then we got a color girl lined up for a camera test on the new French CFS 23, and if there's time—"

He broke in. "There *isn't* time. Who's directing?"

"Jim Botsworth."

"Call him and tell him I'm on the way over with an urgent break-in to feed to the Coast."

"All right, Mr. Ball."

"And if anyone should ask you what this is all about, just tell them it's something the Old Man wants rushed through, no discussions."

"Yes, Mr. Ball."

"Thank you, Marty."

He hung up, found a blank sheet of white paper in a side drawer, uncapped a heavy black Flair pen, and printed a title page: BACKGROUND FOR S.S. TITANIC. Then he thumbed through the Xeroxed pages, found a half dozen mentions of the S.S. *Marseille* and obliterated them with black ink.

Thelma Stutz was on long distance as he came up to her desk. "Tell him to hold on," he whispered urgently.

"Sir? . . . Sir? . . . Can you hold it just one second please?" She covered the mouthpiece with her hand and looked up. "It's Tony."

"I want you to call Brian Joy also," he said. "I think I may have forgotten to tell him he's supposed to be doing a special for us."

"You didn't forget."

"Call him," he said.

He heard her talking to Salmagandi again as he hurried out of her office and started down the hall to the Flash Studio.

They gave him the aggrieved look as he walked into the crowded little room, its concentration and purpose broken now by the director's voice on the intercom telling them to hold everything.

"Sorry, fellas, sorry," Leonard Ball said to all the faces.

The lean young Italianate one in the sweatshirt and jeans and the layer of dark pancake said in an ugly voice, "What is this bullshit?"

Ball gave him a cold smile. "Listen, buster, we don't say bullshit around here until after ten p.m. There's liable to be some small child out in the corridor who might overhear you talk like that and go out and bullshit someone."

The pancake face looked at him, then turned to the stage manager. "You'll find me in the loo when you're ready." And he walked out.

"Actors," said Ball. He handed the Xeroxed pages to the stage manager. "Set these up on an easel, will you, Henry?"

"Sure thing," Henry Simon said.

"What the Old Man wants immediately, the Old Man gets immediately."

"Oh, I see."

Ball shrugged. "What else?"

He left the studio, went down the hall, and entered the control room.

"Sorry, Jim," he said to the director.

"Sorry-shmorry," said Botsworth, a bald-headed hulk of fifty, seated between the audioman and the videoman, his stubby fingers drumming impatiently on the console as his eyes darted over the bank of monitor screens before him. In the dark far corner of the room, Larry Edwards, the associate director, was talking *sotto voce* to the Coast on the open phone line.

"He just walked in," Leonard Ball heard him say.

"You put him away beeyootiful, old buddy," said Botsworth in his growl of a voice.

"Oh, you heard?" said Ball.

"The faggoty prick," said the director.

The men on either side of him mumbled something that sounded like "nice going" and Ball said, "Hi, fellas." To Botsworth he said, "Henry Simon is setting up a hundred and sixty-one pages on the easel. We have to feed them to the Coast right away."

"I'm with *you,* pal. How do you want it?"

"Nothing fancy, just very clear. No art, just information. Give me about eight seconds on each page."

"Will you settle for four?"

"All right, four."

The director hit the Talk-Back. "Henry, are you set up?"

"Yes, Mr. Botsworth," said the stage manager's voice.

"Joe, go in full frame. We'll do four seconds on each."

"Gotcha," the cameraman replied.

Ball saw his title page come up on the center monitor screen.

"The *Titanic,* for chrissake," muttered Jim Botsworth. He hit the Talk-Back again. "Is that as tight as you can get?"

"If I go any closer, I'll be on the other side."

"Heh-heh. By the way, we're feeding sunny California with this, Henry."

"I know, Mr. Botsworth."

"You guys don't need a director. I'm obsolete. Mr. Ball, it would appear that we're ready to go."

"Just a second." Ball turned toward the man at the telephone. "Find out if Tony Salmagandi is at the tape machine out there, will you?"

"Salmagandi . . . chocolate candy," said Jim Botsworth to no one in particular.

The man at the telephone called out, "Yes, he's there, Mr. Ball . . ."

"Good."

"But he wants to speak to you."

"Oh, shit. Sorry, men." Ball walked over to the associate director and took the phone from him. "Yes, Tony?"

"Leonard, what the fuck's going on?" whined the distant voice.

"Wait a minute. Didn't my girl explain everything?"

"To *me,* yeah," cried Salmagandi. "But not to Lester Hammersmith."

"Hammersmith?"

"The new Vice President of Programming. Where the hell have you been?"

"CBS News. What do *we* know?"

"He's in the next room calling the Old Man in New York right now, because he can't believe that *anyone,* not even the Old Man, would authorize the bumping of a screen test that's gonna leave a six-hundred-thousand-dollar production shooting tomorrow with no goddamn male lead set."

Ball swallowed the dryness in his mouth. "Tony, you guys out there just don't know the Old Man like we do. Now will you stop wasting time, before the network goes back up and we're *all* dead?"

"Leonard, this could cost me my ass."

"I'll buy you a new one. Now put the tape man back on and hurry." He handed the phone to the associate director, who was watching him tensely. "Let's go."

The other man nodded, spoke into the phone. "Jack? . . . Right. Roll the tape." He placed the phone down, called out, "Rolling."

Botsworth punched the Talk-Back. "Rolling."

The associate director clicked on a stopwatch.

Ball watched the center monitor screen, aware of his own body sweat. The image was sharp and clear. "That's very good," he said.

"I get very good money," said Jim Botsworth.

"Right," said Ball, watching.

"Four seconds," said the associate director.

Botsworth hit the Talk-Back. "Next page."

Ball stared at the monitor screen, felt a drop of sweat rolling into his left eye, jabbed at it with a finger.

"These jokers were on the *Titanic?*" said Jim Botsworth.

"Four seconds."

"Next page."

On the eighty-ninth page, the interoffice phone near the door started ringing.

"For chrissake," Jim Botsworth growled.

"Keep going," Ball said quickly. He went to the phone, picked it up. "Yes?"

He knew well the voice and its imperious, womanly politeness. "May I speak to Mr. Leonard Ball please?"

"I'm sorry. He's not here."

"To whom am I speaking?" inquired the voice.

He hesitated a moment, then broke the connection. The Old Man's executive secretary would now be staring at her phone. Now she would be hanging up. Now she would be deciding to dial again. Ball removed the receiver from its cradle and placed it on the surface of the console. Then he turned his attention to the monitor screen, to the list of W's in the passenger configuration of a ship that was not the *Titanic*.

They were nearing the end now, just about finished.

So, in all likelihood, was he.

He thought about that for a moment, searching for apprehension, and found instead a pleasurable feeling of anticipation and excitement beginning to well up inside of him. It started in his loins and went right up to his head and came out in a secret, silly grin.

What a helluva day this one had been so far.

He needed more like it.

CHAPTER TWENTY-EIGHT

Latitude 20° N., Longitude 53° W.—4:50 P.M. From outside, beyond the double glass windows their table was facing, you could hear the thunder of waves exploding on the bow, and the hiss of spray. But in here in the Méditerranée Room there was only the soft murmur of voices and the tinkle of teacups against saucers. Julie glanced quickly through the four pages that Yves Chabot had taken from his breast pocket and placed before her. "My God," she exclaimed, "what in the world do you *do* with all this stuff?"

The Frenchman smiled. "That is nothing. I could have prepared a small *book* if I had included all our remedies for *mal de mer,* backache, headache, toothache, overeating, hangovers and such. What you have there are only the most potent chemicals in our arsenal, the ones to be used for all the heart attacks, kidney failures, epileptic seizures, cerebral hemorrhages, insulin shocks, skull fractures, and suicide attempts that never, never happen on the *Marseille.* They wouldn't dare."

"You've got more ampules and tablets and vials and capsules

here than all the doctors in Beverly Hills put together." Julie glanced up. "And sometimes I'd *like* to put them all together—and drop them into the same hole."

Chabot wagged a finger. "Your husband, madame, your husband."

"Billy included," she said. "Most of their medical practice consists of trying to cure their patients of the side effects of each other's prescriptions."

"Nevertheless, my lovely lady, you *will* give that list to Dr. Berlin to send out on the air, as soon as you finish your tea."

"Of course I will. He'll love it. Some men read *Playboy*. My husband reads pharmaceutical brochures and QST."

The ship's doctor stared at her for a moment. "Despite your lack of confidence in medicinal preparations *or* in the men who prescribe them, I must tell you we are all hoping that somewhere in that list lies the answer to our biggest problem . . ."

"You mean, how to overcome bullets with aspirin tablets?" She couldn't resist the trace of sarcasm.

"Not aspirin tablets, my dear. Perhaps one of the cyanides." He shrugged. "Who knows?"

Her eyes widened. "Cyanide? You *don't* have things like *that* on board."

He nodded.

"Good heavens, what for?"

"Extreme fumigation and other forms of necessary extermination. The Compagnie Française does not like to talk about some of the exotic winged creatures and crawly things and four-legged little animals—rodents, if you will—that invade the *Marseille* during some of its stopovers on the annual round-the-world cruise . . ."

"Ugh," Julie shuddered.

He smiled mysteriously. "Also, sometimes these chemical compounds are the only cure we have for a cynical wife."

"I deserved that." Julie shook her head in mock despair. "Once a bitch . . ."

"Absolutely not." Chabot smiled. "The diagnosis is that you are not a hopeless case, but trying very hard to be one. Now, suppose you put the information away in your handbag, and tell me your timetable so that we can be in quick communication if necessary."

"Well, directly to Billy first, with all these delicious poisons . . ." She slipped the pages into her bag. "Then, let's see, I promised

Harold Columbine I'd have cocktails with him in the Verandah Lounge at five-thirty. After that, no plans."

"I would invite myself to your dinner table tonight," he said, "but I think it would be unwise."

She smiled at him. "You mean, people will talk?"

"Not people. Our enemies."

Her smile faded. The doctor rose to his feet and looked down at her. "Do take care of yourself . . . please."

"I will," she said, in a small voice. She had been feeling so unrealistically better, almost carefree, sitting there having tea with him. Now, as she watched him walk away, she felt a slight, premonitory chill.

She picked up her glass, took a sip of water into her mouth, and surreptitiously swished it around to cleanse her teeth, a habit she was secretly ashamed of. Then she noticed the two attractive, thirty-ish women, obviously Americans, sitting at the small table near the entrance watching her and smiling. She quickly swallowed the water, got up, and started away, feeling their eyes still on her as she came abreast of their table.

A soft, pleasing voice called out, "Hi, there, Mrs. Berlin."

Julie stopped and looked down quizzically. "Hello . . ."

The woman on the left had long, jet-black hair and wore over-sized tinted glasses. The other one, who wore a cute, short, blond wig, smiled at Julie. "You *are* Julie Berlin, aren't you?" She had marvelous white teeth.

"Indeed I am." Did she know them? Yes . . . No . . .

"Don't be too bewildered," the soft-voiced woman said. "I'm Edith Carter and this is Jill Pleasance."

"How do you do?" Julie nodded.

"The Purser told us who you were."

"Oh, am I famous or something?"

"No, but you *are* from Bel Air and quite stylish to the eye, if you'll pardon my saying so . . ."

"Pardon granted."

"And don't think we haven't noticed and envied you and that gorgeous hunk of a ship's doctor."

Was that it? "Girls, if it's an introduction you're after, just do as I did. Get a sore throat and have *him* examine you personally."

The two women laughed, and Jill Pleasance said, "We're married to a couple of guys who are gin rummying their way clear across the Atlantic on this trip, and it would serve both of them right. However, Dr. Handsome is not what's on our mind right now. Could we go somewhere and have a little chat with you, Julie?"

"I'd love to," Julie said, "but I really must get back to my cabin."

"We need a little *expertise*," Edith Carter persisted. "It won't take long."

"I hate to sound unfriendly. Perhaps some other—"

"No problem," the dark-haired woman interrupted. "Come on, Jill, move your derrière." She quickly pushed the table back and looked at Julie as she rose. "We'll go along with you and discuss our little problem on the way."

"No, really . . ." Julie fumbled for words, but the two women were already going past her to the entrance. She followed them, irritated with herself for having been lonely enough to stop and talk with strangers, and weak enough not to be able to shake them off at will. She was *not* going to have them trudge along to the cabin, that was for sure.

In the lurching corridor, Jill Pleasance said, "Hang on for dear life, ladies. This boat is making moves like my husband makes after three drinks."

"My husband isn't making any moves at all," Julie said rather loudly. "He's in bed with a horrible case of the flu, just waiting to give it to anyone who comes near him."

"I never catch anything," Jill Pleasance said.

"What we wanted to talk about," the woman with the black hair and the tinted glasses said to Julie as they moved with careful steps toward the elevators, "well, it's . . . we feel, Jill and I, that our charming Captain is always stuck with giving parties for the passengers on these crossings, but nobody ever does anything for *him*, and that's just not fair. So Jill and I thought, wouldn't it be marvelous to get a group together and throw some kind of unusual surprise party for him . . ."

"Wonderful," Julie said.

"Only trouble is, I'm from Fort Worth and Jill's from El Paso and between us we can't think of *one* idea that doesn't have *barbecue sauce* all over it."

"And so I'm *it?*" Julie asked.

"Exactly," replied Edith Carter. They arrived at the closed elevator doors, and she pressed the DOWN button. "If Bel Air can't come up with a terrific party idea, then I've been misled by *Women's Wear Daily* and I'm going to cancel my subscription."

"Okay," Julie said. "Why don't I give it some thought tonight?"

The woman with the short blond hair said, "I always say there's no time like the present."

And Edith Carter gave Julie a big, pleasant smile and added, "Now that we've got you, we're not going to let you go, darling."

"You don't seem to understand." Julie felt a strange urgency in her voice. "I was *serious* about my husband's flu and—"

"Then we'll go to *Jill's.*" The dark-haired woman turned to her friend. "Okay with you, doll?"

"Dreamy," Jill Pleasance said.

"But not for *me.*" Julie shook her head wearily. They were like *glue.* "Not right now."

The elevator arrived, empty, and she went in quickly.

"Wait for us." They followed her in.

She pressed one of the buttons. "I'm going to the Première Deck. What about you?"

"Wherever you go, we go too," Edith Carter said, pleasantly.

Julie's lips tightened. She turned, saying, "Now listen to me, please—" But stopped suddenly, seeing their faces as they stared past her out of the elevator. She turned sharply and saw the olive-skinned woman in the white gabardine suit rushing toward the closing doors calling out, "Hold it, please hold it . . ."

Quickly she punched the OPEN button and the doors sprang back and the woman entered the elevator all breathless and smiling, saying, "Thank you, thank you . . ."

Then Julie recognized the finely molded features of the ship's hostess. "Hello, Miss Shanneli . . ."

"Oh . . . Mrs. Berlin . . . *Hello* . . ." Olga Shanneli's dark eyes brighted. "Do press A-Deck, won't you? It's down to the lower depths for *me.*" Julie pushed the button and heard the woman saying, "By the way, did they find you?"

The elevator doors started to close.

Julie looked at her. "Who?"

"Those two lovely American ladies who were so taken with our little du Barry creation last night. I gave *you* all the credit. After all, *I* didn't *wear* it."

Julie's heart sank even faster than the elevator.

And then the woman was glancing behind her and exclaiming,

"Good heavens, so you *have* found each other. I didn't even recognize you two, forgive me. But you've changed your *hair* or something, haven't you?"

Harriet Kleinfeld's voice was cool and casual. "We just flipped our wigs a little," she said.

Olga Shanneli laughed.

The elevator doors slid open onto the Première Deck and Julie stood motionless, drained of blood, drained of everything but the growing dread that was paralyzing her.

"This is Première, Julie," said Betty Dunleavy quietly behind her.

Julie did not move.

"Shall we?" the quiet voice persisted.

Julie waited, and the doors closed again.

Olga Shanneli glanced from the two expressionless faces at the rear to the ashen, stricken profile near the doors, and she was gripped by a strange uneasiness. "Well, my dears," she said, "what have we all planned for *this* inclement evening? A champagne and dramamine party, perhaps?" No answer. Only the soft clicking of the descending elevator. "Have no fear. Shanneli will think of something to fit the occasion." She looked at the profile. "Is anything . . . is there something I can do, Mrs. Berlin?"

"Yes!" Julie whirled suddenly. "Yes!" Seizing the startled woman as the elevator stopped, hurling her violently into the two who were starting forward, hearing their stunned cries of pain and outrage as their soft bodies hit the unyielding metal of the car's rear wall. And then the doors were open and she was out and racing along the endless swaying corridor, bouncing off the side railings, moaning to herself, dropping her bag and its precious contents, stopping, falling to her knees, clutching at it, scrambling to her feet, running again, running, looking back, seeing them pushing past Olga Shanneli and starting after her.

"Billy . . ." she heard herself crying. "Billy . . ."

The door—COMPANIONWAY—she pulled it open, saw the staircase, went through.

Up. She had to go up. Keep going. Not Main Deck. Higher. Not Promenade. Not this one. Keep going, Julie. Première Deck. Hurry . . .

"Billy . . ."

Oh Christ, her ankle.

I can't . . .

Yes.

She fought the stairs—would they ever end?—and her pounding heart.

I can't, Billy . . .

She heard them.

They were behind her. Below her. Their scrambling footsteps were coming closer. Stumbling on the stairs, their voices harsh . . . "Goddamnit, come *on* . . ."

She saw the gray door, ran to it, pulled it open.

Première Deck. Yes. Deserted corridor. Which way? Right? Left?

Left.

She started forward. The ship lurched. She fell back, braced herself, pushed off and ran . . . faster . . . eyes searching. Where *was* it?

One-sixty-four . . . One-sixty-four . . . Ninety-four . . .

Oh God, wrong direction.

She turned, clutched at the side rail, started back, rushing past the gray door, hearing their voices on the other side.

Hurry.

One-seventy-two . . . seventy-one . . . seventy . . . One-sixty-nine . . . eight . . . seven . . .

She heard them come through.

She'd never make it.

One-sixty-five . . .

They spotted her, called out something.

One-sixty-four.

Pound it, pound it. "Billy, open up, hurry! . . ."

Coming toward her in the swaying corridor, wigs slightly askew.

"Billy! . . ." Pounding, pounding.

His muffled voice. "Julie?"

"Hurry! Open it, open it!" Pounding, pounding.

"Is that you?"

"Yes! Hurry!"

The rattling of bolts.

"Open it!"

Seeing them lurching closer.

"Don't you come near me!"

Hearing the latch click, and then she was crashing through, knocking Billy aside, slamming the door shut, throwing the bolts into place, turning, clapping a hand over his open mouth, staring into his startled eyes and feeling her whole body trembling as she held his face in a viselike grip.

The pounding on the door began.

She looked into his eyes, shook her head, waited.

More knocking, louder, impatient.

"Mrs. Berlin? . . ." The soft-voiced one, not so soft. "Mrs. Berlin? . . ."

Julie held on to Billy, staring at the door, waiting.

A few more raps on the door, and then the other voice. "We'll see you later, Julie."

Waves boomed distantly against steel. Spray hissed somewhere like steam. The cabin groaned.

She took her hand from his face.

"They're gone," she whispered.

His eyes searched hers. "What the hell *is* it? What's happening?"

She began to fumble in her handbag. "From Dr. Chabot . . . The hospital list . . ."

He took the list from her, still puzzled.

"You're to send it to Brian Joy immediately, along with the names."

"I was just trying to raise him." He gestured to the transceiver on the table.

"Then go on, hurry."

He took her arm. "Aren't you going to tell me what's going on?"

"Yes, yes, of course I will. Now will you get *to* it?" She turned her head away, feeling the tears coming.

"Julie?"

"Oh God, Billy, it's no good . . ." She began to weep softly. "It's no good out there . . . and it's not going to get any better . . ."

And then she didn't resist it any longer, and he put his arms around her and held her while she cried.

The hot California noonday sun had burned off the morning fog and was slanting into the den, bouncing off the brown spackled top of the Signal One into Brian Joy's squinting eyes. If he'd had ten seconds, he would have jumped up and gone around the desk and yanked the blinds shut, but there wasn't time for anything now except the impossibility of trying to keep up with the distant voice coming out of the loudspeaker, of trying to get down on paper all the unfamiliar pharmaceutical terms that would have been gibberish even *without* the damnable summer static crashes and the unwitting interference of other stations. As his pen moved swiftly over the yellow pad he felt new respect for all the secretaries, past and present, who had uncomplainingly absorbed his own rapid-fire dictation down through the nervous years.

". . . Verutinium . . . Vinyl Ether . . . Xylocaine Hydrochloride for spinal anesthesia . . . Zarontin . . ."

Zarontin? It *sounded* like Zarontin . . .

That goddamn carrier tuning up, and the New England accent asking, "Is this frequency occupied?"

He threw down the pen and grabbed the mike. "Yes, this frequency *is* occupied. Why don't you *listen* before you tune up?"

"Sorry, old man. QSY-ing up five."

Up yours.

Billy Berlin had gotten lost in the exchange. Brian Joy waited for an opening, then broke in fast. "W6VC maritime mobile. W6LS. QSL everything through spinal anesthesia. Please repeat all after, starting with Zarontin. Go ahead."

Billy came back a solid five and seven now, and resumed his relay of the *Marseille* hospital list. They had both decided to throw caution to the winds of the southern Atlantic by discarding their elaborate code and using circumlocutions instead. There was too much data to bounce across the thousands of miles between them, and too little time in which to do it. "Eric and Charlie and Frances and Charlotte" and all the other first-name phantoms had become "the friends back home" to whom Billy was sending his regards from the *Flying Unicorn*. And "strychnocyanate-K, intraval sodium, meticortelone acetate," and a few hundred others sounding exactly like that (or so it seemed) were simply some medical props that the vacationing doctor was suggesting to Brian Joy for the hospital scene in that new pilot he was working on.

He angled his head now, ears cocked, straining, feeling his fingers beginning to cramp, tiny rivulets of sweat staining his cotton shirt, his mind already starting to anticipate the questions Billy would be asking when this transmission was over, and the answers he would give him without lying more than was necessary.

". . . Zarontin . . . Zinc Sulfocarbolate . . . Zolamine, Injectable . . . Zylofuramine Hydrochloride . . . Okay, Brian, that's it. That's about all I can suggest for now. W6LS. W6VC maritime mobile Region Two aboard the *Flying Unicorn*. Go ahead."

Brian Joy went right back to him, and because the frequency was clear he steered their comm cycle into short fast breaks. "Roger on everything, Billy, and thanks a million. I'm going to pass all your ideas on to my colleagues at the network, and I may even give you a little credit. Okay?"

"Affirmative," Billy Berlin said. "Now, Brian, do you have any specific good news for me? Is anything positive happening with those matters we discussed in our last QSO?"

"Yes, Billy, the answer is yes. Everything is coming along beautifully." A bell started ringing in the room, as though his lie had set off an alarm, and it took him a moment to realize that it was the telephone. He turned his head and shouted, "Maggie?"

"Yes!" From somewhere in the house . . .

"Get the telephone!"

"It's probably for you!"

"Answer the goddamn phone!"

He turned back to Billy's voice, lost in the speaker. The ringing stopped. He pressed the mike button. "Sorry, Billy. Land line. I missed most of that. Please repeat."

"I was saying that the conditions here, the weather and things like that, you know what I mean, Brian, the *conditions* are not very good." Despite the static, the anxiety in the voice was unmistakable. "The sickness, the seasickness, you know, what I told you about yesterday, it's all become very, very serious, and I don't know what else to tell you except that I'll be guarding the frequency and looking forward very eagerly to our next contact. But please have something for me, Brian. There is much worry here—I mean about my signals and all—and the next time I talk to you I want a good report, do you know what I mean? We need a good report, Brian. Go ahead."

What could he say to him? Even if the band *weren't* filled with a thousand inquisitive ears . . . even if there were *no* chance in a billion that someone in the radio room of the S.S. *Marseille* was casually eavesdropping on an amateur radio contact between a nearby freighter and a stateside station . . . what good would it do Billy, how would it raise the morale of Captain Charles Girodt and his staff to be told that well-intentioned men and women on two continents were striving to save them by running with the ball in different directions and getting no closer to any goal lines? So he said, "Yes, Billy, I understand what you're trying to tell me. I want you to know you have been very, very helpful. All the information you have transmitted has been used and will be used, and I can guarantee you that all problems will be solved. Did you copy that?"

"But, Brian," the voice quavered, "look at that digital clock on your desk and keep looking at it. Do you know what I'm talking about?"

"Of course I know what you're talking about," he shot back, with a trace of anger.

He turned at the sound behind him. Maggie was standing in the doorway.

"It's Tony Salmagandi," she said.

"Christ, I almost forgot about that." He pressed the mike button. "Billy, hang on a minute, will you? QRX." And to Maggie: "Is he on?"

"No. He just said to tell you to get in the car and come down to CBS right away. Something's coming through from Leonard Ball."

"Good. Don't go away."

He got rid of Billy fast, blaming it on changing band conditions, leaving him with a few more glib reassurances. Then he snapped off the equipment and started to gather up his papers, saying to Maggie, "I hope you're going to stay close to home while I'm gone."

"If I have to."

"Yes. Important."

"How did Billy sound?"

"Terrible. I don't think he believes a single lie I tell him."

"Neither do I," she said.

He grabbed his jacket from the chair, stuffed the *Marseille* medical supply list into the inside pocket, went up to Maggie and gave her a sweaty kiss on the lips.

"What's that for?" she asked.

"For putting up with all this shit."

"Who said I'm putting up with it?"

"And also for having any phone call that comes in from Lisa Briande in Paris transferred to Lloyd Shipley's office at Remo . . ."

"You can have your kiss back."

"I'll be there in about an hour."

"What in the world are you going to Remo for?"

"A think tank is for problem-solving, isn't it? And have we got a problem."

"How come we never took our marriage there?"

"Funny." He grazed her chin lightly and hurried out, hoping there would be enough lunch-hour traffic on Beverly Boulevard to get him riled up and make him forget the anxiety in Billy Berlin's voice.

Harold Columbine was of the firm belief that any girl who was twenty minutes late for a date with him was sending him a message that she was sorry she had made the date in the first place. He didn't like that message, not from Julie. So he tore it up and decided to give her another five minutes, letting the slow roll of the ship and his second martini have their way with him. After a while he had had enough, not of martinis but of waiting. He called the bartender over and asked for a telephone.

"And while you're up, you might as well bring me another one of these."

"Shall I make it a double, m'sieur?"

"That's a helluvan idea."

She answered the phone on the first ring with a rather nervous "Who is it?"

"Mrs. Berlin, sweetheart, this is your Prince Harold, and my wristwatch says ten to six and I'm getting more than impatient for the sight of you."

"I should have called you, Harold. I can't make it." Her voice sounded tight.

"Do you know what you're doing to me, baby, leaving me alone here at the mercy of a willing bartender?"

"I'm sorry," she said flatly.

"Not only that, but there's a chick at the other end of the bar who's been giving me a very obvious eye, and the only reason I've ignored her is because I can't bear to be unfaithful to my own true love." And he was amazed to realize that he almost wasn't kidding.

"I have to hang up now," she said.

"You sound strange," he said. "What is it?"

"When I see you," she said.

"Dinner? *Please* now."

"If I . . . if it's safe to come out."

"You're in danger, right?"

Silence at the other end.

"Your husband and—?"

"No," she said quickly.

He said, "They've found Madame du Barry."

She didn't answer.

He said, "I'm picking you up at nine. You need a bodyguard, and I can't think of a guard I'd rather body."

She didn't say no. She didn't say anything. So he said goodbye and hung up and decided to wait until nine o'clock before worrying about this new threat to her, and to him, too, for that matter. And he knew that it would be easier not to think about it if he became preoccupied with something else, and if he put the brand new double martini where it belonged, instead of in the glass.

The something else had swung around on her bar stool so that he could see her legs now. They were bare and slender and deeply tanned, and the beige shorts she was wearing made them look even longer and darker than they really were. She wore a man's shirt, unbuttoned down to her brown midriff, the shirttails tied together in a saucy little knot over her navel. Her face, with its high cheek bones and large dark eyes framed by feather-cut short black hair, was the color of tea. He stared at her and decided that she was somewhere in the vicinity of thirty-second street, which was a neighborhood rich with experience, and for a few moments he made a mild pass at psyching himself out, saying softly: no, Harold, no, Harold, you mustn't, goddamn it. But then she looked slightly past him, took a deep suck on her cigarette, parted her lips, and let the smoke curl out slowly over her moving tongue, like a long kiss, and he knew then that there was no way he was going to be able to rise above the Harold Columbine he had known so well for so many years, Julie Berlin or no Julie Berlin.

He got to his feet, picked up his drink, and walked it over to where she was seated, losing a few splashes of precious gin to the drunken roll of the ship.

"May I?" He slid onto the stool beside her.

She looked at him and smiled, and he saw the crow's feet at the corners of her eyes and moved her up to thirty-eighth street, which was still fine with him, because now he was close enough to her to smell the musky odor of her body, and nothing about her could have put out his fire.

"I'm Harold Columbine," he said.

"I know you are," she said. "You think I pick up any old riff-raff?"

"Oh, a star-fucker, huh?"

She didn't even blink. "Who said anything about fucking?"

"I think I did," he said. "And incidentally, you didn't pick me up. I'm picking you up."

"In that case, you can buy me another vodka on the rocks."

He caught the bartender's discreetly inattentive eye. "My sister will have another. I'm fine."

"Louise Campbell," she said.

"Missus?"

"Mizz."

"Hi ya, Lou."

"Hal."

"Are you making this crossing by your lonesome?"

He thought he saw her flinch slightly. She looked down into her empty glass and said, "Yes."

"And we don't like that very much, do we?"

She closed her eyes and shook her head. "Unh-uh."

"We going to do anything about it?"

She gave him a quick glance. "That's up to you."

He stared at her mouth. "You couldn't be in more loving hands."

Her drink arrived and she seized it quickly and took a large gulp, gasping a little when she came up for air.

He took her hand in his and felt marvelous tingling circuits closing between them. "Where you from, honey, Dallas or Fort Worth?"

"Houston," she said. "That obvious, huh?"

"Charming. I love it. Have you read any of my books?"

"No, but I know all about you." She gave his hand a little squeeze. "You're really wicked."

"And I can prove it. That is, if you'll let me."

She intertwined her fingers in his and stayed with her drink until she had almost finished it.

"Will you let me?" he asked.

She looked into his eyes and brought his hand to her mouth and bit him gently and then licked his palm.

"Christ, don't," he groaned.

"Why not?" she smiled, and did it again.

"That kills me," he sighed.

"I'd like to," she said.

"Here?"

"Not exactly," she said.

He looked at her and felt the sweet ache in his balls. "Are you for real, baby?"

"I don't know," she said, meeting his gaze. "Suppose we find out."

He poured the rest of his drink into himself and got to his feet and leaned over her, putting a hand on her thigh and the other on the bare back of her midriff, and he loved the way she turned her head and tilted it up to take his opening mouth with hers, and then he grew so dizzy with gin and lust and the damp musky smell of her that he couldn't stand it any longer, and he murmured into her open mouth, "Oh baby, you're too much, I can't stand it."

And her tongue caressed his and she murmured, "You better lie down then."

And he said, "Not without you," and then he felt a key being pressed into his hand.

"Give me five minutes," she whispered, breaking the kiss. She slid off the stool and walked away, leaving him standing there flushed and swollen with excitement, holding on to the bar to steady himself, his eyes going to the bartender who was watching him.

"Hey, do something about this glass, will ya? It's too goddamn empty."

Oh Jesus, this was going to be beautiful . . .

While two decks below, her heart racing with fear and anticipation, she waited for the steward to unlock her cabin door. "My husband is expecting a visitor and doesn't want to be disturbed tonight for any reason."

"Very well, Mrs. Campbell, but if the night maid—"

"For any reason," she said.

"I understand, madame."

You understand nothing, you French faggot. She went inside and shut the door in his face and then she stepped to the porthole and pulled the blinds closed before going over to the dreaded desk. You would never understand why the clothes of my husband that hang in the closet will never be worn again, or why I take this gun out of the drawer, or why there is a wetness between my legs that even I do not understand.

She grasped the cold steel in her moist hand and looked down at the silencer, feeling herself going off balance, not with the roll of the ship so much as with the giddiness of the vodka that was stealing into her brain in a most surprising and delicious way. And when she fell back onto the bed, she didn't move, but decided to stay there instead, yes, lie there, her beautiful legs—God, so gorgeous and tan—beautiful legs sprawled out invitingly, and then she decided to shove the gun under the pillow where she could easily reach it with her right hand. And in making those decisions, which made no sense really because she had planned to execute him from a standing position the moment he entered, she understood the wetness now and knew that she was going to allow herself to go part of the way with it and enjoy it, yes, take it, throbbing in her hands, and put it inside of her yearning hunger and enjoy it to the very edge of exquisite agony, no farther, just to the edge, before reaching behind her and, yes, she had a *right* to enjoy it, she had a right to anything that would make her forget the grief and horror, they would understand and be happy for her, they would want that for her because she wanted it for herself, oh God, how she wanted it, needed it, God, *deserved* it, she was earning it and she'd have it, she'd have it and then she'd kill it, she wanted to have him and then kill him, that's what she wanted, to *have* him, right now, she wanted him, right now, the hairy stranger, right now, her hand fumbling with the buttons of her shorts, stealing to the naked mound between her spreading thighs and caressing it lovingly, mouth opening, eyes closing, tongue flicking out to find him, to find anyone in the emptiness above her as she lay there slowly moving with herself and moaning, fuck me, darling, oh husband darling, fuck me, fuck me . . . until the creaking of the ship and the distant slap of waves against steel became the sound of a key in the lock and the door opening and closing, and she withdrew her hand and rested its fragrance on the pillow beside her, leaving her buttons open so that he could see her glistening hairs when he peered through the mysterious gloom of the darkened cabin and saw her lying on the bed.

"Oh, that I like," he said thickly, moving toward her.

She held out her hand to him, and he came slowly to the side of the bed, his heavy-lidded eyes fixed on the silken down below her midriff. "Hello, honey," she whispered to him and shuddered with delight as she felt his hand gently grasp her there and his fingers go inside of her and then he bent over her and took her waiting, open mouth with his.

"Oh baby," he murmured into her, stroking and exploring her deeper and deeper.

"Ah, yes, Harold, yes, oh, yes," opening herself wider to him.

He removed his mouth with a wet sucking sound, and she mourned the loss of his hand for a moment, and then both of his hands were peeling her shorts away from her arching bottom and down along her yielding thighs, and she raised first one leg and then the other until he had her naked save for the shirt she was wearing and the shoes that he was removing now and tonguing the soles of her captured feet, her ankles tight in his grasp.

"Oh, lover," she sighed, and closed her eyes and allowed him to kiss the insides of her bronzed and naked thighs as he spread her legs wide and up over his shoulders and went down to his knees on the bed and his mouth engulfed her vulva and his teeth held the lips gently for his probing, thrusting tongue, and she reached down and pressed his head to her as if she would take him, all of him, inside of her, and then she pulled his head back and away, gasping, "Harold, I want to see you, please, I want to look at you," and she watched him with lascivious eyes as he straightened up and backed out from between her legs and came around the side of the bed, tossing his shirt aside and standing naked and hairy above the waist, beautiful black-hairy male, close enough to her so that she could smell the sweat of his body as she grasped his belt and pulled herself up and around to a sitting position, head swimming, her bare legs and thighs on either side of him, and she began to kiss his warm naked belly while she opened his bulging trousers and waited for a moment as he leaned down to pull them off and get rid of his socks and shoes, and she was waiting, she had a right to this, they would understand, she was waiting for it, her hands were waiting when he straightened up, oh lovely cock, so that her palms on the smooth hard roundness of his ass with the gentlest of pressure could bring his upthrusting pulsating erection into her hungry mouth, and she heard his gasping sigh, "Oh, beautiful, baby, beautiful," as she began to feast with infinite pleasure on his sweet-tasting maleness and fondled the hairy velvet sac and felt his uncontrollable hands wandering over her head and shoulders. "Ah, beautiful . . . beautiful . . ."

They would understand and forgive her, yes, they would understand that it was perfectly right for her to be licking her own saliva from the quivering tip of this male-smelling stranger, and sliding her encircling lips slowly back and forth around the swollen throbbing shaft that was beginning to move with a rhythm of its own in the grasping, sucking wetness of her mouth. It was perfectly right that she should be doing this, because she deserved it and needed it and loved it, oh God, how she loved it, God, how she loved it, and what difference did it make that he was moaning with the same heavenly agonies as she, it only heightened her excitement, it only made more unbearably beautiful this reward she was giving herself for doing their bidding, for blowing his body apart and ripping the life out of him after it was over. And this renewed conviction, this wonderful certainty of the utter rightness of what she was doing to him now, and wanted him to do to her, sanctified her lust and set free every animal hunger that was in her in a way she had never known in all her years, not with any of them, not even with her husband, God forgive her, not even with him . . .

And she felt the convulsive hands rubbing and pressing on her head, and heard his voice groaning with pleasure. "Oh God, your mouth, your beautiful mouth, oh baby, your mouth," and he pulled back carefully and slipped out of her lips and away from her following tongue, and reached down and lifted her gently to her feet facing him and put his hands on her ass and, crouching, brought her tight against him with his cock between her legs, and then he put his mouth on hers and she placed her hands on the back of his head and they began to kiss each other slowly and deeply, their tongues loving each other with sinuous passion, their saliva intermingling so that she could taste her own cunt in his mouth and he taste his cock in hers. And when the hardening nipples of her swelling breasts brought her hands down from his head to grope with the knotted shirttail at her midriff, he relinquished her mouth and whispered, "Let me, baby, please," and she whispered, "Yes, lover, yes," and watched him work the knot open while she held his throbbing phallus in her hand and rubbed the purpling tip against the wet yearning lips of her vulva, whispering over and over, "I love your cock, Harold, oh God, how I love your cock," until he was slipping the shirt off her trembling shoulders and throwing it aside and falling to his knees and fastening his mouth on her breasts so freshly exposed, tongue licking her nipples, lips sucking, devouring, moaning with delight, his hand stealing between her legs and taking possession of her swollen clitoris, stiff and erect, and she threw her head back, eyes closed, mouth open, wide-spreading crotch undulating slowly against the divine intervention of his knowing fingers, hands clutching his slow-moving wet-tongued head, and she moaned, "Yes . . . oh yes . . . oh God . . . oh honey . . . beautiful Harold . . . oh God . . . oh baby . . . oh God, I think I want to fuck you now . . . oh God oh Harold oh God, I want to fuck you now . . . baby oh please oh yes, I want to fuck you now . . . yes oh yes oh God, I want to fuck you now . . ."

Feeling him rising and enveloping her in his powerful embrace and his tongue coming into her open mouth and his hands wandering over her silken ass and his cock slowly thrusting in her grasping palms and the smell of his sex on his breath as he groaned, "Oh baby, I'm going to fuck you now, is it all right if I fuck you now, darling Louise, I'm going to put my cock inside of you and fuck you now . . ." And she cried, "Yes, honey, yes," and fell back slowly down onto the bed and opened her arms and her thighs and her cunt so that he might come to her and fill the throbbing emptiness of her womb with his pulsating organ, all hot and alive, not cold and lifeless like the metal she felt now underneath the pillow, and brought her hand away from it quickly to receive him above her, his knees between the welcoming spread of her thighs, his elbows resting beside her pointing breasts, his hands cradling the back of her head, and the velvet tip of his cock entering ever so gently and pausing within the lips that would draw him into the warm and loving moistness of her vagina, as his eyes looked down into hers, heavy with desire, and she gazed up into his eyes and met his desire with her own, and it was more than either of them could bear and so they brought their mouths together and began slowly and rhythmically to suck on each other and break apart and moan meaningless sounds of passion, and join tongues again and suck each other and break apart and moan and fasten lips and suck on each other again and again, while her legs slowly folded over his hairy thighs and her hands on the back of his buttocks drew his prick further up inside of her loving clasp, and they kissed each other and sucked each other until she felt the quivering tip of him all the way up as far as it would go, and then she locked her legs around him, murmuring, "Honey, oh honey, oh God," and he looked deeply into her eyes and murmured, "Warm . . . wet . . . soft . . . beautiful cunt, I'm going to fuck you now," and she breathed, "Yes . . . oh yes, fuck me," and knew in her swoon that there was something she should remember, and then she felt him begin to move inside of her with slow and purposeful insistence, thrusting and withdrawing, bathing himself in her fragrant honey, rooting and searching and gliding inside of her, filling her womb with a savage and insatiable hunger for more of him, more of him, meeting him, taking him, holding him, clasping him, wanting him deeper and deeper and deeper, moving her hips in a soft rolling circle to his slow demanding rhythm and his devouring tongue and the unbearable caresses of his roaming hand. "Oh wonderful cock, oh fuck me, you beautiful cock . . . oh Jesus, oh God, I'm dying, you beautiful cock . . ." And the answering groan in her ears, "Oh baby . . . oh baby . . . I'm going to shoot into your beautiful cunt . . ."

"Oh yes, honey, shoot into me, fuck me and shoot into me . . ." And hearing the words, she remembered suddenly, and her hand left his back and writhed into the air, clutching convulsively at the darkness above them as though it would escape its owner and save her as she plunged closer and closer to the edge of ecstasy, and somewhere deep down in the thrilling delirium of her soul she knew that she was trying to stop, to back away, to stop, but her brain was fainting and swooning with voluptuous joy and her voice was crying, oh fuck me, oh fuck me, oh yes honey, fuck me, and her body was answering the hard-driving thrusts of his quickening rhythm and it was heaven, oh God, it was heaven, and the independent hand searching under the pillow was finding and seizing the cold hardness of steel before it was too late, yes, hurry before it was too late, and coming out with it in her grasp, and his frenzied torso was thrusting deeply into her soul and her liquid womb was preparing to expire with unbearable rapture that must be stopped, must be stopped . . . Oh God, I think I'm, hurry, oh God, finding the hole between the driving cheeks above his swollen sac . . . Hurry, oh God, oh hurry because she had no right to this, it was too, oh God . . . working it in past the yielding sphincter . . . it was too beautiful, oh you cock, fuck me . . . "Jesus, that's so cold, what the hell are you—?" No right to enjoy this, she didn't deserve this, oh God, I think I'm going to oh God I'm oh hurry they'd never forgive her oh God, I think I'm going to come, I didn't mean, oh God, I never meant, oh God, I'm going to come, oh heaven, oh beauty, they'd never understand never forgive, do it to him before you GOD, I'M GOING TO COME . . .

And he was groaning, "Oh Jesus . . . oh Jesus . . . oh baby . . ." and his body was shuddering in its final great thrust and his ass was clamping down tightly on the cold hardness inside of him, and he cried out, "Oh Jesus, I'm oh baby, what are you *doing* to me oh God here I OH CHRIST I'm going to shoot now oh what are you OH CHRIST I'M COMING," reaching back behind him as his brain exploded and his cock burst open and his semen began to spurt into her as he gasped, "Oh . . . oh . . . oh . . ." And her fingers groping for the trigger and the swooning brain that was trying to save her from herself could do nothing to help her now because his hand was already upon hers and making its discovery and ripping the alien thing from his body, and his uncontrollable cock was pouring his juice into her and her own moment of ecstasy was already upon her, flooding her whole being with such irresistible waves of indescribable pleasure that nothing on earth could have prevented her from giving herself over to them and convulsively embracing the beautiful sweating maleness that was transporting her to heaven with his liquid spasms even as his back-reaching hand was tossing the cold steel prick to the floor with a thud, and she couldn't care about anything now but this soaring wonder inside of her soul as she grasped him tightly in her powerful thighs and squeezed his juice into the mouth of her clasping womb, crying, "Oh my God . . . oh my God . . . oh my God . . . oh my God," and hearing his own groans of ecstasy as he shuddered and throbbed inside of her, spending, spurting, shooting inside of her, and when finally their rapturous outcries died away and became sighing gasps of exhaustion, and their hot wet bodies grew limp in each other's arms, she felt him slowly pulling out of her, and his body rolling off hers onto his back, and then she turned her head to him and kissed his breast, smelling the perfume of her sex upon him, and she sighed, "Oh God, that was so beautiful . . ."

And then, after a long and foreboding silence, she heard his voice mutter in the darkness, "All right, just what the hell is going on around here?"

But she felt so much at peace, so filled with contentment, that she did not want to say anything right then, she just wanted to lie there in heavenly bliss, and it did not even matter that she knew with every fiber of her being that it was time for her to die.

"If I wasn't so goddamn drunk," he was saying, "I would've known you were one of them. You were too goddamn easy . . ."

She rested her head on his shoulder and felt the tears coming to her eyes, and from the distance outside, she heard the angry crashing of the sea against the unyielding plates of the doomed ship.

"One thing I'll say for you," he said, "you're the best piece of tail I've had in the past twenty minutes . . ."

"Please don't," she pleaded softly, letting her tears stain his matted chest.

"You know what you can do with that gun, don't you, you can shove it up my ass . . ."

"Please . . ." she cried.

He pushed her face away from him, and his voice was filled with resentment. "Are you going to start telling me about it now, or am I going to have to fuck you again just to get you to open your mouth?"

She lay there beside him, weeping softly, mourning the irrevocable loss of herself.

"If they ask you what happened," he said, "tell them you suck a pretty good cock but you're from nowhere when it comes to a ream job."

Oh help me, someone help me . . .

"I mean, I don't mind them wanting to kill me, hell, they're not the only ones, I got ex-wives, and we all gotta die sometime, but what I don't like, I don't like being made a fool of. You want to be a star-fucker, you gotta learn not to fuck around with the stars, baby . . ."

"Stop it," she cried in anguish and, rising, tried to drive her clenched fist into his hurtful mouth, but his hands were too quick for her and captured her wrists and pushed her back down, and then he was forcing her over onto her belly and coming down heavily on top of her, and she felt his flaccid organ hardening against her buttocks and his hands parting her cheeks and his bitter, wounded voice in her ear saying, "I mean, how would you like it if I did the same thing to you?"

Afterward, after he had left her cabin, taking the gun with him, she lay there until her tears had dried and the terrible ache in her flesh had subsided, grateful that his harsh, insistent questioning had drawn from her nothing that he did not already know. It was the least she could have done for those she had failed.

She got off the bed, drained of all feeling now, and found her shorts and her shirt and her shoes and put them on, even though her body stank of his sweat and her own, and the hair of her crotch, matted with his fluids. She would cleanse herself . . . But first a scribbled note to Craig, to leave on the pillow.

Outside on deck, everywhere she looked, she saw passengers chatting and laughing with each other as they took their last lurching walk before dinner, oblivious to the heaving seas around them, acting just as though they would live forever. She walked through them and past them, paying them no mind, and if they noticed her at all, they did not remember it afterward when word spread among them about what she had done.

She walked toward the rail at the open stern, no longer caring whether the others would understand and forgive her. There was nothing they could ever do that would help her to forgive herself. She had failed them, and she had soiled herself, that was all there was to it. She had soiled herself deeply.

And she was terribly lonely.

She rose up on the rail, her lithe slender body poised for one last moment in an attitude of exquisite grace as she said goodbye to herself and to the world, and then, with a great soaring leap, she gave herself to the angry cleansing waters and plunged into the icy killing depths, and at the last instant, just before her lungs finally burst, she knew with great joy that she would never feel sorrow ever again.

CHAPTER TWENTY-NINE

LLOYD SHIPLEY, sweating profusely, watched the president of the Remo Corporation listening to Brian Joy, and did not like what he saw. Terrence Dunlop was shifting uneasily in his desk chair, looking alternately from his public relations director to the television man with equal annoyance at both. Shipley had seen that same look on Dunlop's face before and had never liked it, the last time only a few weeks ago when Senator Burch, bored with Disneyland, had dropped in to inform Dunlop that Armed Services was thinking of chopping Remo to twenty million in the next budget.

Brian Joy was pressing on to the end of his lurid recital of the plight of the *Marseille,* shifting his gaze slightly to the right of and past Dunlop's left shoulder, looking off at the distant waves of Malibu rather than into the man's eyes as he eased into the more difficult part, the outrageous plea for all-out assistance. Dunlop listened impatiently, fussing with his horn-rimmed glasses and the empty pipe in his mouth, feeling the conviction stealing over him that he was doomed to smoking his first cigarette in four weeks, maybe a whole goddamned pack, before this day was over. Anger at this impending degradation finally overcame him.

"Excuse me, Mr. Joy," he interrupted, and turned his steely blue eyes on his corpulent public relations man. "Lloyd, can I ask you a simple question?"

Shipley nodded. "Please do, sir." A former newspaperman, now fifty-five and constantly awash in straight bourbon, he no longer cared much about anything but a continuity of paychecks. But he did feel for Brian, a nice sort of schlump, always had been.

"Why have you brought Mr. Joy here to see *me?*" his superior was saying. "I mean, why me? You have cronies in the Federal Bureau of Investigation, you play poker with everyone in the District Attorney's office, and you go skeet-shooting with the Chief of Detectives of the Los Angeles Police Department. Why not them? Why me?"

Brian Joy quickly rose to his feet saying, "I'd like to answer that if I may." Lloyd Shipley shrugged be-my-guest. "I can't go to the FBI with this, Mr. Dunlop. I can't go to *any* of the authorities. In fact, nothing I've told you can leave this building. I sort of hoped you *realized* that total secrecy is the condition that prevails."

The Remo director removed the pipe from his mouth. "Mr. Joy, I don't mean to sound cold or callous or indifferent to the danger to all those innocent people, but I do think we have to be a little more realistic here . . ."

Lloyd Shipley looked away. He knew what was coming.

"I'm answerable to the board of directors, and I cannot ever allow myself to forget that. Remo's *raison d'être* is strictly research and development, and only in those fields affecting national interest and U.S. strategic policy. We are not, never have been, and never will be actively involved in crime prevention, crime detection, or anything else pertaining to law enforcement. There is no way on earth, I regret to say this, no way Remo can violate its charter or its purposes by sticking its nose into your unfortunate situation. I'm sorry, but I hope you can understand my viewpoint."

"Well, *I'm* sorry too, because frankly *no,* I *can't.*" Brian Joy found his voice growing hoarse with anger, or weariness, he wasn't sure which. "I'm not asking Remo to stick its neck out or its nose into anything. I'm not even asking you, as president of this organization, to reply to me as president. I'm asking this of you, man to man—"

"The answer is still—"

"—The Captain of the *Marseille has* to know which of his two thousand passengers are conspirators. The Chief Medical Officer of the ship *has* to be advised how to liquidate this group. They've got to know this by twelve noon tomorrow at the very latest. And I can't think of anyone, any organization, more logical to turn to, considering the need for secrecy and instantaneous problem-solving. I can't think of any single complex of buildings in the *country* that has a greater collection of diversified brain power within its walls, not to say the most sophisticated and far-reaching memory banks and computers on earth, than Remo . . ."

"That may be true, Mr. Joy, but—"

"All I want you to do, Mr. Dunlop, is give Lloyd Shipley and me permission to try to round up, strictly on an unofficial basis, a dozen or so of the best people who happen to be on the premises today. We'll set them up as a brainstorming group. We'll ask them to do it as non-Remo, private citizens, on a personal, voluntary basis. I'll give them whatever data I have. I'll give them this passenger information list. And they can spend the rest of the day and night right here on the premises with their brains and your computers. The outside world won't even know what's going on here—"

"Lloyd, maybe you can explain . . ."

"You can't say no," Brian Joy cried. "You can't."

The buzzer sounded on Terrence Dunlop's desk. He picked up the telephone with an alacrity that suggested he welcomed the interruption. "Yes?"

"I have a call here for Mr. Brian Joy from Mrs. Joy," his secretary said. "I wouldn't have interrupted, but she indicated it was urgent."

"All right, put her on." He looked up at Brian Joy. "It's your wife calling."

"My wife?"

"Would you like to take it in private?"

Brian Joy stared at the phone for a moment. "No, that's all right." He took the receiver from the man. "Yes, Maggie?"

"Can you talk?"

"Yes. Go ahead," he said.

"She called again from Paris, while you were in transit."

"Lisa?"

"How about Miss Briande?"

"I thought you were going to shift the calls to here." What the hell was he getting angry about?

"She couldn't wait for you to get there," Maggie said evenly. "She said she had to go off and find someone named Raffin . . . the Sûreté? She said you'd know."

He glanced at the watching eyes of the other two men in the office and said to Maggie, "So what's up?"

"Do you have the passenger list there?"

"Yes. Why?"

"I have some names for you to cross off. They're either passengers or crew."

"I see." He didn't like the sound of it. He moved the PIL sheets closer to him on the desk. "Go ahead."

"Mr. and Mrs. G. Parker," Maggie said.

He found their names and crossed them out. "Okay."

"H. Grabiner. That's G-R-A-B."

"Okay."

"D. Campbell."

"All right."

"F. Mandrati."

"Wait a minute. Must be crew."

"B. Crepin. C-R-E-P-I-N."

"Crew."

"E. Senestro."

"Also crew."

"That's it. Those are the seven," Maggie said.

"Why am I crossing them out?" he asked, not wanting to hear her reply.

"Because they're dead," she said. "Executed, as a warning."

He closed his eyes. "Christ."

"Brian, are you all right?"

"Yes," he said.

"Neither am I," she said. "Call me when you can."

"Stay there," he said, and hung up. Dunlop and Shipley stared at him, waiting. He tossed the PIL sheets back on the desk and ran a hand over his eyes. He didn't feel like saying anything, but he knew he had to. "Look, Mr. Dunlop, I really don't want to lay this on you but . . . my wife just got the news from my contact in

Paris. They've murdered four passengers and three of the crew, as a warning."

"Son of a bitch," Lloyd Shipley muttered under his breath.

Terrence Dunlop rose slowly to his feet. His face was pale, and his lips were compressed in a tight, thin line. He looked wordlessly at Brian Joy, then at Lloyd Shipley, who averted his eyes. The president turned and went to the window and stared out. The only sounds in the room were the low hiss of air conditioning and the distant hum of traffic on the Pacific Coast Highway. When Dunlop spoke finally, he kept his back to the other two men.

"I'm going to leave now, Lloyd," he said in a strained voice. "I'll be at the center in Santa Barbara if you need me. But I don't think you'll need me. It will look better afterward if it turns out that I wasn't here while you and Mr. Joy were instigating unauthorized use of our facilities."

"I understand, sir," said Lloyd Shipley quietly.

"Mr. Dunlop, I don't know how to thank you enough," Brian Joy said to the man's back.

Dunlop wheeled around, and his face was flushed. "Don't thank me, Mr. Joy. Do you think I would permit this if I could figure out a way to say no and still live with myself?" Without waiting for a response, he went quickly to the door and walked out.

Brian Joy turned to Lloyd Shipley. "I'm a hell of a friend. This could cost you your job, couldn't it?"

The public relations man looked at him and frowned. "Don't bother me with trifles, will you?"

The Chinese-red elevator doors slid open and Julian Wunderlicht stepped out into the lobby of the Hotel Prince de Galles. A brief inspection of the area convinced him that his colleagues were nowhere about. They had gone ahead to the restaurant without him, thank God. They would be into their food when he joined them, their mouths full, as usual. There would be less need or time to listen to their vulgar conversation. As he crossed the lobby to the newsstand, he wondered whether they had become aware of how bored he had become with them. He preferred to think of it as boredom. He could not wholly confront the truth that it was their blatant Germanism that repelled him and made him ashamed to have been one of them once upon a time.

The front pages of the evening newspapers, he was pleased to note, contained no stories that included the words "S.S. *Marseille.*" Dechambre and Sauvinage were apparently behaving themselves.

On the sidewalk before the hotel entrance, he paused for a moment to breathe deeply of the cool night air. The nap had definitely helped him. His crotch no longer itched, and the exhaustion of a day of prowling the museums and walking the lovely streets of Paris was gone. He glanced with automatic interest at the luscious bottom of the girl with the vaguely familiar figure who had just come out of the hotel and was now moving away from him. Then he looked across the street at the restaurant Au Vieux Berlin and felt an almost sexual hunger at the thought of the native dishes that awaited him there.

The hotel doorman said, "Taxi, m'sieur?" and Julian Wunderlicht replied, "No, thank you. I'll walk," smiling to himself, pleased with his own humor as he stepped off the curb and waited for the flow of traffic to subside. It wasn't until he was halfway across the avenue that he remembered who the girl was, and it didn't bother him at all.

Yvette Goutay had arrived at the Mercedes Benz parked beneath the trees, and leaned into the open front window.

"That's him," she said to Jean-Claude Raffin, pointing.

The head of the Sûreté Nationale peered through the windshield and saw Wunderlicht cross the far sidewalk and enter the restaurant.

"Are you certain?" he asked the whore.

"It's only between your legs that you men all look alike to me," she said. "The faces are something else again, especially that pig's."

Raffin peeled off two 100-franc notes and thrust them through the open window. "Give your back a rest tonight. Go to a flick."

Yvette Goutay uttered an obscenity, snatched the money from his hand, and walked away. Within a block of the Champs-Élysées, she had a Belgian with watery eyes and a bulging crotch sniffing around her.

Gritzen's hairless pink dome glistened with sweat, and Freuling's thick lips never stopped moving as the two men tore at their *Matjesfilet Hausfrauenart* with a silent, ravenous greed that positively disgusted Wunderlicht. He looked away from them, allowing his gaze to wander over the dimly lit dining room with its dark leather banquettes and flowered, upholstered chairs tucked under the still empty tables. It was a little early for the smart crowd, the supper crowd. Within a half hour, he was sure, the room would be filling up with them. And no doubt that some of them would be members of the gendarmerie, come to look him over.

An awareness of his own power and invulnerability surged through his body and made him giddy. Let them come, he thought. That was the beauty of this game, to know that their coming, their taking him into custody, their interrogation of him would lead them nowhere except to the realization that there was nothing they could do. He was untouchable. And those two fools at Françat would be made to squirm for whatever they had done to put the little cunt on his trail tonight. Wunderlicht did not believe in coincidences.

He looked up idly at the waiter who had arrived at the table with the *Berliner Erbsensuppe,* and he addressed him in French.

"You are not the same waiter who took my order, no?"

"That is correct, m'sieur," the man replied.

"The chef, Henry Bamberg, is a dear friend of mine. Would you please tell Herr Bamberg that Willy Fields of Leipzig says hello?"

"I will do that, m'sieur. Certainly. The plate is very hot. Please be careful."

"Thank you," Julian Wunderlicht said, and watched him return to the kitchen.

The whore must have worked fast. Already they had someone in here posing as a waiter. If they hadn't been in such a hurry, the man might have taken the trouble to learn the name of the chef.

Wunderlicht took a sip of the steaming *Erbsensuppe* and placed his spoon down. "Listen to me, chums," he said in German to Freuling and Gritzen. The men grunted without looking up from the mounds of herring on their plates. "There will be a slight change in our plans for tonight." He paused until they finally glanced up at him, their full mouths still masticating. "You will put your forks down, both of you, wipe the sour cream from your lips, get up from the table and walk out of here as unobtrusively as possible . . ."

"But what about my supper?" demanded Klaus Freuling. "We only just—"

"You will go to the Lido on the Champs-Élysées," Wunderlicht continued, softly but firmly. "Anyone can tell you how to find it. The most beautiful girls in all of Europe. Bare breasts and naked legs up to here. That should take care of your appetites." He shoved five hundred francs across the table at the men. "Stay there until one o'clock, then return to the hotel. Not before."

Freuling's florid face broke into an uncertain grin as he took the money. Wilhelm Gritzen scowled across the table.

"What the hell is going on here?"

"Ask me your questions at one o'clock," Wunderlicht snapped. The two men rose to their feet and glanced at each other.

"Get moving or you'll miss the show," Wunderlicht said. "And keep your hands off your cocks. We wouldn't want you getting picked up by the police for indecent exposure, would we?"

Freuling chuckled. The other man followed him out to the street, still scowling.

Wunderlicht picked up his spoon and turned his attention to his *Erbsensuppe,* telling himself that he had had a perfectly legitimate excuse to be rid of their company. True, they knew nothing of importance yet, not even where they were to fly the plane, should they ever be taken into custody and tortured. Actually, it was that he preferred to be alone when he finally met up with his adversaries. He had no wish to share his impending glory with those two louts.

In quiet comfort now, and at his own leisure, he would follow the soup with some delightful *Rheinischer Sauerbraten,* follow that with a platter of *Gemischter Viäseteller,* and top it all off with an orgiastic *Eisbecher Viroahbeere,* and who knew, maybe even a cognac with his cigar. After that, he would stroll out onto the Avenue George V and walk, belching, into their waiting arms.

Aristide Bonnard reached across the supine body of his wife, Althea, and brought the ringing telephone into bed. He knew the call would have some measure of significance, because nothing insignificant ever reached him on this most private of private lines. It was the Director General of the Sûreté Nationale, wanting him to be the first to know that the man called Julian Wunderlicht had been picked up, and was about to be questioned, in the strictest secrecy, in the basement of Police Judiciaire Headquarters on the Quai des Orfèvres. The President thanked Raffin profusely, and returned the telephone to the bedside table. His elation at the news was tempered somewhat by the fact that, in the process of receiving it, he had unaccountably lost his erection.

Why was it, he wondered, as he lay back on the damp sheets again, that so few people realized that heads of state went to the toilet just like everyone else did, and even made love to their wives sometimes a few hours after dinner?

They were dressed as ship's officers, and they held their arms stiffly to conceal the bulk of the sawed-off weapons hidden beneath the jackets of their uniforms. Entering the card room of Tourist, they put on their most benign expressions, came to a stop and glanced about. The tables were all occupied. Husbands and wives, mostly in their forties and fifties, fresh from the first dinner sitting. You could tell the bridge players by their silence, the poker players by their taunting chatter as they tossed their chips into the pot. Amateurs, obviously.

Lou Foyles and Wendell Cronin looked them over for a moment or two, feeling comfortably clean of anxiety or trepidation. They had shared a joint of Acapulco Gold just before coming down, and that had put the icing on the cake. Not that they had really needed anything. This would be just like the good old days, like spilling gook blood in the rice paddies of Hon Quan. The group would never have selected them with such unanimity if both men hadn't long ago established their reputation for being unfailingly strong of stomach.

It was during that meeting that Craig Dunleavy had, for the very first time, seen the possibility that he and Kleinfeld could some day conceivably lose control of the entire group to the domination of the Hot Heads, so violent had the group's reactions been when he had read aloud Louise Campbell's farewell. He had been certain they'd want Columbine's head before anything, gun in his possession notwithstanding. But Dunleavy had underestimated their rage and their thirst for a larger vengeance. So had Kleinfeld. Both men had sensed simultaneously, with only an exchanged glance between them, that it would be prudent to step back and let the group have its way, whatever the larger dangers. And so they had allowed them to vote for the more drastic punishment.

"Ladies and gentlemen, excuse me for the interruption, please." Lou Foyles laid a heavy French accent on his Southern drawl. "May I have your attention for a moment?"

His voice was loud, but most of the card players were too absorbed in their games to become aware of him. He raised his voice almost to a shout. "Ladies and gentlemen . . . if you will . . . *please* . . ."

Heads finally turned. The card room fell silent. There was only the sound of a fat woman muttering, "Hey, I've got a straight here."

Foyles stepped forward, smiling. "First Officer Bergeron and I have been asked by the Captain to carry out a little project for him tonight, somewhat like a survey, and the results will be featured in the ship's newspaper. With your cooperation, we will try to make this interruption as brief as possible. Will that be all right with you?"

No one said anything, until a man named Milton Tempkin, who was certain he was holding four no-trump in his hand, called out, "Go ahead. Get it over with."

"Thank you," Lou Foyles said. "Now, first of all, how many of you nice people are husbands and wives, married to each other? May I have a show of hands please, and please keep them raised."

The two men in uniform counted forty-eight.

"All right, now of this group, which of you are traveling without, I repeat, without children?"

The count went down to thirty.

"And how many of you have no children back home, or elsewhere? In fact, no children?"

More hands were lowered.

"All right," Lou Foyles said. "You eighteen good people, would you be kind enough to write your names down on a slip of paper. Anything will do. And First Officer Bergeron will take them from you. The rest of you please continue with what you were doing, and may you all be winners."

The room began to buzz again. Wendell Cronin moved among the eighteen who were childless, took the slips of paper that were handed to him, leaning over and quietly saying to each of them that, as soon as they finished the hand they were playing, he and his fellow officer would be needing them for about five minutes of picture-taking elsewhere.

Claire Rogers, a trim little woman of forty wearing large attractive eyeglasses, protested with a sour smile. "I'm on a hot streak, mister. I bet this'll change my luck."

"For the better, madame." Wendell Cronin smiled.

Stanford Whitman, an attorney from Evanston, Illinois, did not try to conceal his irritation. "Do you mind telling us what the hell this is all about?"

"Oh, stop it, dear," his wife said.

"After the pictures are taken, sir," Cronin replied, most pleasantly. "Right now it would spoil the effectiveness of what we're trying to do."

He walked over to Lou Foyles and handed the big man in the gold-braided uniform the slips with the names, muttering under his breath, "Pain in the ass . . ."

Foyles consulted the pieces of paper and called out, "Just as soon as you're available, would the following please join us here? Mr. and Mrs. Rogers, Clayworth, Whitman, Sneed, Holdorf, Tempkin, Lockhart, Rice, and Willow. Thank you."

When they finally had them all together, they divided them into two groups of five couples and four couples, and took them by separate elevators three decks below, and then led them, chattering and bantering about the inconvenience and mystery of it all, to the garbage disposal area at the stern. Two crewmen in sweaty T-shirts were hurling refuse into the thundering sea through the huge opening just above water level. Foyles left the passengers with Cronin and went over to the crewmen, very close to them so that they could hear him above the sound of the rushing waters beyond them.

"Beat it," he said in French. "Get lost, both of you."

One of the men looked at him with disbelief. "What?"

"You heard me," said Foyles. "Out of sight, or I'll blow your heads off."

The two crewmen looked at him for a moment, then set their pails down and hurried away.

Foyles returned to Cronin and the passengers, who stood in awkward silence, waiting to be told what to do. Foyles said to them, "All right, for the first picture, I want you all to stand over there near that opening, but not too close to the edge now, facing me. First Officer Bergeron will arrange you. Okay?"

The passengers looked puzzled. They moved uncertainly to the opening.

"My God, it's cold here," Margot Whitman said.

"I know," Foyles said.

"This whole thing is ridiculous," said Claire Rogers's husband, Gary.

The others shrugged, or grinned foolishly. The experience was totally alien to any they had ever had, and they were left without familiar reactions to bring into play. They felt like children.

"Wives in front," Wendell Cronin directed them. "Husbands stand behind your wives, and put your arms around their waists, gentlemen."

The passengers jostled each other, getting into place, some of them laughing to cover their embarrassment.

Tom Rice grabbed his wife and leered comically. "This could lead to something big."

Maxine Willow frowned. "I don't see any camera. Where's the camera?"

"That's very good," Lou Foyles said. "Stay like that." He and Cronin backed up about four yards.

Larry and Maxine Willow were on the extreme left. Tom and Adele Rice were next to them. Next were Edgar and Sue Ann Lockhart. Then came the Tempkins, the Sneeds, Frank and Millie Holdorf, Gary and Claire Rogers, and Ned and Myra Clayworth. Stanford and Margot Whitman were on the extreme right.

They were given practically no time to react. So swiftly did Lou Foyles and Wendell Cronin open their jackets and bring out their engines of death that the fading smiles and the disbelief had little time to change to fear and horror. Only a few outcries managed to escape . . . "Wait a minute . . . What is this? . . . My God, don't . . . Oh please . . . *Don't*—" before the machine guns chattered and hissed and spit out their leaden agony, the women's hands caught on the way up and out as if to hold back the hail of bullets from their faces, the men torn apart as they instinctively tried to shield themselves with the crumpling, dying bodies in their arms.

It was over very quickly.

The two men in officer's uniforms stepped up to the tangled, bloody, sprawling heap and pushed the victims, one by one, using their rifle butts and their feet, over the edge and into the churning wake of the great ship. Then they looked about for a mop or a hose to clean up the blood and the waste matter on the deck, but they soon abandoned the idea and departed.

Much later that night, both of them would have to drink themselves into a state of insensibility to wipe out the bad feelings that came over them when they started to obsess on the fact that several of the bodies had still been twitching when they kicked them into the sea. They had thought, at the time, what difference would it make? But that had been a mistake. They should have shot them all in the head, and saved themselves a bad night and a terrible hangover the next morning.

CHAPTER THIRTY

———————

OH GOD IN HEAVEN, if anyone heard him this way or saw him now, the Commandant of the great *Marseille,* a contemptible, slobbering weakling. He hadn't wept like this since his poor mother had been lowered into her grave in Orléans, and that had been seven years ago. But he had kept a grip on himself that day. He had stood straight, head unbowed, eyes unflinching though tearful. He had been a true man, worthy of her years of respect. But this now, this horrible sobbing was too deep, too unexplainable, and it frightened him to know that he was totally out of control. It reminded him too much of the first few nights at that place in Switzerland, before Henri Cachon had arrived with his blessed needle. Would he never be able to stop this outpouring of anguish, these wracking, wrenching animal sounds that came welling up from the depths of his being? He caught sight of his wet, contorted face in the mirror on the wall, and was horrified and filled with shame.

He stumbled to his bedroom door and locked it from the inside, and fell face down onto the bed and lay there for several minutes crying into the cushions. It wasn't my fault, there was nothing I could have done to save them, his disordered mind kept telling him. (*Stop this, stop it, stop it!*) They were total strangers. They were only names on pieces of paper, delivered in a sealed envelope by that terrible Dunleavy man. I never knew them. I don't even know what they looked like. (*Stop it!*) I wonder what they looked like as they— (*Stop it!*) Just before they— (*Stop it!*).

Quickly he rolled off the bed to his feet, holding his tear-stained face in his hands, cursing God through his fingers, calling up every obscenity he could think of. This too, he thought, with fear in his heart. Something else to add to all that he would never be able to forget, this vile blaspheming of God. Suicide flashed through his mind and frightened him. He went to the dresser and hastily uncorked a bottle of cognac and drank from the bottle, choking and gasping on the fiery liquid. I need a doctor, he thought. I will collapse and die of an exhausted heart. Where is Chabot? No. I don't want him to see me this way. Better to die. He took another great swig and put the bottle down.

Time passed, lost in his aimless shuffling back and forth. He heard the sounds of the sea beyond his cabin growing more violent, but he did not care. And then he was listening to himself, and took note. Could it be? Was it ending finally? The weeping and the sniveling were dying down, fading. The animal sounds had come to a stop. Was it over? Yes. Suddenly there was no sorrow left in him, only this overpowering disgust with himself.

He went into the bathroom and pulled huge wads of toilet paper from the roll and blew his nose endlessly, and then he turned on the faucet and doused his face with handfuls of cold water, looking into the mirror and cursing not God but himself, hearing the brandy in his voice and feeling it in the dizziness of his brain.

Why not? he said out loud to the walls of the bathroom. I am the Captain of this ship, am I not? And then he said it again. I am the Captain of this ship. The courage of cognac was better than none at all.

He dried his face briskly, threw the towel aside, went out to the bedroom, unlocked the door and pulled it open. And for a startled instant, he tried to shut it again, but he knew he was too late. The man had seen him. And besides (it suddenly occurred to him), he had *sent* for the man, hadn't he? Of course he had. He had wanted to see the American instantly, in the first heat of rage and panic and grief. Let it be his own appalling secret that the Commandant of the *Marseille,* under sufficient stress, was capable of losing even his memory tonight.

He went into the office and approached the man. "How long have you been waiting out here?" he asked warily.

"No bother," Harold Columbine said, leaning back against the desk, his arms folded, eyeing the older man quizzically. The novelist's smoothly shaven face showed little trace of his brush with death and too much gin. A good orgasm and a cold shower had always done wonders for him.

"Did you just arrive?" Girodt *had* to know.

The other man shrugged. "You sent for me, and I'm here."

"That isn't what I asked you, Mr. Columbine." Already he could feel the alcohol fueling his anger.

"All right, if you insist. Yes, I *did* hear you carrying on in there. And I'm sorry. I didn't mean to—"

"You're sorry?" Suddenly Girodt hated this man in the black velvet dinner jacket and the patent-leather loafers more than he hated Craig Dunleavy. "You damned well should be sorry—"

"What am I supposed to do?" the American flared. "Wear ear plugs or something? I walk in here and you're—"

"Do you realize what you have done with your arrogance and your meddling—?"

"Wait a minute, for Christ's sake, you've been boozing it, haven't you? I can smell it all the way over here—"

"Do you know how many innocent people have died because of you, Mr. Columbine?"

The writer looked at the Captain with angry puzzlement. "What the hell is this, Girodt? Are you all right?"

"You were with a woman this evening, a passenger named Louise Campbell . . ."

Harold Columbine started to smile, thought better of it. "Yeah. She tried to kill me. She's one of them."

"And you have a weapon that belonged to her?"

The novelist opened his jacket, bared the object tucked under his belt. "You mean this?"

"I know you think you are very clever, much smarter than the rest of us, Mr. Columbine . . ."

"Not at all. Just lucky, knock wood. I'm trying to *survive* on this unpleasant little pleasure cruise."

Charles Girodt looked at him with piercing eyes. "Louise Campbell is dead. She committed suicide tonight. Because of *you.*"

"Dead?" Christ, how could that be? He could still feel his cock inside of her.

"And because of that, because of you, they have taken husbands and wives, eighteen innocent people . . ." Girodt's voice faltered. He turned away. "They have slaughtered them, Mr. Columbine, executed them . . ."

Girodt heard the man moan and, when he turned around, saw him sinking into a chair, his head in his hands. "Dirty cocksuckers." His voice was low. "I'll kill those fucking animals . . ."

Charles Girodt's voice shook. "Haven't you killed enough for one night?"

Harold Columbine looked up sharply. "What did you say?"

"Exactly what you think I said. You have been taking things into your own hands, *constantly,* while those of us in authority on this ship have been treating the situation with delicacy and caution, trying desperately to avert a catastrophe—"

"Now wait a minute—"

"You have taken it upon yourself to interfere at every opportunity, and to antagonize the very people who have our lives in their hands. And now *this* . . . this senseless horrible murder of eighteen defenseless men and women . . ."

"You're not going to lay this off on *me,* goddamn it!" Harold Columbine was on his feet, trembling with fury. *"You're* the one who's supposed to be in charge around here. It's *your* responsibility, not mine, to see that no harm comes to the passengers, to *any* of us, including me. And what are you doing about it? Not a fucking thing, Captain. You've lost control of your own ship, and people are dying because of it, because of *you,* not me. So don't try dumping this into *my* lap, because I'm not going to let you get away with it."

Charles Girodt stared at his accuser, his face pale, his eyes cold. "I do not intend to answer your charges now, or defend myself in any way. I think there is something particularly distasteful about getting into this kind of vulgar squabble when the circumstances are so tragic . . ."

"You started it," Harold Columbine retorted.

"Then I will end it." Charles Girodt held out his hand, spoke quietly. "Give me the gun."

The American looked at him. "Sorry. No."

Girodt kept his hand outstretched, waiting. "I am exercising the very authority you have indicted me for not using. You can't have it both ways, Mr. Columbine. Give it to me."

The novelist shook his head slowly.

"The *Marseille* has a jail," the Captain said. "Must I have you imprisoned?"

Harold Columbine patted the bulge at his waist. "I don't think that would be possible, Captain. At any rate, not very wise."

Girodt's lips tightened. "I ask you to go to your cabin and stay there until all this is over. Will you do that much?"

Harold Columbine took the hard edge off his voice, but his tone was still firm. "Look, Captain, despite what I said, I respect your authority. But that doesn't mean I'm going to do just anything you say, regardless of whether I think it's right or wrong. Those bets are all off, under the conditions that prevail. I'm not going to give up this weapon, because it may help me, and some others, to stay alive. I don't know of anything or anyone else who can offer that help right now, including you. And I am not going to stay in my cabin. They could find me there if they wanted to, so what the hell difference would that make?"

"It would keep you from the apparently irresistible temptation to incite our enemies to further acts of destruction," said Charles Girodt with bitterness.

Harold Columbine shrugged. "You want to cling to that viewpoint, you're welcome to it. As for me, I'm going to take Mrs. Berlin to dinner tonight. I'm going to take her away from that cabin where her husband has the radio. Yes, she's told me about it. She's as much of a marked woman as I'm a marked man. So if they're going to make any move against her, I don't think we want them going to her cabin and finding out what Dr. Berlin is up to. Let them see her out in the open with me. Let them see that there's no *reason* to go to her cabin. I don't mean that her life isn't important, God bless her beautiful face. But that radio is even more important. That's what we ought to be protecting beyond all else. Besides, the little lady will be a damned sight safer out in the open with *me*, because I'm armed, and they goddamn well know it. Have I made myself a little more clearly understood, Captain?"

Charles Girodt regarded him for a moment in stony silence. Then he stepped to the desk, picked up the envelope that Craig Dunleavy had delivered to him. He would be glad to get it out of his sight. There was no way he could get its contents out of his mind. "The names of the unfortunate victims are in here," he said coolly, handing the envelope to the novelist. "I would like Mrs. Berlin's husband to have them. He will know what to do with them."

Harold Columbine nodded and put the envelope in the inside pocket of his velvet jacket as Girodt continued: "Please don't take my asking you to do this as some indication that I approve of any of your actions or plans."

Harold Columbine's lips twisted in a smile. "Hell, no. You've made your position very clear, Captain. The way to win out over these dirty bastards, the most strategic device to overcome them and save us all, is to put me behind bars."

Charles Girodt's fists clenched. Then he turned on his heel and walked quickly into the bedroom and slammed the door shut behind him.

The cognac stung his throat and burned its way down into his stomach, but he had little confidence that it would help. It would take more than alcohol to make him forget what the American had said about him, and with how much of it he had secretly agreed.

CHAPTER THIRTY-ONE

THE BASEMENT OF Police Judiciaire Headquarters was hot
and airless, and the cell was humiliatingly small. His wet shirt stuck
to his back, and the naked overhead light was harsh in his eyes. But
Julian Wunderlicht betrayed no outward signs of discomfort.
Equanimity, he knew, was his strongest weapon right now. "I must
tell you," he said to his inquisitor, with mild indifference, "I am
sorely disappointed in the executives of the Compagnie Française
Atlantique, specifically Monsieur Dechambre and Monsieur Sauvinage. They knew full well what the consequences would be if they
went to the authorities."

Jean-Claude Raffin spoke quickly, with too much urgency.
"They went to *no* one. Do you hear me? They do not have the
faintest idea that I so much as *know* of the peril to the *Marseille,*
much less that I have found you, that I am holding you here."

Wunderlicht smiled inwardly at this inadvertent display of anxiety on the part of his captor. "Am I supposed to believe that you
simply stumbled over me while you were out shopping for a good
restaurant? Come now, Monsieur Director General. I not only *saw*

that whore you put on my trail, I smelled her."

"It is perfectly understandable that you would jump to the wrong conclusions, and doubt anything I say to you. After all, you have never met me before . . ."

"Some pleasures come to a man late in life," said Wunderlicht.

Raffin allowed a moment of silence to go by, while he refined the lies that would be necessary now. "I am an ambitious man, Wunderlicht. Keep that in mind," he said. "My present position in the government does not provide sufficient power or importance to satisfy me, and I have every intention of moving upward as rapidly as possible."

"Congratulations."

"When I accidentally became aware of certain confidential communications passing between President Bonnard and the Caissier General regarding the urgent transfer of a huge amount of gold bullion to an unnamed destination, I decided to conduct my own— shall we say *private,* unauthorized—investigation of the matter, and quickly learned enough of the details to realize that I had in my hands the opportunity to score a personal victory of such magnitude that my political ambitions could take a sudden quantum leap forward. There, I have let you in on a little secret that even the President of France does not know."

Wunderlicht regarded the head of the Sûreté with cool gaze. "I would find it easier to appreciate these shared intimacies if we were sitting at a table at Maxim's, instead of in this degrading cell, Monsieur Raffin."

The official shrugged helplessly. "As I told you, I too am dissatisfied with my present lack of status. I am merely an exalted policeman. Someday, who knows, my meetings will be taking place in the Élysée Palace."

Wunderlicht offered a cynical smile. "I should feel flattered that a man of my insignificance could turn out to be an important figure in the political history of France." He paused. "Unfortunately, there is little chance of that happening."

Raffin's expression showed nothing. "Why such pessimism, Wunderlicht?"

"This personal victory you referred to." Wunderlicht shook his head slowly. "I'm afraid you're not going to have it, at least not through *me.*"

"I'm not?"

"Unh-uh." Julian Wunderlicht brought a flame to his damp cigar and crossed his legs, wondering when the man was going to make his move. He was tired of all this sparring, and the stool he was sitting on under the glaring light did not agree with his behind. "You see," he said, through clouds of gray smoke, "there is nothing really that I can do to make you a hero, and nothing that you can do to *me* to change that."

Raffin controlled his anger, with only partial success. "I could take you to one of our more interesting laboratories here, and apply anywhere from one to two hundred and forty volts to your testicles. That's one thing I could do. However, I hope to avoid that, if at all possible."

Wunderlicht smiled coldly. "I share that hope, Monsieur Raffin, though it would be one of the few forms of genital stimulation I have not yet sampled." He shrugged. "But what would it avail you? To break me down? To hear me scream? What would you learn from me, what could I tell you that would lead you to this 'personal victory' you are seeking? Surely you must realize that all you have to do is throw one monkeywrench into the machinery of my sea-going colleagues, in fact, all you have to do is let one word out that I am being held prisoner here, even that I am being *questioned,* and you will have caused the instant destruction of the *Marseille* and several thousand lives. I hardly see you running for high office on *that* platform. Of course, I don't profess to know the political climate of this country. Maybe the saving of thirty-five million dollars in gold for your bulging treasury is all that means anything to the French people, *including* you."

Raffin raised his hand as though to slap the German's smiling face, then dropped his arm and abruptly turned away. Wunderlicht watched him take out a pipe, jam it back into his pocket, find a pack of cigarettes there, withdraw one and light it with trembling hands, before turning back to him. "Let me make sure you understand this, Wunderlicht. The gold is going to be paid. Bonnard has already arranged that for the people over at Français. Nobody is planning to do anything to cause a disaster at sea."

"Excellent," said Wunderlicht briskly. "That is the kind of intelligent thinking I like to hear about. Now, perhaps, you will follow suit and let me go on my way. The night is still young enough for me to enjoy it." He rose to his feet.

"Sit down, goddamn it," said Raffin wearily.

Wunderlicht sighed, and sank down again on the uncomfortable stool.

"Now listen to me," the police official said, with slow deliberation. "Just as a doctor finds it almost impossible not to prolong the life of his patient even when he knows the case is hopeless, the Director General of the Sûreté cannot force himself to let a self-admitted criminal walk out of custody Scot-free, even when he knows not to do so can have dire consequences. The world is full of irrational men, Wunderlicht, and I am one of them. The sooner you realize that, the better it will be for the both of us. Putting it simply, you are going to rot in jail for the rest of your life unless you can find a way to deal with my irrational compulsions, unless you can come up with some kind of scenario that will appease not just my peers and superiors, but my own perverted conscience as well."

Wunderlicht eyed the man with an impassive countenance. "Are you suggesting a deal with me, monsieur?"

Raffin bristled at the word. "I have already told you *my* goals, Wunderlicht. *Your* goal is your freedom, is it not, guaranteed, now and forever?"

Wunderlicht pursed his lips. "In return for what?"

"Talk," Raffin replied with great intensity. "Tell me everything I must know, and quickly. My men can bring you to the edge of death if you insist, but that takes too much precious time, and besides, it is needlessly messy."

Julian Wunderlicht sucked on his cigar, then withdrew it from his mouth and examined the wet tip with elaborate care. What a marvelously sinister influence this police official was having on him. By automatically assuming his, Wunderlicht's, capacity for disloyalty to his colleagues, the man had stirred up the very worst that had lain hidden within him, something that Wunderlicht could feel growing now, in a matter of moments, into the beginnings of an incredibly evil plan. Later, when he was far away from this confining cell, he would give the plan more thought, perfect it, luxuriate in it. But right now, he would first have to go through the necessary motions to satisfy his unwitting Dr. Frankenstein.

"God help me," he said, finally. "I find myself willing and prepared to trust you, Monsieur Raffin."

"Good." The head of the Sûreté moved forward eagerly. "The conspirators. Who are they?"

"I warn you that you are going to be disappointed with me,"

Julian Wunderlicht replied. "But that is the bargain that you have made. It was not my idea."

"Who are they, Wunderlicht?"

"I know only the names of their leaders, and not much else," he said. "Craig Dunleavy and a Mr. Kleinfeld, two Americans. I am nothing more than a well-paid hired hand who was dealt with, for the most part, by telephone and the mails."

"What about their motives?"

"The gold. That simple . . ."

"Go on. What else do you know?"

"There are, in all, one hundred and seventy-four of them," Wunderlicht continued. "Who they are, what they are, where they came from, I cannot tell you because I do not know."

"You expect me to believe that?" said Jean-Claude Raffin angrily.

Wunderlicht shrugged. "As I see it, you wish to save the *Marseille,* its passengers, and its crew. You wish not to lose for France the sum of thirty-five million dollars, and you would like to capture and punish the conspirators. Quite understandable—"

"You are not helping me, Wunderlicht—"

"But I must tell you, Monsieur Raffin, that I would also find it understandable if you harbored secret dreams, despite your guarantees, of some day in the future tracking me down, and perhaps my two friends, the former German pilots, though they have not yet committed a crime, and then throwing us all in prison." Raffin started to protest, but Wunderlicht gave him no chance. "If you will be patient now, and stop interrupting me, I believe I can show you how to achieve all of your goals save one—that one, of course, being the jailing of *me.*"

The official pulled his sleeve back, looked at his wristwatch, muttering, "Time, damn it. *Time* . . ."

Wunderlicht exhaled a perfect smoke ring. "You have handed the baton to me, Monsieur Raffin. If my tempo seems a little too slow for your taste, it is only because you are impatient to get to the end, while the conductor is more concerned that you hear every note, every cadence, every subtle shading. He thinks it is critically important that you understand what you are listening to—"

Raffin hurled his cigarette to the stone floor of the cell and ground it out with a violent twist of his shoe.

"I, Julian Wunderlicht, am the only one who can assure those on board the *Marseille* that their instructions are being carried out, that the gold bullion has been transferred to the 747, that the plane is in flight and on its way to the distant landing field where the trucks await it to transport the gold to its hiding place . . ."

"Where? Await it *where?*" demanded Raffin.

"Please." Wunderlicht raised a hand to silence him. "I am trying to make you realize the absolute necessity of your keeping me and my two air-minded friends alive and healthy so that the gold can be safely flown to its destination. Once this has been done, the group at sea will be notified, and they will leave the *Marseille* for good. Should you suffer a change of heart, a lapse of judgment, and permit something to happen to me, it is true you will have thwarted the conspirators, but the price of that satisfaction, as I have already told you, is the death of the ship and all on board."

"I don't think you have to make that point again and again," snapped Raffin.

"I'm glad to hear you say that," replied Wunderlicht. "It will work out so much more smoothly for you, if you bide your time and wait for the *Marseille* to be safely rid of her enemies. Immediately, you can then alert the local authorities at the plane's destination, and they will seize the trucks and the gold for you. I, of course, will be untouchable, for I am an American citizen, and this landing I speak of will take place in a country that is extradition-proof for me."

Jean-Claude Raffin rubbed his chin reflectively. He searched the bland, expressionless face of Wunderlicht as though trying to fathom concealed intentions. "Tell me this," he said quietly. "Why could you not accomplish all this for yourself *and* for me by taking off in an empty plane, by flying off *without* the bullion? Upon landing, you notify the *Marseille* that all is well, and walk away a free man. So simple, Wunderlicht. So much cleaner."

The German smiled. "It would not work."

"Why not?"

"Because I am not the one who has been chosen to notify the *Marseille,* at that stage of the operation." Wunderlicht saw the puzzled frown on Raffin's face. "At the landing point, there will be a man waiting whose assignment it is to oversee the transfer of the bullion from the plane to the trucks. After that has been completed, and he has made a count of the gold bars, he will then make the call to the ship. *He* will, not I. So you see, an empty 747 without its precious cargo would be a disaster."

Jean-Claude Raffin turned away from his tormentor and paced back and forth in the little cell, muttering to himself, "Why should I believe any of this?"

"Only because you have no choice," Julian Wunderlicht offered.

The official turned, looked down at him. "Would you allow us to put two Air France pilots aboard as passengers?"

Wunderlicht glanced up sharply. "For what purpose?"

"To fly the plane and the gold back to Paris," the other man said evenly.

Wunderlicht stared at him. "They would have to stay so perfectly hidden that no one at the landing point would be aware of their presence until the local authorities had seized the gold . . ."

"I'm sure we can arrange that," Raffin said, too quickly, too eagerly.

Wunderlicht eyed him coldly. He did not like the idea of this man taking him for a fool. "No," he said. "It is too much of a risk. I cannot approve of such a notion."

"But I assure you—"

"The answer is no, Raffin." He was sick and tired of this game. He wanted it to end. He wanted to be off some place by himself where he could think about what he already knew he was really going to do.

Raffin's face was a grim mask. "Suppose you tell me now—or am I rushing you too much?—who is this man who oversees the transfer of the bullion and notifies the ship?"

"I take it then," said Wunderlicht, "that you are in total agreement with my suggested plan?"

"You have already said it: I have no choice," the police official said.

Wunderlicht nodded. "His name is Otto Laneer. He is a local importer of farming implements."

"L-A-N-E-E-R?"

"Correct."

The head of the Sûreté drew a deep breath. "And what is the plane's destination?"

Julian Wunderlicht examined his cigar. It had gone out again.

He placed it back between his lips, unlit. "Brazzaka," he said. "The capital city of the Republic of Libwana."

"Naturally." There was deep bitterness in Jean-Claude Raffin's voice. "That pig Aramis will take anyone into his country."

"Only if they come with guns or gold," said Wunderlicht, deciding to overlook the personal insult.

"And how do the others, the conspirators, expect to get there?"

"The boat which they have arranged for to take them off the *Marseille* will deposit them on a group of islands that are unknown to me," Wunderlicht explained. "From there, they will inconspicuously make their way to many different destinations, none of which has been divulged to me. Eventually, the gold is supposed to catch up with them."

"Not they with it?" said Raffin.

"No," said Wunderlicht.

The police official frowned, puzzled. There was a thought in his head that was trying to make its way to the surface, but he somehow couldn't find it, or formulate it, and it slipped away. "I don't understand how these people could have reasonably expected to get away with such a foolish plan. What is to prevent the Sûreté and the authorities in the United States from tracking them down, one by one? After all, *they* will be the one hundred and seventy-four passengers who sailed from New York on the *Marseille* and were missing when it docked at Le Havre. We will know whom to search for no matter how carefully they have changed identities, or forged their passports, or used all the other tricks that are child's play to professional law enforcement agencies. And we'll have several thousand witnesses to help us identify the missing fugitives."

Wunderlicht shrugged. "I must admit to you that I myself have never been able to figure that one out either. I can only assume that they have devised a plan which they believe to be foolproof."

What Julian Wunderlicht did not tell the man was that, once or twice, he had found himself privately speculating on the possibility that Craig Dunleavy might be planning to destroy the ship and its human cargo no matter *what*. But he had quickly banished the thought as being unacceptable, and inconsistent with his peace of mind. No doubt the possibility would eventually occur to this French official too, if it hadn't already, and he too would probably banish it from his mind as being unacceptable, for even to think of it would paralyze him. If the *Marseille* never arrived at Le Havre, if it were blown up at sea and went down in the southern Atlantic, who but the hungry sharks would know which ones were missing from the platter?

Wunderlicht rose to his feet briskly, and with clear intention. "In my opinion, this meeting will prove to have been highly constructive for the both of us. Do you not agree, Monsieur Raffin?"

The Frenchman's lips tightened. "Time will tell," he muttered.

"You know, of course, where to find me if anything else should occur to you," Wunderlicht said rather breezily. "I don't have to tell you that no one must know of my involuntary visit here. If they already do, I assume you will seal their lips. Also, I strongly urge you not to put any tails on me. The shadowy presence of the police in my vicinity will only arouse suspicion."

Jean-Claude Raffin bristled. "Do you have any *further* instructions for the Sûreté Nationale?"

Wunderlicht grimaced with mock sorrow. "It pains me that you have such little regard for what you have accomplished here tonight."

Raffin bowed elaborately, and his voice was cruel. "Forgive me, sir. It is gross misconduct on my part. I have been trained over the years never to inflict pain on a common criminal in my hands, no matter how vile and loathsome his crime." Abruptly he turned away and called out to the guard at the end of the corridor to come unlock the cell door.

Julian Wunderlicht forced a smile to his face as he stood there waiting, hoping the smile would induce in him a quick flush of elation and triumph to wipe out the sudden sinking feeling in the pit of his stomach brought on by Raffin's ugly remark. But the smile congealed, and by the time he had mounted the stairs and reached the entrance and walked out into the night air, he knew he was going to have to use some woman's body to help him get rid of the nasty discomfort within him.

He wondered if the lovely young blond girl seated behind the wheel of the little red Peugeot, parked at the curb in back of the Mercedes Benz that had brought him here, might be a waiting whore. He moved toward her thinking, my God, what a beauty, it could never be, and he saw her head turning to him. Her pale green eyes looked up at him and he felt faint.

"Yes, what is it?" she said to him, so cool, so direct.

"I was thinking," he said. "How about you and I . . ." His voice faltered. "How about us having a drink somewhere . . . together?"

The girl seemed to look right through him for a moment. "What else did you have in mind?" she said.

Wunderlicht's heart leaped. "I will allow my imagination to run riot," he said, with a gaiety that surprised him.

The girl smiled. "Where are you staying, honey?"

He loved the "honey." She made it sound so personal. "The Hotel Prince de Galles," he said. "But I have friends there. They would interfere with our privacy. I was hoping perhaps *you* had a place."

"I do," she said. "But I have to . . . uh . . . wait here for a girlfriend who's supposed to be bringing me some money she owes me . . ."

"I see." Wunderlicht hesitated.

"Would you mind waiting for me in the lobby of your hotel?" the girl added quickly. "I'll come over and pick you up. It shouldn't be long."

Wunderlicht frowned. "You're not giving me the brush-off now, are you?"

"Now why would I want to do a thing like that?" She smiled again. "You look sufficiently prosperous for my requirements, and I think I'm going to enjoy myself with you very much."

"Good. I like that," Wunderlicht murmured, feeling it between his legs. "The Prince de Galles . . ."

"I know. You wouldn't want to give me your name, would you, just in case?"

"In case what?" he said. "Don't worry, I'll be there, and you'll be there."

"Then get moving," she said, "before the police nab us both."

"Right." Wunderlicht grinned and walked on, believing in miracles.

A long shot at best, Lisa Briande told herself, but who could afford not to cover every horse in the race? She had noticed him emerging from the building out of the corner of her eye, and when he had come up to her car and had spoken French with a German accent, something had told her not to lose this man completely. Hadn't Max Dechambre mentioned that the conspirators' contact in Paris was a German? And hadn't this man just come out of the very building where Jean-Claude Raffin was closeted even now, keeping her waiting interminably?

She tossed the remains of what must have been her fourth or fifth cigarillo out of the window, and examined her face in the rear-view mirror. Tired and drawn, that's what she was. Too little sleep. Who *wouldn't* take her for a Paris streetwalker?

She spent a few minutes feeling sorry for herself, then glanced toward the gray façade of the dimly lighted Police Judiciaire Head-quarters and suddenly there he was, moving wearily toward the Mercedes Benz. She had seen his photograph in the magazines and in the morgue of her own paper often enough to recognize him instantly. She clambered out of the Peugeot and ran toward him, calling out, "Monsieur Director General . . ."

The chauffeur was holding the rear door open. Halfway into the Mercedes, Raffin drew back and turned. Lisa had her wallet out and ready, opened to her press card. She thrust it at him, saying, "Lisa Briande of the *Herald Tribune.*"

Raffin glanced down at the card, then at her face. "It is late and *I* am late," he said coldly.

"I have to speak to you," Lisa said.

"That does not mean that *I* have to speak to *you.*" Raffin moved to get into the car, but she took his arm and held him there.

"Monsieur Raffin, I *know* what's going on here in Paris and out at sea, and I want to talk about what *you* are up to."

Raffin quickly turned to his chauffeur and told him to wait in the car. Then he moved a few steps away from the Mercedes, Lisa moving with him.

"Miss Briande—that *is* your name, isn't it?"

"Yes."

"Listen to me carefully." His voice was low and razor-edged. "Whatever this thing is that you're referring to—and I absolutely refuse to talk about it—"

"There's no sense in your refusing because—"

"If you or your newspaper divulge one word, just *one word* that would jeopardize our present plans, you will not live to see next week, is that clear?"

Lisa laughed, but she could feel her face flush. "I don't believe this. Did I just hear the Sûreté threatening a reporter with murder?"

Raffin's lips twisted in a sardonic smile. "You members of the press are always hearing things, and imagining things . . ."

"Yes, well I'm also imagining some of the talk that must have gone on between you and that German who was in there with you tonight," she shot back at him.

Raffin's look of alarm betrayed him. "Forget the German, do you hear me? Forget everything you think you know, because if you don't, you are a blond corpse lying in the gutter with your lipstick smeared."

He turned away from her angrily, strode to the Mercedes, slammed the door shut behind him, and in a moment the car was speeding off.

Lisa couldn't help smiling as she quickly climbed into her Peugeot, started the motor, made a sharp U-turn and headed for the bridge that would take her to the Hotel Prince de Galles. She didn't need Jean-Claude Raffin. He had given away all that she had to know. Her long shot was no longer a long shot now. He was the odds-on favorite, and she was going to play him with everything she had . . . which, tired and drawn face notwithstanding, was still not all that bad. She thought about herself for a moment. Not all that bad? Hell, it was terrific.

When the Director General of the Sûreté Nationale arrived at 11 rue des Saussaies and let himself into his locked, darkened office, he went directly to his private telephone and awoke Aristide Bonnard out of a light, troubled sleep in his bedroom at St.-Germain-en-Laye. Raffin had already contacted Arsène Schreiner of Interpol before leaving Police Judiciaire Headquarters, and within twenty minutes had received confirmation of the existence of one Otto Laneer in Brazzaka. Raffin therefore spoke with some measure of assurance in his voice when he informed the President of the French Republic, without giving him lengthy details, that it would regrettably be necessary to ship the gold bullion to Charles de Gaulle Airport after all, and allow it to be flown away, as agreed upon with M. Dechambre of Françat. And before the sleepy President could protest, Raffin quickly added that, not only would the *Marseille* be saved by this necessary move, but also, most happily, he, Raffin, had worked out a plan with the conspirator, Wunderlicht, whereby the gold would be easily and completely recovered within twenty-four hours of its departure.

The President's reaction to this news struck Raffin as being somewhat less enthusiastic than he had expected. And when Raffin then politely informed Bonnard that it would be necessary for the President to telephone immediately Patrick Hennessey, editor-in-chief of the *International Herald Tribune,* either at his residence at 24 Quai de Béthune or at his office at 22 rue du Berri, wherever he was, and order him, in the name of national security, to withhold from publication in the *Tribune* for the next forty-eight hours, anything whatsoever relating to either the Compagnie Française Atlantique or any of its ships, particularly its ships at sea, Aristide Bonnard bristled and demanded to know the reason why he was being asked to degrade and humiliate himself in such extraordinary fashion.

"Monsieur le Président," Jean-Claude Raffin replied, with extreme delicacy. "First, you must trust me when I tell you that my request is not only well-founded but urgent. Second, believe me when I say that it is better for you, better for your future credibility, that I do not go into details, particularly on the telephone. And finally, I humbly ask you not to be upset with me now when I tell you that I believe it would be unwise for us to have any communication other than the most urgent for the next few days, until all our problems, maritime, monetary, and otherwise, have been successfully resolved."

Raffin heard the long and probably angry silence at the other end, and then Aristide Bonnard's begrudging, "Very well, Raffin, if that is the way you see it. Good night, and good luck."

"Good night, Monsieur le Président. And thank you." Raffin hung up, feeling vaguely guilty, instead of proud, or victorious. He had no way of knowing that the lack of grace exhibited by his chief executive was due, in part, to the fact that the President had had a rather poor time of it in bed earlier that night with the First Lady of the Republic.

Raffin sat at the antique desk, lost in thought, his fingers nervously drumming the smooth surface of aged walnut. That blond bitch from the newspaper still troubled him. True, he should have been congratulating himself now for having found out about her in time to suppress whatever it was that she knew. And yet, her very existence pervaded his senses as a threat, a toothache that he knew would not go away. Faces and names flashed through his mind, ugly and dangerous men who would do anything they were asked to do if it meant earning a little respite from the law. His head filled with the terrible sounds of squealing tires and cars smashing into each other and blood-curdling, high-pitched screams ending in the sudden silence of death.

Quickly he got to his feet and fled the office. In the back seat of the Mercedes Benz on the long drive home, he convinced himself that he was suffering from exhaustion and needed only a good night's sleep. He would be all right in the morning. The sun would be shining, and he would be sane again, and decent.

But then, Julian Wunderlicht crept into his thoughts, and he began to try to recall what it was, why it was, that he had decided to trust the man. And when he could come up with nothing, no basis on which to have made so fateful a decision, he ordered the chauffeur to turn the car radio on to one of those all-night jazz stations he abhorred.

But the music was not loud enough. Not loud enough at all.

CHAPTER THIRTY-TWO

─────────────

JULIAN WUNDERLICHT, naked and relaxed, lay back on the rumpled bedsheets sucking idly on a cigarette, listening to the sporadic traffic going by on the rue de Sèvres and re-enacting in his mind each exquisite moment of his recently completed fornication with the blond darling who called herself Simone.

When he heard the door buzzer sound, his first impulse was to let it keep ringing until whoever it was went away. He glanced toward the closed bathroom door and knew that the girl, standing under the full blast of the shower, was unaware of her late-night visitor. The buzzer sounded again. Wunderlicht tamped out his cigarette in the ashtray on the night table, got off the rumpled bed, wrapped a towel around his midsection, and padded to the door, chuckling inwardly when he realized that he was nurturing a faint hope that it would be still another beauty. The last magnificent ejaculation was still vivid in his memory, and here he was wanting it again, feeling deeply in his loins that he had one more good shot left in him tonight.

He unlatched the chain and opened the door and found himself staring into the surprised face of a thin young Frenchman whose lips and cheeks bore unmistakable signs of inadequately erased cosmetics. The man eyed Wunderlicht with pained distaste and said, "Is she in?"

"Who?" said Wunderlicht. "Simone?"

"No," the Frenchman said with impatience. "Miss Briande."

"Miss who?"

"Briande. Lisa Briande. She lives here."

"Oh, Lisa Briande," Wunderlicht said, with a certain wonderment.

"Well, who did you think I meant, Alice B. Toklas?"

"May I ask who you are . . . at twenty minutes past one?"

"The name is Jimi Brocke, at this time or any other time. I'm a copy boy at the *Herald Tribune,* and I happen to have a message for Miss Briande from her editor. Now am I coming in or not?"

"Not," said Wunderlicht, the truth dawning on him far too swiftly. "I am a friend of Miss Briande and will be happy to relay the message, unless it is too confidential."

Jimi Brocke stared at the German, his full lips twitching with outrage. "Very well. Tell Miss Briande her editor has been trying to reach her for twelve hours without success. Tell her he said that if she wants to remain incommunicado indefinitely, the *Tribune* will find someone else to fill her brassiere."

"Miss Briande does not wear a brassiere," Julian Wunderlicht offered.

"It was meant as a figure of speech," Jimi Brocke replied savagely.

"Forgive my stupidity. I will give her your message."

"Fucking asshole," said Jimi Brocke, turning away.

"No thanks. I'm not in the mood," Wunderlicht said as he shut the door. He listened for the man's footsteps receding down the stairway. Then he started back to the bed, frowning. He lay back, sighing, and realized that he was singularly unsurprised at what he had just found out. It restored him comfortably to his lifelong disbelief in miracles. At the worst, he had a little handling to do now, another game to play and win, when just a few minutes ago he had been enjoying the luxury of contemplating further erotic sport. By the time the shower had fallen silent, and the assorted fragrances of talc and eau de toilette had found their way to his nostrils from the bathroom, he considered himself prepared for anything within reason, though he was not fooling himself. He knew that some part of him simply had no heart for what was to follow. Some part of him wanted something far different. But what? Was it love? Romance? Endless lust? What was it? And was it with any woman? Or was it with this woman?

Lisa Briande. How beautiful. But a reporter. How sad.

Watch yourself, Wunderlicht. A cunt will be your undoing.

Presently, she emerged from the bathroom, naked and soft and tawny gold, and his heart died a little as he gazed at her.

"I had too much Calvados," she said. "My head is all woozy."

"Bring your woozy head over here," he said, struggling feebly against the onset of horniness.

"Did I hear you talking to someone?" she asked.

"Yes," he said. "Myself. Telling myself how lucky I am. You're too good for me. I don't deserve you."

"I agree with you," she said. "Not at these prices, anyway. What are we going to do about it? I mean, to make it fair all around?"

He eyed her from the bed. "You French girls are all alike. But I'd hate to have it any other way."

She looked at him. "Before I put my clothes on, while I'm all nice and fresh and perfumed and clean, is there anything I can do for you?"

"Yes. You get dressed, if you insist, and I'll watch you, and I'll talk and you'll listen, and if I go too fast, or you don't understand what I'm saying, you'll stop me. Okay?"

"Sounds too easy."

"Maybe. Maybe not." He lit another cigarette and made himself comfortable against the pillows and gazed with heavy-lidded eyes at her lovely legs as she started to draw on her flesh-toned pantyhose. He wanted her. He wanted to fuck her again. But he had to do what had to be done. He had to talk. "I speak French with an accent," he began. "A German accent yet. Nothing could tend to make me sound less shrewd, less intelligent than I am, unless the accent were American."

She didn't say anything for a moment. Then, without looking at him, she said, "Accent or no, I haven't noticed you making one dumb move yet."

He exhaled noisily. "What do you call my mistaking you for a whore? Do you see me getting the Nobel Prize for that?"

"I'm sorry if you think I was lacking in expertise." She was slipping into a sheer white blouse, leaving the buttons open. "If you didn't want to come that quickly, you should have said something. I could have made you last forever."

He felt a little sorry for her. It was too easy, too unfair. "Look, I'll waste just a few more moments making myself sound brilliant, because my ego always throbs a little bit after it has been taken for a sleigh ride. Then I'll get down to business. Brilliant observation number one: whores don't get moist as quickly as you did, if at all, and believe me, I do not have a history of being sexually irresistible . . ."

"I believe you," she said.

"My cock is long, but somewhat thick and unappealing, I am told . . ."

"You can't please everyone." She picked up a comb and began to run it through her crackling hair.

"Observation number two: the moans and cries and thrashings of a woman faking an orgasm are as familiar to me as the performances of my favorite movie stars. Whereas *your* gasps, dear girl, your beautiful involuntary obscenities, the bite of your fingernails on my back, the bone-cracking clutch of your legs and thighs at that moment of moments, and those divine spasms deep inside of you, were all genuine enough to hang in the Louvre alongside the *Mona Lisa*."

"I don't think da Vinci would like that," she said.

"You do get my drift, do you not?" He blew a gentle cloud of cigarette smoke and watched her toying with her hair.

"It's a helluva world is all I can say," she sighed, "if a girl gets branded as an amateur and loses her status as a whore just because she decides for once to enjoy a good fuck. You *are* a good fuck, you know."

He nodded in appreciation, and continued. "Another observation. Not too many more, I promise. That typewriter over there on the desk is a little too battered, a little too lived in. It doesn't quite make it as something to write letters home to Mamma. It looks to me more like it means business. The writing business maybe, huh?"

She hesitated for an instant before replying. "You want me to listen and keep dressing, or you want me to answer questions? Which is it?"

"A little more listening, and then we'll make it a two-way deal," Wunderlicht replied softly. "Incidentally, you needn't put any more clothes on. I like you just as you are."

Lisa set the comb down. "Before I forget it, or get talked into insensibility, you *are* going to leave a handsome sum of money on the table, right?"

"But certainly."

"Even a whore who you insist isn't a whore expects to get paid for her services."

"Have no fear. And now, in conclusion, it is my firm belief that your parking outside Police Judiciaire Headquarters tonight was about as accidental as the setting of the Reichstag fire."

"I wouldn't know. Adolf never did confide in me about that one."

Wunderlicht decided he had massaged himself long enough. "You're an American girl, my young lovely, or an English girl—I lean heavily to American, because the English often smell under the armpits, and you are sheer heaven there. So that means the odds are in favor of your working either for United Press International or for the *Herald Tribune* here in Paris. In my head I toss a coin and it comes up *Herald Tribune*. No further questions, Your Honor."

She turned sharply to face him, shaking her golden mane into place with an angry twist of her head, trying to clear the Calvados from her brain. "Okay, Sherlock Holmes, I think you've displayed enough brilliance to heal your wounded ego and maybe even grow some hair on it. Where would you like the medal pinned, on your navel?"

He smiled easily. "Holmes, my backside. You know damned well what my name is, Miss Lisa Briande."

She sucked in her breath. "I know damned well what name you're *using*."

"You can just call me Julian."

"Whatever you say, Mr. Wunderlicht."

"Lisa Briande. I like the name, by the way . . ."

"Goodie."

"How much do you know?"

"About what? Life? Man's fate? The world?"

"About the *Marseille*."

"Oh, *that* . . . everything."

"No you don't. Nobody knows everything."

"I mean, everything that's happened so far, up to and including your tête-à-tête with Jean-Claude Raffin tonight. All I *don't* know is the future, how everything is going to work out, or come apart. I mean, suppose there's upper air turbulence and the 747 loses a wing, or Aristide Bonnard substitutes lead for the gold, or Max Dechambre, in a fit of madness, telephones the whole story to French television just before hurling himself from a window of the Tour Française, or suppose your people on the *Marseille* get cold feet and turn themselves in to the Captain? Not even God has those answers, so what is there to know that *you* know that *I* don't know? Nothing. In a word, I know everything."

And he marveled that she almost did. "Why haven't you used it?" he said. "Why hasn't any of it been in your paper?"

"All blondes aren't dumb, Mr. Wunderlicht."

"All blondes don't make love the way you do either. Take it from an old blonde-fucker."

"Flattery will get you nowhere."

"I don't want to get anywhere. I like it here. I'm not budging."

"Don't bet on it, Julian. Life can be full of surprises."

"So I have discovered. You know everything, and you're not using it. Why did you pick me up then? What would you want with *me?*"

"Nothing. I got lucky, that's all. For once I was in the right place, for the wrong reason, at the right time."

"You mean, you weren't waiting for *me?*"

"Nope. For Raffin. He ran like a frightened gazelle. The thought of the press knowing what's going on . . ."

"Well, naturally, it could ruin everything, for innocent people, for my friends, for me, everybody."

"I know that."

"Then what are you up to, Miss Briande?"

It sounded plausible to her even as she was about to say it. She simply hadn't had the time to let her mind travel in that direction yet. "The big score, just like you and your friends," she said. "Only with me, it's going to come out of that typewriter. A book. A big one. The whole story, by one who has been in on it, from the inside, in ways you could never even dream of, mister, from the very beginning. And there's still more to come, plenty left to be played out, and I intend to go on being part of it until it's all over."

"What about the *Herald Tribune?*" he inquired coolly.

"They've been exploiting me for five years, ever since I hit this city of light." It was true, by God, it was true. "Look at the way I live. And it would be even worse if I were ugly, or refused to take whatever gifts come my way to keep me willing, and quiet."

"You're a woman after my own heart, Lisa Briande."

"I'm after more than that, Mr. Wunderlicht. I'm after what's left of this story, and I intend to get it, and all the millions of francs in royalties and serialization rights that go with it, and that may mean not letting you out of my sight."

He smiled. "Much as the thought of continuing our relationship excites me, I must say that I truly do not understand your thinking. Don't you realize that I am capable of killing you?"

She laughed without mirth. "Anybody could do that to anybody. Why would you want to do away with *me?*"

"First of all, for having tried, unsuccessfully, to deceive me. You never would have told me who you were or what you were about."

"That's hardly a capital offense."

"And suppose you just don't fit in with my plans? Suppose you are a dangerous impediment to me?"

"Ridiculous," she said. "Why would I do anything to get in your way when all that would do is spoil *everyone's* hopes, especially mine, because out the window would go my marvelous book? So far, I think you've got to agree, I've got two pretty damned good acts. All I need now is the grand finale. Will the bullion be delivered? Will the bad guys release the ship? Will everybody get away, with gold coming out of their ears? Or will the authorities foil the villains and bring the dastardly creatures to justice?"

Wunderlicht regarded her with a slightly quizzical expression. "For a girl who is in a mighty precarious situation, you talk quite frivolously, Miss Briande."

"I don't see anything all that precarious about my position, Julian. I would say *you* are a helluva lot closer to being in boiling water than I am."

His voice hardened. "You could be an unnecessary burr up my ass, if you will pardon the expression. Burrs I don't need, and burrs I don't intend to have. Do I make your situation a little clearer to you?"

"You are in no position to threaten me, sir."

"Right now I am flat on my back and enjoying the sight of your lovely body, which it would be a pity to rearrange, but the position is deceptive, because it does not take into account the handgun with its Maxim silencer in the left side pocket of my trousers on the chair here." He gestured idly with his right hand.

"I fail to see your trousers on the chair there," Lisa said. "And you will too, if you bother to look."

Wunderlicht turned his head, and his face went blank. When he turned back to Lisa, he saw the gun held loosely in her hand. His mouth opened. "What the hell have you done with my clothes?"

She smiled. "Well, you see, while our johns go rushing off to the bathroom to wash their precious little dicks, we amateur whores don't just lie around shoving wads of Kleenex up our vaginas. Your clothes, with the exception of your shoes and that bulging wallet, have gone on a little toboggan ride down the chute to the incinerator, where by now they have joined the universe. Poof."

He sighed wearily. "Oh, my silly little bitch, you didn't."

"Uh-huh."

He started to rise.

"Stay where you are, Julian."

He stared at the gun, sank back on the pillow. "That's no toy. It's been known to go off, you know."

"Not unless I pull the trigger. And I have no intention of doing that unless you force me to in self-defense. So just lie back, please."

He threw the towel aside, exposing himself. "What am I supposed to do now, spend the rest of my life as a nudist?"

"Have you ever thought of going in drag?"

"I'm too old to change my lifestyle." He shook his head impatiently. "Now look, what do you plan to do with me?"

"Well, it *is* getting late, and eventually we're both going to have to get some sleep. You in here, locked in, of course, double-bolted, I might add, in case you have any notions of streaking through the streets of Paris."

"I have no desire to leave you," Wunderlicht said.

"I'll sleep in the next room, where the telephone is."

"I have two colleagues, the 747 pilots, at the Prince de Galles. They'll miss me."

"You'll call them and say everything is fine. And of course you'll remember to call Georges Sauvinage at Françat at twelve noon tomorrow on schedule. You can do that from here . . ."

"Is there *anything* going on in this sordid enterprise that you don't know about?"

"Apparently there is, according to you. Which is why I'm going to start asking you some pertinent questions now—"

"I thought we were going to sleep . . ."

"—and you're going to give me straight answers."

"Suppose I tell you nothing but lies. How will you know the difference?"

"I don't recommend it, Julian, but try it and see how far you get. How many bullets are there in this thing? One? Two? Four? Six?"

"Six. Fourteen. Twenty-four. What's the difference? You're not going to shoot me and you know it. And I'm not going to do anything to harm you, and you know that too. We both happen to need each other much too much, my dear. And right now I need you for something very specific, and if you will be good enough to oblige me, I promise you I will answer any questions you put to me, with total truth and sincerity. Come over here, please, and sit down like a good little girl and stop pointing that damned thing, will you?"

"What do you want?" She moved slowly toward the bed, feeling the brandy in her head.

"What do you think I want?" Wunderlicht said, reaching a hand out toward her. He found the sight of her in pantyhose and an open blouse totally captivating.

"You are crazy, Mr. Wunderlicht."

"Sit down and shut up," he murmured.

She sat slowly, at a cautious distance.

"I've been letting you go on and on this way," Wunderlicht said softly, "not that I have found you boring, or even uninteresting, but I've let you go on and on to give myself time to assess how I really feel about you, because part of my own private fantasy includes you in with me on the remainder of this adventure, with a great deal of wealth being put in your hands to make it worth your while should you find me something less than the man of your dreams . . ."

"We're wasting time and I've got things to find out . . ."

"And you will, you will, if you stroke me the right way. Need I be more explicit? At any rate, as I was saying, I was assessing you and my feelings about you, and just as I was beginning to decide finally that I didn't like you, tits and ass aside, that you are like most young, well-educated, well-endowed, aggressive, on-the-make career girls, a pure and simple smart-ass, I noticed that this damned thing between my legs was beginning to get hard again—look at it, will you—and it just won't stop getting bigger and harder and I've got to tell you it's got me plenty confused because obviously I like you a hell of a lot more than my head knows about—"

She found herself unaccountably staring at the "damned thing" with too much fascination. "Look," she said, "why don't you just take it in your hands and get rid of the confusion, and I'll watch?"

"Aren't you being slightly cruel?" Wunderlicht murmured. "Is this the way to persuade me to be cooperative?"

"Just use the old mitts, Julian, you'll love it."

Wunderlicht sighed with resignation and seized his pulsating erection with some embarrassment. "I'm not sure I remember how to do this."

"No one ever really forgets," Lisa said. "It'll come back to you, like riding a bicycle."

Wunderlicht labored, but without enthusiasm. "I think it's that gun in your hand. I can tell you right now, this isn't working very well."

"You're doing fine."

"What do you mean, I'm doing fine? I'm going absolutely nowhere. Lisa, help me, please."

"Help you?" The man was *insane*. And *she* was drunk . . .

"Come on . . . please . . ."

"Another two hundred francs?" She giggled inadvertently.

"This is no joke. For God's sake, Lisa, help me . . ."

She leaned over and took him in her left hand. "How's this, you crazy son of a bitch?"

"Oh, both hands . . . please . . . Use both hands, Lisa . . ."

"Take what you can get, you greedy bastard."

"Oh Christ, that *is* good . . . Oh Jesus, you're wonderful . . . Oh God . . . yes . . . yes . . . yes . . . Oh my God, guess what's going to happen . . . Oh guess what's going to happen . . . What's going to *happen* . . . Oh . . . Oh . . . OHHHH . . . OHHHH . . . OHHHH . . ." His legs and thighs locked convulsively around her waist. "OHHHH . . ."

"Wait a minute . . . I can't—" she gasped.

"OHHHH . . ." he shouted.

"—breathe . . . Julian, I . . . can't . . ."

"Oh, that was so good," he groaned. "I'm sorry to be so ungrateful."

"Loosen your . . . Oh, don't . . . I can't . . . my ribs . . . oh God . . ." She dropped the gun.

"A little tighter, baby? How's that? A little tighter? Anything cracking yet?"

"Oh . . . oh . . . please . . . can't . . . stand it . . . oh . . . oh . . . I'm going to . . . die . . . Oh please . . . stop . . ."

"Promise you'll just roll off onto the floor?"

"Oh . . . *don't* . . . OH!"

"Promise? Huh? More? Tighter? Huh?"

"I'm . . . dy—"

"The floor! Promise! The next squeeze will kill you! Yes or no? Yes or no?"

"Yes . . . yes . . . I . . . yes . . ."

"Good girl." He opened his legs and she fell to the floor, gasping and wheezing hysterically.

"Stop making such a fuss. You'll live," he said, wiping himself with the towel as he reached for the gun and got off the bed. "Breathe deeply. That's it. Take it in. It's good stuff. You're doing fine. Inhale, exhale. Inhale, exhale. Gun two three four. Gun two three four." He cackled. "Well now . . ."

Slowly she got to her hands and knees, moaning, "You miserable, treacherous prick . . ."

"Pretty good, huh, for a middle-aged schmuck who just shot his second load of the night? There's thigh muscles in the old boy yet, huh?"

She was on her feet now, holding her sides. "If you've broken any of my ribs . . ."

"Stop worrying. I had you by the diaphragm, that's all. It's good to give up breathing now and then. It makes you appreciate being alive. I figured I had a better chance of staying that way if this thing is in *my* hands instead of yours. Women have a way of acting hysterically when they feel a trigger against their finger. Wedding rings sometimes do the same thing to them."

Lisa lay down on the bed and began to weep softly, more out of humiliation and anger at herself for drinking too much than with pain. Wunderlicht padded into the next room, found the telephone, dialed the Prince de Galles, and asked for his suite.

Klaus Freuling came out of a deep sleep to answer.

"Don't say anything, just listen to me and do as I say," Wunderlicht said with sharpness and authority. "In my bedroom closet, and in the top drawer of the dresser, get my brown suit, a white shirt, a brown tie with green dots, some brown socks and a pair of jockey shorts. Bring them in a sack or a laundry bag . . . whatever. Take a taxi and pull up in front of Number Two rue Récamier. It's off the rue de Sèvres on the Left Bank. Do you have that so far?"

"Yes," said Freuling. "But what—?"

"A woman wearing some kind of hat and a dressing gown, or maybe a raincoat, will come out on the sidewalk when you pull up. Open the door, hand the clothing to her, and drive right back to the hotel and go back to sleep. Everything is fine, and all systems are go."

"What's happening?" asked Freuling.

"Will you hurry up, please?" Wunderlicht hung up and went back into the bedroom. "Get me a hat, any hat, and a long raincoat if you have one. If not, a long robe or dressing gown will do."

Lisa's back was to him on the bed. "Get it yourself," she muttered.

He went to her closets, flung them open, and rummaged through her things. "I'm going to have to tie you to the bed while I go downstairs. Afterward, I'll let you sleep in comfort."

She turned to him, her eyes drying. "I take it we're spending the night here."

"Correct," he said.

"And tomorrow?"

"You're going along with me. Where I go, you go. You wanted to be in on everything, for that big book. Well, I'm not going to disappoint you."

"Do I have a choice?"

"None. You're going with me."

"Am I allowed to ask where to?"

"You can ask anything you want. Now and then you may get an answer."

"You know, Wunderlicht, your whole personality took a change for the worse when you got your fat hands on that gun."

"I don't think it's that. I find it always happens to me after I've purged myself of the last drop of sexual desire. Physiologically I go soft. Philosophically I stiffen. It's a nasty trait, I admit, and it has made lasting relationships with women very difficult, if not impossible. Tell me, do you have any sizeable luggage around here, for me and for yourself?"

"All sizes, all kinds. Am I going on a trip?"

"Yes," Wunderlicht said, "with an empty suitcase."

He had already decided how he was going to use her . . . before he did away with her. She was lean of limb and had the deceptive appearance of fragility. But after tangling with her in bed and feeling the powerful thrust and clench of her body, he had no doubt at all that she'd be able to carry one hundred pounds, give or take a little huffing or puffing.

At the current world price of gold, that would mean more than a quarter of a million dollars extra for him.

CHAPTER THIRTY-THREE

JAMES BAGGETT, former linebacker for the University of Maryland, one-time second-in-command of Gerald Ford's White House Secret Service detail, and now a security officer at the Remo Corporation, frowned as he looked up from his desk through the open doorway of his cubbyhole and saw Arkady Slocum, Remo's venerable computer specialist, limping down the basement corridor toward the room that housed the great 307 facility. Baggett rose from his chair, moved swiftly out of his office, and arrived at the locked door to 307 one stride ahead of the other man.

"I can't let you go in there, Dr. Slocum," Baggett said, politely but firmly.

"Not to worry, Jim." Slocum was a mild-mannered, bespectacled man of sixty who had walked with a cane ever since a childhood battle with polio. In his left hand he was clutching the folder containing the one hundred sixty photocopied pages of the passenger information list of the S.S. *Marseille*, together with the inventory of the ship's medical supplies. "I'll be in and out in no time."

"That's not the point." Baggett's face took on a pained expression. "I don't think it's *right,* it just doesn't make *sense,* security not knowing what the hell is going on around here."

The older man feigned surprise. "Didn't the president tell you?"

"Nothing. The only word *we* got was that you and those others in the war games room were to have the run of this wing until tomorrow morning."

Arkady Slocum shrugged and took a white magnetic card from his pocket. "That's the whole story, Jim. There isn't any more to know."

"Bullshit, Doctor."

"Isn't everything?" Slocum sighed. He moved around and past the security man and inserted the magnetic card in the slot.

"Now lookit here . . ."

The steel door was swinging open. "Not to worry, Jim. Not to worry." Slocum quickly shuffled inside and heard the door clang shut in the face of a very worried James Baggett.

The room, if such it could be called, was functional and disproportionately ugly, with the accent on temperature control devices, ventilating ducts, smoke and flame detectors, and an overhead carbon dioxide fire-extinguishing system built into the distant, neon-lit ceiling. All this for the comfort and protection of the room's sole occupant, the superstar, Remo's 307, fifty feet high, thirty feet wide, its steel feet planted firmly on the basement floor, its aluminum head high up in the clouds at the third floor level, on its facing surface a plexiglass window through which you could peer into its soul. To Arkady Slocum it was the most beautiful beastie in the whole world.

He went to the workbench, placed the folder on it, hooked his cane onto the back of one of the two wooden chairs in the room, sat down on the other, and, reaching out, pulled the portable terminal over to him on its ball-bearing rollers. The keyboard was creamy white. The CRT monitor screen above it had a dark background to give contrast to the bright green letters with which 307 did its answering back. Slocum shook his hands loosely, like a concert pianist limbering up, and addressed his first query to the giant computer via the keyboard.

"Are you occupied?"

"Define occupied," replied 307.

Slocum smiled. "Are you busy right now with remote access service?"

"Affirmative," said 307. "Aberdeen, Baltimore, Houston, Milwaukee, Colorado Springs, and Pasadena."

"How quickly can you complete present phase of all assignments and interrupt?"

"Between two minutes twenty seconds and three minutes five seconds," came back the swift reply.

"Continue service, interrupt as soon as possible, then advise."

"Command acknowledged. In process."

Slocum waited, listening to the faint whirring of the electric motor driving the huge magnetic disc pack behind the plexiglass window at thirty-five hundred revolutions per minute. Presently the CRT screen flashed: "Done."

Slocum punched rapidly on the keyboard. "Until further notice, refuse to acknowledge any outside terminals attempting to dial in."

"Define outside," replied 307.

Slocum shook his head slowly. "Everything outside this room."

"Understood," said 307. "Will advise current terminals I must go off line for maintenance."

Slocum thought, why didn't I think of that? and said, "Excellent."

307 said, "In process," paused, then flashed, "Done."

"Stand by," said Slocum.

He took up the folder from the workbench, reached for his cane, rose to his feet, and went over to the Optical Character Reader, a steel-gray rectangular device resembling a portable Xerox machine. Like the CRT, it too was connected to the 307. Slocum removed the one hundred sixty sheets comprising the passenger information list, raised the lid of the OCR device, and carefully placed the stack inside. He pressed a button activating the automatic page-flipper, went back to the keyboard, and sat down before it.

"Are you ready?" he inquired.

"Affirmative," said 307.

"Acquire all information now in OCR," he ordered. "Store names in alphabetical order."

"Command acknowledged," said 307. "In process."

The OCR had a capability of reading one thousand characters per second. Within five minutes, the computer had absorbed the contents of the entire list into its memory bank.

"Done," 307 announced.

Slocum nodded, as though to another being. "The collection of information you have just acquired is our data base," he said through the keyboard. "It will henceforth be referred to simply as PIL."

"PIL," responded 307. "Understood."

"Now restore access to all terminals in war games room, but to no others."

"Terminals 119 through 140," said 307.

"Affirmative," said Slocum.

"Done," said 307.

Arkady Slocum rose to his feet, removed the PIL from the Optical Character Reader, put the stack back in the folder, and threw a farewell glance at his giant friend before going to the steel door. James Baggett was standing outside in the corridor, cracking the knuckles of the hands that had once beaten Navy with a fourth-quarter interception and had pushed Ford out of range of an empty water pistol.

"Now that wasn't so bad, was it?" Slocum said to him.

Baggett shook his head wonderingly. "You guys . . . I mean it . . . you guys . . ."

"I know," Slocum said. "We're very naughty boys." He limped away toward the war games room, glancing at his digital wristwatch as he went. He would have liked to spend the rest of the day, the whole night if necessary, alone with 307. 307 was so calm, so direct, so unemotional, so devoid of ego. It troubled Slocum that he would now have to sit in a room with other men, not one of whom was very good at listening without interrupting, or at taking commands and carrying them out without antagonism. There were times when Arkady Slocum wished he could remote access all of life instead of *being* there, living it. This would be one of those times.

He entered the war games room and heard their chatter die and felt their eyes go to him as if they were expecting him to return with some kind of announcement that it was all over, everything had been miraculously solved. But all he said to the room was, "Okay, we've got something to start with now." And to Al Santley, his assistant and genius-in-training, thirty years his junior with two good legs, he said, "Al, let's have every terminal in here log onto 307 like maybe we're going to make its head spin from overwork."

"Right arm," said Santley brightly, springing to his feet.

"You took ten minutes," said Mike Keegan with almost friendly sarcasm. "You're slowing up, Arkady."

"I had to do the six-foot hurdles over security, what do you want?" Slocum sank down into one of the black leather chairs, already hating this windowless concrete room with its celotex-lined walls and overbright neon and the massive CRT projection screen that dominated one wall. Ashtrays everywhere were still filled with the stale butts of the Red and Blue teams that had just been kicked out in the middle of constructing the defense of New Orleans as the new seat of government after Washington, D.C., and eighty percent of the continental United States had been destroyed by the Enemy. Slocum glanced around him at the other men who, like himself, lounged about facing the large screen. They were all in shirtsleeves, ties still on, not even loosened. Like Slocum, they had been seduced by Lloyd Shipley and his overwrought friend from television into lending themselves to this dubious venture of saving the *Marseille*, out of mixed feelings of guilt, challenge, romanticism, and the need to break out of the personal ruts of their own lonely projects. "Okay, gentlemen," Slocum said. "You were foolish enough to appoint me the leader of this group, so that gives me the power to ask questions. Here's my first. Anybody around here got a bright idea?"

Angelo Martini, a lean, sallow-faced behavioral psychologist out of Berkeley by way of the Center at Princeton, raised his hand. "Nothing exactly bright about this, but I gotta say it anyway. No group planning a crime of this nature is going to be collectively stupid enough to let the French Atlantic Line, of all people, find out anything significant about them. Therefore, I can't see this passenger information list doing anything for us but wasting a lot of precious time. Personally, I think it's a crock, and the sooner we start using our own brains instead of the steel and copper and aluminum kind, the better off we'll be."

"Talk about wasting time," Mike Keegan broke in, bristling. "Where the hell does *that* kind of talk get us, Martini? If you got nothing concrete, nothing positive—"

"Come on, Mike," Arkady Slocum quickly interrupted. "Really now . . ."

"Well, shit . . ."

"Nobody around here has the right to play dogcatcher," Slocum said. "Muzzles are out. Disagreements are in. The name of the game is Anything Goes."

"Time is our biggest enemy," Keegan countered hotly. "Talk talk talk."

"All right, Mike," Slocum shrugged. "Impress us."

"Okay," Keegan snapped. "I say we decide on a list of every data bank in the country that could conceivably have information helpful to us, keeping it down to a reasonable minimum, and program 307 to access each and every one of 'em."

Slocum's eyes narrowed. "Can you give me an idea what you have in mind?"

"Well, naturally the first thing *I'm* gonna wanna know is possible criminal records, arrests, convictions, acquittals, dropped charges, any brushes with the law, on any of those two thousand names."

"Naturally," Slocum said. Keegan was the former head of the Criminal Intelligence Division of the Los Angeles Police Department. It was no surprise to Slocum that a CID man would expect a crime of this magnitude to be carried out by criminals. "But the Captain's radio message indicated that he didn't think the conspirators were criminal types."

"What the fuck does a ship's captain know about things like that?" Keegan said with impatience.

Slocum eyed him. "Let's hear your list."

"All right," said Keegan. "Number one, I want in on the linkup that connects the files of every bureau of the FBI . . ."

Slocum felt a knot slowly forming in his stomach. "Go on."

"Next, we access the State Department's passport files, to see if any of these passenger names are phonies. That would be a dead giveaway. We'd have them cold, and we'd be home in time for dinner."

Slocum nodded, lips tightening.

"Then the Social Security bank—I'm talking about nation-wide—for everything it's got. Talk about *information*, how about IRS, all regions? This so-called confidential PIL of the French Atlantic Line is piffle, mere garbage, compared to what *Washington* has on its loved ones . . ."

"Well, didn't I say *just that?*" demanded Angelo Martini angrily.

Keegan ignored him. "Then gimme motor vehicle bureaus, state by state . . . the Central Credit Reference Bureau . . . What *they* don't know ain't worth knowing. And let's not forget the CIA's baby at Langley . . ."

"The CIA is strictly foreign," Slocum said, without blinking. "Not domestic."

"Hah," said Keegan.

Slocum turned away from him. "Does anybody have anything else to add to this list? Let's go clockwise."

"Yes," said Rudi Fleischman, a retired cryptanalyst formerly with the National Security Agency. "I would like to log onto the air carrier central reservations bank and the space bank of U.S. hotels and motels."

"What the hell for?" Mike Keegan demanded.

Fleischman, a corpulent man, smiled blandly. "I haven't the faintest idea, Keegan. But if I don't touch all bases now, how can I hope to be blessed with serendipitous insight later? When it happens, you'll be the first to know."

"I'm serious, goddamn it," said Keegan.

"So am I, goddamn it," said Fleischman, still smiling.

Arkady Slocum glanced about. "How about you, Irving?"

Irving Harris had published many lurid and imaginative novels, but none so lurid and imaginative as the secret project he had been working on at Remo for over a year now, "Outer Space Avenues of Non-Violent Acquisition of Middle East Oil Fields Without Unacceptable Loss of Future Productivity of Wells." The novelist scratched his shaggy gray mane and said, "I'm doing a lot of listening and a lot of thinking, fellas. So far the only ideas that come to my head are too depressing to mention. So if you don't mind, I'll pass for now."

"Before anybody else around here gets too depressed, like Mr. Harris," interjected Frank Skinner, a sandy-haired, loose-limbed statistician who had played the numbers game everywhere from the International Monetary Fund to the New York Stock Exchange to Equitable Life, before taking up the California sunshine and solitude of Remo as a place to die, "let me point out that we're not going to be dealing with two thousand people, so let's, for crying out loud, stop bandying that number about like it *means* something. Certain elements have to be accepted as *facts* even though we are not sure they *are* facts. If the captain of that ship says the bunch we're after are probably all Americans, that means we've got to start off by automatically ruling out all *non*-Americans. Also, I feel that if any of those passengers are under eighteen or over sixty

. . . pick any numbers you want . . . they should be taken off the list to *begin* with or we'll be here through next Christmas. We may be talking about only nine, twelve, fourteen hundred people to sort out, not two thou. And we got the name of at least one guy, their ringleader, Craig Dunleavy, and how many first names, fourteen, twenty-four? It isn't like we've got *nothing* to start with."

"All right, Frank," said Mike Keegan, "this is going to be such a lead-pipe cinch, why the hell are we wasting precious time *talking?* Arkady, shouldn't we start getting into these banks immediately?"

Slocum stared at the CID man. "I was *wondering* when you were going to get around to asking 'shouldn't we,' Mike."

"What do you mean?" Keegan flared.

"You don't know what I've been working on for the past three years?"

"Of course I do."

"And it doesn't mean anything to you?"

Keegan's face flushed. "Listen, I didn't *have* to come down here from Oxnard this afternoon. I could still be out in the sunshine shingling my roof and enjoying a couple of cold beers. But when Shipley called me and said we're dealing with life and death, I climbed down that ladder and *came* . . ."

"And we're all grateful, Mike . . ."

"Then please don't throw any moralistic crap at me *now,* at *any* of us, Arkady. *We* know how much of your life has gone into fighting illegal invasion of privacy. But I'm assuming that a man who has spent three years figuring out how to prevent unauthorized parties from getting into remote data banks has also learned *exactly how it's done.* And I'm also assuming that, considering the situation we're all into here—we *are* all in this together, for Christ's sake— you're gonna do what has to be done even if it means breaking a few goddamn laws and fracturing your precious code of ethics. So maybe you'll be hauled before some congressional committee. Maybe you'll even go to jail." His craggy face broke into a grin. "We'll bake you a cake every visiting day, won't we, fellows?"

He glanced around. No one was smiling.

Arkady Slocum spoke quietly. "Not just me, Mike. All of us. Maybe we'll *all* go to jail." He sensed a restless stirring in the room. "Now that's perfectly all right with me. I just want to make sure that that's perfectly all right with *you,* gentlemen."

Nobody spoke for a while, and there was some clearing of

throats, and then Frank Skinner drawled, "Oh, what the hell . . ."
And Rudi Fleischman said, "I could *use* a vacation."

Arkady Slocum's gaze swept the room. "Any further comments?"

"What, and waste more time?" Angelo Martini snapped, looking directly at Mike Keegan.

Lawrence Wibberly, gray-haired, rumpled, but distinguished-looking, tapped his pipe on the table beside his chair and said, "If I may, please . . ."

Slocum nodded. "Professor."

The astrophysicist had spent years on Mount Palomar gazing up at the heavens, but whenever he spoke he had the unaccountable habit of looking down at the floor. "One night," Wibberly said, "I was searching for a brand new supernova and I knew exactly where it would be, so that's where I looked and everything was fine, except that, as it turned out, it wasn't there at all. And that's how I happened to discover, by pure accident, the black hole in the vicinity of Cygnus. After that incident, I started looking everywhere in the skies for *more* black holes, and to this day I have never found another one. But in the process of searching, I did stumble across two undiscovered quasars."

Mike Keegan shifted uncomfortably in his seat. "Can you come back to earth, Professor, where we mortals live?"

Wibberly frowned. "I am merely suggesting, gentlemen, that if you are looking for something very desperately, with great purpose and high intention, and with the aid of all your marvelous technology, it would be wise always to leave yourselves open to the possibility that the seemingly right direction you are pointing in will turn out to be the *wrong* direction, and that you will not discover what you were seeking, but perhaps something even more significant."

"I think that's damned good advice, Dr. Wibberly," Arkady Slocum said, not knowing exactly what the hell all *that* was going to do for them. "May I assume you are with us as we start on our journey to Leavenworth penitentiary?"

Wibberly stared down at his Earth shoes and managed a smile. "My wife has taken our grandchildren to Disneyland for the afternoon and evening, and my stomach rebels at the thought of a lonely TV dinner. Nothing could drive me from this room except the eventual, but highly unlikely, success of our mission."

"Thank you for the cue, sir." Arkady Slocum rose. "Gentlemen, consider yourselves temporarily driven from this room. I'm asking all of you, with the exception of Al Santley, to please get lost for about ten minutes. Get a candy bar from the machine, take a leak, do anything you want, but don't wander down the hall and antagonize Jim Baggett if you can help it."

"How do you like this baby?" Mike Keegan grumbled as the men slowly got to their feet. "He actually thinks we'd peer over his shoulder and steal some of his dirty tricks."

"I wasn't thinking that at all," the computer specialist said evenly, as he and Santley moved toward the main terminals. "I'm giving you men an out when you find yourselves on the witness stand. You didn't know what I was doing in here. You would never have permitted it."

"Don't crap a crapper, Arkady," muttered Keegan, trailing the others to the door. "You just don't trust us, that's all."

Arkady Slocum waited for the door to close, then turned quickly to his assistant and spoke briskly. "First thing I want you to do is instruct 307 never, under any circumstances, even if so requested by any terminal in this room including you or me, never to repeat or acknowledge or duplicate on the screen any dialing sequences or log-on instructions we are about to program in."

The younger man looked at him and smiled knowingly. "Me neither," he said. "Not one of them . . . not as far as I could throw him."

"Step two," said Slocum. "Unless previously commanded, 307 is to destruct the entire program at twelve noon tomorrow and have no memory of its prior existence."

Santley glanced up and frowned. "Seriously, boss. *That* dangerous?"

"You should study some of the new legislation," the older man replied. "We could be in deep yogurt here. Very deep yogurt."

"One more question . . ."

Slocum gestured impatiently to the terminal keyboard. "Please get *to* it."

"How come?" Santley persisted. "How come nobody talks about how in hell we're gonna *kill off* these bastards once we identify them? Why aren't we also feeding that list of drugs and chemical compounds into the computer?"

Arkady Slocum felt his face reddening. "Do I have to draw you a picture of a cart before a horse?" The trouble with Santley was, he was too goddamn young, there was still too much he didn't understand. Remo was a place where you came for refuge, not for reality, where you could spend undistracted years setting up exotic clay pigeons and shoot them down with your elegant brainpower, telling yourself you were making important contributions to the military defense of your country and the future betterment of mankind. None of the regulars around here, and Slocum knew he was included, none was ready yet to shoot at *live* bodies, to confront anything as real as mass murder. They would come at it slowly, circuitously, reluctantly, and maybe never at all if they couldn't first find some way of viewing it as just another game. "And if you have any more questions, don't ask me, ask 307," Slocum snapped irritably, and turned away.

Santley glanced down at his keyboard feeling vaguely uncomfortable, sensing that he had just learned something painful and sad from the sudden anger of a man he admired. He'd think about it later. Right now he had work to do.

His fingers began to move over the keys with practiced grace and speed.

CHAPTER THIRTY-FOUR

Latitude 17° N., Longitude 52° W.
Luxembourg Dining Room—9:40 P.M.

"The stabilizers on this boat must be Polish, and your Dramamine is from Warsaw, too. It does *nothing* for me."

"Craig, you really shouldn't mix so much alcohol with it."

"You're all *shouldn'ts* tonight, Betty."

"Don't turn around."

"What is it?"

"Them. They're just coming down the staircase together."

"Columbine and the bitch?"

"Yes."

"Right on schedule."

"Don't sound so *happy* about it."

"You think he's balling her while her husband is balling the flu?"

"Will you *please* leave that stuff alone?"

"What've you got against brandy?"

"It's not just the brandy, it's the *martinis* and the *wine* and the brandy. Why don't you tell me what's gotten into you, what's wrong?"

"I've got to get through this night, that's all. Where are they now? Am I allowed to turn my head, pretty please?"

"No, don't. They're at her table now. I want to know, Craig."

"What, damn it?"

"What you plan to do about them. Why you men met without the women tonight, for the first time ever."

"We're male chauvinist pigs, you know that, Betty."

"I'm not going to let you do this. The others yes, but you're not going to bullshit *me.*"

"What are they ordering?"

"I swear to God I'll throw this in your face if you take *one more.* Now *tell* me, goddamn it, what's been going on?"

"Oh, Betty, Betty, Betty . . ."

"Don't Betty me. Come on."

"Must I?"

"Yes."

"All right. All right. Jesus. All right. We had to . . . *handle* eighteen of them tonight. There."

"Eighteen what?"

"People. Passengers. Husbands and wives."

"What have you done with them? Where did you put them?"

"You're not understanding me, Betty. You don't *want* to understand me. Which is to be expected. Which is why we didn't want you girls in on it tonight."

"What in heaven's name are you—?"

"They were hostages."

"Craig, what are you . . . ? *Craig . . . !*"

"I think you got it."

"Oh my God . . . *Oh . . . no . . .*"

"Here."

"I don't want it."

"Take it."

"I don't want it."

"Don't give me that look. You know goddamn well we're not playing pattycake. What's the difference if they go now or tomorrow?"

"None."

"All right. Then don't do this to me."

"I'm not doing anything to you."

"The fuck you're not."

"You're drinking, and I'm sick in my heart and my stomach. What am I supposed to do?"

"Help me. Support me. Especially when it gets unbearable. See me through it. Can't you tell when I need your help?"

"Yes . . . yes . . . I'm sorry . . . You're right, darling . . . I'm sorry."

"Better. That's better. Are you okay?"

"Yes. I just want to forget it."

"This helps."

"You. Not me."

"Chacun à son goût."

"But did you have to, Craig?"

"If it's any consolation, I was against it. So was Herb. The others were beyond reason."

"I guess we better stop talking about it."

"All right. But it concerns me, Betty, it really does, that the fellows think you and Harriet and the others couldn't have been able to confront it, and I thought they were right and now I *know* they were right, and that brings us to tomorrow. You're going to have to be able to look *that* in the face, honey. All of us are."

"I know. I know. Somehow I'm assuming it'll be different."

"How different?"

"We won't . . . *be* there . . . when it happens. It'll be, I don't know, something in the head, an idea, an ungraspable idea, like how much is a trillion, or how many miles is it from here to the nearest star."

"That's fine. Anything that works for you is fine."

"I hope so."

"I *know* so."

"Craig, I think I *will* have some of that after all."

"Good girl. How's this?"

"Keep going."

"So?"

"Fine."

"Cheers."

"Cheers."

"Here's to escape, and all its many different hatches."

"Ugh. Tell me something I still don't understand. Why were those two not included tonight, and please don't turn around?"

"We decided it was more important for us to try to find out how much they know."

"But we *know* how much they know."

"Not really, Betty. How can we know for sure what Louise volunteered, or Columbine forced out of her, before she took her final bath? And too many of our friends at the masquerade ball were stoned for us to be one hundred percent certain they didn't let some very large cats out of the bag when the little lady you won't let me turn around to look at infiltrated us behind that fucking mask."

"I thought all she got was some of our first names."

"That's what we *think*. But were *you* there, was *I* there, to guarantee that no one cracked?"

"So that's why you wanted Harriet and me to bring her in?"

"More or less. Yes."

"But they go with the others tomorrow anyway, right?"

"Right."

"Then what's the difference what they know or don't know? Where are they going to go with it that isn't straight down?"

"You're making a dangerous assumption, Betty."

"I am?"

"Suppose one or both of them have somehow found out what our true intentions are, and have passed that on to the Captain?"

"Oh my, yes, but I'm not sure I . . . I mean, what could *he* do?"

"We don't know. We can only speculate. At the very least, a trapped rat, a few thousand of them, could make tomorrow a *very* uncomfortable day . . ."

"Craig, I don't *like* this . . ."

"At the very worst, Girodt could, he just *could,* play it cool, lie low, pretend to believe us, and then *not* go along with our defusing instructions. Suppose he waits till we leave and immediately orders the lifeboats lowered? This whole goddamn ship can be emptied in less than fifteen minutes, you know."

"Good God . . . when I think of all the stupid, meaningless, senseless deaths so far . . . Why were *those* two allowed to live for *one extra moment* after they became *known* to us as active enemies?"

"Now that's unfair, Betty. That's just plain below-the-belt hindsight and you know it."

"No, I *don't* know it. All I know is that you and Herb have been selling us all a bill of goods. He's too *famous. She* has been *seen* with him too much, this famous fool, by *too* many passengers. They're a *pair,* a *couple.* People will *talk* if they vanish."

"Monday morning quarterbacking."

"Where the devil did those two, of all people, come off to have charmed lives, for God's sake?"

"Make a long distance phone call to hell and ask Don Campbell. Ask Louise. They *tried,* didn't they?"

"And you *opposed* it all the way . . ."

"All *right.* Nobody's perfect, not Don, not Louise, not *any* of us, certainly not me."

"For sure."

"Just the same, we've made damned fewer mistakes than anyone could've predicted. No really big ones . . . I don't think."

"You don't think."

"Scratch that."

"Look at me, Craig. I'm scratching that."

"Hey, take it easy, will you? You'll be useless. We *are* going to have to hook into them, you know, join them for dessert or follow them to a bar or something, and we'll both have to have our heads on straight if we're going to make it come off."

"What about Louise's gun?"

"Stop worrying. This is bullet-proof brandy."

"Darling . . . ?"

"Mm?"

"I'm unforgivable, I know it, but I do love you."

"I know that, sweetheart."

"I don't want us to die any other way than together."

"Or not at all, if it's all right with you."

"If you insist."

"Why don't we order a *cappuccino* to clear the cobwebs, then go over to that table and see how the other half lives?"

"Yes."

*   *   *

"Baby, you're not listening to me . . ."

"I *am*. Go ahead. And stop calling me baby, Harold."

"Then you're deliberately trying not to dig what I'm saying."

"She keeps staring at us."

"So what? Let her stare."

"She gives me the shivers."

"You're got *me* to keep you warm. Now, are you gonna go along with me on this and trust me?"

"If you'll be more clear about what I'm going along *with* . . ."

"I can't be, because I don't even know myself yet. A lot depends on *their* attitude, what *they* say. You just ad lib along with me, swing with it, hang loose, and suddenly we'll know where we are and who we are and what we're playing, and we'll be carried along by our own momentum. It works. You watch."

"This is the way you write your novels?"

"Only sometimes. When the hangover is of a certain magnitude, or I've got too much on my mind for anything as orderly as rational creative thinking."

"So you end up with a Book-of-the-Month Club selection, *that* I can understand. But what is *this* game going to do for us tonight?"

"The answer to that is a multiple choice of five. Only one, or all, or none of them, is correct. (A) Anything we do that keeps them away from your cabin is desirable; (B) Maybe we find out something significant, by sheer accident, slip of the tongue, whatever, that can be fed to the Captain and/or your husband's radio; (C) You or I or both of us together achieve the impossible, to wit, we convince them that their scheme is so hopeless they all should give themselves up; (D) They'll find us so charming and lovable, they won't want to kill us; and (E) If we don't spend time with *them* tonight, then I'm going to find myself doing nothing all night except trying to lure you into my bed, and that would be most unfair to you because I intend to be irresistible. Okay, you have thirty seconds."

"What did you think of Billy when you met him tonight?"

"Twenty-four seconds."

"Harold?"

"I've been married four times. What I know about spouses and the mating game you can put in the head of a pinhead."

"So what did you think of Billy?"

"Jesus, *I* don't know. What did I have with him, *twenty minutes,* while he's trying to radio that death list to the friend who wasn't there? Okay, he twirls a great radio dial. Lots of grace under pressure. Probably a fine doctor. Very serious, very earnest—"

"Very dull?"

"Loves you, adores you, would never cheat on you, will be there at your fiftieth wedding anniversary. Ten seconds."

"But all wrong for me, right?"

"All *right* for you. Wrong."

"You're a liar."

"Your time's up. What's the answer?"

"You're afraid to be real with anyone like me, aren't you, Harold? You could never handle it. You might have to love and be loved, instead of fuck and be fucked . . ."

"Don't *use* words like that, goddamn it."

"You've heard fuck before."

"I mean love. The answer is, all five are correct."

"Why is he so right for me?"

"Because of guys like me. The woods are full of us. We know what we are and we like it. The way to a woman's heart is through her vaginal itch, that's how we nail them. But the smart women, like you, see right through us, and they either say, who needs it? and blow, or they say, *I* need it, and get their itch scratched for a while and *then* blow. But they always blow, and you don't want that kind of life, blow after blow. You want—what? Continuity? I give you the good doctor. From him you ain't gonna blow, lady."

"What about the middle ground? You talk in such ridiculous extremes, Columbine."

"Middle ground, my ass. It's all a matter of degree, but putting it as simply as possible, which is the only way to reduce anything unfathomable to something that makes sense, there are only good guys and bad guys. For you, it'll always be a good guy, and you've got one. However, this is not to say that you won't hump anywhere from four to a dozen of the other kind, along the bridal path that leads but to the grave. *I'd* just like to be the *first*."

"You've got a fucking nerve."

"For saying four to a dozen?"

"No. For assuming you'd be the first."

"Wrong?"

"Right, damn you."

"The nose knows . . ."

"Prick."

"And God how I love that fragrance."

"Will you *listen* to us? Those poor people horribly murdered like *minutes* ago, and Billy scared out of his gourd trying to reach the States with the news, and those two right across the room from us, and what are we talking about? I mean, listen to us."

"Is there some particular virtue in dining in silence?"

"No."

"Would it make you feel better if we recited prayers for the dead over this caviar?"

"The least we could do is be serious."

"I can't think of anything more serious than what we were talking about. It's like plane talk."

"Not so plain."

"Plane. *Air*plane. The kind of conversation you have with the total stranger sitting next to you on the 747 thousands of miles and forty thousand feet from anywhere, because you both know that you'll never see each other again, so it's perfectly safe, and because way deep down, you both are wondering if maybe you're not going to crash and die in the next hour or two . . ."

"That's us, all right. You're a barrel of laughs tonight, Harold."

"There's something I gotta tell you, Julie."

"Really?"

"Yes. I've got a gun on me. Loaded. A Magnum, with a silencer."

"Where on earth did you get it?"

"Remember I told you about a girl at the bar eyeing me, when you stood me up this afternoon?"

"Vaguely."

"I went to her cabin and . . . uh . . . slept with her . . ."

"Just a few hours ago . . ."

"Yes."

"Thanks, Harold."

"I was pissed . . ."

"I'm sure."

"And when I found out she was one of them, setting me up to kill me, I took her gun away and then I . . . Jesus, I can't believe it . . . I buggered her. You hear what I'm saying?"

"Yes."

"It must have destroyed her. Louise Campbell. She was the one who jumped overboard this evening."

"Why are you telling me this?"

"Because I don't want to have any secrets from you, Julie. I want you to know exactly who I am."

"I already know, Harold. So stop trying to be someone you're not."

"Can *you* stop trying?"

"I guess not."

"Then shut up."

"Harold . . ."

"What?"

"They just got up. They're leaving."

"So?"

"I think they're coming over here . . . to us."

"Perfect. Stop trembling."

"I hate you. Hold my hand."

"Hi, I'm Craig Dunleavy. This is my wife, Betty."

"Yah. I'm sure you know who *we* are."

"Oh, yes."

"Care to sit down, join us?"

"All right, yes, for a few minutes. We've *had* dinner."

As they sat down, Betty Dunleavy looked at Julie and said, "I'm sorry about this afternoon, really."

"You mean you're sorry you weren't wearing your running shoes," Julie said.

"How about some booze?" Harold Columbine said.

"No, we're fine," Betty Dunleavy said quickly.

"All right." Harold Columbine said. "What can we do for you, Mr. Dunleavy, aside from dropping dead?"

Craig Dunleavy smiled. "All we really wanted to say to you two is, how about a truce, an armistice, a peace settlement of some sort?"

"Meaning?"

"You lay off us, we lay off you . . . for the duration."

"We haven't done a thing except stumble into your operation. No harm, no foul."

"That may have been true at first, Mr. Columbine. But then you set out to deliberately interfere." Dunleavy glanced at Julie. "Especially you, honey."

"You're so right, mister. Anything for a little excitement on this dull voyage."

Dunleavy's smile was disdainful. "Please don't take me for a fool, Mrs. Berlin . . ."

"I wouldn't take you for anything, Mr. Dunleavy."

"You've been trying to get information about us," Craig Dunleavy said.

"To stick in an empty wine bottle?" Julie said. "And cast it adrift in the ocean?"

"No, I think you've been feeding whatever you could pick up to the medical officer on board, for him to relay to the Captain . . ."

"So *he* can put it in a wine bottle."

"Am I correct?"

"Yes," Harold Columbine took over. "You're correct. Next?"

"How much have you found out?"

"About what?"

"Us."

"Plenty. You're a bunch of amateurs who drink too much and kill too much, and if you think for a minute that we believe this cockamamie story about your caring how much we've found out, you're a worse amateur than I thought, Dunleavy. Strictly bush."

Craig Dunleavy blinked rapidly. "What do *you* think I want, Mr. Columbine?"

"For one thing, our help . . ."

"How can you help us, other than by staying out of our way?"

"Exactly."

"Any other way?" Dunleavy said.

"Louise Campbell's gun," Harold Columbine said.

"Inconsequential," Craig Dunleavy said.

"In the long run, maybe. But I don't think you like the idea of some crazy nut having the capability of taking six of you with him as he falls."

"How melodramatic."

"I'm a writer. What line are *you* in, Dunleavy?"

"Getting rich quick. Want to hand it over?"

"Unh-uh."

"I think maybe you better."

"Or?"

"See that waiter standing over there watching us?"

"Mm-hm."

"He doesn't work for the French Atlantic Line."

"I wonder what he could do fast enough to prevent me from pulling the trigger of this thing I am holding under the table aimed at—forgive me, ladies—your balls?"

"I don't know about you," Betty Dunleavy said to Julie, "but I find this macho talk pretty boring."

"I agree," Julie said. "Harold, put it away, will you?"

He looked at her. "You believe everything I say?"

"What about my peace offer, Columbine?" said Dunleavy. "Yes or no?"

"You said something about 'for the duration.' How long is that?"

"Until we leave the ship."

"Which is when?"

Craig Dunleavy looked at him without expression. "I think you already know that perfectly well."

"So waste the words anyway," Harold Columbine said.

"Tomorrow afternoon."

"Good. We were afraid you were going to take us on a trip around the world. I don't think I could have stood that."

"Not enough champagne and caviar aboard," Dunleavy said.

Harold Columbine looked at Julie and waited for her eyes to meet his. "That doesn't give us much time then, honey." He held her puzzled gaze. "Lucky we ran across these people tonight . . ." Julie nodded uncertain agreement. He said, "You want to start?"

Julie flushed. "Me?"

"Yes."

"No, I . . . uh . . . I'd find it too . . ."

"Awkward?"

"You could say that. Yes, awkward."

"What the hell are you two talking about?" Craig Dunleavy said.

"Look, Dunleavy, I know you and the missus here and who knows *how* many of your confederates (what a word) think that Julie and I have been messing around just to spoil your act, so it's going to be pretty hard for me to sell you on the *real* reason . . ."

"Try us," Craig Dunleavy said.

"Honey, sure you don't want to take it?"

"No. Please, Harold. You're doing fine."

"Would you rather I discuss this when you're not around?" he said to her.

"What do you mean?" Julie said.

"You could leave the table for a while and come back, or he and I could leave the table."

"No." Their eyes locked. "Don't worry about me, Harold. Just say it."

"Okay." He turned away from her. "Plain and simple, Dunleavy. We want to make a deal with you."

Craig Dunleavy exchanged a glance with his wife. "We're listening," he said.

"Julie and I have managed to collect the first names of over twenty of your colleagues . . ."

"You worked long and hard," Dunleavy said.

"She did most of it."

"And you've turned the names over to the Captain, so that when the *Marseille* docks at Le Havre, he can start the ball rolling that will eventually flatten us all."

Harold Columbine shrugged. "If I did that, what would I have to offer you now?"

Craig Dunleavy looked at him. "You haven't turned us in?"

"Correct."

"Why should I believe that?"

"Because it's the truth."

"All right. Go on."

"That's *our* end of the deal. The list would be yours."

"What about other copies, what about your powers of recall?"

"Our lips would have to stay sealed, because we'd be implicated so heavily."

"By what? I don't follow."

"You don't get the list for nothing, Dunleavy."

There was a pause before the other man spoke. "Of course. How much? Ten grand? Fifty? Ten percent of our take, deposited in a Swiss bank?"

Harold Columbine shook his head slowly, and his eyes went to Julie. "Not a penny," he said.

Craig Dunleavy said, "Did you hear that, Betty?"

"I heard," she said.

"How do we get it, Columbine?"

"Shall I, honey? Last chance. Yes or no?"

"It's your decision, Harold."

"I don't want it to be mine. I want it to be ours together."

"I know you do, but I don't want it that way. I want it to be yours alone."

"Let's have it," Craig Dunleavy said impatiently.

Harold Columbine turned to him. "Her husband."

"Dr. Berlin . . ."

"The one with the flu."

"So?"

"It's a self-limiting disease," Harold Columbine said. "He's gonna get better."

"Yes."

"We don't want him to. Excuse me, *I* don't want him to."

"Get better," Craig Dunleavy said, blinking.

"That's right," Harold Columbine said, not looking at Julie.

"Craig . . ." Betty Dunleavy said.

"Hold it. And you want us to—?"

"Yes," Harold Columbine said. "Select him at random, like you did the others."

"Craig, this is—"

"No one will ever suspect anything," Harold Columbine said.

"You've got the Magnum," Craig Dunleavy said. "You could do it yourself and they'd think it was us."

"We've discussed that—" He heard Julie's little moan. "Don't shake your head, honey. We *did* talk about it. Face it, we *did* . . ."

Craig Dunleavy said, "And?"

"It would never happen," Harold Columbine said. "I don't have the stomach."

"Craig, I want no part of this . . ."

"Haven't you two ever heard of divorce courts?" Dunleavy asked.

"Yes. You ever hear of life insurance policies?" Harold Columbine replied. "Big bunch."

"I see."

"How about tonight?"

"How about stop pushing me? Betty, what do you say?"

"I don't believe him for a minute, and if I did, the whole idea is too disgusting even to *think* about . . ."

"You're a hell of a one, Mrs. Dunleavy, to be talking about what is or isn't disgusting."

"Take it easy, Columbine."

"Fucking holier-than-thou bullshit."

"Did you hear me?"

"Yes or no? You want the list? Yes or no?"

"Do you have it on you?"

"No, but I can get it."

"Tell you what. Let me discuss this with my people and get back to you."

"Tonight."

"Tonight. Where will you be?"

"At the bar of the Montmartre Cafe. Give me a signal and we'll join you somewhere. I don't think we should be seen together."

"Agreed. One thing I know, they're going to say you'll have to turn over the Magnum as part of the transaction."

"Never."

"Powerful word."

"I might have to develop a strong stomach, if you guys fail to come through."

Betty Dunleavy rose quickly and started from the table muttering, "Sick . . ."

"Betty?" Craig Dunleavy scrambled to his feet, muttered "See you later," and went after his wife.

Harold Columbine and Julie watched them go.

"The elevator, or walk?"

"Walk. I need air badly."

"What the hell *is* it with you, Betty?"

"I don't know. It's all getting to be . . . too much."

"You *said* you didn't believe a word he was saying . . ."

"That's what I *said,* yes."

"Well, you were right. He writes bad, he lies worse."

"How do you know, Craig?"

"To high heaven, I'm telling you. Oh, yes, he's got a list all right. Unimportant whether he has or hasn't given it to the Captain. I say has. But they can wipe their asses with it . . . if they hurry. As for the stuff about him wanting us to take care of her husband, that's a crock, a crap suzette, sweetheart."

"Can't you get out of the bathroom?"

"They were just inventing a reason to develop some kind of relationship with us, anything to maintain contact with us for whatever it might be worth to them."

"All right. So what did we accomplish, what did we find out that made it worth sitting with that repulsive man?"

"This: they have no idea what's going to happen tomorrow. If they did, he wouldn't have thought that a list of names would be something of value to the Captain, and therefore to us. Get it?"

"Okay, what are you going to do about him, *and* her?"

"I thought you felt that tomorrow was good enough for them."

"I just want to know what you're planning to do. I don't want any more surprises, Craig."

"Speak to Herb, that's what I'm going to do. You wanna come?"

"Yes."

"Horrible," she said.

"I rather liked it," he said.

"You would."

"It was so . . . logical."

"Suppose they accept your offer and want to go through with it? Then what, Harold? Give me the logic."

"Stop worrying, will you, baby? He didn't swallow a thing I said. Even if he did, he'd want the list first. We're in control. Now lay off for a second and let me think, will you please?"

"Also, I had the ugly feeling that you meant every word of it."

"What is it? . . . What is it they're afraid we've found out? They have no idea that we have a means of communication with the outside world. Still, they're worried that we *know* something, and whatever it is must be something that could ruin their scheme and stop them cold, or they wouldn't care all that much. It's the only reason they came over to the table, the only reason we're still alive. Goddamn it, what could it be?"

CHAPTER THIRTY-FIVE

MAGGIE JOY turned the flame lower under the chicken caccia-tore and answered the ringing telephone. The operator said she had a collect call for Mr. Brian Joy from Tampa, Florida.

"Who's calling?" Maggie asked.

"The party said he's a ham radio operator in contact with a ship at sea," the operator replied. "Is Mr. Brian Joy there?"

"Yes, he is," Maggie said. "Hold the wire please."

She went quickly to the den and saw him with his ear to the speaker beside the Signal One transceiver, his left hand nursing the dial of the VFO with the delicate touch of a safecracker.

"A ham in Tampa, Florida, on line one," she said. "It's collect."

"Hey." Eagerly he snatched up the phone on the desk. "Hello?"

"Mr. Brian Joy?"

"Yes, speaking."

"I have a collect call for you from Tampa, Florida. Will you accept the charges, sir?"

"Yes, yes, put him on."

"Go ahead, sir," the operator said.

"Hello? Is this Brian, W6LS?" The voice was middle-aged, easy-going.

"Yes, it is."

"My name is Jim Hogan, K4 Kilowatt Romeo, in Tampa . . ."

"Yes, Jim. What's up?"

"I'm in a QSO here with your friend Billy, W6VC Mickey Mouse, on 14,220. He said he heard you very weakly calling him, but you're obviously not hearing *him*, so he asked me to relay. He's got traffic for you."

"Terrific," Brian Joy said. "Much appreciate."

"No sweat," the Floridian said. "Want to try hooking up with me on twenty, or shall we stay on the Lima Lima and play it safe?"

"The land line, by all means," Brian Joy said.

"Roger. Stand by now."

Brian Joy looked up at Maggie, watching him from the doorway.

"Anything?" she asked.

He shrugged. "I don't know yet. Can I have a drink?"

"No," she said.

"Thanks," he said.

"What time do you want to have dinner, if at all?"

"Of course we'll have dinner. Sevenish. Something like that."

"Let me know if anything . . ."

"Don't worry, I will."

She left him and went back to the kitchen. He held the phone tightly, waiting, thinking about the men at Remo, wondering if he'd ever hear from them. What an unimpressive bunch . . . nebs, losers, all of them. His thoughts went to Paris, to Lisa Briande. One-thirty in the morning there. She was probably asleep. He wondered with whom, and felt a pang. The voice from Tampa came back on the line.

"Brian?"

"Yes. Go ahead."

"Your friend gave me some names. He wants you to take them down. Got a pencil?"

"Yes. I'm ready."

The man in Florida slowly read eighteen names, nine men, nine women, and Brian Joy wrote them down on the yellow pad. "I've got one more name," the voice said. "It's Louise Campbell."

"Got it," Brian Joy said.

"He said that *that* one, that last one, is definitely one of them, and you'd know what that means."

Brian Joy circled Louise Campbell and said, "Would you please ask Billy what about these names, what am I supposed to do with them?"

"Oh, sorry, pal, forgot to tell you. He said the first eighteen names should be scratched from the list. I assume you know what list he's talking about."

Scratched from the list? Brian Joy swallowed hard, wishing his phone would suddenly fail. "Ask him if they are all silent keys," he said finally.

There was a long pause at the other end. "You mean *dead?*"

"*Ask* him, will you, Jim?"

"Sure, pal, sure. Hold on."

He felt the dread rising in his stomach. He called out, "Maggie? . . ."

"What is it?" Her voice drifted in from the kitchen.

"Pour me a drink and bring it in here right away."

"The hell you say."

"Will you bring me a drink, goddamn it?"

The voice from Florida said, "Brian?"

"I'm here," he said into the telephone.

"The answer is yes," the voice said.

Brian Joy hesitated. "Silent keys?"

"Yes, all eighteen of them, plus the lady named Louise Campbell."

He tried to say something, but nothing would come out.

"What's this all about?" the voice asked.

"Nothing . . . Just a game . . . Listen, Jim, I better hang up now. This collect call is costing a fortune . . ."

"Yes, I know, but before you go, your friend wants to know if you have any news for him."

"No. Nothing. Wait a minute. Yes. Tell him we're working on everything. Tell him I'll look for him on our regular schedule every hour." Tell him anything . . .

"Roger. Will do. Well, nice meeting you, pal. Maybe we can meet on the air some day and you can fill me in on all this. It sure sounds—"

"You bet, Jim, sure thing, and thanks a hell of a lot for the relay."

"My pleasure," the man in Florida said.

Brian Joy hung up and stared down at the pad, sick at heart. He tore off the yellow page, pushed his chair back from the desk, rose to his feet and made his way slowly to the kitchen.

The afternoon fog had come in from the ocean as if on cue. Maggie was standing at the stove with her back to him, the bitch.

"Why the hell don't you turn a light on in here?" he said.

"Why don't you?" she said, not turning.

He snapped on the lights. "And when I ask you to pour me a drink, the least you can do is *do* it. I don't need this kind of shit from you, not today."

"I'm trying to keep you alive, you asshole," she said quietly.

"Fuck." He uncapped a bottle of Sauza Gold, poured four ounces into a tumbler, took the orange juice pitcher from the refrigerator and splashed some into the glass. He threw a few ice cubes in, added a dash of grenadine syrup, stirred with his index finger, then picked up the glass and drank it all down in one continuous gulp, sighing, "Ah Christ," after the shock wore off.

He reached past Maggie, took the wall phone off the hook and dialed the private line in the war games room at Remo.

Arkady Slocum picked it up. "Is that you, Brian?"

"How are you guys doing?" he said.

"I told you I'd call you if we—"

"I know. So how's it going?"

"We're down to less than four hundred possibilities. I'm inclined to view that as progress," Arkady Slocum said coolly.

Brian Joy's lips tightened. "I've got some news that might interest 317, which is why I'm calling."

"You mean 307," Arkady Slocum said.

"Excuse me," Brian Joy said. The tequila was already pissing on his brain. He could feel it making him angry. "The name of one of them, and this is definite, is Louise Campbell."

"Hold it a minute," Arkady Slocum said. Then he said, "Yes, we already have her as a probable."

"She's dead," Brian Joy said, hearing Maggie's stirring spoon suddenly slow down. "Don't ask me how or why."

"That's odd," Arkady Slocum said.

"Yeah, hilarious," Brian Joy said. "For 307, if you will . . . the following eighteen names . . . in alphabetical order . . ." He paused.

"Go ahead," Arkady Slocum said.

"Ned and Myra Clayworth . . . Frank and Millicent Holdorf . . . Edgar and Sue Ann Lockhart . . . Tom and Adele Rice . . . Gary and Claire Rogers . . . Walter and Geraldine Sneed . . . Milton and Ruth Tempkin . . . Stanford and Margot Whitman . . . Lawrence and Maxine Willow . . ." He stopped.

"What about them?" Arkady Slocum asked.

"Passengers to be removed from consideration," Brian Joy said. "Scratched from the list, as it were."

Arkady Slocum cleared his throat. "Do you mind telling me why?"

"Not at all, Dr. Slocum, I'd be delighted. They are dead . . . D-E-A-D . . . or, as we say in television, they have been canceled."

"I understand," Arkady Slocum said quietly. "Is there anything else?"

"Yes," Brian Joy said with bitterness. "Wake me when it's over." He hung up, and saw Maggie starting to turn to him. Fuck it. Who needed her sympathy?

"Brian? . . ."

He reached for the Sauza. She whirled and grabbed for the bottle and he struggled with her, crying, "What . . . the . . . hell . . . are . . . you—?"

"No, goddamn it," she said, wrenching the bottle from his grasp.

"Give it to me." His voice was hoarse. He watched dumbly as she poured his life's blood down the sink drain. "What are you *doing,* for God's sake?"

"I don't know," she moaned. "I don't know . . ."

He turned away, and heard her beginning to weep softly. He walked slowly, without purpose, back to the den. The orange-lighted numbers in the digital frequency readout of his transceiver were winking silently in the fog-shrouded grayness of the room. He sank down in the desk chair, stared unseeingly at the flickering lights and slowly closed his eyes.

Julie Berlin and Harold Columbine sat at one of the small tables in the Montmartre Cafe until well past midnight, waiting for Craig Dunleavy to appear. They drank too many stingers, lit too many cigarettes, and skirted too many personal issues, both of them realizing that they had said far too much to each other earlier that night, far more than either found comfortable to live with now. Small talk was worth its weightlessness in gold, and when it became clear that Dunleavy was not going to show, Harold Columbine called for the check, and a waiter brought it to the table, along with a note which he said had just been delivered to him by a stranger. Harold Columbine waited for the waiter to leave, then opened the note and read it aloud to Julie.

"Your offer is accepted. Bring the list to my cabin, Main Deck 405, as soon as possible. Also the key to *his* cabin, and enjoy yourselves elsewhere until 1:30 a.m. We aim to please. Signed— C.D."

Julie's face turned pale. "Now what?"

"Easy does it." He patted her hand comfortingly, welcoming the rolling thunder of the angry sea and the persistent clanking of the *Marseille*'s bones. Perhaps she wouldn't hear his own heart pounding now. He turned things over in his mind with first-draft speed, then scribbled on the back of the note: "Sorry, you'll have to come to *my* cabin to get it. I'll call you as soon as I get there. H.C." He showed the note to Julie, put it in the envelope and summoned the waiter back.

"Give this to the man who sent it," he told him.

"But, m'sieur, I do not know who he is," the waiter said.

"How do you say bullshit in French?" Harold Columbine said. "Deliver it."

The waiter took the envelope with sullen expression and walked away.

"Let's go."

He took Julie to her cabin door and waited there with her as Billy struggled with the lock and finally opened up and let them in. The young doctor's face had the glassy pallor of a man who hadn't slept for a year. He looked past Julie and said, "I got through to him."

"I knew you would," Harold Columbine said. "Did he have any encouragement for us?"

"Yes, he said everything was coming along, they're working on things."

Harold Columbine smiled at Julie. "See? What did I tell you?"

She looked at him worriedly. "What are you going to do now, Harold?"

"I'm going to my cabin. A real heavy date. As for you two, don't either of you open this door for *anyone* tonight. And I mean *anyone,* including the Captain. See ya."

"What's going on?" Billy Berlin said quickly.

"Your wife will tell you about it, but Doctor, you ain't gonna believe it." He chuckled and turned to leave.

"Harold? . . ."

The look in her eyes was worth anything that could possibly happen to him. "What, Julie?"

"Will you call me?" she said.

"When?"

"In an hour?"

"And wake you up?"

"I want to know that you're all right," she said.

He glanced at Billy, watching them. "I'll be all right," he said.

"Call me," she said.

He went out and waited until he heard the door being bolted. Then he hurried away down the lurching corridor.

The passageway outside his own cabin was deserted. He unlocked the door and pushed it open into the darkened room and stood outside for a long moment before entering slowly, the automatic gripped tightly in his right hand. He snapped on the lights, closed the door, searched the cabin with what he felt was sufficient thoroughness, even peering under the bed, then tucked the gun back in his belt.

He picked up the telephone and called Craig Dunleavy's cabin. Betty Dunleavy answered.

"Hello?"

"Did he get my message?"

"Yes," she said.

"Put him on please," he said.

"He's not here."

He hesitated for a moment. "When will he be back?"

"That's up to you," she said.

He frowned. "I don't understand." He heard her hang up. And then he heard another sound, behind him. He turned and saw Dunleavy standing in the open bathroom doorway, his suntanned face without expression.

"You forgot the shower stall," Dunleavy said.

Harold Columbine's right hand started a small movement toward his belt.

"Unh-uh," Dunleavy said.

The hand gave up. "Would you mind aiming that thing some-place else, please?" Harold Columbine said.

Dunleavy walked over and unbuttoned Columbine's jacket and removed the automatic from his belt and dropped it into his own pocket and buttoned the jacket again. "There we are," he said.

"I'm glad you did it," Harold Columbine said. "I might have shot someone and hurt him."

"Yes, and we wouldn't want that, would we?" Craig Dunleavy said.

"I suppose you want the list now . . ."

"What list?" Dunleavy started for the door.

Harold Columbine swallowed the dryness in his mouth. "What are you going to do now?"

Dunleavy opened the door and turned. "I don't know about you, Columbine, but *I'm* going to bed. It's been a busy day."

"You don't have a chance of getting away with any of this, Dunleavy. You know that, don't you?"

"Of course." Craig Dunleavy smiled. "But not getting there is half the fun." He walked out and closed the door.

Harold Columbine quickly went over to it and locked himself in. He turned and caught sight of himself in the mirror on the opposite wall.

"Harold Kornbloom," he said. "You are a *putz.*"

France slept fitfully. The night was disagreeably warm and airless. At 4:32 a.m. in St.-Germain-en-Laye, Aristide Bonnard awoke with a start and quietly slipped out of bed. The sentinel in his brain that never slept had just decided that the President could not afford one more second of irresponsible forgetfulness.

Bonnard found his slippers in the darkened bedroom and put them on, listening to the slow, measured snoring of his sleeping wife. Then he went down the stairs to his study and telephoned the Élysée Palace, keeping his voice low.

Marcel Fleck, a nervous man with a slight speech impediment under stress, was the highest ranking aide on presidential duty at this unseemly hour. Aristide Bonnard could hear the paralysis of anxiety in the man's voice when he recognized his caller.

"Y-y-yes, Monsieur le Président."

"Fleck, the following message is to be sent at once to the President of the United States at the White House, using Code Blue. Repeat please."

"C-c-c-code Blue."

"For his eyes only . . ."

"For his eyes uh-uh-uh-only . . ."

"The text . . . Ready?"

"Yes, Monsieur le P-président."

"Problem in Atlantic has been solved. Period. All arrangements concluded. Period. Tomorrow brings freedom. Period. Will notify you. Period. Signed, Bonnard."

Marcel Fleck read the text back to the President without error.

"Good," said Bonnard. "I want the message dated yesterday, ten p.m., and tagged 'Delayed in Transit.' "

"B-b-b-but there will be no d-d-delay, Monsieur le—"

"Do as I say," said Bonnard.

"Y-y-y-yes, Monsieur le Président."

On the way back up the stairs to his bedroom, it occurred to Aristide Bonnard that perhaps he hadn't really *forgotten* to notify his American counterpart. Perhaps he had been subconsciously waiting for some word of concern and sympathy from him. It was the least the man could have done. He felt himself growing increasingly angry as he entered the bedroom and carefully lowered himself to a sitting position on his side of the bed.

"Miserable son of a bitch," he muttered, half aloud.

In the darkness, Althea Bonnard stirred. "Yes, my sweetheart," she murmured dreamily, then quickly fell back into her measured snoring.

At approximately the same time, as if linked by some extrasensory chain of communication, Max Dechambre, the Director General of the Compagnie Française Atlantique, lying in his separate bedroom on the second floor of his home in Neuilly, rose out of the third-stage sleep of an unpleasant dream, turned over to his other side, and sank swiftly into the fourth-stage sleep of deep nothingness, while in his flat in the 15th Arrondissement of Paris, his assistant, Georges Sauvinage, grumbling as he always did under the same nightly circumstance by which anyone could have set their clock, so regular was the occurrence, padded slowly to his darkened bathroom, threw back the toilet seat and began to relieve his tormented bladder. For *this,* he thought, the wine makers of Bordeaux fight to the death with their Italian competitors?

Meanwhile, on the Left Bank, in Lisa Briande's disordered apartment overlooking the rue Récamier, Julian Wunderlicht and his soft, warm-skinned captive slept reasonably well, if not comfortably. Wunderlicht had found some strong cord in the little kitchen and had bound Lisa to him in such a way that any attempt on her part to escape him would have awakened him instantly. They lay facing each other on the disheveled bed, his right hand grasping the gun beneath his pillow, his other hand resting gently on her right thigh. Just before falling off to sleep, Lisa had observed that their position would hardly find its way into the sex manuals. To which Wunderlicht had replied, I have already seen it, only the gun was not loaded.

As for Jean-Claude Raffin, Director General of the Sûreté Nationale, he was nowhere in this universe, or in any other for that matter, having rammed not one but two suppositories of hypnotic oblivion up his rectum, before falling into bed in his residence at Vincennes, muttering to himself, Shutup, for Christ's sake, shut your damned head up . . .

Four thousand one hundred miles to the southwest, the *Marseille* cleaved through the roiling Atlantic seas at three-quarter speed, her bows dipping in graceful, rhythmic accommodation to the swelling, smashing enemy, screened off from the curious moon and stars by a heavy canopy of low-scudding clouds. Musical aggregations played long and hard in her several nightclubs, bartenders splashed generous doubles to the sound of laughter, and at least three hundred passengers of various sexual persuasions clung steadfastly to the night, unwilling to give up hope of adventure. Those who had long ago gone to their staterooms to attempt sleep were the very young, the very old, and the very married.

In his own stateroom, Billy Berlin sat before the transceiver beside the bed, staring at it as though his eyes could magically coax from it some friendly single sideband voices, preferably Brian Joy's. But the twenty meter band had gone completely dead, and there was only the steady hiss of a failed ionosphere in the cabin, and the soft, regular breathing of Julie on the other side of the bed, where she had dozed off with a magazine still in her hands.

Harold Columbine paced back and forth in his creaking, air conditioned cage with intolerable restlessness. There were live bodies out there on those dance floors and he knew it, and their hips were swaying in his head to a mélange of rhythms that were driving him up the fucking wall. But you're unarmed now. Christ knows what dangers are out there. Haven't you had *enough?* He savaged himself with the question, knowing that the answer never had been, never would be, yes, *yes.* He went to the phone, dialed Julie's number, got Billy instead.

"Yes?" A whisper.

"Columbine."

"Oh?"

"Can I speak to her?"

"She's asleep, Harold."

"I see . . . well . . . I just want to tell her I'm okay."

"If she wakes up, I'll . . . I'll let her know."

"She wanted me to call her, you know."

"Yes, I know. If she wakes up, Harold."

"Thanks."

Prick. He hung up and started to undress quickly, as though that was going to save him, tossing his velvet jacket and the tie and the shirt on a chair. But then he moved to the mirror and stood looking at his bare chest. He unzipped his trousers, took out his cock, gazed at it in the mirror, held it in his hands, waited, felt it stir, burgeon. He smiled, his eyes bright but fearful. He tucked it back in, reached for his shirt and started to put it back on. Fuck it, they can't touch me, I own the world. And the very idea of that went right where he wanted it to go. His fingers trembled with eagerness as he hastily buttoned his shirt and reached for his tie.

In Charles Girodt's living room, the Commandant of the *Marseille* sat slumped in a club chair, feigning alertness and attentiveness as he listened to the individual situation reports of his executive staff. But the narcotic effects of the alcohol he had consumed earlier in the evening were more than his brain could overcome. His unusual behavior did not escape the attention of Yves Chabot, whose expression showed increasing pain every time his superior offered a few slurred words of comment. Nothing came of the meeting other than repeated statements that the coming of daylight would be crucial, that total cooperation with the criminals was still official policy, and that the passengers remained remarkably calm and oblivious to their circumstances. Apparently none of them had made inquiries regarding the whereabouts of certain missing shipboard acquaintances. At the mention of this, Yves Chabot, seeing Charles Girodt's features suddenly begin to disintegrate, quickly rose to his feet and forcefully proclaimed the meeting concluded.

"Immediate sleep is the prescription, gentlemen," he said to the somewhat startled men. "We must be at our best, come breakfast."

"But, Dr. Chabot, what about the radio, and word from our friends on land?" demanded Pierre Demangeon.

Chabot eased the Chief Engineer to the door, saying, "When there is something definite to report, you can be sure we will all share it together, Demangeon. Pleasant nightmares, gentlemen."

He closed the door on the last of them and turned to the Captain, who sat with his hands covering his face. Chabot snapped off the overhead lights, moved around behind the club chair, and placed his hands gently on Charles Girodt's shoulders.

"Come, my dear friend, I will help you to bed now."

"Oh God, Chabot . . ." The voice was muffled behind the shielding hands.

"It will be all right, I promise you," the doctor said softly, wondering to himself how long his captain would be able to hold himself together. Chabot would have to take some Valium when he got back to his own quarters. His concern for Charles Girodt was a secret anxiety that had been growing in him like a cancer. He had shared it with no one but Christain Specht.

Craig Dunleavy stood outside one entrance and Herb Kleinfeld was posted at the other. Though the last screening had ended at midnight, the lobby still had some lights on, and there was no difficulty scrutinizing each face that passed them on the way in. No words were exchanged. By 12:50 a.m., all members of the group, with the exception of those on active duty, had filed into the darkened, empty theater and had taken seats down front. There were a few lighted candles on the apron of the stage, just to keep anyone from breaking a leg in the dark. A few of the women carried small flashlights. It was an eerie scene, unintentionally ritualistic in mood. Dunleavy had requested total darkness not only because he had felt it would be safer, but more importantly because he had felt that some members would feel less inhibited if their faces were unseen while they spoke out. Some might dare to reveal last-minute secret fears and doubts.

He and Kleinfeld posted Lou Foyles as a guard, then came down the aisle to the front and turned to face those they could barely make out in their seats.

"We can make this short and sweet," Dunleavy began. "I know I don't have to say it, you couldn't care less, but I'm going to say it anyway: you've all been terrific. I'm proud of you . . ." He waited for the short burst of soft applause to end. "Is there *anyone* who isn't *totally* sure of his or her individual assignment tomorrow?"

There was only silence. "Okay. Now don't be angry. I've gotta ask you this. Is there anyone who would like to come up here and try to convince us all to change our minds while there's still time?" He paused, and the silence was broken by a voice he recognized as Charlotte Segar's.

"Craig?"

"Yes."

"Is there absolutely no way we could put all the smaller children into a lifeboat and cast it adrift?"

"Let me answer that this way . . . Children grow up, and their memories never fade."

"Yes. All right."

"Any more on that, Charlotte?"

"No. That's it. Thank you."

"Anyone else?"

More silence. Dunleavy turned. "Herb?"

Kleinfeld cleared his throat, faced his audience. "I'm a pain in the ass. Don't know how many times I've said the following. Maybe a thousand. So what's one more time? Do not leave anything of a personal nature behind, and by anything I mean *anything*. What you're not taking along must be dumped overboard tonight. I know what you're thinking. *I'm* thinking, ten years from now they'll discover a method of deep salvage that's going to go so far down, they'll be able to bring up China. Have I forgotten anything, Craig?"

Dunleavy looked out at the faces. "Has he forgotten anything?"

The voices were a soft chorus of no's.

"Friends, what do you say we all go to bed?"

There was a rustle of bodies rising and seats thumping back. Kleinfeld blew out the candles. Dunleavy removed them from the stage and followed him out. Within minutes, the theater was dark, silent, empty.

To Leonard Ball, it was that simple . . . he couldn't have lived through the night without her. Words like "tormented with desire" on a network show, even on a daytime soap, would have made him wince with embarrassment, but, by God, that's exactly what he had been, *tormented by desire,* starting the moment he had washed his hands of the passenger information list and departed the Flash Studio control room and remembered, suddenly, the violet eyes and the rustle of silken thighs and the clouds of Je Reviens. No way could he have waited until lunch the next day. No *way.* And so the call to Peter Broussard's office, and the teasing, tantalizing duel of love on the phone with her, during which, for one disastrous moment, he had almost come in his gabardine trousers right there in his office, with Thelma Stutz not twenty feet away. And then the quick arrangement of lies, relayed to Amanda in Old Lyme by the coldly disapproving Thelma, and at last, the delirious hand-holding, knee-holding, eye-holding hour and a half at Elaine's, where he hadn't cared *who* saw them, he was so inflamed with her . . . "Leonard, baby, what's old at CBS News?" . . . "Gordon, say goodbye to Hélène Maurais."

And now he was in the phone booth outside the john, waiting for the operator to put through his credit-card call to the Coast, his heart only half in it, a sure sign he was slipping as a newsman, his whole body, his very being, pulsating, practically *pointing,* toward the closed door of the ladies' powder room behind which, he was sure, the most enchanting girl ever born on French soil was performing all necessary intimate ablutions with a foreknowledge born of instinct and plenty of sleeping around that neither she nor her lover would get anywhere *near* a bathroom, much less a bed, when they arrived at his Park East apartment, before they tore each other's clothes off and fell to the carpet and fucked each other to death. If Leonard Ball had any problem at all at the moment, it was to figure out how not to blow his load in the back seat of the cab. Maybe if they both sat up front with the driver . . .

When the telephone rang, Brian Joy was seated opposite Maggie at the kitchen table, picking at his chicken cacciatore in the sullen silence of enforced sobriety that was as thick as the deepening Beverly Hills fog outside the windows. She watched him, waiting. Defiantly, he made no move. Finally she said, "Well, it sure as hell isn't for *me*."

He reached across to the sideboard without getting up and brought the receiver to the table. "Yes?"

"Brian, this is Leonard Ball in New York . . ."

"Yeah, Leonard?" Flat, without enthusiasm.

"Am I interrupting something?"

"Not a thing," Brian Joy said. "We just happen to be in the middle of a dinner that my wife has been working on the whole goddamn day. You're not interrupting anything."

"Stop that," Maggie said.

"I'm sorry," Leonard Ball said. "I just called to find out how everything was going."

"Which everything did you have in mind?" Real shitty, like it was CBS News that was denying him his alcoholic fix.

"What the hell did you *think* I had in mind? The *Marseille* . . . the think tank group. Any developments?"

"Not one fucking development," Brian Joy said. "The ship is still floating and the tank is still thinking. Don't call me, I'll call you."

"Well, I did what I could . . ."

"I suppose I should thank you."

"You don't have to, but you can if you want," Leonard Ball said.

"Tell him about the deaths," Maggie said.

"Hold it, Leonard . . . What?"

"Tell him about the deaths."

"What for?"

"You owe it to him."

"But *not* to CBS. Will you forget it?" And to the phone, "Leonard, where will you be tonight in case I should want to reach you?"

"Well, to tell you the truth, I kinda don't think I *can* be reached tonight." Leonard Ball chuckled. "I'm going to be, shall we say, pleasantly occupied?"

"Anyone I know?"

"Let's say you'd like to."

"I'm very happy for you," Brian Joy said bitterly.

"You live on the wrong coast, kiddo."

"By the way," Brian Joy said. "They murdered twenty-six men and women on the ship who got in their way today."

"What did you say?"

"You heard me, Leonard, and you heard it right. Twenty-six. I gotta hang up now."

"Wait a minute . . ."

"Have fun." He hung up quickly to break the connection, then took the receiver off the hook again and set it down on the sideboard, muttering under his breath, "Cocksucker."

Leonard Ball opened the door of the phone booth and rose to his feet dazedly, aware that no part of him was pointing any longer, nor would be for the rest of the night. Few men knew the vagaries of their apparatus better than Leonard Ball did, and as he left the booth, he was already working on the lie he'd have to tell the French girl when she emerged from the powder room giving off that goddamn female fragrance.

"Why did you treat him like that?" Maggie said.

"He's of no further use to me," Brian Joy said. "Besides, I'm underslept and all fagged out and I'm not interested in meaningless calls from New York City when I'm sitting around waiting for the call from Remo."

"Or Paris."

"I knew you'd say that."

"How do you expect to get a call from *anyone* with the phone off the hook?"

He replaced the receiver in its cradle.

"Go to bed and get some sleep," Maggie said, without looking at him. "I'll guard the phone."

"You will? How come?"

"Because I can't stand the sight of you or the sound of you this way for another second. It's disgusting."

"Thanks a lot," he said.

"You're welcome," she said.

He got up from the table and went upstairs to bed.

The patterns had kept tantalizing them, seeming to come into focus at times, only to blur again into meaningless confusion. Craig Dunleavy had been easily linked to Herb Kleinfeld by probing back through a sufficient number of years to find them both working for the National Aeronautics and Space Administration, then more recently, along with wives, living in close geographical proximity. But, strange to understand, no reasonably convincing cross-references had shown up as yet to link the two men with anyone else on the ship, nor did anyone else link up with others. Mike Keegan's early hope that a flurry of criminal records would flash onto the CRT projection screen of the war games room and bathe the conspirators in the glare of discovery had come to nothing. The S.S. *Marseille*, it turned out, carried a passenger list of crushing respectability. And even more discouraging had been the time-consuming scanning and the ultimate feedback from the State Department's data banks that every man, woman, and child on the ship had sailed with a legitimate passport. It was then that Arkady Slocum announced to his team that, if they were going to get anywhere, they had damned well better start resorting to desperation rather than inspiration.

The first apparent breakthrough was Angelo Martini's. It sprang more from his family life than from his expertise in behavioral psychology. "You know what would keep *me* from trying what those fools are attempting? Not morality, not a fear of danger, not a distaste for money. One thing. My kids. Two boys and a girl."

"Translate, Angelo," said Mike Keegan.

"Give me only the childless, I mean the swinging singles, the sterile marrieds, whatever they are as long as they're without living bundles from heaven."

Keegan looked at Arkady Slocum. "Can you do it?"

"No," the computer specialist said, "but 307 can. Al?"

Santley hunched over the keyboard, slithered into the PIL, then went visiting IRS, Social Security, Central Credit and back to the PIL, and inside of thirty minutes, knocked 725 names off the 1,400 they were dealing with at that time.

"Anybody else feeling constructively desperate?" Arkady Slocum said, looking around the neon-bright room.

"Hunger," offered Rudi Fleischman. The cryptanalyst leaned forward in his black leather chair and patted his ample belly. "A full stomach keeps people home, or sends them to the French Riviera to overeat and fall out of their bikinis. But real economic hunger, the psychic wrinkles in the belly, could put them on the *Marseille* with guns in their hands and gold in their eyes."

"Mind if I use that line some day?" Irving Harris inquired.

"Be my guest." Rudi Fleischman smiled at the gray-thatched novelist.

Twenty-five minutes later, after Al Santley had punched 307 in the face with a stiff order, the giant machine came back with the answer. Of the 675 names under consideration, 580, either singly or as part of a married, jointly filed income tax return, showed net incomes for the year past of $20,000 or less.

"Why don't we go for *all* the marbles?" Irving Harris suggested, glancing around at the others. "If Rudi's thinking is right, twenty thousand still buys far too much food."

"I'll buy that," Frank Skinner said quickly. Mike Keegan grunted agreement, so Arkady Slocum gave Al Santley the signal for another go.

This time 307 shrank the list miraculously by another 180. There were 400 passengers aboard the *Marseille* who had earned less than $11,000. And another quick look into IRS for the year before that showed the same 400 in the same financial pickle. The fact that Craig Dunleavy and Herb Kleinfeld were right there in the barrel with the other 398 caused the first cautious stirrings of optimism in the room.

Irving Harris clambered to his feet so quickly, his knee joints popped. "On two hundred a week income you couldn't even book a *toilet* on the *Marseille*. I tell ya, fellas, something's not kosher here."

"Unless you happen to be independently wealthy," Lawrence Wibberly said to the floor. "Some of this country's most distinguished ingrates earn millions on tax-free municipals and don't have to report *any* income. They wouldn't have to hold the *Marseille* for ransom. They could *buy* it outright."

"Don't be a spoilsport, Dr. Wibberly," Frank Skinner said. "To me, the statistics look favorable. I say we go with the four hundred as our new data base. But first, and more important, who's going to call Colonel Sanders? I've gotta have some Kentucky fried, or I'll drop."

It was while they were eating dinner that Brian Joy's call came with its death list. That turned the chicken rancid.

At nine-thirty-five, Tony Kuhn, who had taken over Security from Jim Baggett, came into the war games room with two thermos pitchers of black coffee. At ten-forty, Arkady Slocum, thoroughly caffeinated, decided suddenly that no group as large as the one that had taken over the *Marseille* could have formulated its plans without having meetings first, but he said nothing about it until he had spent an hour in a furious duet with 307, playing imaginative tunes on the console with the distant air carrier central reservations bank and the U.S. hotel space bank, searching them both out over a period of two years and making notes along the way. Then, slightly flushed with discovery, he reached for his cane, pushed himself to his feet and faced his bedraggled team, the sheet of paper in his hand trembling slightly.

"Would someone please wake Rudi up?" he said.

"I'm not asleep." Rudi Fleischman quickly opened his eyes and rose to a sitting position on the couch.

"This is curious, gentlemen, most curious," Arkady Slocum began. "I'll try to give it to you in short takes." He cleared his throat. "A year ago last May, the fourteenth, to be exact, Mr. and Mrs. Craig Dunleavy checked into a large motel in Twentynine Palms, California. On the same day, Mr. and Mrs. H. Kleinfeld arrived at *another* motel in Twentynine Palms. At the same time, many other men and women were checking into five other motels in and around Twentynine Palms. You follow me so far?"

"Nothing to follow," Mike Keegan said.

Arkady Slocum continued, "The following September—two days before Labor Day—the Dunleavys and the Kleinfelds decided to spend the weekend at the Broadmoor Hotel in Colorado Springs. So did a few hundred other lucky people. And among those lucky people, thirty-six women and forty-two men turn out to have been in Twentynine Palms the previous May fourteenth. Seventy-eight people have *twice* been in the same place at the same time as the Dunleavys and Kleinfelds . . ."

"Jesus," said Irving Harris.

"I like it," said Frank Skinner quietly.

Arkady Slocum held up his hand and went on. "This past April, on the day before Easter, the Dunleavys arrive at the Marlin Inn in Baja California, the Kleinfelds show up at the Fisherman's Lodge in Baja, and the seventy-eight men and women who had been at Twentynine Palms a year ago last May, and in Colorado Springs the following Labor Day weekend, check into the Holiday Inn . . ."

"In Baja," Frank Skinner said.

Arkady Slocum nodded.

Rudi Fleischman said, "Arkady, you're incredible."

"Not me. 307. And wait, that's not all. There were *other* guests at the Marlin Inn and the Fisherman's Lodge and at Holiday Inn this past Easter in Baja. Several hundred, in fact. And ninety-two of them—forty-four married couples and four single women—show up on the list of the hundreds of lucky people who had spent the previous Labor Day weekend at the Broadmoor Hotel in Colorado Springs . . ."

"One seventy-four," Frank Skinner said.

"You're ahead of me, Frank," said Arkady Slocum. "Including Craig Dunleavy and his wife, and Herb Kleinfeld and his wife, 307 now has the names of all of the conspirators, one hundred seventy-four of them, *most* of whom attended all three of what I believe to have been planning meetings, and *all* of whom were present at the last two . . ."

"We got 'em," Rudi Fleischman chortled.

Mike Keegan pounded a fist into his open palm. "The ball game is over."

Arkady Slocum looked at the group with a rueful smile. "I'm afraid not," he said gently.

There was a moment of stunned silence.

"What are you doing to us?" Irving Harris demanded, frowning.

"I'm feeding this to you slowly and carefully, in a way you can digest, and I've saved the dessert, the bad news, for the last . . ."

"Oh, shit," Mike Keegan growled.

"All right, I'm a sadistic son of a bitch, but here it is," Arkady Slocum said. "We've got the names of the one hundred and seventy-four conspirators. Right?"

"Right," said Frank Skinner.

"The worst of the news is not that these names fail to appear among our four hundred probables." Arkady Slocum drew a deep breath. "With the exception of the Dunleavys and the Kleinfelds, these names do not appear anywhere on the entire passenger list of the *Marseille*."

An audible, collective sigh of disappointment rose above the soft whistle of air conditioning.

Irving Harris started to laugh.

Mike Keegan said, "What the hell is so funny, Harris?"

"Who said anything's funny?"

"Then shut up, for chrissake."

"I'm sorry, but I'm sitting down," Arkady Slocum said.

Frank Skinner ran a hand through his sandy hair. "Let's not panic, huh?"

"Please tell me why I shouldn't," Rudi Fleischman said.

"They attended the meetings using assumed names," Skinner said.

"Dunleavy and Kleinfeld didn't. Why not?"

"I don't know."

"Maybe the names were legitimate, and the ones they're using aboard the *Marseille* are phony," Angelo Martini said.

"But the passports have all been authenticated," Irving Harris said, his voice rising.

"Irving," Arkady Slocum spoke quietly, "if you believe that computers are always smarter than desperate men, and that no forger is clever enough to outwit an electronic scanner, you are a naïve young man."

"I'm getting older by the minute."

"So where the fuck *are* we now?" Mike Keegan demanded.

"Give me a few minutes and I'll answer that," Arkady Slocum said.

"I got all night," Mike Keegan shot back.

The computer specialist turned to his assistant. "Al, do a random sample on the hundred and seventy-four who attended the meetings. All I want to know is, do they exist, are they real people or fictitious identities?"

"Right, sir."

Presently, 307 responded: "GENUINE."

Arkady Slocum turned to the others. "Okay then. Who is our most probable probable on the ship?"

Angelo Martini said, "Craig Dunleavy, of course."

"Come on, Angelo, I mean *aside* from him and Kleinfeld."

"Louise Campbell, then," the behavioral psychologist said.

"All right, Al, tell 307 to give me her address and telephone number."

"But Louise Campbell is dead, sir."

"Will you please do as I say?" Arkady Slocum rubbed his eyes wearily.

307 flashed a Portland, Oregon, address and phone number.

Arkady Slocum direct-dialed and switched on the speakerphone so they all could hear.

The woman who answered had an elderly quaver in her voice and sounded frightened. "Yes? Hello?"

"Is Louise Campbell there?"

"Yes, this is Mrs. Campbell. Who—?"

"Louise Campbell?"

"That's right. Who is this?"

"Mrs. Campbell, this is Lieutenant Slocum of the San Diego Police Department . . ."

"Oh, dear me . . ."

"Now there's nothing to be concerned about . . ."

"Is my nephew in trouble again?"

"No, Mrs. Campbell, I just want to ask you a few questions, and then you can go back to sleep . . ."

"We're not asleep. My husband and I are watching Johnny Carson . . ."

"I'll let you get right back to him."

"Oh, that's all right, the commercials are on."

"Good. Good. Mrs. Campbell, aren't you supposed to be on a ship bound for Europe?"

"Heavens, what ever gave you that idea? Mr. Campbell never likes to travel, not ever. I can't even get him to visit my sister in Seattle. He's a stick in the mud, Donald is."

"Do you happen to know, or have you ever heard of, a man named Craig Dunleavy?"

"Craig who?"

"Craig Dunleavy."

"Young man, what did you say your name was?"

"Lieutenant Slocum, Mrs. Campbell."

"Well, you've got the wrong party, Mr. Slocum, and the commercials are over."

"Thank you very much, Mrs. Campbell."

"You're very welcome. Good night now."

Arkady Slocum hung up and looked at the other men. "I think we're learning something," he said.

Frank Skinner's eyes brightened. "Try another one."

"Did you notice her husband's name is Donald?" Rudi Fleischman said. "We have a Don Campbell on the ship . . ."

"Who is reported dead," Al Santley said.

"Let's not confuse ourselves, shall we?" Arkady Slocum said.

"So far we have two passengers listed who are using the identities of others."

"Try another one, will you, Arkady?" Frank Skinner said impatiently.

"Al, on that list of first names, which would be the best stab in the dark?"

"Well, sir, there are three Erics aboard, eight Charleses, two Charlottes . . ."

"Give me a Charlotte."

Santley queried 307 on Mrs. Charlotte Fox, got back an Alexandria, Virginia, address and two phone numbers.

Neither number answered.

"At three in the morning she could be asleep with the phones shut off," Irving Harris suggested.

"Or legitimately in the middle of the Atlantic," Angelo Martini countered.

"Try the other Charlotte, Arkady."

"Would *you*, Frank? I'm exhausted," Arkady Slocum said.

"Aren't we all," Frank Skinner said, reaching for the phone.

Al Santley played the keyboard again, and 307 flashed Charlotte Segar's address and telephone number in Boise, Idaho.

A sleepy male voice answered on the speakerphone.

"Good morning, sir," Frank Skinner said. "I'm sorry to call you at this hour. This is Captain Skinner of the Los Angeles Police Department and I have to ask you a few questions of extreme importance."

"You're making some kinda mistake, Captain."

"That could very well be. Is this Mr. Segar?"

"Yeah, that's right."

"Is Charlotte Segar on her way to Europe at this moment?"

"I don't know what the hell you're talking about. My daughter, Charlotte, is asleep in the next room with her leg in a cast, unless this damned phone woke her up."

"Does she or you know anyone named Craig Dunleavy?"

"No, she doesn't and I don't and you people in Los Angeles are a bunch of crazies, do you know that, mister, anyone ever tell you that?"

"All the time, sir. I'm sorry if—"

Boise, Idaho, hung up.

Frank Skinner turned to the group. "I think I can now safely state the following as *fact* rather than supposition: the names used in Twentynine Palms, Colorado Springs, and Baja are the real names of the one hundred and seventy-four who have taken over the *Marseille,* but they aren't worth a damn to us or to the Captain of the ship, because one hundred and seventy of those persons are using entirely different names and matching passports out there at sea. And that so-called list of probables we worked up is relatively valueless now, because it was based on data pertaining to a passenger list that contains one hundred and seventy names of people who are actually on dry land. Would you agree with me, Arkady?"

"More or less," the computer specialist replied.

"Can I ask a question?" Irving Harris said. "What made the conspirators choose certain specific real people and take on *their* identities, give *their* vital statistics to the passenger information list? Is there a connection between the woman on the ship who called herself Louise Campbell and the *real* Louise Campbell in Portland, Oregon? I mean, I am a very confused Jew."

"*I* don't have those answers for you, Irving," Frank Skinner said.

"Are we in a position to *get* them?" Irving Harris said irritably.

"I can't answer that either."

"Jesus Christ . . ."

"The answer is probably yes," Arkady Slocum said quickly, "but it could take forever, and I *mean* forever. Conceivably, 307 could do an exploration and workup on each of the authentic names and come up with a capsule biography of every one of them, and then try and find some common links with some of those two thousand passengers on board the ship . . ."

"Blue-sky bullshit. I don't like it," Frank Skinner said.

"I agree with you," Arkady Slocum said instantly. "So top me."

"Fellas, look, you know what we're gonna have to do, don't you?" Mike Keegan's voice was heavy with gloom. "Al Santley and 307 are going to have to feed us names and telephone numbers, and the rest of us are going to sit on individual extensions and call the homes of every goddamn passenger on the list until we find out which names are truly at sea and which names are on land, because the names which are on land are the names being *used,* right now, by the guilty parties on that ship. There's no other way to do it."

"Why didn't we think of this before?" Rudi Fleischman said, with unaccustomed enthusiasm.

Frank Skinner held up a hand. "Let me give you a little simple arithmetic. If each of the six of us calls three hundred different numbers simultaneously, and conservatively takes five minutes to establish the number, dial it, get an answer, and nail down the facts at the other end, that's fifteen hundred minutes, which is twenty-five hours . . ."

"Twenty-five?"

The lean statistician nodded. "And we've got less than twelve hours to the deadline."

"So we'll do it in *two* minutes a call," Mike Keegan offered, with bluster but no conviction.

"With no rest, no sleep, no wrong numbers, no nothin'? Impossible," Angelo Martini said.

Arkady Slocum rose unsteadily to his feet. "Look, gentlemen, we've already got a head start with some first names, and we *may* get lucky and fill in the whole group by the time we've covered the first four or five hundred passengers. So let's stop beating our gums and start dialing. But first, maybe we all ought to take a leak. That's an order. Let's go." He took his cane and started for the door. "That includes you, Dr. Wibberly."

The astrophysicist had not said a word for several hours. He had sat there scarcely listening, sucking on his unlit pipe, his eyes on the floor, his mind roaming through the galaxies, pretending to be searching for supernovas and quasars and black holes. Just around a corner of the universe he knew that something unpredictable, undreamt of, was waiting to be stumbled upon, and it would be the key to the whole problem that was the *Marseille*. And he was not going to give up now, to play their silly game. He would keep going, wander the cosmos and wait for the happy accident to happen to him, confident that it was no more than a few light years away.

"I'm sorry, gentlemen," he said to the room, his eyes downcast. "I'm afraid you'll have to do your telephoning without me."

Arkady Slocum wheeled around at the door. "*Without* you?"

"Jesus, Professor, five of us can't *hack* it," Mike Keegan exclaimed.

"I cannot interrupt what I'm doing," the astrophysicist said quietly.

"And what the hell is *that?*" Mike Keegan demanded.

Lawrence Wibberly looked up from the floor and met his eyes. "I'm thinking," he said.

The lookout on this watch was the Baby Bull, the Angry One, Nick Moustakos. High up in the pitching crow's nest of the *Angela Gloria,* wet and cold and bone-weary beneath his oilskin hat and poncho, he cursed the vile night and the shrieking winds and the persistent slanting rain that stung his eyes as he peered into the blackness to the north and saw nothing. Over and over he shouted the same epithets, bitter that only he could hear them, for it would have pleased him immensely if the ears of Panos Trimenedes could have borne the brunt of his invective.

His captain was a filthy Greek liar, that's what he was, and his freighter was a filthy Greek pile of rusting shit, and if there was any good reason for this filthy Greek pile of rusting shit to be struggling to maintain sixteen knots against the mountainous swells that assailed it, he, Nick Moustakos, had a right to know what that reason was. It was *his* stomach up here in the crow's nest, not Panos Trimenedes's. That filthy Greek liar lay below in his warm bunk, dreaming of fat ugly women with their legs spread out and ouzo all over their cunts.

Nick Moustakos did not believe the story the Captain had told his crew as they were quietly stealing out of Paramaribo in the middle of the night. Even if she loomed out of the darkness right then and there, or appeared out of the grayness that would come in less than an hour, even if she suddenly materialized before his very bloodshot eyes and knifed right through the *Angela Gloria*'s decks below him, he would not believe that the great French ocean liner, the S.S. *Marseille,* was planning to rendezvous with this Greek rust-pile in order to hand over some passengers who were suffering from food poisoning or something.

Never mind where we will put them, we will *do* it, the filthy Greek liar had shouted to them, and we will take them to the Kokones and the Montureses so the planes can get them out.

Nick Moustakos bared his teeth to the night in a knowing leer. Cocaine, heroin, opium . . . the devil *himself* couldn't guess what contraband was in those crates in the hold beneath him. Whatever it was, only a fool could fail to figure out that Panos Trimenedes was in a desperate hurry to get to a safe port and turn his cargo into gold. And there was no lie the pig wouldn't invent to spur his men on and make them break their testicles to move the shit-pile to its groaning limits.

Are you out there, *Marseille?* Nick Moustakos shouted into the rain-swept wind. Let me see the shape of your ass, you dirty French whore that doesn't exist . . .

The wind laughed in the Angry One's face, and slapped his mouth shut.

BOOK THREE

THE FINAL DAY

"Oh build your ship of death. Oh build it!
For you will need it.
For the voyage of oblivion awaits you."

D. H. LAWRENCE

CHAPTER THIRTY-SIX

───────────

LISA BRIANDE first became aware that it was morning, and that she was in her own bed in her own apartment at 2 rue Récamier, and that she was in the process of awakening from a long deep sleep, when she heard the familiar clamor of traffic from the rue de Sèvres and found herself recalling a vivid dream in which she was being bound to a stake or something, and then . . . and then suddenly she became totally awake and tried to sit up in bed and knew that it had not been a dream after all, for she was lying spread-eagled on her back with her wrists and ankles securely tied with clothesline to the four corners of the bed.

"I'll be goddamned," she said in a loud voice.

She writhed about to no effect. She undulated her hips to see how much free motion she had. Not much at all. Then she raised her head and looked past her naked torso and saw Julian Wunderlicht's message, printed in large bold letters on a sheet of white typing paper and scotch-taped to the foot of the bed facing her: YOU ARE DELICIOUS AND FIT TO BE TIED. DO NOT PANIC. I WILL RETURN QUICKLY . . . J.W.

She let her head fall back on the pillow and said to the ceiling,

You fascist son of a bitch, feeling the dull, drugged headache of too much brandy and too much Ritalin-fueled excitement the day and the night before. She wondered when the German had left her, where he had gone and when he would return. "Quickly" could mean five minutes or five hours, depending on how badly you needed to go to the loo or have a cigarillo or a cup of steaming black coffee, all three of which she would not want to do without now for more than, say, twenty minutes.

She sorted out the events of the night before as quickly as they would come to mind, and decided that it actually was more valuable to her, and just possibly to those aboard the *Marseille,* if she stayed with Wunderlicht rather than try to get away from him and thus miss being eyewitness to the climactic events she believed would transpire this day. Not that she had all that much choice in the matter, she mused, tugging gently at the rope around her right wrist. While she sensed that she was in clear and present danger, her innate optimism prevented her from taking it as seriously as her conscience told her she should, and she could feel the first wispy stirrings of the guilt that always nagged her when she refused to treat real or fancied threats to her survival with sufficient alarm. Besides, she told herself, any man who likes to fuck as much as he does can't be all bad, can he? (Yes, Lisa, he can.) Still, it gave her an odd feeling of safety, knowing she could have him, literally, by the balls, any time she wanted to.

She recalled the last, and only time she had been bound to a bed like this. The Plaza-Athénée, two summers ago, August, when there had been only two consenting adults left in all of Paris, the other three million preferring to do it on the Côte d'Azur . . . she and Gaston B. Hart, American maker of quickie films and even quicker ejaculations, poor thing. Jimi Brocke used to call him "your open-fly-by-night producer," probably green with envy that *he* wasn't getting past that unzipped Talon-fastener himself. Those had been the dog days, when she was taking anything that could move or pick up a tab.

And, baby, look at you now, you've really come a long way, she thought bleakly. The new journalism incarnate. Let the others sleep with generals and foreign ministers and aides to the President. Lisa Briande fucks a middle-aged hijacker, masturbates a sweet-talking gunslinger, to get a good story. She lies in her own bed with her legs spread apart, waiting for him patiently, hoping this time she'll get lucky. Maybe this time he'll pull out his leather belt and lash her until the blood shows and she begins to scream . . .

The first sharp ring of the telephone beside the bed brought her back to reality. She strained against her bonds, knowing it would do no good, as the phone pierced her ears repeatedly. Hennessey? Jimi Brocke? Max Dechambre? Brian Joy in California? Leonard Ball from New York?

There's nobody home, she shouted. But the phone kept ringing anyway. And finally fell silent.

Julian Wunderlicht hung up and stepped out of the temporary phone booth beside the construction shack into the cacophony of automobile traffic and jackhammers and cranes and earth-scoopers, handling his new blue-gray attaché case with extravagant care. He had had great faith in his ability to tie a good sound slip-knot, yet it was comfortably reassuring to hear no voice answering Lisa Briande's phone, especially not *her* voice. He could take his time now when he got to the Galeries Lafayette. He would browse through their electrical department until he found everything he needed, the wire, the mercury batteries, the timing mechanism, everything.

He made his way along the temporary wooden sidewalks that had become a permanent eyesore to the thousands who toiled in these towering skyscrapers, pleased with the irony of his situation, but knowing it was more than his passion for irony that had led him to this vast area of demolition and construction known as La Défense. He arrived finally at the parking area where he had left the rented Fiat station wagon. He would be glad to get away from these monstrous steel girders that were everywhere, from the endless machinegun bursts of the riveters, from the rape of a beautiful city.

Just for a moment, he glanced up at the topmost floors of the Tour Française looming before him, and he thought briefly of Dechambre and Sauvinage up there, no doubt brooding over the call they hoped to get from him at noon. Then he opened the door of the Fiat and got in, as he heard once again the dull boom of chained-down dynamite tearing at the granite heart of Paris. A chilly smile came to his face.

It would serve them right, the rapists, the careless, negligent fools . . .

Wunderlicht returned to Lisa Briande's flat directly from the department store. He placed his newly acquired packages and the attaché case on a table in the foyer and went to the bedroom. The nude, spread-eagled body on the bed looked distractingly inviting to him. He wished this were going to be a different kind of day.

"Have you no shame?" he said, walking over to the bed.

"If you don't untie me in a hurry, I'm liable to pee right in your face," Lisa said.

He chuckled, leaned over her, undid the rope around her ankles, then unbound her wrists and stole a quick kiss of her lips before she could protest. "You can go do your thing now," he said.

"You're so good to me," she said with bitterness, swinging to her feet beside him.

"Please be ready to leave here within the hour," he said, and patted her warm fanny.

"How shall I dress?" she asked, ignoring his hand.

"Informally," he said. "A jump suit would be perfect. You can forget the parachute." He waited until she disappeared into the bathroom and locked the door. Then he went quickly to the foyer, retrieved the attaché case and the packages, took them into the living room and opened them, sat down on the sofa, removed the wirecutter from his pocket and began to prepare the assembly, surprised at his own dexterity and sure-fingered ease.

Seated at his operating position in the stucco building at Audierne on the west coast of France, Bernard Delade swung the rotary Yagi beam almost due south and tuned his powerful Raytheon receiver to each of the assigned frequencies of FNRC and heard nothing but summer static. There had not been a trace of the ship, at least not in this station, in over thirty-six hours, and if Paris was not concerned, why should he be? That's what he kept asking himself, but the question did nothing to dispel his uneasiness.

He got up from his chair and went over to the window and looked out through the opened Venetian blinds. The morning sky was gray, with black clouds near the horizon. There had been humidity in the air on his way to work. Delade began to think of the possibility of thunderstorms. His uneasiness fed on the thought. No number of lightning arrestors, no depth of perfect grounding, would ever rid him of his lifelong fear of electrocution from the sky.

He turned and walked over to the telephone to do something

about his growing anxiety. He called Poste-Téléphone-Télégraph at St.-Lys. They were sorry but they had not received any position reports from the *Marseille,* was there anything wrong? No, Delade replied, and hung up quickly. He called PTT at Le Conquet and at Boulogne and received the same negative responses. He ran a hand through his hair, then went over to the teletype machine, sat down and banged out a short message to Georges Sauvinage at Françat in Paris: CONTINUED SILENCE FROM FOXTROT NOVEMBER ROMEO CHARLIE. IS THERE ANYTHING I SHOULD KNOW? DELADE.

He knew the telex was useless. He would probably not even receive a reply from that fat-faced son of a bitch. But he already felt better for having sent the message. When he sat down before the Raytheon receiver again and turned the volume up, he was not even thinking about the possibility of thunderstorms any more.

Maurice Boulot, Director of Intercontinental Operations for Charles de Gaulle Airport, found it easy to empathize with the suspicion and distrust of the man at the other end of the telephone. Boulot had reacted in like manner when, previously, he had been given his orders and instructions by the Minister of Transportation.

"I am not at liberty to give you their names," he explained patiently. "You will have to accept my word that they are both qualified to fly wide-bodied aircraft."

André Delaporte's voice rose with annoyance. "My controllers will laugh at me, and I do not blame them."

"Tell them they are laughing at the President of France," Boulot replied.

"Charles de Gaulle Airport cannot authorize the takeoff of a 747 with a fictitious flight number, no flight plan, no destination, and two unnamed pilots," the Chief of Air Traffic Control insisted.

"In this case, my dear Delaporte, I am afraid you not only can but you will. Air France Flight 1000 is to be cleared to take off at any time the chief pilot makes the request. He will give the tower a heading and will announce a cruising altitude. Your men are to create absolutely no delays, no difficulties whatsoever, and there are to be no questions asked *by* anybody *of* anybody. The flight is a personal, private mission of our President, and that is only *our* business, yours and mine, not the business of TWA or Pan Am or any other carriers. If I haven't made myself clear, my dear Delaporte, please tell me now."

There was a long silence at the other end of the line. Then André Delaporte said, "It is totally ridiculous."

"But clear?"

"Yes. Very clear."

"Good," said Maurice Boulot. "If all goes smoothly, I will personally commend you to the Minister and he, I am sure, will pass the word to the President."

"You can tell them both I said the whole thing is ridiculous," said André Delaporte.

"Thank you and good morning," Maurice Boulot said, and hung up. He took out a handkerchief and wiped the perspiration from his forehead. He started to put the handkerchief back in his pocket, then thought the better of it and placed it on the desk. He would probably need it again after he got through ordering airport security to take a three-hour lunch, as it were, on a moment's notice.

He sighed as he picked up the telephone again.

Something woke Harold Columbine up . . . the movement of another body in the bed, a getting-out-of-the-bed movement. He came back from some place in outer space and opened his eyes and saw her standing beyond the foot of the bed getting into her panties in the gray morning light coming through the uncurtained porthole window. Her fair skin glistened with a thin film of perspiration, and her perfume permeated the warm cabin. He must have forgotten to turn the air conditioning back on. And that wasn't all he had forgotten last night. He propped his head up and watched her fondling her breasts as though to reassure herself that they were still there.

"You still got 'em," he said aloud.

She glanced sharply toward the bed and gave him that toothpaste-ad smile that absolutely killed him. "You got 'em too," she said, "if you still want 'em. I thought you were dead."

"Christ, that grass. Jesus."

"The best." She knelt down and found her bra on the floor and started to put it on as she straightened up.

"Must you?" he pleaded.

"Gotta," she said.

"Why?"

"Gotta wake up in a respectable place."

"Where?"

"Home."

"Where's home?"

"A-Deck. A-42."

"It's Terri, isn't it?"

"Good for you."

"Short for tall, tempting, and terrific."

"You said it, Harold, I didn't."

"Terri Worthington?"

"Montgomery. Where'd you get the Worthington from?"

"Beats me. Where did I get Terri Montgomery from?"

"Man, you are something." She sat down on the foot of the bed and put her hand lightly on the sheet covering his genital area. "Place Pigalle in Tourist. At the bar. You tried to light a cigarette with my lipstick."

"What else did I do?"

"I'll tell you what you *didn't* do."

"Oh-oh. Don't tell me."

"You didn't get *this*," she squeezed him gently, *"up."*

"Oh, shame on you, Harold. Shame shame shame. That stuff couldn't have been grass. What the hell was it? What did you slip this helpless stranger, Terri?"

She smiled. "Just good old plain Colombian. I told you two hits were enough. You went at it like there was no tomorrow."

"I guess I was wrong, 'cause here it is, and it's today." He moved his body slightly under her hand. "So why don't I make amends right now for letting you down?"

"Oh, you didn't let me down, Harold. You were beautiful."

"Really?"

"You haven't got a head on your shoulders for nothing, honey."

"That's very true. Sometimes I even use it when I'm writing. Incidentally, if you're gonna insist on leaving, I suggest you take your hand away from there."

"Sorry about that." She got up and resumed dressing.

He watched her with undisguised admiration.

"Did you tell me what you do for a living?" he asked.

"I did," she said, stepping into her wedgies.

"Model?"

"Uh-huh."

"That's nice," he said.

She fastened the belt that matched her rust-colored silk sheath, slipped the rope of pearls around her neck, ran a comb through her long auburn hair, retrieved her purse from the dresser, turned and blew him a kiss.

He sat up in bed quickly. "Am I ever going to see you again?"

"Tonight," she said. "Same time, same place."

He grinned. "Look, just in case I get all tied up with some friends of mine I sort of promised—"

"No problem," she said. "I'll wait at the bar until you get untied, no matter what time it is."

"Are you always this terrific, Terri?"

"Only on water." She went out to the sound of his laughter.

He lay back, smiling. Then suddenly he remembered where he was and what day it was and why this trip wasn't supposed to be fun, was supposed to be a deadly, dangerous game and he was in the middle of it. What the hell was he doing *smiling,* for Christ's sake? He reached for the phone beside the bed and dialed Julie Berlin's number.

She answered cautiously.

"How're you doing?" he asked cheerily.

"All right," she said. Her voice sounded strangely flat.

"Any change in your husband's flu? I mean, any medical bulletins during the night?"

"No. He says it's too early in the morning for anything to . . . uh . . . happen. He doesn't think that he can take a turn for the better until another hour or so. He's in the bathroom now, taking a shower."

"I get it," he said.

"It was nice of you to call here last night to let me know you were safe and sound in your cabin."

"It was the least I could do," he said.

"I woke up right after you called, and called you back. There was no answer."

"That's funny," he said.

"I was concerned, so I slipped on a coat and went over to your stateroom and knocked on the door, but you weren't in."

He hesitated a moment. "You shouldn't have done that. It was dangerous."

"Where were you, Harold?" she asked evenly.

"Oh, just prowling," he said.

"Prowling?"

"Yeah, about the ship."

"For what?"

"Now you know everything," he said. "I'm a jewel thief."

She said nothing. The silence grew endless and heavy.

"That's an old joke," he offered.

She didn't reply.

"Will you have breakfast with me?" he asked.

"I've already had it," she said.

"Will you sit with me while I have mine?"

"What for?"

"You can blow on my coffee and cool it for me."

She didn't say anything for a moment. And then suddenly her voice came at him with a low but intense fury. "You *are* a bastard, and I hate you, you son of a bitch—"

"Hey—"

"—Not because of what you are but because you make me hate myself. Can you understand what I'm talking about?"

"Don't say that, honey, now come on." He was going to feel awful. He already did, but he could tell it was going to get much worse. "Please don't—"

"I am such a fucking fool . . ."

Oh God, she was crying. "Honey, will you please stop that? Honey? . . ."

He heard a voice in the background, Billy's, saying, "Who is it?" And getting no reply, "Julie, who is it? . . . What's wrong?" Then Billy's voice came on the line. "Hello?"

"It's Harold Columbine," he said.

"What's happening?" Billy demanded.

"Nothing. She's upset, that's all."

"About what?"

"Isn't there plenty to be upset about on this ship?"

"Listen, Columbine, listen to me. I know you've been trying to be helpful, but do me a favor, will you? Stay away from my wife, okay?"

"What the hell are you—?

"Okay?"

"Haven't we got more important things to talk about than this petty bullshit?"

"Just stay away from her, do you hear me?"

"Yeah, I hear you," he said. "Roger, over and out."

He hung up the phone and rolled over onto his stomach and buried his face in the pillow. He had never wanted to hurt Julie, never, never. He hadn't even known he *could*. Oh Jesus, he felt awful. He felt *terrible*. He'd never be able to get through the day feeling like this. He'd have to get totally smashed or something. He'd have to get up and shave and shower and get dressed and go out there and find some of them, any of them, and kill them, or get himself killed, that's what he'd have to do, get himself killed . . . on second thought, not get himself *killed,* but at least do *something* dangerous, something gutsy, something that would make him feel less like the shit that he was . . .

Plowing a white furrow through the swelling seas under a cover of low-flying heavy black clouds, the S.S. *Marseille* plunged onward toward its hoped-for rendezvous at a speed of 31.7 knots. Ninety feet above the observation deck, his eyes straining with tension as he squinted through the eyepieces of his powerful binoculars, a man who called himself Paul Tendler braced his feet on the small deck of the dizzying crow's nest and sucked in his breath as, at long last, something just below the horizon to the southwest began to come into his field of vision.

Tendler's lips tightened with fierce concentration. He focused and refocused the glasses, saw the curling black smoke of a vessel coming up over the distant curving sea. Now he began to see the superstructure of what appeared to be a freighter. Then finally he managed to make out the hull of the ship. And tiny as it was in the distance, the completed picture in his prismatic vision told him that the configuration was the one he had been searching for, waiting for, since daybreak. Filled with elation, he picked up the telephone at his side and called his colleague far below him on the bridge.

"*Angela Gloria,* about twenty-five miles just off the starboard bow."

Craig Dunleavy was in his stateroom, waiting, when word reached him. His first call was to Kleinfeld, his second, to Charles Girodt.

"I need your Chief Radio Officer in the communications room immediately."

"Very well," said Girodt tersely.

"I'm told you were indisposed last night, Captain. I want you to know that this is going to be a good day, for you as well as for all of us."

"I am not interested in your assurances, only in your departure," Charles Girodt said.

Christain Specht was in the communications room when Dunleavy got there. Dunleavy picked up a note pad and pencil and started writing as he talked. "I'd like you to break radio silence for one short message, Mr. Specht."

The Chief Radio Officer nodded without expression.

"Use 2856 kilohertz, CW. The ship you will contact is using the call sign ELHX. Do not sign the call letters of the *Marseille*. Use the call of the *Bordeaux,* Fox Mary Baker Baker. Just get an acknowledgment of this message, then go off the air."

Specht took the sheet of paper that was thrust at him and read it quickly: STAY WITHIN 20 MILES, NO CLOSER. FOLLOW US IF WE PASS YOU. He looked up. "I'll handle it myself," he said.

"Good." Dunleavy went to the telephone on the wall and dialed the wheelhouse. "John?"

"Speaking."

"Craig Dunleavy. Reduce speed to twelve knots."

"Twelve knots. Roger. And congratulations."

"For what?" Dunleavy snapped. "We're still on board."

He hung up and walked back to Christain Specht's operating position. "Mr. Specht . . ."

"Yes, sir?" The Chief Radio Officer turned to him.

"Not that I don't have faith in the abilities of my own men, but I want you personally to supervise the guarding of the ship-to-shore radiotelephone channel. I am expecting a call to come through from Paris. I don't have to tell you how important it is that I get it."

"That's correct. You don't have to tell me," Christain Specht said, turning back to his receiver.

Something in the man's voice did not please Dunleavy. He decided to stand there and wait to see for himself and hear with his own ears the delivery of the message to the *Angela Gloria.*

Except for the morning traffic which kept speeding by in both directions, the little sidewalk table at the Café Bar de la Banque gave Wunderlicht a splendid vantage point from which to observe the gratifying bustle of activity going on behind the double gates of the courtyard of the Banque de France across the rue de Valois.

And he had only to turn his head and glance over his left shoulder to see the red Fiat station wagon containing all of his necessities parked around the corner on the rue Coquillière. He consulted his wristwatch and saw that it was sixteen minutes past eleven, well ahead of schedule. He felt Lisa's eyes on him, and glanced up to see her looking at him over her café espresso. It was her third cup. He wondered how she did it without getting the jitters.

"Why do you look at me that way?" he asked.

She smiled. "What way?"

"As though you found me amusing."

"Hardly," she said. "I was admiring your cool. How do you manage?"

"Very simple," he said. "I drink Perrier water when others pour espresso into their veins. A lesson you would do well to learn."

"Thank you," she said. "I appreciate your interest."

He shrugged, and allowed himself to gaze at her loveliness for another moment, knowing it was bad for him, the wrong thing to do. She was wearing a charming blue denim jump suit with four slanting zippered pockets. Her shoulder bag was white leather, matching the little peaked hat perched atop the long golden hair that framed her smooth fair skin and the pale green eyes, altogether more than he could bear. This was no time to be torn between longing and anguish, not now, when there was so much to be done. There would be time for the pain later—quick, sudden, terrible, over with—when it could no longer be avoided.

He forced his eyes to look away from her, and peered across the rue de Valois at the squat, severe, immensely long building underneath which lay France's precious hoard of gold. A goodly portion of that hoard was even now making its way up from the basement vaults by elevator to the platform in the courtyard where two gray armored Citroën trucks stood waiting. It was a sight to make the blood sing. Wunderlicht allowed his body to tingle with secret pleasure. The Perrier water in his mouth was sweet ambrosia, and warmed his stomach like cognac.

"How long is this going to take?" he heard Lisa saying.

"Each gold bar weighs twelve kilos," he explained, without looking at her. "There are five bars in each gray metal case. It will take five hundred bars, or one hundred cases of five, to make up the value of thirty-five million dollars. All in all, over six-and-a-half tons of gold will have to be loaded into the two trucks."

"I'm sorry," she said. "I left my pocket calculator in the office."

"If you will watch carefully," he said, still not looking at her, "and observe how long it takes for them to place one metal box in one truck, and then multiply that by one hundred, you will have your answer."

"The reason I ask, Julian . . . I have to go to the john."

He glanced at her briefly and frowned. "You'll wait," he said, and turned his gaze to the other side of the street.

Six men in blue workman's garb were moving back and forth swiftly and surely between the elevators and the armored trucks under the close surveillance of a black-suited bank official. Wunderlicht surmised that he represented the Caissier General, who would have had to authorize the transfer of the bullion after receiving direct orders from President Bonnard himself.

The workmen completed their task in less than twenty minutes.

Wunderlicht nodded approvingly as a gray-and-blue uniformed policeman of the Garde Républicaine came forward to the towering steel gates and slid a long horizontal iron bar to his right. Another policeman stepped to his side, and together they pushed on the gates and swung them open. Two drivers got into the front seat of each truck and the engines started. Four black-clad armed guards suddenly emerged from the bank building, mounted motorcycles parked near the loading platform and gunned their motors with a roar. Slowly, two of the motorcyclists drove through the yawning exit of the courtyard and swung to their right onto the busy rue de Valois. Then the first gray armored truck emerged from beneath the tricolored flag of the Banque de France and followed the lead motorcycles. Then the second truck appeared, and finally, in the rear, the last two armed motorcyclists. Slowly, inconspicuously, the convoy moved off into the stream of traffic and began the long journey to Roissy, to the waiting 747 at Charles de Gaulle Airport.

Wunderlicht grunted with satisfaction. He got to his feet and dropped a 10-franc note on the table. "Now we can visit John," he said.

Lisa rose, and he led her inside, holding her gently by the arm.

The cafe was empty, except for the waiter and a tall, sallow-faced man behind the bar who seemed much too young to be the proprietor. Wunderlicht approached him.

"Have you a lavatory, monsieur?"

The man pointed to the rear.

Wunderlicht walked ahead of Lisa, opened the door, snapped on the light and peered into the little bathroom. There was a sink, a small mirror over it, and a toilet—but no window leading out. He turned to her.

"Perfect."

She looked at him with bemused expression. "Even if I wanted to escape from you, which I don't, I'd never dream of trying to outrun a well-concealed snub-nosed revolver."

"I admire your judgment," Wunderlicht said. "Take your time. I have several calls to make."

She stood there and waited until he turned and was walking back to the sallow-faced man at the bar. Then she quickly stepped to her right to the supply table along the rear wall and removed two folded cloth napkins and a large water glass. She took them with her into the lavatory and locked the door.

Glancing about, she saw at once that the water glass was unnecessary, and placed it on the sink. The mirror above the sink was not only cracked, it was loosely bracketed to the wall. In no time at all, with very little effort, she had wrenched the mirror free. She wrapped both of the cloth napkins around it, kneeled down, set one end of the mirror on the wooden flooring near the toilet, leaned the other end against the wall at a low angle, straightened up, reached out, depressed the toilet-flusher, waited a moment until the noise of the churning water reached its peak, then raised her right foot and stomped down hard, and felt the satisfying crunch of breaking glass.

Her heart was pounding, for no reason at all.

Stop it, she said to herself. You're doing fine.

She leaned down and carefully took up the napkins and their contents and set them down in the small metal wastebasket beside the sink. From the roll next to the toilet she unfurled yards and yards of coarse brown paper, tore the streamer in half, and folded both halves into two thick paper wads to protect her hands. Kneeling down, she gingerly unfolded the cloth napkins and examined her handiwork.

The mirror had broken into several irregular shards of glass, one of them about six inches long and three inches deep, its inside edge razor-sharp and lethal. Using one of the wads of toilet paper as a handle, she picked up the jagged shard and placed it in her shoulder bag, cutting edge down, wadded paper handle intact. She stuffed the cloth napkins and the second wad of toilet paper over the remains of the broken mirror in the wastebasket and pushed the receptacle under the sink. She straightened up and turned on the faucet. She let the water run for a few moments, then turned it off, unlocked the door, glanced about, turned out the light, opened the door, and stepped outside.

Julian Wunderlicht was nowhere to be seen.

She walked slowly toward the bar. The sallow-faced man turned to her without expression and gestured over his shoulder with a jerk of his thumb. Then she saw the open door of the little office past the end of the bar. Wunderlicht was seated with his feet up on the desk, talking on the telephone and, with his free hand, waving to her to join him. She went in and remained standing near the doorway, listening to him.

She knew very little German, enough to deduce that he was talking to one or both of his colleagues, the two pilots, giving them instructions. Several times he repeated himself, urging them to listen, not talk. He glanced up and looked directly at Lisa when he advised them not to be surprised to see a strange woman with him when he joined them on the plane. Then he became irritable at their reply, muttered a curt goodbye and hung up.

"How did you get the use of a private office and telephone?" she asked him. "Old snub-nose?"

"A hundred francs is more effective and makes less noise," he said. "Sit yourself down please."

"Yes, Mein Fuehrer." She sat.

His eyes glinted. "That is the first thing you have ever said to me that I detested."

"I'll make it up to you, Julian."

"Don't make it up to me. Just don't do it again."

"Yes, Julian."

She already knew how she was going to make it up to him. What she didn't know yet was exactly *when*. If she did it too soon, she would never know what his plan was. If she did it too late, she would never get to do it at all. He would already have done it to *her*.

She saw him glance at his wristwatch, then pick up the phone and start to dial.

"You're early," she said.

"Don't worry," he said. "At Françat, they have ants in their crotches."

The call from the Caissier General at the Ministry announcing the departure of the gold had galvanized Max Dechambre into a monomania of aggressive optimism. He paced back and forth now before the windows of his office in the Tour Française with such an excess of nervous energy that Mrs. Grillet simply gave up in despair and sank into a chair clutching her steno pad.

"Please, monsieur, I'm sorry, I missed that last," she said, trying not to whine. He *hated* her whining.

"Blume. Blume. Mary Blume. The *Herald Tribune*," Dechambre snapped savagely. "And speak to *her,* not her secretary. Extend my deepest apologies and say I am not responsible for telephonic malfunctions on ships of the Compagnie Française. However, when service is restored—and it *will* be this afternoon—"

"It will?"

"—I shall personally serve as her ship-to-shore operator and place the call myself, and if that doesn't satisfy her, I will have her flown by Sikorsky helicopter to the deck of the *Marseille* to *meet* this damned author, whoever he is—"

"Oh, now Monsieur Dechambre—"

"Do as I say."

"Yes, monsieur."

"Next, call the directors, everyone on the board, no exceptions, wherever they are. Same message to all. Quote. You will enjoy your dinner tonight. That is a promise. And you must promise, underline *you,* you must promise not to say a word to any member of the press until after tomorrow's meeting. Unquote. Got it?"

"I think so . . ."

"You *think* so?"

"Yes," she cried out. "Yes, yes, I have it."

"Stop whining, Mrs. Grillet." He pulled at his goatee. "By any chance, has there been a call for me from Miss Lisa Briande?"

"I'm afraid not, monsieur."

"Why is that something for you to be afraid of?" he said sharply.

"I only meant—"

The intercom sounded. He strode to the desk, flipped the switch. "Yes, what is it?"

"It's him," said the voice of Georges Sauvinage.

"Who, damn it?"

"Wunderlicht."

"Wunderlicht? But it's only—"

"He's in a hurry, m'sieur."

"Have the call transferred and get your behind up here right away."

There was no response.

"Did you hear what I said?"

"Yes, m'sieur."

Dechambre released the switch, felt his heart skip a beat. What was he worried about? Everything was going splendidly. He turned to his secretary. "Go out and take the call that's coming through. Stall until Sauvinage gets here."

"Will there be any more—?"

"No, you have enough." He waved her to the door.

She rose quickly and fled the office.

He felt his pulse.

Racing, damn it. Watch it, Dechambre. Still a few good years left.

From outside, he heard the ringing phone. He held on to the side of the desk, impatient. He tried to wait, but couldn't. He pressed the button. "Put him through."

"But you said—"

"Put him through."

The phone buzzer sounded. He picked up the receiver. "Max Dechambre speaking."

"Good morning, sir," said the smooth voice of Julian Wundericht. "I trust you are well today."

"Considering the circumstances of the past twenty-four hours, Wunderlicht—"

"Forty hours would be more accurate."

"—I have never felt better in my whole life. I hope that meets with your approval."

"It warms me to the depths of my being, Herr Director General."

"Thank you."

Sauvinage came bursting through the door, wheezing breathlessly, his face damply pale. Dechambre pointed sharply to the telephone beside the club chair, as Wunderlicht continued speaking.

"Inasmuch as this will be the last occasion on which I will be speaking to you, Dechambre, or to my dear friend Sauvinage, who breathes so heavily as he no doubt listens on the extension . . . yes, Sauvinage? Are you there, comrade? Speak to me. Hello? Sauvinage? Say something. I command you."

Dechambre snapped his fingers angrily.

Sauvinage murmured into the phone. "What is it?"

Wunderlicht chuckled. "There you are, my ample one. And how many others beside you? Would the Sûreté Nationale care to say a few words? Monsieur Raffin? Jean-Claude? Come now, blow your whistle . . ."

"Stop this nonsense, Wunderlicht," interrupted Dechambre. "There is no one else here but Sauvinage and me. Now what is it you wish to say or to know? Fire away."

"The plane," said Wunderlicht.

"Air France 747, designated Flight 1000, Runway S-801, fueled for nine thousand miles at a load of seven tons . . ."

"You have done your arithmetic with the gold and its traveling companions very well, Dechambre. Congratulations."

"What else?"

"Security."

"None."

"Good. My pilots will be wearing Air France uniforms."

"Life is full of temporary desecrations."

"Profound. Now about the gates . . ."

"What gates?" Dechambre demanded.

"In the cyclone fences that surround the farthermost boundaries of the field," Wunderlicht replied.

"You never said anything about gates."

"I am saying it now. I want every one of them unlocked and swung into an open position."

"For what reason?"

"To let the breezes in. What's the difference? You're going to do it anyway, because I tell you to do it. Please don't make our last conversation together anything but a warm and friendly one, Dechambre."

"All right, all right, the gates will be open. You overwhelm me with trivia. Why don't you ask me about the bullion?"

"I don't have to," Wunderlicht said. "Though it is not *you* that I trust, Dechambre, only my eyes."

"Thank God we are not dealing with a *total* cynic," Max Dechambre said. "May we now talk about the release of the *Marseille?*"

"There is nothing to discuss. You know the conditions. Besides, I am not through with you yet."

"Oh, I beg your pardon, Mr. Wunderlicht."

"There is the matter of ground crew personnel."

Dechambre bristled. "What personnel? You specifically stipulated that no one but the men to start the engines was to be within a thousand yards, or was it a thousand miles of the plane, did you not?"

"May I have the Director General's permission to change my mind?"

"Continue."

"A small oversight," Wunderlicht said. "I need one man, two at the most, to close and lock the cabin door from the outside, and to drive the loading steps clear of the plane before it taxis."

"You and your flight crew, if I may call them that, can secure the door from the *inside* of the plane just as effectively," said Max Dechambre.

"Arguments, Dechambre. Arguments. Sauvinage, are you there?"

"Yes," said Georges Sauvinage.

"You heard my demand?"

"Yes," said Sauvinage.

"Please see that your superior carries it out."

"Yes," said Sauvinage, feeling Dechambre's glare.

"And I want those men waiting out of sight, in the terminal building, until five minutes after the jet engines have started. Is that clear?"

"Yes," said Sauvinage.

"One final request," Wunderlicht said. "The loading steps are to be placed on the *south* side of the cabin—"

"Look here, Wunderlicht—" Dechambre tried to interrupt.

"—all loading, all entry into and out of the plane is to take place on the south side," Wunderlicht persisted.

"How can you expect us to do this on such short notice? The gold is already on the way," Dechambre said angrily.

"Sauvinage, see that it gets done, will you?"

"Yes," said Georges Sauvinage.

"That appears to be it then, gentlemen," said Julian Wunderlicht.

"Wait a minute," Dechambre said quickly. "Can't you give me *some* estimate, some approximate time when we can all breathe freely again?"

"It is simple mathematics, Dechambre, consisting of takeoff time, flying time, headwinds, tailwinds, crosswinds, landing patterns, gold transfer, ship-to-shore phone connections, disembarkation time. Unfortunately, each element is somewhat uncertain. Therefore I cannot give you what I know you want. You will have to be patient, and you will have to pray that while you are standing by waiting for the good news, no one makes the mistake of trying to bring any personal harm to me."

"What do you mean, harm to you?" Dechambre's voice rose. "You will be on the plane. How can we harm you?"

"Just heed my warning, and remember it well," said Wunderlicht. "As for your breathing freely, Dechambre, I think our friend Sauvinage is doing enough breathing for the three of us. *Au revoir,* pals. *Auf Wiedersehen.* Ta-ta."

"Wunderlicht?"

The phone clicked.

Dechambre slammed the receiver down, turned to Sauvinage. "All right, you know what he wants. Do it. If anyone gives you any trouble, let me know immediately."

Georges Sauvinage stared at his superior, unmoving. His moist white face was without expression, but his full lips quivered slightly.

Dechambre went behind the desk and sat down, trying to banish nagging thoughts. Why had that damned German referred to Jean-Claude Raffin, of all people? What were the wide-open gates and the south side of the plane all about? And why was Sauvinage still standing there with that strange look in his eyes?

"Well, what *is* it?" he said to him sharply.

"I am leaving," Georges Sauvinage said quietly.

"Yes, and hurry, for God's sake." Dechambre gestured toward the door.

"The company, monsieur," said Sauvinage.

Dechambre looked up and frowned. "What are you talking about?"

"My resignation, monsieur, effective immediately."

Dechambre cackled, "At a time like *this* you are going to have your period? Come now, Sauvinage, get to your office and make those calls, and we'll talk about your personal problems over a champagne celebration tonight."

Georges Sauvinage struggled to keep his voice from cracking. "It is not because you have disobeyed the wishes of the board of directors in the *Marseille* affair," he said, "and operated in total secrecy behind the backs of everyone, including me——"

"That is none of your——"

"Or because of the humiliating manner in which you dismissed me from the restaurant yesterday so that you could climb between the legs of that woman——"

"Just a minute now, Sauvinage . . ."

"Or because of your rudeness and vulgar ways with everyone from Mrs. Grillet to Madame Dechambre herself——"

"Why you insolent son of a bitch——"

"No, Monsieur Dechambre, I believe it is because of your reference to my *behind* that I am leaving the company now. Get your behind up here right away, is what you said to me, Monsieur——"

"And you can get it out of this office immediately," Dechambre shouted.

"You did not know that I am very sensitive about the fatness of my ass," Sauvinage said. "It has assumed its vast size because of all the food I have stuffed into my mouth in a vain effort to compensate for the deep wounds you have inflicted on my soul, Monsieur Dechambre, and because of all the sitting I have done on that ass while waiting interminably for the occasional bark of your unpleasant voice from the intercom on my desk——"

Dechambre grabbed the telephone and pressed the button savagely. "Get me Maurice Boulot at Charles de Gaulle Airport or wherever . . . Yes, yes, *Boulot*. It's urgent." He slammed the receiver down and said quietly, "Now get out of here."

Georges Sauvinage started for the door, his body stiff and awkward, on his face a twisted smile. Dechambre looked after him with grim expression.

"You're right," he said. "It *is* fat."

"Goodbye, Monsieur Dechambre," Sauvinage said quietly as he opened the door.

"So is your head," said Dechambre.

The phone buzzer sounded.

Georges Sauvinage walked past Mrs. Grillet's desk and out into the corridor. He did not go toward the elevators. Instead, he opened the door to the stairway and started down the stairs. He did not begin to cry until he had passed the twelfth floor.

CHAPTER THIRTY-SEVEN

SHE HURRIED INTO the pitch-black bedroom, switched on the overhead light, and went over to the bed where he lay sprawled on his stomach on top of the covers, snoring the sleep of the dead.

"Bri? . . . Bri? . . . Get up . . ." She grabbed his left foot, tugged on it. "Did you hear me?"

Brian Joy convulsively pulled out of his wife's grasp and grumbled in his dream.

Maggie went to the head of the bed and handled him roughly around the head and shoulders. He lurched up, startled.

"What the hell . . . ?"

"Get up, Brian. They called."

"Who?" He glanced around, bewildered. "What time is it?"

"Three-fifteen. Remo. They have the names."

He swung his feet to the floor saying, "I didn't hear any phone."

"I switched it off up here. I've been dozing in the den."

He stared at her with begrudging admiration.

"Will you go on?" she said. "Slocum wants you to call immediately."

"Yeah, yeah." He rose to his feet, half awake, scratching his body.

Maggie looked at the bed. "Maybe I could sleep here now."

"No, I may need you," he said. "Go downstairs and get out a fresh yellow pad and some Flair pens while I throw some cold water on my face."

At 3:21 a.m., California time, the voice of Arkady Slocum, hollow with fatigue, began to dictate over the telephone the shipboard names and cabin locations of the one hundred seventy-four men and women who had taken over the *Marseille*, four of them now dead. Brian Joy, listening on the extension beside the sofa in the den, repeated each name and cabin number out loud for verification, while Maggie, seated at the desk telephone, wrote down the information.

When Arkady Slocum came to the end and said, "That's it," Brian Joy, rubbing his eyes, said, "Yeah, but what about the extermination plan? How is the Captain supposed to deal with these people?"

"We're working on it, Brian." Arkady Slocum sounded irritated. "As soon as we come up with a solution—*if* we do—I'll call you."

"Yeah, well . . ."

"You've got work to do. Better get to it."

The phone clicked. Brian Joy replaced the receiver in its cradle. "What the hell's the matter with *him?*"

"They did the impossible and you didn't say anything." Maggie rose with the yellow pad in her hand. "You didn't even thank him."

He stared at her. "Put some coffee on, will you?"

"It's already perking," she said, and dropped the pad in his lap.

He riffled through the pages, glancing at the list of faceless men and women. "So these are the bastards who are fucking up everybody's lives."

"Including ours," Maggie said.

He beckoned to her. She leaned down and he kissed her on the lips. Then he got up, took the pad over to the desk, sat down, punched the AC button of the Signal One, watched the digital readout spring to life, turned the VFO dial slowly, and heard exactly what he expected . . . no signals.

"Too early. I need sunrise. I could have slept another two or three hours, goddamn it."

"Poor thing," Maggie said.

"Shit."

"I have an idea," she said.

He turned his head, looked at her. "Go ahead."

"I'll tell you, if you promise to ask how Julie is."

"Promise her anything, give her a kick in the ass. I'm waiting."

"Call Mort Styne."

"Mort Styne? In Woodmere?"

"It's three hours later there, isn't it? He's three thousand miles closer to Billy Berlin, isn't he?"

"Christ, you know Mort. He'll want to know everything."

"What are you, a helpless child?"

She was right, goddamn it. He hated her always being right. "Well, don't just stand there," he said. "Get me a cup of coffee. Make it a mug."

He direct-dialed Long Island. Mort Styne had sold more life insurance than any man in America, retired at forty-five, and was probably the only ham radio operator on the planet who owned every item of electronic station equipment in triplicate. "So I'm insecure, don't bother me," was his standard explanation. Well, this was going to be a different variety of bother now, truly worthy of his filthy extravagance.

The maid answered the phone.

"Is Mr. Styne there?" Brian Joy said.

"Who's calling please?"

"Just tell him a friend. It's long distance."

"Oh, one moment please."

Then Mort Styne came on, New Yorkish as all hell. "Yeah?"

"Mort? Brian Joy."

"Brian. I don't believe it. It's what, quarter of four out there? I get it, you haven't been to bed yet. What's up? How's Maggie? How are *you,* for chrissakes?"

"In a hurry. I need a big favor, Mort."

"How much?"

"I got a friend at sea, a maritime mobile in the southern Atlantic, looking for me on 14,220, and I have urgent information for him which I've gotta get to him right away, and the band is as cold as Kelcey's out here and—"

"Hey, Brian, hey, baby, little Mortie has three duffers waiting for him right now on the first tee at the Woodmere Club and I'm only fifteen minutes late *already* and you're talking QSOs and a *relay* yet—"

"Mortie, you *gotta,*" he shouted into the phone.

"I gotta?" Mort Styne asked quietly.

"Yes, you gotta," Brian Joy said.

The pause was a long one. "You're right," Mort Styne said finally. "I gotta."

"His call is W6 Victor Charlie, Region Two. Point the beam southeast. He's on 14,220," Brian Joy said quickly. "Name is Billy."

"Is that all you're gonna tell me?"

"Until you manage to hook up with him. Then I'll give you the information for him."

"What about information for *me,* like what gives here?"

"I'm sorry, Mort. You're gonna have to go along with me on this and not ask questions."

"I'm gonna *have* to?"

"Yes, Mort."

A pause. "You're right." The shrug was in his voice. "I'm gonna have to."

"Call me on the land line when you get him, okay?"

"Brian?"

"Yeah?"

"Is it all right with you if I phone the Woodmere Club first?"

"Must you?" Brian Joy said.

Mort Styne chuckled. "You son of a bitch, you."

The only condition of his immediate environment that pleased Jean-Claude Raffin here in the control tower of Charles de Gaulle Airport was the incessant babble of voices. The chatter of the traffic controllers delivering instructions into their microphones, and the answering squawks of flight radio officers coming from the loud-speakers above the radar screens, served as a cover for the muttered curses that kept escaping from the Director General's lips as he peered anxiously through his glasses at the great silver bird, sitting on the ground in impressive isolation three quarters of a mile away. The two armored trucks and the four motorcycles from the Banque de France were at rest beside the plane, that much Raffin knew.

And the guards were going up and down the steps to the cabin, loading gold bullion into the passenger compartment, that he knew too. It was the fact that he couldn't see a damned bit of it going on with his own eyes that irritated him to distraction.

He cursed the smoked glass in the windows of the tower for cutting down the amount of light that could reach his straining eyes. He cursed Bausch and Lomb for not inventing binoculars that could see through aluminum. But above all, he cursed the nameless functionary at Air France who had decided to run the loading steps up to the cabin door on the *far* side, the south side of the aircraft, out of his view.

Who am I fooling? Raffin asked himself. And the answer was, no one. It was *himself* he was cursing, for not knowing what he expected to accomplish here at Charles de Gaulle in the first place, other than to discover, perhaps, some sickening verification of his gross stupidity in trusting Julian Wunderlicht the night before.

The blue and white Air France jeep that was cruising along the distant borders of the field did not catch his attention until it had made several stops at the steel-wire fence that marked the boundaries of the airport. He swung his glasses off the 747, refocused, and saw that the driver of the jeep, a man in white coveralls, had alighted and was unlocking the padlock on a gate and swinging the gate open, then returning to the jeep and driving on. Raffin quickly moved the glasses in a wide arc to the left and to the right, and saw immediately that there were wide-open gates in other areas of the field.

He lowered the glasses, frowning with puzzlement, and breathed deeply to soothe his nerves. He promised himself that, once this day was over, he would take a long vacation, if he wasn't fired first. But he had no time to give the matter further thought, for suddenly he was back in his symbiotic relationship with the binoculars, watching something new on the field—the motorcycles of the Banque de France, four of them, zooming out from behind the huge aircraft and speeding away, soon followed by the two gray Citroën trucks, traveling at the leisurely speed of armored emptiness.

Raffin gazed for a moment at the winged monster that was Air France Flight 1000, and in his mind's eye he saw the rich golden gleam of its interior. Then, lowering the glasses, he strode to the nearby telephone that had been reserved for him by André Delaporte and dialed a number that was known to few men.

The familiar voice answered, and Jean-Claude Raffin said, "Monsieur le Président, Madame has asked me to inform you that, in the matter of her dental work, the inlays are now in place."

"It is most thoughtful of you to let me know," Aristide Bonnard replied, and immediately terminated the call.

Why do I sit here as though I were hypnotized by him or handcuffed to him? If I got up from this sofa and walked away, what could he do, shoot me right here in the lobby of the Hotel George V, in full view of a hundred people? No, Lisa told herself, he would not shoot me, for the simple reason that I would not get up and walk away, and *he* knows that just as surely as I do, because, yes, I *am* handcuffed to him, by my need to know what he intends to do. Of what possible use can I be to anyone on the *Marseille* if I have no hard facts, no new information for Brian Joy to relay? And let's not forget Page One of the *Trib,* and maybe, who knows, the book.

Her gaze went to the window where Wunderlicht was standing now, waiting impatiently for the telephone operator behind the glass to execute his call to the ship. She thought of her California co-conspirator, and silently said to the sleeping stranger (who was not sleeping) six thousand miles away, I don't know a damned bloody thing.

Well, that wasn't *completely* accurate. She did know that Max Dechambre's dream of ransoming the *Marseille seemed* to be coming true. The gold *was* probably at the airport by now. But there was an aura of duplicity about Wunderlicht, something about his behavior that would have paralyzed Dechambre with fear had he been around the German last night and today, as she had been. She wondered if Wunderlicht's cryptic telephone call had shaken up the goateed Director General of French Atlantic, or was he lunching this very moment in naïve tranquility at his favorite restaurant with his unfavorite assistant, the leaden Sauvinage? She decided not to think about him further. Why spoil his day, even in her thoughts?

She heard Wunderlicht call her name, and looked up to see him beckoning to her with urgency. She got up quickly and crossed over to him.

"The call is about to go through," he said to her. "You might as well listen, at least to my end."

"What you really mean is, you can't keep an eye on me if I'm not in the phone booth with you."

"Lisa, please stop showing off. We know how bright you are." He took her arm and moved her along with him to the very same booth he had used for his original call to the *Marseille*. He had explained to her that the Hotel George V was on their way to the airport anyway. But the real reason he had wanted to place the call from here was that he had been confident—as it turned out, correctly so—that he would be able to persuade one of the three women behind the glass to route the call through Madrid. Radio FFL at St.-Lys would never have found the errant ship. However, it had taken far too long for the connection to be made. He had felt himself growing irritable and apprehensive during the agonizing delay.

He entered the booth, left Lisa standing in the partly opened door, and picked up the phone.

"Your party is listening, m'sieur," said the lovely operator who had accepted his two hundred francs of persuasion.

"Hello, Dunleavy, is that you?" He heard his own voice through the earpiece, hollow and time-lagged by a fraction of a second.

"This is Dunleavy speaking," came the echoing reply, a ghost of a voice, scarred by static, a far cry from the Craig Dunleavy he had known in California.

"Uncle Julian here," said Wunderlicht, seeing Lisa watching him intently, listening. "Can you hear me?"

"Yes, Uncle Julian, go ahead please," said the ghost.

"The bird has wings of gold," Wunderlicht said. "I will repeat that. The bird has wings of gold."

"Wonderful. Are you looking at it, Uncle Julian? Can you see the bird?"

"With my own two eyes," Wunderlicht lied.

"And when does it fly away with you?"

"In another five minutes, ten at the most."

"That is excellent, truly excellent," said Craig Dunleavy from the southern Atlantic. "Well done, Uncle Julian. I commend you."

"Thank you, Dunleavy, and good luck to you, to all of you."

"You too, Uncle Julian. Happy landing."

"*Auf Wiedersehen,* dear friend."

Wunderlicht heard the connection broken, then a Spanish-speaking male voice coming on, probably Madrid. He hung up, aware that he was sweating profusely and feeling cramps in his intestinal tract.

"That's that," he muttered, as Lisa stepped back to let him out of the booth.

"What's going to happen in five or ten minutes, Julian?" she asked him quietly.

Wunderlicht walked past her to the glassed-in communications desk, mopping his face with a handkerchief.

"You didn't speak very long, m'sieur," the girl smiled at him. "Three hundred and fifty francs please."

Wunderlicht scowled and savagely thrust some bills through the opening in the glass. "Who says talk is cheap?"

The girl's smile vanished. "I'm sorry, m'sieur."

Sorry? What did *she* know about being sorry? Had she ever taken the first steps on the road to betrayal?

He turned to Lisa, who had come up behind him. "Let's get going," he said brusquely.

They walked through the crowded lobby together in silence. Near the entrance, Lisa gave him a sidelong glance. "Julian, what's going to happen in five or ten minutes?"

He looked at her with anger. "It was a forward projection of what will happen when we get to the airport," he said impatiently. "And the fewer questions you ask, the sooner we will get there."

He pushed through the door and went out ahead of her, moving quickly toward the station wagon, eager to be alone, away from her, if only for a few moments. Her probing eyes, and his own nagging thoughts, were going to make the heavy traffic seem even heavier now.

They worked their way swiftly through the deepest compartments of the ship, without undue nervousness, exercising extreme care in what they were doing. The call from Paris had galvanized them into a controlled frenzy of long-planned action, the final release from tension. Anthony Palazone, Al Tomlinson, and Carmen Ferrante covered the portside. Ed Lambert, Floyd Jackson, and Carroll Wright took care of the starboard side. The timing boxes were no larger than the smallest cooking timer found in the average kitchen, but the similarity ended there. The differences, and there were many, lay in a printed circuit whose only original copy was the one that had been grooved in the brain traces of Leonard Horner.

Their hands sure and steady, the men would stop before each little red box they came upon, kneel down and carefully twist the black dial clockwise. They would then remove the dial, rise, and move on, looking for the next box. In the twin boiler rooms, in the twin engine rooms, under the four great dynoturbines, beneath the nine thousand tons of fuel-oil tanks, against the steel plates of keel and bulkheads and double-bottoms, beside the propeller shafts, in the central security control room, along the banks of generators and turbo-alternators, in the electrical distributing station, inside the air conditioning and ventilating plants, inside each and every vital organ that made the *Marseille* a living, breathing thing and kept her head above water, these men dispatched by Dunleavy's orders set the timing mechanisms that would flash their simultaneous and instantaneous electrical commands to the vast network of grayish-white, innocent-seeming putty that had been so carefully implanted several days before.

They were highly visible, these delicate red boxes, but the soft clicking inside of them was barely audible above the subdued, vibrating hum of the great ship, slowed down now to less than half her speed.

Charles Girodt's crewmen saw these strangers, saw what they were doing with the little red boxes, but said nothing and did nothing. Some even walked away. For they knew there was nothing they could do. The dials were being removed. And affixed to each box, printed on a metallic plate in bold black letters in French, English, Spanish, and Italian, was a clear warning to all of them: DANGER—DO NOT TOUCH.

The boxes were now set for 1600 Zulu, less than five hours away.

Julie Berlin stood at the porthole window staring out at the ugly sea and the leaden sky, trying to feel sorry for herself, but somehow it wouldn't wash. There were too many things going on right now that seemed just a little bit more important than Harold Columbine or *her* hurt feelings. Like the *Marseille* slowing down to a cakewalk. That had to mean something. And that freighter on the horizon off the starboard side, dogging their tail with unmistakable persistence. And Billy on the bed, hunched over the Atlas-210, earphones clamped on his head, scribbling away furiously on sheet after sheet of French Atlantic stationery as he talked, mostly listened, to that friend of Brian Joy's in New York, Mort Styne.

"How many more?" Billy was saying into the hand-held mike. "Great. Go ahead."

She went over to the bed and said, "Can I help?"

Billy said, "QRX a minute" into the mike, ripped off the earphones and looked up at her. "I can't hear you with these things on, you know that."

She said, "Can I help? That's all."

"In a couple of minutes, you sure can. Now sit down, will you please?" He pressed the mike button and said, "Carry on, Mort. Everything after E. Carroll Wright." And quickly jammed the headphones on again.

Maybe, she thought, his jealousy wasn't the *worst* thing that could have suddenly crept into their marriage. Trouble was, he was so hopelessly preoccupied, it was coming out as irritation, instead of new-found appreciation. She watched him doing what he did so well, ears sharp, fingers fine-tuning the receiver with a surgeon's deftness, and wondered why she still found it so hard to accept self-evident truths. He was a grownup man, the one man on this paralyzed ship who had been capable of providing a possible lifeline for three thousand helpless people. And yet she still persisted in seeing him as a little boy, playing little boys' games.

What was there about her that felt less threatened by a little boy than by a grownup man?

Fuck it, she said, and lit a cigarette and blew smoke into her eyes, knowing that Albert DeGrooning would have been ashamed of her.

She heard Billy signing off with Mort Styne. She watched him take the earphones off and pull the jack out and throw the receiver back onto the speaker, with the volume low. And then he folded the thick wad of writing paper and stuffed it into a white envelope and rose from the bed, his eyes gleaming with excitement.

"We got it," he said. "We got it."

"What?"

He waved the white envelope at her. "Their names and their cabin numbers. Every goddamn one of them . . ."

"My God," she exclaimed. "Why didn't you tell me?"

"I'm telling you now. A hundred and seventy-four of them, four of them dead."

"I had no idea . . ."

"You couldn't hear *his* end of the QSO. You wanted to help— get to it, honey. Put this in your handbag and get it to the Captain fast. But for Christ's sake, guard it with your life."

She took the envelope from him and tucked it away at the bottom of her carryall, saying, "Don't you think I should call him first?"

He scratched his head for a moment. "You may be right," he said. "But don't *say* anything."

She picked up the phone and dialed Charles Girodt's office. Leon Carpentier, the Captain's aide, sounded muffled and strange. "The Commandant cannot speak to anyone now."

"It's very important," she said.

"I'm sorry," he said stiffly.

"Well, is it all right if I come up there for a brief visit? A minute or two at the most."

"No, I'm afraid not," Leon Carpentier said.

"It's *urgent.*"

"I'm sorry. No."

She heard the phone clatter down. She hung up and looked at Billy. "Something's wrong."

He grimaced. "That's putting it mildly."

She dialed another number.

"Who're you calling?"

"Yves Chabot."

The Chief Medical Officer's head nurse was strangely unfriendly. "I'm sorry, madame. The Doctor is in a staff meeting with the Commandant."

"May I come over and wait for him?"

"I do not think that would be advisable," Genvieve Bordoni said.

"Well, suppose I were ill or something?"

"I would send someone to your cabin, madame."

"Never mind," Julie said, and hung up.

She saw Billy back at the transceiver with his ear to the speaker. "I'm going to take this over to the Captain right now," she said to him, "no matter what. It's too important."

Billy raised his hand. "Hold it a minute," he said. "I think I hear someone calling me. He's very weak. I think it may be Briney's friend again."

Three minutes later, with the earphones back on, he was listening to Mort Styne's voice coming through heavy interference, and the voice was saying: "I don't know what this means, fella, but Brian said you'd understand. It just came through from Remo, whatever the hell *that* is. He called it the E-Plan."

Billy Berlin gestured urgently to Julie to sit down.

Dunleavy glanced from one to the other of them as he spoke, enduring their hard, cold eyes and their stony expressions, knowing that they hated him for being the cause of their unmanly helplessness. "The cutting of one wire, the severing of one electrical connection anyplace in the entire circuit we have rigged, will automatically trigger all detonators. So please, gentlemen, I beg of you, don't make any foolish errors. And you, Captain Girodt . . . don't let any of your men try to become a sawdust hero . . ."

Charles Girodt took another sip of the mild sedative powders that Yves Chabot had dissolved for him in some Perrier water, set the glass down on his desk and stared at the suntanned man who sat across from him, issuing instructions to him and his staff with such soft-voiced arrogance. It was difficult, well nigh impossible, for Girodt to accept the fact that he would never be able to wreak vengeance on this stranger who had irrevocably ruined his life. Irrevocably, because he knew that he would never be the same again, even if they hailed him as a national hero in France when he finally steamed into Le Havre.

"Your concern for our safety, now that you are planning to leave us, is touching, Mr. Dunleavy. But let me assure you that no one in this room, and I think I can speak for all of us, no one in this room has anything but the utmost contempt for you and your band of murderers, and nothing you say now will soften our resolve to bring you to justice. So you see, *you,* Mr. Dunleavy, are not safe at all."

Girodt fancied he saw Yves Chabot glancing at him and shaking his head imperceptibly, but he did not care. Let them all . . . Leboux, Specht, Demangeon, Vergnaud, Ferret, Dulac, Plessier . . . let them all sit there in careful silence. He, Charles Girodt, master of the *Marseille,* would not let this cheapjack American gangster get away without being told what scum he was.

"Before this day ends, you and your filth will all be dead," he went on, with an uncontrollable tremor in his voice. "You will all—"

"Commandant, excuse me . . ." Yves Chabot interrupted.

Girodt turned sharply. "What is it?"

"If you do not finish that . . ." He nodded toward the glass on the desk. "The fizz will be gone."

"To hell with it," Charles Girodt snapped.

Craig Dunleavy cleared his throat. "A question, sir, if you don't mind, about one of your lifeboats . . ."

Girodt turned away. "Tell him, Ferret."

"What is it you wish to know?" said First Officer Henri Ferret.

"The large one with the enclosed cabin, the powerboat cruiser . . ."

"Yes, m'sieur?"

"Are the diesel engines fueled and ready to go?"

Henri Ferret stiffened with pride. "Naturally. What kind of—?"

"Take it easy," Dunleavy said. "Have the cruiser lowered to the Boat Deck and prepared to take on passengers at a moment's notice."

"Very well, m'sieur." The First Officer remained seated.

"Do it now, Mr. Ferret."

"Now?"

"Yes, Mr. Ferret. Use the telephone."

Henri Ferret glanced uncertainly at his captain, then got to his feet, stepped to the desk, picked up the white telephone, and issued orders to René Derbos, officer in charge of Station 23.

"It is done," Ferret announced, and sat down again on the leather sofa.

Dunleavy got slowly to his feet and addressed the room. "We will be relieving you of our presence just as soon as I receive the message from one of our representatives on land that the gold has reached its destination safely. After we arrive at the freighter, we will send back to you very specific instructions for the safe disarming of all explosive devices . . ."

Pierre Demangeon's face showed instant concern. "After you leave the *Marseille?*"

"Correct," Dunleavy said.

"It was my understanding," said the Chief Engineer, "that you people would remain on board until you received this call you speak of, and that once you received it, you yourselves would then disarm and remove the explosives, and then remove yourselves. No?"

"I'm afraid that was a misunderstanding on your part, sir," said Craig Dunleavy. "We intend to put a lot of miles between our freighter and this beautiful ship before the timers run out at 1600 Zulu and make it possible for you to follow out our disarming instructions. While those timers are ticking away, no one, not even my men, could disarm the plastic network. Once the timers have run their course, anyone who knows exactly what to do can turn the network into a mass of silly putty."

Charles Girodt broke in, his voice shaking. "And where will all this cleverness get you, Mr. Dunleavy, when we contact land and send the air force and naval planes after you?"

Dunleavy smiled. "In case you're thinking of any tricks once we're in the powerboat, Captain, let me tell you that we intend to take a few of your passengers along with us as hostages. When we reach the freighter and climb aboard, they will be permitted to make their return to the *Marseille* in the powerboat. We'll have no further use for it. I think you'll welcome their return, inasmuch as *they* will be the ones carrying back our instructions for disarming the explosives." His eyes turned hard. "As for your contacting land, Captain, or anyplace else, I'm afraid that's going to be kind of difficult for you, because we're going to destroy every piece of communications gear on this ship before we leave it." He paused to let it sink in. "You'll talk to the seagulls, sir, until you reach Le Havre."

Charles Girodt stared at him for a moment, and then his lips began to curl in a curious smile. He exchanged a glance with Christain Specht, and he looked over at Yves Chabot and back to Dunleavy, and he started to speak. But before he could say a word, Chabot sprang to his feet crying out, "Give me that, Captain, will you?" and snatched the glass of sedative powders from the startled Girodt's hands.

A fleeting look of puzzlement crossed Dunleavy's face. "What is this?"

Charles Girodt saw the stern warning in Chabot's eyes, and his smile died.

Christain Specht looked down at his hands.

Dunleavy waited, but nothing came to him. He went to the door, opened it and called out, "Okay, you can come in now."

Lou Foyles and Wendell Cronin left their positions beside Leon Carpentier's desk and entered the room, tucking their ugly Baretta handguns out of sight as they moved. They did not look at the ship's officers sitting about, but went quickly to the bank of telephones on Girodt's desk, seized them by their cords and began to wrench them from their connections at the base of the wall.

Charles Girodt stared at the men, his face white with anger.

"I hate to be so destructive," Craig Dunleavy said. "It happens to be necessary. Oh, and one more thing. I'm going to have to ask all of you to remain in this room until we've left the ship. It shouldn't be more than an hour or two . . ."

"But we are needed elsewhere, all of us," Pierre Demangeon insisted.

"Not as much as I need all of you right here." Dunleavy looked at Charles Girodt. "Goodbye, Captain."

The Commandant turned away, and in a low and terrible voice said, "Get out of here before one of us kills you with his bare hands."

"My friends here will be standing guard outside your door, Captain, to see that you don't do anything childish."

Girodt whirled with contorted face and moved suddenly at the other man, but Yves Chabot quickly stepped between them. "Go," he said quietly to Dunleavy.

Dunleavy glanced away, ignoring them both. "Goodbye, gentlemen," he said to the others. "I would like to say that it has been a pleasure, but why damage my credibility at a time like this?"

He walked out quickly, followed by Foyles and Cronin carrying the crippled telephones.

Leon Carpentier's face paled as he saw the men coming toward him and tossing the damaged instruments on the sofa. He heard Dunleavy's voice. "You, too."

"What, m'sieur?"

"In there. Quickly."

Carpentier rose and hurried inside.

Dunleavy closed the door and looked at the two men. "Be god-damn careful," he said. "The pricks may be up to something."

He turned, and then he saw her . . . just at the moment that she had entered and had seen *him,* and was now backing away and turning quickly . . .

"Hold it," he called out. But she had run out to the corridor.

He heard Lou Foyles behind him saying, "Shall I?"

He glanced back, decided no, turned and moved forward to the corridor in time to see her hurrying down the long, endless tunnel of dim lights and closed doors. Beyond her, a man in officer's uniform was approaching slowly, wearing sunglasses.

Sunglasses?

"Stop her," Dunleavy called out to him.

The man in uniform grabbed Julie as she tried to get past him.

"Let go of me . . ."

"It's okay, Craig," the man called out. "I got her." And taking her forcibly by the arm, he began to hustle her away from the waiting Dunleavy.

"Where you going?" Dunleavy called out, puzzled.

"To lock her up," the man called back, dragging Julie along.

"Charlie?"

"Yeah?"

"You sound funny. What is it?"

"Sore throat, Craig."

Dunleavy saw them disappear through the passageway to the elevators. He looked after them for a moment, sorting out his priorities, then turned and started away in the opposite direction. It was only a three-hour flight from Charles de Gaulle to Brazzaka. He wanted to be available to his men in the communications room, ready and waiting at his telephone when the call came through from Otto Laneer.

The voice hadn't fooled him. Even coming from a sore throat it hadn't sounded like any Charlie *he* knew. He thought about it a while, and he wasn't even angry. He even allowed a small smile to come to his face as he hurried on, looking forward to the call that would come later and free them all to climb into the powerboat and escape this cursed doomed ship.

And he knew now who the two hostages would be.

Perfect.

"Don't squeeze my arm, damn it. I'll be black and blue."

"You ought to be glad you're alive, you little bubblehead."

"Don't talk to me that way, just because you're wearing that idiotic uniform. Where did you get it?"

"Officers' dry cleaning shop."

"What for?"

"I feel safer in it, not that it's going to fool anyone like Dunleavy for long. But I'll bet *some* of them think I'm one of them when they see me."

"Don't count on it."

"Fooled *you.*"

"Until you opened your mouth. Look, you can let go of me now. We're out of sight."

"I want to talk to you, Julie."

"I'm sure you do. I'm sure you want to beat your breast and tell me what a horrible man you are but, shucks, you can't help yourself, and then you want to get down on your knees and beg me to forgive you—*ow . . . don't . . .*"

"You gonna cut that out, or you want me to break your arm? I'm not your husband, you know. I mean, who the fuck do you think you are to pass judgment on me all the time?"

"Well, well. We actually know how to get angry. We don't just slobber and whine with guilt every time we get caught doing something shitty. We even beat up on women, provided they're not too big . . ."

"I'm warning you, Julie . . ."

"Don't worry, I need you, or I *wouldn't* stop."

"Nevertheless, I apologize, I'm truly sorry I upset you. Okay? Now, can we talk?"

"Not out of choice, only because I have to. And not about you and not about me. Where can we go?"

"My cabin? . . . Well, don't look so frightened. I'm not going to touch you."

"You'd look frightened too. They've got the Captain and his staff under lock and key, incommunicado. We're going to have to do it ourselves, Harold, you and me."

"Do what?"

"When we get to your cabin."

Genvieve Bordoni, her dark hair pulled back in a bun beneath her smartly visored nurse's cap, looked up and saw the uniformed man in dark glasses coming through the entrance to the waiting room, and knew immediately that he was not a legitimate officer of the ship. The unpleasant man who had occasionally stood guard in her area had wandered off. This one was obviously his replacement. He came up to her desk, glanced about at the passengers who were sitting patiently waiting to be treated for their imaginary ailments, and spoke to her in a low voice, using heavily American English.

"I have to speak to you in private. Where do we go?"

"I'm sorry, m'sieur, but I cannot leave my desk now."

"Do as I say," he said quietly, "and hurry up about it."

The arrogance of these gangsters. Would they never leave the ship? She got up, gestured with her head for him to follow her, walked away from the watching eyes of the impatient hypochondriacs, and led him into an unoccupied examining room. "Very well," she said, turning. "What is it you want?"

The man took out a slip of paper and handed it to her. "This," he said. "All you've got."

She glanced down at the writing, then handed the slip of paper back to him. "I'm sorry. Only Dr. Chabot can authorize issuing a preparation such as this." Two days ago, these people had roamed through the hospital and decided its medicines were harmless. Had they changed their minds?

"Right now your good doctor is in no position to authorize the dispensing of an Alka-Seltzer," the man said gruffly. "You're wasting time, Miss Bordoni."

"What have you done with him?" she said, her voice trembling a little.

"We've put him away with the Captain and a few of the other superstars to keep them from getting themselves into trouble. You'll have him back in a couple of hours, don't worry. Bet you two fool around a little, huh?"

She slapped his face as hard as she could. He laughed at her. She swore at him in French. The only word he recognized was *merde*.

"Nice girl," he said. "You got quite a staff here, Miss Bordoni. Couple of female nurses, a male nurse, Christ knows how many assistants to the boss man behind those closed doors. You don't wanna see them suffer, do you, along with yourself? Or do you happen to like the sight of blood?" He seized her arm in a fierce grip. "Now come on, goddamn it. You gonna get it for me?"

She stared into his dark glasses for a moment, then wrenched her arm free and said, "Come with me."

He followed her down the corridor to a closed door at the rear of the hospital. She took a set of keys from the pocket of her white smock, unlocked the door, went inside, and snapped on the lights.

The supply room smelled of ether and demerol and whatever antiseptic detergents and sprays they used to get rid of the odor of ether and demerol. She opened the door of a shallow closet, went in, stooped down, and picked up a small portable cabinet, which she brought out and set down on the floor. With another key she unlocked the cabinet, opened it, reached in, and withdrew an eight-ounce vial of a substance that resembled coarse table salt. Handling the vial gingerly, she placed it on the white metal top of the cabinet.

The man in uniform stared at it. "Strychnocyanate-K?"

"Yes," she said.

"Soluble crystalline form?"

"Read the label," she said.

He looked at her. "Is that all of it?"

She hesitated a moment, then reached in and withdrew a second vial and set it down and closed the cabinet. "Sixteen ounces," she said, and then, with bitterness and contempt in her voice, "but a *hundred* ounces will do you no good. Ten-pound rats will die on contact, but human beings will shrug it off, and we *are* human beings, m'sieur. You will have to kill us some other way."

"Save the speeches," he said, and handed her another slip of paper. "Now get me this."

She read the slip of paper quickly and gave it back to him. "We do not have it."

"You're lying. You have twelve four-ounce bottles of parahoxy-dil HCL concentrate around here somewhere. I want one of them. Now hurry."

She stared at him, tightlipped, then turned, stepped into the closet again, and presently came out with a small bottle of clear, syrupy liquid. She set it down beside the vials of the crystalline substance and said, "If you do not know what to do with this, I would like to suggest that you take it as an apéritif, preferably on an empty stomach."

"You'd make a lousy bartender," he said. Then, slowly, he took off his braided officer's hat and his dark glasses, and a smile came to his face as he looked at her.

Genvieve Bordoni's eyes widened. Her expression softened. "Good heavens . . . M'sieur Columbine . . ."

"Sorry about that," he grinned.

She quickly closed the door of the supply room and came back to him. "You shouldn't be here. It could be dangerous."

He was stuffing the two vials and the small bottle into the pockets of his uniform, saying, "You swear beautifully, honey."

"I'm afraid you earned it," she said ruefully.

"Now tell the truth," he said. "Would you have handed this stuff over to *me*, Harold Columbine, if I had asked for it?"

"Never," she said. "I am under the strictest orders. All of our compounds, no matter how seemingly innocuous, can be dangerous if misused."

"If misused in the right *way*," he said meaningfully.

She eyed him shrewdly. "Just what are you planning to do with these two substances, m'sieur?"

"Combine them," he said.

"For what? They are entirely dissimilar in chemical structure and in use."

"I guess you'd say that what I had in mind is to create a very bad case of contact dermatitis. I'm talking about the kind where the victim is out of all misery in anywhere from five to thirty minutes."

She frowned with puzzlement. "With rats, yes, as I already indicated, instantaneous death after touching a microscopic speck of the strychnocyanate, but . . ."

"I'm talking about *human* rats, Miss Bordoni . . ."

The color seemed to drain from her face.

He nodded. "With them it can happen too."

"No," her voice faltered, "that is not—"

"*Yes*. Provided the exact amount of this parahoxydil whatchamacallit is added to create the proper synergistic effect, and provided the solution in water is just right, not too weak, not too strong." He shrugged. "Only problem is, it'll take a little longer to happen."

Genvieve Bordoni's eyes slowly widened with horror as full realization came to her. "M'sieur Columbine, you *mustn't* try anything like that. *Please* don't fool around with things you know nothing about . . ."

"*I* may not know, but somebody back in the United States apparently does, and that's the number we're betting on," he said with grim purpose.

She stared at him speechlessly.

He had no way of knowing that that somebody back in the United States, that number he was betting on, was 307.

René Derbos was an able officer and an intelligent man. He was not the kind of person who would waste his courage on what he thought was an impossible situation, merely to prove to himself that he had courage. When the man wearing rubber boots, rubber gloves, and the soiled apparel of an ordinary seaman came up to him at Station 23 on the Boat Deck, where he was guarding the sleek, white power cruiser, he knew that the man was one of them even before he set down the pail of water he was carrying and opened his mouth to speak. No French Atlantic seaman, this one. A Chicago thug, like you see in the flicks.

"This the boat we're leaving on?" the man demanded.

Derbos nodded.

"How many does she hold?"

"Two hundred," Derbos said.

"We don't trust you frogs," the man said in an unpleasant voice. "We're gonna wash this thing down from stem to stern, and when I'm finished, nobody goes near it or goes on board, and that includes you. Do you understand?"

"Certainly, m'sieur," said René Derbos.

"Anybody touches any part of this baby or puts one foot inside, he gets his head blown off, and it's gonna be up to *you* to see that it doesn't happen. Gimme a Roger on that."

What a vulgar man. Derbos blinked. "A Roger?"

"Say yes, say okay, say *oui*, goddamn it," the man said fiercely.

"Yes, m'sieur," the officer said quietly.

"Yes, what?"

"I understand your request."

"Okay, open the gate for me."

René Derbos swung back the four-foot section of railing on its hinges.

Harold Columbine, swathed in all the protective garments Genvieve Bordoni had been able to find for him, tucked the long-handled toilet-bowl brush under his left arm, and with his rubber-gloved right hand slowly raised the pail that was three quarters filled with a 12 percent solution of strychnocyanate-K combined with 72.8 cc. of parahoxydil HCL concentrate, and carefully made his way onto the twin-engined, diesel-powered cruiser that hung from its davits, swaying slightly above the sea that was rushing by a hundred feet below.

He knew that Julie Berlin was standing in the shadowed entrance to a passageway less than twenty feet away, ready to shout a warning if Craig Dunleavy should be seen catastrophically approaching. But the knowledge of her presence did not lessen the mortal terror that gripped his intestines, nor stem the flow of fear pouring down his forehead and into his eyes as he began to swab the interior of the power cruiser with the lethal solution.

He covered the ceiling and the floorboards of the vast cabin. He bathed the walls, the six circular windows, the handrails, the benches, and the bucket seats. He anointed the instrument panel, the throttle, the steering wheel. And almost as fast as he applied the murky, colorless liquid to wood and metal and plexiglass, it evaporated in the briskly moving ocean air, leaving a thin and all but invisible residue behind.

Now he picked up the empty pail and stepped off the powerboat onto the Boat Deck and went past René Derbos, who was watching without expression, and he moved quickly to the passageway where Julie was hiding and set the pail down and carefully picked up another one, three quarters full.

She looked at him worriedly and all he could say was "Christ . . ." dry-tongued and quavering.

He returned to the powerboat and began to work with desperate care on the outer deck that surrounded the cabin, swabbing the entire railing, starting at the bow, making his way to the stern on the starboard side and back to the bow on the portside. Then he followed the same route as he swabbed the hardwood planks of the deck itself.

His hands were shaking now, and the sweat stung his eyeballs, and he dripped some of the liquid onto his right trouser leg just above the top of the rubber boot and his heart leaped and he let out a hoarse involuntary gasp that embarrassed him. But it was not enough to soak through.

Maybe Julie had been right.

"We *know* their cabins. The doorknobs will do it."

But he had overruled her, after seeing the powerboat poised on its davits, ready to go. "We can't be sure of getting every last damned one of them with doorknobs, and certainly not all at the same time."

Smart-ass that he was, he'd wind up getting himself instead.

He finished in less than fifteen minutes.

Julie Berlin never shouted once.

Craig Dunleavy was occupied elsewhere, thinking about the call that would come from the communications room, looking forward to the moment when he would be told by a faraway voice that a plane had landed in Brazzaka and thirty-five million dollars in gold was rumbling in trucks to its hiding place. Through his porthole window Dunleavy stared off at the *Angela Gloria* about twenty miles off the starboard side, as the *Marseille* glided southward, its turbines under forced restraint. He felt relaxed, and confident.

Standing at the rail of the Greek freighter, gazing with bitterness and awe at the beauty of the distant liner to the east, Nick Moustakos knew that somehow, before this day was out, he would have to get very drunk, or die. He could not much longer stand the chagrin and the humiliation of having to admit to himself that his pig of a captain, Panos Trimenedes, had not lied to his men after all. It was typical of that filthy Greek to betray his crew any way that he could, even with the truth.

CHAPTER THIRTY-EIGHT

THOUGH DAWN HAD NOT YET diluted the darkness of the Southern California sky, the gentle morning air bore promise of a pleasant day. Driving south on the San Diego Freeway, Lawrence Wibberly felt comforted by the peaceful silence within his car, by the absence of any appreciable traffic in either direction. It was the kind of surcease his nervous system had been craving all night. Soon, he knew, the Freeway would become horribly alive with the early-shift mob, pushing their infernal machines to sixty and beyond and getting away with it. By that time, Wibberly hoped to be safely in Palos Verdes, nestling between the cool sheets in his darkened bedroom lying beside Clara, who would not even know that he had come home, much less bother him with questions. She slept with pink wax plugs in her ears and a pink satin sleepshade over her eyes. See no Wibberly, hear no Wibberly, thank God for that.

The elderly astrophysicist drove very slowly, his hands gripping the steering wheel of the ten-year-old Pontiac as much to keep himself upright as to control the destiny of the car. He stared straight ahead at the monotonous ribbon of roadway and forced his dry and irritated eyes to remain wide open for fear that if he relaxed the effort, they would close completely. He was agonizingly weary, and not just from lack of sleep.

Wibberly had stayed awake many times before for much longer periods than the endless hours he had just sat through in the air conditioned, windowless war games room at Remo. There had been times on Mount Palomar when he had literally forgotten to go to bed for as much as two days and nights, without feeling this kind of exhaustion. In fact, he had usually known great exhilaration. But those occasions had had a fundamental difference. The stars had no voices. The galaxies never talked back to him. The heavens were silent. That was why he had been attracted to astronomy from the very beginning. He had never been able to think effectively in the midst of too much input. His brain had always had a way of turning off at the sounds humans made when two or more of them were placed in the same room together.

He drove on, oblivious to the occasional car that approached from the rear and swung out to pass him on the right. He was thinking about his dismal experience as a member of Arkady Slocum's now-disbanded team, wondering whether he wasn't artfully constructing a defense for his own failure. It would not be the first time he had caught himself doing that sort of thing, nor would it be the last, he was sure.

He had sat among them under the neon lights before the CRT projection screen, sucking on his pipe, gazing at the floor and roaming through the universe seeking some exotic solution to the predicament of the *Marseille* that would have permitted him to dazzle them with his brilliance. But no supernova had exploded, no black hole had lighted up. He had come up with nothing, absolutely nothing. And to make matters worse, he hadn't even cooperated with them on their own mundane, practical approach. Yet here he was, blaming his poor showing on *them*, on their distracting crosstalk with all its petty jargon, the computerese, the brainstorming, the quick and dirty studies, the simulated games, and, worst of all, the interminable phone-calling that had finally cracked it, at least for them. A think tank was a place where you couldn't hear yourself think . . .

His eyes were drawn to the rear-view mirror and for a moment he was unable to comprehend the two red lights that he saw directly behind him. And then his weary brain put the picture together and he understood that the lights were mounted on the handlebar of a motorcycle and behind the handlebar was a khaki-uniformed officer of the California Highway Patrol and he was making pointing gestures with his gloved left hand indicating that he wanted Wibberly to pull over to the shoulder at the extreme right-hand side of the Freeway.

Lawrence Wibberly felt his heart sink with involuntary guilt. He glanced hurriedly over his right shoulder, turned the steering wheel sharply, and swerved across three lanes to the right and brought the Pontiac to an awkward stop, thinking, what a fitting climax to the whole miserable night.

He lowered his window and brought his wallet out of the inside pocket of his rumpled jacket and picked through his credit cards and membership cards, half expecting to find that he had lost his driver's license, because that would have been fitting too. But he found it and pulled it out and sat slumped over the wheel, waiting for the Law to make its unhurried way from the now-parked motor-cycle to his open window. He had no idea, as yet, how thoroughly annoyed and irritated he was at this humiliating interruption of his homeward-bound train of thought.

He saw the young face encased in the blue-and-gold helmet peering in at him through the open window, tanned and fuzzed with blond hairs where stubble should have been. The pale blue eyes were vacant. "Good morning, sir," the face said pleasantly.

"Good morning," Lawrence Wibberly said, looking away as he handed his license to the man.

The officer glanced at the license. "You were driving rather slowly, Mr. Wibberly . . ."

"Doctor Wibberly," he said wearily.

"Thirty-nine miles an hour, Doctor."

"Well, that's a damned sight better than sixty-nine," Wibberly said, a little surprised at the testiness in his own voice.

"Not always. No sirree, not always." The officer smiled. "Especially when you're in the fast lane. You were in the fast lane, Doctor. You were obstructing the free flow of traffic. You were forcing other cars to pass you on the right. Sometimes that creates unnecessarily hazardous conditions. You understand that, don't you, sir?"

Give me a ticket and let me alone, Lawrence Wibberly thought, but he said, "Yes, you've got a good point there, officer. No arguing that."

"I'm glad that you agree with me."

"I don't think I'll do it again," Wibberly said. "I appreciate your pointing this out to me. Now, if I can have my license back, maybe I can get moving again."

"Have you been drinking, sir?"

"Drinking? Have I been drinking? Yes, I've been drinking. A lot of water, and a half a dozen cups of coffee. But that's not what you meant, is it?"

"No, it isn't. What about dope?"

"What *about* dope?" Wibberly said.

"Did you have any drugs last night or this morning?"

"Do I look like the kind of man who takes drugs, I mean at my age?"

"Your eyes look kind of funny to me, sir."

"Look here, young man, I'm sleepy. I'm tired. I've been up all night. That's why I was driving so slowly and carefully. If I broke the law, why don't you just give me a ticket and let me go? All right?"

"What's your hurry, sir?"

"I'm not in a hurry. If I were in a hurry, I would have been driving fifty-five."

"Where are you going now?"

"Home to bed."

"You work nights, sir?"

"I'm an astrophysicist. We do a good deal of our work at night because that's when the stars are out, know what I mean?"

"They weren't out last night, sir, not around here. The low clouds came in from the sea early in the afternoon."

"I wasn't looking at the stars last night, officer."

"Oh? What *were* you doing, Dr. Wibberly?"

"You really want to know?"

"Yes, I do."

"Well, I was with a group of men, scientists mostly, and we stayed up all night trying to determine whether the universe is a closed system or an open system, and we decided finally that it's a little bit of both."

The officer stared at Wibberly. "You shouldn't be out on the Freeway in your condition, sir."

"I agree with you," Wibberly said. "That's why I want to get home. Are you going to let me get home, or are you going to keep me out here on the Freeway in my condition?"

The officer's lips tightened. He pointed his index finger at Wibberly. "You just sit right there, mister, okay? You just relax and stay right where you are until I come back."

"Whatever you say, officer," Wibberly said. "If I'm asleep when you return, would you be good enough to wake me?"

The officer started to say something, thought the better of it and walked away, back to his parked motorcycle. Wibberly watched him in the rear-view mirror, and suddenly he was seized with an impulse to back up, run the man down, jump out of the car, grab his driver's license and the citation pad, and speed away with them, with no motorists passing by to witness his act. He would be forever free of suspicion, detection, or pursuit. His slow driving in the fast lane, his crime, would cease to exist. A tree falling in the forest— and Wibberly had always believed this—makes no sound unless there are ears there to hear it.

He cringed with guilt at his horrible thoughts. He wished the young man no harm. After all, fear of the consequences of a traffic citation for a moving violation, a slow-moving one at that, was hardly justification for the destruction of the witness and the evidence, even in fantasy. On the other hand, he mused, if he had hijacked an ocean liner on the high seas and murdered dozens of innocent people . . .

A quasar flashed onto the screen of his mind and vanished. His head nodded toward the steering wheel and his leaden eyelids began to close. Instinctively he fought the sweet sleep, straightened up, drew deep breaths, and shook his head sharply from side to side, trying to become one of the conspirators for a few moments, trying to plan it as they must have planned it, confident that all radio communication from the ship to the outside world could be cut off at will, never suspecting the accidental presence of an amateur radio operator and a secret transmitter.

A black hole disappeared, in its place a ray of light. Wibberly looked into the rear-view mirror, and instead of seeing the young blond officer holding a microphone to his mouth, he made himself see three thousand men in uniform leaning over three thousand motorcycles writing out citations for murder, for which the fine would be life imprisonement or death . . .

Three thousand witnesses?

Never.

The plan could never have permitted that. The witnesses would have to be wiped out, or the planners would never be free of suspicion, detection, and pursuit. And whatever evidence existed would have to be totally destroyed too. That had to be the fundamental prerequisite. He was sure of it.

It *had* to be.

A supernova exploded and for an instant took on the unmistakable shape of an ocean liner blowing up, and in his weary head Wibberly heard echoes of Arkady Slocum's soft laughter and Irving Harris's raucous cry of triumph and the rasp of Mike Keegan's profanity and the voices of all the others, back-slapping each other with words of congratulation. And he remembered his own uneasiness in that war games room because he hadn't done anything to earn those congratulations, and he realized now that the uneasiness hadn't been guilt or envy, it had been his own nagging doubts, his own persistent feeling that identifying the conspirators and formulating a plan for their possible liquidation might not be what they should have been seeking.

Beyond all other considerations, they should have been searching out and determining with utter certainty the ultimate intent of the conspirators. Without that knowledge, all their instructions to those on the ship were wildly dangerous and irresponsible, for those instructions had not included considerations of the ultimate intent.

And the ultimate intent—he saw it clearly now—was ultimate disaster.

Lawrence Wibberly knew that as surely as if it had been written in the stars.

He started to wonder if there was still time, and suddenly sleep caught him unawares. His head dropped forward. He began to dream. Less than two minutes passed, but he couldn't have known that. He was jolted back to consciousness by the sound of a car door slamming. He opened his eyes with difficulty, remembered where he was, and heard voices behind him. He turned his head and saw a black-and-white patrol car parked beside the motorcycle. The young blond officer in the blue-and-gold helmet was talking to a handsome black man in a dark blue uniform. Another man in a

dark blue uniform was sitting behind the wheel of the patrol car,
listening. Then the young blond officer was coming toward Wibberly's open window with the black man.

"Dr. Wibberly, how you doing?"

Wibberly tried to say something, but merely nodded sleepily.

The officer thrust Wibberly's driver's license through the open
window and said, "Here you are, sir. This is Sergeant Hudgins. He's
going to drive you home."

"No, not yet," Wibberly protested. "I . . . uh . . . I have
to—"

His door was pulled open and the Sergeant said, "All right, pops,
move over and fasten your seat belt like a nice fellow," and eased
him over and got in behind the wheel.

"I have to get to a telephone right away," Wibberly said.

"Goodbye, sir," the blond officer called to him. "Take care of
yourself now."

Wibberly saw the patrol car pull out onto the Freeway and start
south, and then he felt the Pontiac surging forward and falling in
behind the lead car.

"Young man . . ." he said to his driver. He wanted to sleep, but
he *didn't* want to sleep. He wanted to call Arkady Slocum and wake
him up and make him realize that they had to reach Brian Joy
immediately and tell him to try to warn the *Marseille* without delay.
"Please take me to the nearest telephone," he said to the Sergeant
behind the wheel of his car.

"I'm takin' you home, pops," the handsome black officer said
quietly.

"This is very important," Wibberly said, feeling his eyes closing.
"We have to warn them to . . . warn them not to trust the situation . . ."

"I know how it is," the Sergeant said.

"No matter what they say . . . don't trust them . . . We have
to tell them that."

"Uh-huh."

"Please," Lawrence Wibberly said weakly. "I have to . . . telephone . . . to . . ."

"When you get home, pops, you can do all the telephonin' you
want," the Sergeant said, and then decided not to say another
word.

He didn't want to wake the old gentleman up.

CHAPTER THIRTY-NINE

RAFFIN RECOGNIZED Klaus Freuling and Wilhelm Gritzen immediately. Overweight and pot-bellied in their Air France flight officer uniforms, they were moving quickly across the field toward the waiting 747 as though running away from someone but afraid to break into anything faster than a hurried walk. He watched them through his binoculars until they disappeared behind the huge silver aircraft. Then he let his mind's eye take over—what other choice did he have?—and pictured them climbing the steps, entering the passenger cabin, mounting the spiral staircase to the lounge, unlocking the door to the flight deck, going inside, peeling off their jackets, and working their aging bodies into the two forward seats closest to the controls.

Good, Raffin thought with cautious optimism. Things are moving toward some kind of end. Maybe, please God, it will be the end that Wunderlicht has promised.

Suddenly he heard the voice coming from the loudspeaker above the radar screen beside him, a voice thick with a German accent. "Tower from Air France 1000."

The air traffic controller, a lean, swarthy Frenchman with thin-ning black hair, said, "Go ahead, 1000."

"We are commencing our checklist," Klaus Freuling announced.

"We need your flight plan, 1000," the controller said.

"I am aware of that," said Freuling.

"Can you tell us what your heading will be?"

"Patience is a virtue," Klaus Freuling replied.

"Shit," the controller muttered under his breath.

Jean-Claude Raffin heard himself blurting out, "What he means is, he doesn't know any more than you do yet."

The controller glanced at the stranger with the binoculars in his hands. "Maybe you'd like to take over this job," he said coldly. "You're welcome to it, you know." Then he turned away and looked down at his radar screen.

Raffin felt his face reddening. He put the binoculars to his eyes to cover his humiliation. The officious little son of a bitch. If he told him who he was, the man's bowels would drop into his pants. He stared with unseeing eyes into the glasses, his field of vision blurred by mortification and anger. And then slowly the pain died and his eyes were focusing again and he was becoming aware of something moving swiftly from left to right on the road beyond the borders of the field, a car, a small red car, a station wagon. He held it in his glasses, saw it turn sharply to the right, shoot through the open fence-gate, and speed toward the waiting plane.

Wunderlicht.

It had to be Wunderlicht.

Raffin felt his body grow tense. He leaned forward, eyes straining with every ounce of visual acuity he could command. Yes, that was Wunderlicht at the wheel. But beside him . . . long blond hair . . . a woman . . . Who was that woman in the seat next to the driver? Was it an accomplice? Wunderlicht had made no mention of any such person as that. Were the wide-open gates and the surreptitious entry because of *her?*

Anxiety crept back into Raffin's soul. Hungering for certainty, he was being fed the crumbs of new mystery. And what was it that made him think he had seen the woman before? The face? No, he could not make out the face. Not the white hat, no, not that. But the long blond hair . . .

The long blond hair?

He groaned with frustration as the silhouette of the plane came up into the field of his down-panning glasses and blotted the approaching car from view.

Wunderlicht, stained with sweat from the tedious drive, started up first and Lisa followed him, keeping her eyes on him, her handbag slung over her shoulder, the empty suitcase in her right hand. She observed how he gripped the attaché case with his right hand, and used his left hand and underarm to manage the two bulky suitcases he was carrying. Obviously the slim attaché case contained something so precious to him that he dared not risk its accidentally slipping out from under his arm.

When he reached the top of the steps he came to a stop, turned, and glanced off into the distance in all directions. Suddenly he heard a muffled cough from beneath him.

"Who is that?" he shouted. "Come out."

Two men in white coveralls emerged from behind the loading steps, their faces showing fright.

"What the hell are you doing here?" Wunderlicht demanded.

"Waiting to seal the cabin door, m'sieur . . . and drive the jeep with the loading steps . . ."

"Weren't you instructed to wait in the terminal until five minutes after the engines were started?"

"It wasn't clear to us, m'sieur . . ."

"Beat it. Go on," he said, and watched them scurry away. "That stupid son of a bitch, Sauvinage," he muttered. Then to Lisa, "Come." He turned and disappeared inside the cabin. Lisa followed him in.

She had never seen anything quite like it. Without the presence of living beings in it, the interior of the plane was immense and ghostly. And on each of one hundred plush red reclining seats in the midsection of the cabin there sat a mute and motionless passenger, a gray metal box containing sixty kilos of gold.

She half expected a stewardess to appear from one of the galleys and offer to lead her to a seat. But there was no stewardess, no one, only Wunderlicht, setting his bags down, stooping over one of the gray boxes, lifting its unlocked lid and gazing at what lay inside with the same lascivious look on his face she had seen the night before, when he had knelt between her welcoming thighs and she had guided him into her.

She shuddered with revulsion, for herself as well as for him. She moved closer, and stared down at the gold. For this, this cold and ugly yellowish metal, men had forever caused terror and bloodshed, and always would. Who was she to think that she could ever stop them?

Suddenly she felt overcome with unreasoning depression, despair . . .

Why try to stop them?

What did it matter?

What did any of them matter?

Not just them . . . she . . . Wunderlicht . . . anyone . . . *Anything* . . .

He was looking at her, his face flushed with excitement. "Put the bag down and come up to the lounge with me."

Dazed, unfeeling, she placed her suitcase down in the aisle near the open metal box. Wunderlicht started up the spiral staircase, gripping the handle of his attaché case as he went. She looked toward the open doorway of the cabin, knowing that she could have run to it, dashed down the loading steps, jumped into the station wagon, and sped away to safety. But she did none of those things. She turned and followed Wunderlicht up the spiral staircase, because he had told her to.

The lounge was empty. The door to the flight deck was closed. Wunderlicht pointed to a swivel chair near the head of the staircase. She sat down in it, turned and watched him pick up the wall telephone near the cockpit door.

"Wunderlicht here," he said into the phone in German, and hung up.

She saw the cockpit door open. A hairless man with a pink head came into view, his shirtsleeves rolled up, his face damp with perspiration. Wunderlicht addressed him as "Gritzen," and took out a sheet of paper and unfolded it, and the man called Gritzen motioned for Wunderlicht to enter the cockpit, but Wunderlicht pointed a thumb over his shoulder and the pink-domed man looked past Wunderlicht and noticed Lisa for the first time and began to question Wunderlicht, and Wunderlicht slapped the paper angrily and told him to look at it and study it. And when the man took the sheet of paper and glanced down at it, he exclaimed, "Brazzaka?" And then another voice called out in German from within the cockpit, and Wunderlicht called in to him that it was time to take off, and while they continued to talk to each other, Gritzen studied the piece of paper in his hand and called out some place names and numbers over his shoulder to the unseen other man whom Wunderlicht referred to several times as "Freuling," and Lisa listened to all this but understood only a little and cared even less . . .

. . . And in the control tower, the thick, German-accented voice coming out of the loudspeaker was ordering the flight controller to have the engines fired up immediately, and the thin-haired, swarthy Frenchman in front of the radar screen was picking up a phone and speaking sharply into it, and then Jean-Claude Raffin, peering through his binoculars, saw the starting-generator truck speeding across the field toward the plane and pulling to a stop, and the mechanic leaping to the ground holding onto the huge plug at the end of the generator cable, and shoving the plug into the receptacle next to the nosewheel of the aircraft. And from the loudspeaker, Klaus Freuling's voice announced: "Flight 1000 will be the next to take off. Our heading will be one hundred seventy-two degrees, cruising altitude thirty-eight thousand feet. Advise all traffic, all carriers, that we expect a clear corridor at least as far as the northern coast of Algeria."

The swarthy-faced controller became agitated. "We do not have the jurisdiction," he cried into his microphone. "I cannot give you any such guarantees."

"But you will, my dear fellow," said Klaus Freuling calmly. "You will."

. . . And just before the first engine fired up, Lisa heard Wunderlicht telling the pink-domed Gritzen to lock the cockpit door because they would be taking off as soon as he went below to seal the cabin door, and then the engines began their slow-rising whine and Wunderlicht turned to Lisa with great urgency and gestured to her to rise and follow him as the cockpit door closed, and he hurried down the spiral staircase, clutching the attaché case in his white-knuckled hand, and when she got to the bottom of the stairs she saw him standing beside her discarded suitcase, pointing to it and shouting, "Open it. Hurry," above the now-screaming engines.

She opened the suitcase and stepped back.

He set the attaché case down with great care, leaned over the open, gray metal box and lifted out two bars of gold and set them down in her empty luggage.

She felt the blood draining from her face. It had nothing to do with surprise. That was what was so shocking to her. She was not surprised at all. She must have known something like this was going to happen all along. Could it mean betrayal and disaster? Was he even lower than the rest of them, this man she had allowed inside her body?

He was removing another gold bar from the container and placing it in her suitcase, and then still another, and then he snapped the suitcase shut.

"Lift it," he shouted above the jets.

She grasped the handle and tugged, straining. "I can't. It's too—"

"Lift it, goddamn it. Take it to the car and wait for me."

"Julian, I can't . . ."

"Do it. You must. Hurry." He was opening his own bags frantically.

She tried with both hands, pulling, straining, groaning with effort. I'll die, she thought. Oh God, what am I doing here? But she knew what she was doing there and she didn't die. She got the suitcase into position and she dragged it to the door, and then she was out on the landing and dragging it down the steps, stumbling and lurching and letting out cries of pain and anguish. And when she reached the bottom she dropped the suitcase to the ground and fell against the side of the station wagon, gasping for breath.

She heard Wunderlicht's voice above the roar of the engines. "Get in," he cried.

She turned and saw him making his way down the steps, his body pulled out of shape, his face straining with agony as he fought to hold on to the loaded suitcases in each of his hands. He grunted with each step and the cords stood out on his neck and he stumbled down toward her, almost fell, then came crashing into the side of the car, propelled by the combined forces of gravity and the three-quarters-of-a-million dollars of gold that greed and lust had placed in his hands. The bags crashed to the ground. He stood there for a moment, fighting for breath.

"Get in the car," he panted, then moved again.

She watched him dragging the bags, one by one, to the rear of the Fiat, opening the hatch, working them inside, groaning with the effort, slamming the hatch shut. She fell into the front passenger seat, pulled her door closed, and then he was beside her behind the wheel, pressing the starter, gunning the motor. She saw the two attendants in white coveralls running across the field toward the plane. The Fiat lurched forward, swerved to the left, and raced away toward the distant open gate.

She turned in her seat, looked back through the rear window and saw the cabin door being sealed, then the attendant clambering down the loading steps that were already moving away on the jeep and the great jet plane rolling forward, gathering speed, engines screaming. Soon it would be gone. Something was wrong. The terrible noise fed her anxiety until she could stand it no longer. She turned to Wunderlicht.

"It's taking off," she said hoarsely above the awful thunder.

"Good," Wunderlicht snapped with savage pleasure.

"But the ransom . . . the money will be short . . ."

"What's the difference?" he said.

"What do you mean, what's the difference?" she cried above the roar of the speeding car and the hurtling jet as the Fiat shot through the wide-swinging gate and onto the road, and the plane thundered down the runway, faster and faster. "Julian . . . answer me . . ."

His face grew tense and ugly. "Not now, for Christ's sake . . ."

She stared at him and the words screamed in her head.

I won't ask again! I don't want to know!

And she heard the answer, *You already know, so don't give me any of that horrified surprise shit* . . . But it wasn't he that was saying it. The screaming was in her own brain, and it was louder than the screaming whine of the four great jet engines as Air France Flight 1000 became airborne at last, climbing, climbing . . .

And then she noticed that the attaché case was missing . . .

. . . Raffin wrenched his glasses away from the rising plane and homed in on the red station wagon speeding off to the left on the distant road beyond the boundaries of the field. Soon it would be out of sight. He would lose all trace of it. He lowered the glasses, his mouth twisting with concern. Had Wunderlicht assured him last night that he would be flying away with the gold, or had he simply assumed it? Was it Wunderlicht driving that car now, or was the girl behind the wheel, without a passenger? Who was she, and why had she stayed at the plane so long? There was too much that he did not know, too much.

Suddenly his eyes picked up the jeep with the loading steps moving slowly toward the terminal. He looked up and saw the plane disappearing into the hazy sky. There would be no answers up there, they had flown away. But down below there were two men in white coveralls, and in front of the terminal his gray Mercedes Benz was waiting. He hurried through the doorway and went to the elevators and pressed the button, but he could not wait and ran down the stairs taking them two at a time.

He had to know.

Once past the village of Moussy-le-Vieux on the outskirts of the airport, Wunderlicht eased back on the accelerator and slowed down to a moderate speed. True, the ancient road he had chosen was devoid of traffic, but if there was one thing he did not need now, it was some senseless, reckless accident that would leave him and a fortune in gold lying in a bloody ditch. Even if those two damned attendants at the field had seen more than they were supposed to see, Wunderlicht felt confident that Jean-Claude Raffin would never risk coming after him while the landing in Brazzaka and the call from Otto Laneer to the *Marseille* were still outstanding, and outstanding was exactly what they would forever be. Besides, there was no reason to believe that Raffin or anyone else suspected that Wunderlicht might not be aboard the plane. Even Freuling and Gritzen in their blissful heaven at thirty-eight thousand feet thought he was aboard. His positioning of the Fiat beside the plane and the leftward arc of his getaway move had been carefully designed to keep him out of their sight.

Driving with the excessive care of the newly rich, Wunderlicht glanced briefly to his right at his silent, moody passenger, the only person who knew most of the truth about what he had done and intended to do. It was even conceivable that she knew or suspected *all* of the truth. And in thinking about that possibility, Wunderlicht realized that he had an overpowering desire for her truly to know it all, for then her death could never be seen by him afterward as unnecessary. It could never haunt him and tinge the remainder of his life with sadness.

Yes, he was resolved that it must not be unnecessary.

He glanced at her again, lovely, delicate of feature, somber now, preoccupied, staring silently ahead at the road, holding on to her white leather handbag as though for warmth and security.

"All right now," he said, all friendly and relaxed. "What's your problem, little girl?"

She did not look at him, or answer him, but he waited, and then she said, "What's going to happen to the ship and all those people when the ransom arrives with . . . how much missing?" Her voice was flat and toneless.

"Roughly a million," he said easily. "But no one will ever know that. The gold is not going to do any arriving, there or anywhere else."

She looked at him briefly, without expression, and then stared straight ahead. "Where did you leave it?"

"Leave what?"

"The attaché case."

"You should be a newspaper reporter. You notice everything." She didn't answer him.

"One of the toilets," he said.

Her lips tightened a little. "Which one?"

"Near the door we came through," he said.

"That's L-1, forward left cabin door," she said.

Wunderlicht shrugged. "If you say so."

"What time does it . . . ?" Her voice faltered.

"Where is more important," he said. "Over water, midway between Minorca and Sardinia."

"What time?"

He looked at his wristwatch. "Another hour or so."

Her voice was unnaturally steady. "If the plane never gets to . . . wherever it was supposed to go . . ."

"Brazzaka."

"What will happen to the phone call to the ship?"

"I guess it will never be made."

"And if it's never made?"

He looked at her. "Boom," he said.

Her breath caught in an involuntary gasp, and for a moment he thought she was about to sob, but then she was under control, without visible emotion. "Who will track you down first?" she said quietly. "Your disappointed colleagues or the international police?"

"My dear sweet girl, you don't understand. Why search for *me?* I died in a midair tragedy at thirty-eight thousand feet. And who will ever know that its cargo was not intact, every ounce of it, when the plane disintegrated in the explosion? Thirty-four million dollars is just about as heavy as thirty-five, and will sink just as fast and lie scattered on the floor of the Mediterranean for years, centuries to come, maybe forever. Who will ever know?"

She turned her pale green eyes on him. "What about me, Julian? I'll be one who knows, always, won't I?"

He looked at her and silently thanked her for saying it. "I can live with that," he said. "That is, if *you* can live with a man whose hair will be dyed black, sometimes brown, sometimes gray, who will wear a matching mustache and horn-rimmed glasses, sometimes steel-rimmed, and travel a lot, far and wide, sometimes on an hour's notice if caution dictates . . ."

She turned away and looked off with thoughtful expression, as though she were giving it careful consideration. He moved his left hand stealthily beneath his jacket up to his belt, certain that she did not see him.

"I know you, Lisa," he said. "And I trust my sense of smell. I like what I smell when I'm in bed with you. It tells me that you've already decided to go along with me, because there could never be anything as exciting ever again in your whole life. I'm right about you, am I not?"

"Yes, Julian," she said in a low voice. "Goddamn you, yes, you've got my number, you bastard. But don't think that that yellow stuff lying on the boards behind us doesn't have something to do with it."

He knew she was lying. What did it matter?

He turned the wheel to the right and swung onto the smaller road, because he felt that it was time now. "Don't worry," he said. "I have no illusions about your feelings for me. Sometimes I think it's your distaste for me as a person that heats you up down there."

"That's funny," she said. "I thought it was your compassion that turned me on, your overpowering concern for the lives of three thousand innocent people, to be specific."

"Yes, let's be sure to be specific at all times." He was glad she was talking this way. He welcomed the hardness in her voice. It would make it easier.

"What's going to happen to them, Julian, now that you've done this? Is there any chance for them, any way that they can live?"

The road they were on now was a deserted ribbon of dirt winding through sparsely inhabited farmland. It looked perfect to him. "Die," he said, without effort. "As it must to all living things, that's what's going to happen to them, Lisa." He saw her flinch. "A little early perhaps, a little watery, a little noisily, a little . . . chokingly? Breathlessly? At least they won't be alone. They can even hold hands as they go down, if they have any hands left." He saw her lips quiver just before she averted her face, and he quickly worked the revolver onto the seat between his left thigh and the door. "You're not going to cry now, for God's sake, are you?"

She shook her head several times and struggled to open her handbag. "I just need a tissue, that's all," she said in a trembling voice.

"I mean, you asked me, so I told you. I could have lied to you but I didn't." He spotted a rutted lane up ahead leading into a clump of trees and began to slow down imperceptibly. "We might as well start learning to live with the truth right now because it isn't going to change."

"Yes," she said quietly, her hand concealed in her bag.

He turned the wheel sharply and swerved into the lane without even bothering to make an explanation to her, and he thought for a moment that it might have been a mistake because she began to scream almost immediately, and he assumed that it was out of fear for what she sensed was coming, but then he saw her left hand pointing to the roof above him and she was shrieking, "Oh my God, what's that?" and he tilted his head back and looked up to see and felt the terrible hot sharp agony in his throat even before he understood the sudden twist of her body and the blurring slash of her glinting right hand or heard his own strangled scream, and then her hand moved again and again, and when he tried to draw breath or speak or go on living and knew that he couldn't, not ever again, his shriek of horror at the realization that she had just killed him rose from the depths of his being and came up out of his severed throat and his soundless, gaping mouth as a huge gurgling gush of his own lifeblood . . .

"Oh God," Lisa cried out hysterically. "Help me, help me," pushing the dying hulk away from the wheel of the runaway car, grabbing the wheel, holding it, kicking the convulsive foot off the pedal, feeling his hot stickiness pouring all over her, screaming incoherently at the horror of it all. "Help me, help me . . ." seeing the trees rushing toward her, trying to avoid them, covering her head with her bloody arms, bracing herself, hearing the shattering crash, head slamming into the dashboard, the blinding concussion, the shower of glass . . .

An instant of silence.

And then the hiss of steam . . .

The gurgle of blood from the open throat . . .

The terrible death rattle beginning . . .

She moaned, fainting from the throbbing in her head, came to immediately, cried out feebly, "Someone help me . . ." and pushed on the twisted, half-open door beside her and found herself on the ground on her hands and knees, gasping with blinding pain, feeling the tears streaming down her cheeks. She reached out, grasped broken metal, pulled herself to her feet, swaying dizzily, held on to the wrecked car, dazedly looked inside and saw the burst suitcases, the sprawling gold, the stiffening corpse in the front seat . . .

"Julian?" she said quietly.

"Julian?" she asked him again.

"Julian!" she shrieked, and looked down at his blood all over her, and her horror was so great that she could not bear another moment of it and started to swoon into unconsciousness again, and then suddenly she remembered.

What time—?

How long had it taken?

How much time was there left?

Before the plane—

She began to run, away from the ruined station wagon, away from the gold, away from the body that used to be Julian Wunderlicht. She had no strength in her legs and her head was spinning but she ran along the rutted lane making incoherent sounds as she went, and when she reached the dirt road she thought of running back in the direction of the airport but she couldn't recall having passed a house or anything else that might have had a telephone and she'd never be able to make it, not the way that she was beginning to lose it all now, her breath, her strength, her will, everything, so she ran in the opposite direction and followed the ribbon of dirt through the farmland, not knowing who she would call or what they could do or whether there was still time, and then she saw through the trees the peeling gray barn and the ruined farmhouse beside it and the old man on the porch rising to his feet, and she stumbled toward him crying, "Do you have a telephone? I have to use your phone, there's been a terrible accident," and the old man who was toothless shouted at her, "Get away from here, what's the matter with you, get away from here," and she ran up to him and he shrank back from her blood-caked hand and her blood-stained clothing and she sobbed, "Please help me, I need your telephone, please," and he pushed her away so hard that she stumbled back off the porch and fell on the hard ground and hurt her shoulder and she saw him rush inside and slam the door and she heard the bolt go into place and she struggled to her feet and stumbled up the steps and pounded on the door and his voice said, "Get away from here," and she went to the window and looked inside and saw him moving with the shotgun in his hands, so she turned and fled from the farmhouse and heard the shrieking of the banshee in the distance, and she ran through the trees toward the terrible sound and found herself on the ribbon of dirt, running toward the rutted lane where the blood was still gurgling and the banshee was screaming, and she felt the world begin to spin and then through the blinding dizzying blur in her head she saw the red station wagon shoot out from behind the trees onto the road and start toward her and it was all bent and misshapen and making a shrieking sound, and Wunderlicht was behind the wheel and his two crimson mouths were grinning at her, and the car bore down on her and there was no way she could escape it, and just as she swayed and started to fall in front of the onrushing car, the banshee stopped and she heard the squeal of brakes and saw the doors flying open and three men jumping out and rushing toward her, and it wasn't a red car after all, it was a gray Mercedes, and the man gathering her into his arms was someone she had seen the night before, it wasn't Julian Wunderlicht, who was dead . . . "I killed him," she sobbed. "I had to," she cried, and began to tell the man about the bomb in the plane and he wouldn't let her alone with his questions, she tried to sink into the blackness but he would slap her face, and the last thing she heard after he set her down gently in the back seat of the car was his voice saying into a telephone or something, "Find Arsène Schreiner at Interpol, and get me the control tower at de Gaulle, hurry . . ." and then she sank into merciful unconsciousness.

Hurtling through the sky, the 747 left the southern coast of France far behind and soared out over the Mediterranean Sea, speeding toward its target in Libwana. In its flight deck, the portly, grizzled veteran, Klaus Freuling, peered off to his left through the sporadic patches of fleecy white cirrus that hung over the blue waters seven miles below and saw the land mass that was Sardinia, flat and formless on the eastern horizon, just where it was supposed to be. So far, everything on this flight had been just where it was supposed to be, provided you didn't include Julian Wunderlicht. It was getting so that the only thing a man could count on any more was his automatic pilot, Freuling told himself with annoyance.

He turned to the bald-headed man sitting next to him and said, "Try him again, Willy."

"Shit, Klaus," said Wilhelm Gritzen, "I phoned every fucking station on this plane. He just don't wanna talk to us right now."

"Why wouldn't he want to talk to us?" Freuling demanded.

"Because he's probably back there lying across three empty seats on top of that skinny blond cunt, that's why," the pink-domed man said.

"Christ, you've got an ugly mouth, you know that, Gritzen?"

Wilhelm Gritzen laughed loudly. He always enjoyed any signs of discomfiture in his older friend. "Tell ya what, Klaus," he said, grinning. "I'll go down and watch them humping for a while. Then I'll tell him you wanna see him. Okay?"

"In a goddamn hurry," Freuling said. "What frequency you guarding there?"

"Eurotraffic. They been calling us like crazy. First Montpellier, then Barcelona." His eyes twinkled. "Shall I answer them?"

"No, no, you imbecile," Klaus Freuling shouted. "They're just trying to get us to reveal our position. Didn't *you* read the instructions to *me?* Don't you understand what radio silence means *yet,* you dummkopf?"

"Oh, yeah, that's right." Gritzen exploded with laughter, then rose from his seat, took off the earphones and placed them on Freuling's gray-thatched head.

"Come right back," Freuling muttered.

"Now, Klaus," Gritzen said, as though talking to a child. "You just sit there and think about all that nice dark meat you're gonna be fressing in Brazzaka."

He unlocked the cockpit door and went out to the lounge and saw that it was deserted. He went down the spiral staircase and glanced in both directions.

No one.

Not in this part of the plane anyway.

Just the cases with the gold in them.

Wunderlicht was probably having the girl back in the tail somewhere.

Gritzen felt the urge to urinate, and stepped into the nearest toilet. When he had finished, he shook the last drops off the tip and shoved it back in his pants, and then his eyes fell on the gray leather box, or whatever it was, sticking out of the towel disposal slot. He pulled it out and looked at it briefly and smiled, and took it with him when he stepped out of the toilet.

If Julian Wunderlicht's briefcase was here, could Julian Wunderlicht be far behind?

"Hey, Wunderlicht," he called out above the steady roar of the plane, as he strode toward the tail section. "I'm coming, Wunderlicht."

But Wunderlicht wasn't there in the tail section. Neither was the girl. And they weren't in any of the galleys or lavatories or any other part of the plane, either.

Gritzen frowned for a few moments, then chuckled to himself when he thought how angry Freuling would be. He hurried back upstairs to the flight deck with the briefcase because he couldn't wait to see the anger on his face.

Freuling was holding the earphones tightly to his head. He seemed very preoccupied.

"Guess who is no longer on the plane," said Gritzen. "The son of a bitch must've beat it before we took off."

Freuling didn't react at all. Gritzen was disappointed.

"Put the emergency frequency on the speaker," Freuling said.

"What for?" said Gritzen, sitting down.

"Radio Barcelona says if we refuse to come back to them, then please listen on the EF immediately."

"Bullshit," Gritzen said.

"Do it anyway," Freuling said, then pointed. "What's that?"

"His briefcase, I think. He left it on the plane when he got off."

"Wunderlicht?"

"Yes."

"Got off?" Freuling's eyes were wide with disbelief.

"Don't you ever listen to a fucking thing I say to you?" Gritzen was hurt.

"Go to 121.5 right away, Willy."

Gritzen sat motionless, trying to understand the urgency in his friend's voice.

"Do as I say, goddamn it," Freuling roared.

Gritzen leaned forward and punched the button that threw the receiver onto the international distress channel, and immediately they heard the voice coming out of the speaker and it was unusually agitated and it was saying in German: ". . . In one of the lavatories near cabin door L-1. The gray attaché case is believed to be an explosive device timed to go off at any moment, at any moment. Do not, repeat, do not open it. Employ any method, repeat, any method to get the bomb off the plane immediately . . . Air France 1000, this is Radio Barcelona. Urgent, urgent . . ."

They looked at each other, white-faced. Gritzen pressed an ear to the leather case. "Holy fucking Christ," he screamed hoarsely.

He leaped to his feet.

"Emergency descent mode," the voice on the speaker was saying. "Use the over-wing emergency exit, repeat, the over-wing emergency exit. Air France 1000 from Radio Barcelona . . ."

"For God's sake, get that out of here!" Freuling yelled, and even before the bald-headed Gritzen ran whimpering from the cockpit with the frightening thing in his hand, the older man was pushing the yoke forward and pulling the power off the engines and lowering the flaps and dropping the landing gear, anything, anything to get the giant plane into a diving descent, anything to get it down where the air pressure could be equalized inside and out, and then struggling to his feet, Freuling fought his way against gravity's pull to the flight engineer's station and pulled hard on the wheel that would open the pressure-release valve, because if Gritzen opened anything in the plane while the cabin was still under high pressure . . .

"Oh Christ," Gritzen moaned as he stumbled down the spiral staircase and lurched down the aisle of the cabin in the diving plane, clinging to the backs of the empty seats, fighting to stay on his feet and keep the horrible thing in his hand from striking against anything, trying to remember the emergency drills, years ago, the drills . . .

"Jesus," he cried, "where is it? Where is it?"

Searching, stumbling, moving forward . . .

Over the wing, you fool, over the wing. It's marked emergency exit. There's a lever. You have to pull it down. The window comes out. It comes flying into the cabin. You can throw the goddamn bomb out through the open window . . .

But wait a minute, that window was designed to work on the ground! The emergency exit was never meant for midair operation! There's a canvas chute connected to the exit window! It unfurls and the passengers scramble through it to the wing! The bomb won't go out into space! It will be trapped in the canvas chute!

But maybe it will drop through and down and hit the wing and bounce off and—

Go off at any moment, the voice in Barcelona had said.

Any moment!

He reached up and grabbed the lever and pulled down on it as hard as he could and heard the explosive impact as the window leaped out of its socket and slammed past him across the aisle and into the empty seats, and the air rushed in past him with a mighty whoosh and the canvas chute shot out of the side of the diving plane. He stood poised for a moment with the briefcase in his right hand like a pitcher on the mound, and he was going to hurl it out of the gaping hole where the window had been and hope that it would tumble down and fall away in the slipstream, anything, anything, because he had to get rid of it before—

"Here it is, Wunderlicht!" he cried out to the betrayer whose life had already oozed away and, rearing back to throw it, Gritzen suddenly separated forever into atoms and molecules and other small particles of varying sizes . . .

And the skipper of the Corsican fishing trawler, *Bastia-Poretta,* who heard the thunderclap and saw the great light in the sky fifteen miles away, thought little of it because something was always happening up there that he could not understand nor explain, like the falling stars that had come every August for over sixty years now, ever since he was a little boy. He could not remember ever having seen a star fall in the daytime though, but there were many things he could no longer remember. Even as he turned away from the light in the sky and the echo of its thunder, he began to forget about it.

The gray-haired man with the weatherbeaten face stood near the long dirt runway under the blazing African sun, squinting up at the sky in search of something that was not there. The flies buzzed around his nose and the sweat ran down his back and belly, staining his white cotton shirt and brown cotton pants. He knew that he would have been more comfortable in the front seat of one of the three trucks parked less than a hundred feet away, but he preferred to suffer out here in the sun rather than sit near one of the drivers and run the risk of their discovering how much he hated the sour smell of them. He could not afford to lose them, not now.

Many times in the two years in Libwana he had told himself to hell with it, he would go back to Buenos Aires and let the hunters have their prey. Nothing they could do to him would be worse than the endless sour stink in his nostrils. But he had never gone back to Buenos Aires, because he wanted to go on living for a while. And the fee he would be getting for this job would put a little style back into that living, too.

He heard the sound of the car behind him and turned with surprise and saw it coming around the side of the tan stucco airport building and moving across the field toward him. As the car came closer, he could see that it was a fairly new American-made vehicle with a white man driving and another white man beside him. He had no idea who the men were, or why they were driving toward him, but of this he was certain: they weren't coming to bring him money, or a safe passage to Australia, or news that Hitler had risen from the ashes.

The car stopped beside him and the two men got out, leaving the motor running. They appeared to be in their late thirties, and had unusually fair complexions. The taller of the two wore a white linen suit and a cocoa-colored straw hat. The other had on a gray seersucker suit and was hatless, probably because he had too much blond hair to take a hat comfortably.

"Are you Otto Laneer?" said the man in the white linen suit, in softly accented English.

"Yes, I am," the gray-haired man replied.

"Would you mind coming with us for a couple of minutes to the airport manager's office?"

"I can't do that right now," Laneer said, before he noticed the Luger pistol in the hand of the smaller man. ". . . unless you insist."

The smaller man pointed casually with the Luger toward the car. Laneer opened the rear door and got into the back seat. He remembered the drivers in the trucks, and poked his head out of the open door and shouted to them in Libwanese that he would be right back. Then the man with the Luger got in beside him and the man in the white linen suit drove the car toward the stucco building.

"Who are you and what do you want of me?" Laneer asked.

"You have a call to make to a ship at sea," the man doing the driving replied, without looking back at him. "We have a circuit all set up for you by way of Tripoli."

Otto Laneer's next statement was made halfheartedly. He knew it would sound foolish to the two men, but he felt he had to say it nevertheless. "I appreciate your help," he said. "But I suppose you know that I cannot make that call until certain events have taken place."

"Yes, we know that," the man in the white linen suit said.

The man holding the Luger smiled, but said nothing. It was the first time his expression had changed.

The car stopped at the side entrance. Inside the building the two men flanked Laneer and escorted him through a narrow hallway to the manager's office. Laneer was surprised to see the building so deserted. The manager was not even there. His desk top was clear of everything but the telephone.

The man in the linen suit picked up the instrument, and while standing beside the desk dialed a local number in Brazzaka. To the person who answered, he said in English, "Please advise the overseas operator Number 67 in Tripoli that Mr. Otto Laneer is ready for the call to the *Marseille* . . . That is correct."

He hung up and gestured to Laneer to sit down behind the desk. Laneer eased his sweating body into the chair, and the man in the gray seersucker suit walked over to him, and Laneer felt the tip of the barrel of the Luger in his left ear.

"You don't have to do that," Laneer said.

The man in the white linen suit said, "Tell them everything has gone perfectly according to their plans. If you say one word that is wrong, you will lose your hearing. Is there anything you don't completely understand?"

"No, nothing," Laneer said.

The phone rang and he quickly picked it up and heard a brief interchange between two operators in a language he did not understand, and then finally he was talking to the ship, and the two men in the office watched him with such intensity, and the metal of the Luger was so cold in his ear, that he was sure he could not carry it off, but Dunleavy's voice was loud and familiar, it steadied him down, he could hardly believe the man was out in the Atlantic some place.

Laneer told him how the plane had arrived and described the transfer to the trucks and said the drive to the hiding place had been so uneventful and easy, maybe they should send down another planeload of the stuff, he even managed to laugh. And when Dunleavy asked to have a few words with Julian Wunderlicht, Laneer had no trouble at all explaining to him that Wunderlicht had gone off to make some arrangements for automobiles for himself and the two pilots, and Dunleavy sounded so high when he said his good-byes that Laneer decided the man must have been drunk or on some kind of drugs.

He hung up the phone and said to the two men, "Well, I did what you told me, didn't I?" But the cold barrel of the Luger was still in his ear and the man in the white linen suit was shrinking back as though he didn't want to get anything on it and Laneer's bowels started turning to water.

"Please don't," he said. "Please don't."

The white linen suit made out all right, but the curtains didn't, nor the whole opposite wall.

The tall man stepped carefully around to the other side of the desk and picked up the phone again, first wiping it off with a handkerchief, which he threw into the wastebasket. He placed another call and said to the person at the other end, "Tell Schreiner it is done."

Then he and the man with the Luger left the building and drove back across the field to where the three trucks were parked, and soon after that the drivers of the trucks lost their hearing too.

CHAPTER FORTY

T HE GOOD NEWS SPREAD to them with incredible speed wherever they were on the vast ship and intoxicated them beyond belief. Nothing could go wrong now. The worst was over. What lay ahead was a happy voyage to a collective dream come true. Somewhere in far-off Libwana, they had been told, in dark damp caves that they had heard about but had never seen, six-and-a-half tons of golden metal lay waiting for them, waiting to buy them freedom and adventure and a brand-new life. So heady was their excitement, they could hardly restrain themselves long enough to go through with the procedures that would be necessary before leaving. But restrain themselves they did. After almost two years of preparation and rehearsal, they weren't going to blow the whole thing out of sheer jubilation, were they?

Not while Craig Dunleavy and Herb Kleinfeld were around.

His eyes feverish bright, his whole being charged with new energy, Dunleavy bounded up the stairway and hurried toward the bridge, letting Otto Laneer's words play over and over in his head like a cheerful broken record, confident in the knowledge that

Kleinfeld was, even now, racing along the Sun Deck rounding up his six-man team to go into action. They both had decided long ago that the passengers would be able to take the mystery and the confusion without any panic, provided that it all happened fast, not too much time for thinking or worrying. By the time Dunleavy reached the wheelhouse and seized the microphone of the public address system, Kleinfeld's men were already beginning their systematic destruction of the ship's communications capabilities, starting with the maze of overhead antennas.

"Attention all passengers," Dunleavy said, knowing his voice could be heard throughout the length and breadth of the *Marseille*. "May I have your attention please. This is your officer of the watch speaking. In a few moments, alarm gongs will be sounding on all decks. When you hear them, will you please drop whatever you are doing and go to your cabins immediately and remain there until the gongs are sounded a second time. There is absolutely no cause for concern, this is merely an equipment check, but it is an important one, and your total cooperation will be appreciated. On behalf of the Captain, I thank you for complying with this request."

He placed the microphone down, reached over and punched the button that started the alarm bells ringing for the next three minutes. Then he turned to the tall blond helmsman and shouted, "All engines dead stop." The startled helmsman hesitated for a moment before pulling the twin telegraph arms upright to the stop position, signaling the distant engine rooms to shut the turbines down. Satisfied, Dunleavy left the bridge and hurried off to his cabin, where Betty would be waiting for him. The others would be leaving their posts too and getting ready for departure. He glanced at his wristwatch and liked what he saw. Fifty-nine minutes to 1600 Zulu. They had plenty of time in which to get out from under.

In the private quarters that had been turned into a prison, Charles Girodt heard the alarm bells ringing, and the distant clash of axes and crowbars ravaging the communications room, and sensed the loss of forward motion of his ship with the dying of its turbines and the four powerful screws. He looked at the faces of his executive officers, seated in the room with him, and a strange glint came to his eyes. "The vermin are deserting the sinking ship, only it is not sinking," he said proudly to his men. But they seemed not to be listening to him. Did they not know who he was?

In his cabin, Billy Berlin frowned at the clamor outside his door and pressed tightly on his earphones to shut out the noise, convinced that he had just heard Brian Joy cailing him from California on twenty meters.

Standing in a doorway of the Boat Deck fifty yards aft of Station 23, from which point they had been keeping a careful eye on René Derbos and the white power cruiser, Julie Berlin and Harold Columbine, who was back in his officer's uniform, suffered the clanging of the bells and made a quick decision. While *he* would be somewhat safe out in the open, she would be far too conspicuous if she failed to vanish into a cabin.

"How about mine?" he said, deadpan.

"No," she said quickly. "Besides, I have to bring Billy up to date," then kicked herself mentally for taking him seriously.

"I was just trying to stay in character," he smiled ruefully.

"What character?"

"Beat it, you. And be careful."

"You too."

She hurried away, and he turned his gaze on the power cruiser once again. So far, no one had even approached the death-laden vessel. He began to think about what he had done, and a nameless dread seized him. Suppose only some of them died, or none of them at all? What if they died too slowly, or merely became ill and realized what had been attempted and retaliated in some terrible, unthinkable way? Quickly he changed the subject of his fantasies to a stunning chick named Terri Montgomery, or was it Worthington, and he decided that he wanted very badly to keep that date with her tonight. It would be helpful if there were a ship afloat on which to keep it.

Eighteen miles to the southwest, Captain Panos Trimenedes stood on the foredeck of the *Angela Gloria* and felt the goose-pimples all over his hairy body as he heard the powerful voice of the *Marseille* calling to him in deep-throated reverberating roars, nine mighty blasts in all from the seventy-foot-high twin funnels, keyed to lower bass A and trumpeting the prearranged summons to a rendezvous. Trimenedes responded to the call by swinging his freighter around and pounding full steam ahead toward the French Atlantic liner, and among those of his men who struggled to unloose the rope ladders in preparation for the great coming together was Nick Moustakos, his brain totally sodden with ouzo. There was no anger left in his soul, for he was a drunken and therefore happy man, and nothing that was going to happen could bother him now. That is what he thought, did Nick Moustakos.

Aboard the *Marseille,* most of the two-thousand-odd passengers went to their cabins with promptness and ease of mind. Some of the first-time sea voyagers, however, the scaredy-cats who saw danger in every ocean wave, doom in every pitch and roll of the ship, laughed and made fun of themselves as they went, too ashamed and embarrassed to admit how grateful they would have been for some kind of explicit and soothing description of the so-called equipment test, and some explanation of the seemingly frantic scurrying about of men on the upper decks, and the strange muffled sounds of hammering on metal and the smashing of glass. As for the majority, their Captain's orders had been simple enough, not really worthy of deep second thoughts, and the equipment test, whatever *that* was, was not going to last forever, for God's sake, so what was there to be upset about? The timing devices in the bowels of the ship moving inexorably onward toward 1600 Zulu were outside their awareness. Therefore their own bowels remained undisturbed.

Only Billy Berlin was in a state of agitation now. And it was not due to what Julie had just told him of Harold Columbine's daring work on the power cruiser. He had even felt a sneaking glimmer of respect for the man, untrustworthy philanderer that he was. What was troubling Billy Berlin right now was the frightening fact that the world in his ears, the world of static and voices and adjacent-channel interference on twenty meters, had suddenly died on him at the worst possible moment, right in the middle of Brian Joy's dimly heard, agonizing transmission: "I've got urgent traffic, an urgent warning, Billy. How do you—?"

Like *that,* without even a chance to say "Go ahead" or "I read you" or "What is it, Briney, what is it?" the receiver had gone dead, and then a quick check of the transmitter revealed that *it* had gone dead too, and in a flash he knew what had happened.

He had no antenna.

Someone must have torn down the antenna.

He bounded from the bed, pressed his face to the porthole window, and looked up. "I can't tell from here," he said.

Julie was on her feet at once. "I'll go up and see what's happened."

He turned sharply. "No, it's too dangerous."

"Billy, we've got to know what that message was, that warning."

"Goddamn it, you'll wait until they've left the ship. You're not going to get killed over some fucking message."

"Everybody dies," she said, and escaped from the cabin before he could stop her . . .

The slamming down of the microphone stand on the desk top sounded like a shot in the early morning stillness of Beverly Hills. "He's gone," Brian Joy said with total disbelief. "How do you like that, he's gone."

"He'll be back," Maggie said.

"But, Jesus, he didn't even fade, he just disappeared."

"Maybe something's happened to him."

"Must you say that?" he shouted at her.

"Yes," she said. "I must."

He picked up the telephone and dialed Arkady Slocum's home. "Bad news," he said. "I couldn't deliver it. He was there for a moment, and then suddenly he wasn't, *isn't*."

"You know this could be the whole ball of wax," the man from Remo said.

"Why couldn't you geniuses have gotten brilliant last night instead of this morning?" Brian Joy demanded.

"We're only computers, Mr. Joy, we're not human," Arkady Slocum said quietly.

"Okay, I'm sorry."

"You'll be sorrier if you don't get to him in time. Is it all right if I go to sleep now?"

"And if I said no?"

Brian Joy got up from the desk and went to the sideboard and poured himself a drink, and it wasn't coffee, and he was hoping Maggie would say something, because he was going to let her have it like she'd never had it before, but she didn't say a word, not this time.

The wise old bitch.

It was like a ghost ship up there on the Sun Deck. The *Marseille* had no motion save the motion of the sea, and there was nobody in sight. Julie moved slowly and carefully and came out into the open, then suddenly heard footsteps behind her and turned and saw the young steward hurrying across the deck toward her, his face chalky with fear.

"You're not supposed to be out here, madame," he said in a tremulous voice.

"I know," Julie said. "I'm going to my cabin right away."

"Please, madame, thank you, madame." He walked away quickly, not wanting to be part of her disobedience.

She waited for him to disappear, then moved forward and craned her neck and looked up at the masts and funnels against the sky. Billy had been right. The antenna to which he had been secretly hooked up was gone. So were all the other antennas. They were nowhere to be seen, probably thrown overboard. She would go back and tell him, but what would he be able to do? Nothing. Not until the enemy was gone.

Her attention was caught by the freighter. She went to the starboard rail and peered off at it. It was heading straight at them now, and coming on fast. Soon it would be heaving to. Soon, those people would be getting into the white boat and lowering themselves to the sea, and then speeding across the water to their rendezvous with a destiny they had never dreamt of. How could they know that the power cruiser would be transporting their dead souls across the river Styx to the other side of hell?

The thought made Julie shudder. She tried to shake it, but it wouldn't go away. Harold was down there, somewhere on the Boat Deck. He would probably see it happen. He would be close enough to see it all, if it happened to them quickly, before they got too far away. She did not envy him. How lucky she was not to be near those men and women when it happened to them.

She realized, suddenly, that she had not thought of them as men and women, as individuals, as human beings. She had thought of them only collectively, as "those people," or as "the enemy." And it was she, Julie Berlin, in a way, who would be killing them. It was she who had given the fateful instructions to Harold. He had only refined them. She could have thrown the plan away, once she realized that the Captain was unreachable. But she hadn't thrown it away. Unconsciously, automatically, she had made the decision that all of "those people" must die, for the safety of the ship, or because of what they had done, or for the sake of those who had suffered death at their hands. There must have been *some* reason why.

She wasn't sure now what it was.

She wondered if Harold knew.

All she was sure of was that she did not want to be a witness to their deaths.

She turned from the rail and started for the companionway, but her thoughts clung to her. Maybe she and Harold had no right to take the law into their own hands. They were acting without authority. The Captain had not issued any orders. He was not even aware of what was about to happen. She and Harold were collaborating in the premeditated murder of one hundred and seventy living, breathing men and women, and she wasn't even sure why.

Harold was down on the Boat Deck. She had to talk to him immediately. Maybe he could give her reassurance. Maybe he could banish these thoughts from her head before they drove her crazy . . .

He heard the pounding on the door, quickly yanked the A.C. cord out of the socket, called out "Who is it," heard the strange voices answering, unscrewed the coax connector, said "Hold it a minute," shoved everything under the bed, went to the door, unlocked it, and saw two men he had never seen before, dressed in ordinary sports clothes.

"Are you her husband?" the first man said.

"Whose husband?" he said.

"Mrs. Berlin," the second one said.

"Yes, I'm Dr. Berlin. What do you want?"

"Your wife. Where is she?"

"Who the hell are *you?*"

"Where is your wife? Where did she go?"

"I haven't the faintest idea. She went out for a walk or something. This is a big boat, you know."

"There were orders given. All passengers to stay in their cabins. Didn't she hear it?"

"Yes, she heard it. She said France is a free country and so are her ships at sea. She went for a walk."

"You're full of shit, Doctor."

"Yes, I know," Billy Berlin said. "I'm working on it."

They turned and walked away.

He shut the door and locked it.

What the hell was happening?

These people were supposed to be leaving the *Marseille,* transferring to the freighter out there. Why were they looking for Julie?

Suppose she had been here right now? What were they going to do to her?

He went to the closet and pulled out some clothes and started to get dressed.

He'd have to find her and warn her.

Harold Columbine wasn't the only man in an officer's uniform moving about the Boat Deck. With all the passengers in their cabins, the crew suddenly seemed more visible. They were all over the ship. And he was just another one of them, looked like one of them anyway, ill-fitting uniform and all. He busied himself with the lifeboat next to Station 23. He pretended to be working on the tarpaulin that covered it, tightening the ties, checking the davits, staying within sight and earshot of the poisoned white power cruiser over which René Derbos was still standing guard.

He knew they'd be appearing at any moment now. The freighter's engines had died. She was standing to quite a distance away, off the bow on the starboard side, far enough away so that the black paint that covered her name on the hull and the fake Liberian flag would be sufficient to hide her true identity. You could imagine the men moving about on her deck, and the rope ladders dangling from her side.

Any moment now . . .

He heard their voices and their laughter before he saw them, and it was like the chattering of a gaggle of geese, it was as though someone had suddenly opened a door and you were hearing the wild merriment of a great social gathering, a cocktail party perhaps, only the cocktail party was in motion, it was coming closer, and then suddenly it burst out onto the Boat Deck, and he saw them pouring through the doorways near the bow and starting in his direction, toward the power cruiser that was hanging on its davits waiting for them. They carried suitcases and cameras and canvas bags, and some of them, not many, carried handguns in full view. The women wore slacks and colorful blouses, and the men were in open-neck shirts and Levis and light cotton pants, whatever would be comfortable and easy, some of them even in tennis shorts and T-shirts, and all of them, all one hundred and seventy of them, wore garish but comical Halloween masks over their faces, and that made them seem even more playful and carefree.

Harold Columbine watched them approaching and thought that

he had heard his name being called out amid the din, but the sound had come from the other direction, behind him, and he turned and looked off down the deck and saw the figure in the pale blue turtleneck sweater and the crisp white jeans, and for a moment he wondered why she wasn't with the rest of the group or carrying any luggage and then, as she came closer, he realized that she wasn't one of them at all. It was Julie, and she was gesturing to him frantically.

He hurried to meet her, and pulled her into a doorway saying, "What the hell are you doing here?"

"I had to see you," she said.

"But now . . . ?"

"Harold, maybe we made a mistake . . ."

"We'll know soon enough," he said, turning. "Look at them. They're getting ready to climb in."

"I meant, maybe we should warn them while there's still time."

He turned to her. "Warn them?"

"Yes."

"What are you talking about?"

"Is it right to kill them, Harold?"

"Yes, goddamn it, yes."

"Why?"

He grabbed her by the shoulders. "What's happening to you?"

"Tell me why, Harold."

He stared at her with growing anger. "Because it's done, that's why. Because you're asking me the question about an hour too late. There's no turning back now."

"Is that enough reason?"

"It is for me."

Her lips trembled. She was looking past him. Neither of them knew what she was going to do next . . .

"Help me, Harold, please . . ."

He hesitated a moment, then slapped her hard across the face. Tears came to her eyes. He struck her again and she gasped, raising her hands defensively.

"Enough . . ."

"Okay then," he said, gently, and he put his arm around her shoulders and pressed her to him. "You're right, Julie," he said. "We shouldn't have, but we did. *I* did, not you. But it's out of our hands now. So ask yourself this: do you want to live out the rest of your long and beautiful life, or don't you?"

She met his eyes silently.

"I do, too," he said. "So just think about what they'd do to you, and to me, if we told them now."

She looked at him with the wide blue eyes of a frightened child.

"Keep thinking about that," he said, "and don't let yourself forget it."

She nodded slowly.

He moved her forward out of the doorway a step or two, because he wanted to watch the noisy group waiting to board the power cruiser. They were clustered in front of the little gate where René Derbos was standing. They looked slightly foolish in their masks, and he wondered why they wore them. Two of the men pulled them off, in fact, and cast them aside on the deck, and he saw that it was Craig Dunleavy and that other man who was always with him, the one called Kleinfeld. Dunleavy gave some sort of command in a loud voice, a cheer went up from the others, and then suddenly they all began to push through the gate and clamber aboard the white vessel, tossing their belongings in ahead of them, reaching out with their hands in the swaying boat and holding on to whatever was nearest to steady themselves, handrails, poles, stanchions, the top surface of the cabin, anything.

Julie turned her head away.

"Don't worry," he said, watching, waiting. "It doesn't necessarily happen that fast. It may not even happen at all. Does that make you feel any better?"

She didn't answer him. She had just noticed the two passengers moving swiftly across the empty lounge, slowing down as they spotted her. She wondered why they had left their cabins, and why they were heading toward *her* now, two men in ordinary sports clothes with tense, determined expressions. She tugged on his sleeve, and he turned just as they arrived and one of them said in a querulous voice, "You people are too hard to find. Why don't you leave word with someone?"

"Maybe we like to be alone," Harold Columbine said, eyeing them carefully.

"Dunleavy wants to say goodbye to you two, okay?"

"No thanks," he said, feeling Julie's startled eyes on him. "You tell him goodbye for us. And goodbye to you too, fellas."

The second man's face took on a pained expression. "Come on,

Columbine, you *know* you're gonna walk over there with us, so don't waste time, huh?"

Julie tried to bolt past them, but the first man seized her without effort and turned her around.

"She'll go," Harold Columbine said quickly. He took Julie's hand in his and they started across the Boat Deck toward the power cruiser with the two men a few feet behind them.

"Harold, what's happening?"

"You heard the man, didn't you?"

"I'm frightened."

"Nobody likes to say goodbye."

The crowd before the gate had thinned out. Most of them were already aboard. Craig Dunleavy turned his head and saw them approaching. His face seemed relaxed and expressionless.

"Hi there," he called out to them. "Be with you in a moment." He was taking an envelope from the breast pocket of his blue denim jacket and turning to René Derbos. "Can I count on you to ease us down gently, sir?"

The officer tried to remain cool. "It is automatic, m'sieur. All our lifeboats make a smooth descent."

"Good show," Dunleavy said. He held out the envelope. "Immediately after we shove off, I want you to deliver this to the Captain. Naturally, it's important."

René Derbos took the envelope. "Very well, m'sieur."

Dunleavy turned with a little smile on his face. "Mrs. Berlin, Mr. Columbine, this is your lucky day. Inasmuch as *someone's* got to return this dandy little lifeboat to its mother ship, you two have been unanimously elected to go along with us as far as the freighter."

"No," Julie said quietly. "No."

"Oh, yes," Dunleavy said, smiling.

"I will not get into that boat."

Harold Columbine felt the dryness in his mouth. "You better pick somebody else, Dunleavy. We won't know how to navigate that thing."

"You'll learn. We'll show you. Get in, please."

"Look, *I'll* go. But leave her here. All right?"

Dunleavy shook his head slowly and in a weary voice said, "Why do you want to keep my friends waiting? Will you two get the fuck into that boat?"

"I am not going," Julie shrieked. "I'm not going."

Dunleavy looked past her. "Sam . . . Jack . . ."

"Harold, tell him!"

Quickly Harold Columbine seized her arm in a viselike grip and led her through the gate, saying with quiet, fierce intensity, "Don't touch anything but *me*, do you understand? Hold on to *me* and *nothing else*."

"Oh God," she moaned.

"Did you hear what I said?"

"Yes . . . yes . . ."

"Stand right there." He held on to her for balance, carefully stepped onto the deck of the swaying white vessel, braced his thighs against the motion, reached out for her hand, seized it, and pulled her in beside him. She teetered for a moment, but he curled an arm around her waist until she was steady, then slowly he led her by the hand to a small, backless bench at the stern, facing into the long wide cabin, and sat her down. He eased himself down beside her, remembering how carefully he had treated this bench, as well as everything else, with the murky solution, and he thought to himself, you could die laughing. "Keep your hands in your lap and don't move from here," he said to her quietly.

"Yes," she said, staring into the crowded cabin with a haunted look on her face.

"Everything's going to be all right," he said. "Long and beautiful, honey."

"Yes," she said, sitting stiffly, unmoving.

Some of the Halloween masks were turned in their direction, and he could feel the eyes peering out with curiosity. The others were too busy to notice them, too busy getting their belongings sorted out and settling into their places on the crowded bench-seats inside the cabin and out on deck, chattering among themselves about the exciting new experience. He saw the men named Sam and Jack clamber aboard, and finally Dunleavy himself, holding on to the side of the cabin for support with his bare hands, standing on the rear deck and answering the scattered applause with a mock bow, and then turning to René Derbos, waiting on the Boat Deck, and calling out to him, "Main floor, please!"

The little officer stepped to the control box at the rail and pressed the button, and the boat started slowly to descend like an elevator toward the water below. Harold Columbine looked past Julie's pale, rigid countenance and saw the puzzled expressions on the faces at the porthole windows of the *Marseille* as the sleek white boat slid down the starboard flank of the liner. He looked down, saw the waves rising to meet them, and put an arm around Julie's waist, holding her firmly. There was a soft thud, a splashing sound, a shudder, and then a cheer inside the cabin and out on the decks as the cables went slack and the boat took on the rolling motion of the sea.

The lines were cleared and the bald-headed man up forward at the wheel punched the starters and the twin diesels roared and fired up. The bald-headed man shoved the throttles open and with a surge of power the big white cruiser leaped forward in the water and foamed a churning arc as it swung over in a southwesterly curve and headed for the freighter that sat waiting in the middle distance, dead ahead.

Using the handrails and fighting the motion of the boat all the way, Craig Dunleavy worked his way over to them and stood swaying, looking down at them. "If you two want to learn to be sailors, you better go forward where the teacher is."

Something in his voice sounded unconvincing, even frightening.

"We'll stay right here if it's all right with you," Harold Columbine said, over the roar of the engines.

Sick with dread, Julie said nothing.

Dunleavy shrugged. "Your funeral."

Harold Columbine looked up at him. "Don't be so fucking sure about that, Dunleavy."

Craig Dunleavy met his eyes for a moment, then turned away and went down into the cabin.

Julie's apprehensive, reproachful glance was brief.

"I know," he muttered defensively. "I know."

Why was nothing happening? Why was it taking so long? What was he doing out here in the first place? This wasn't for him, this was for the other guy. Harold Columbine doesn't sit in a poisoned boat in the middle of nowhere with someone else's woman, trying to keep himself and her alive while surrounded by crazies with guns in their belts. He lies on the beach in front of the Carlton. He does the high dive at Eden Roc. He cruises the Greek islands in his own private yacht with the Playmates of this and every other year. He writes a novel now and then if someone insists. He buys a plane now and then, pays a debt now and then, takes a wife now and then, and never drives anything less than the Silver Shadow, never anything less. Less is strictly for the other guy, like poor is, and sick is, and ugly is, and no broads is. There has been a terrible mistake somewhere. Someone surely must have gotten him mixed up with a whole other fellow, because no way does Harold Columbine wind up on the short end of threats from lunatics and assholes, and worrying whether they're please gonna let him live for another hour or two, please, fellas, I got a date with a warm pussy called Terri Worthingstuff, so don't make me late, fellas, don't make me a no show, I gotta get back to the big boat and climb into that wide one that's waiting for me tonight, I gotta get to the Europes this summer to do the research and the fressing and the fucking that go into the next big one, forty-nine weeks number one this time, none of that number two and number three shit, that's for the other guys, let them choke on my dust and call it emphysema . . .

Dunleavy, Dunleavy, when are you cocksuckers gonna start to die?

He did not want to listen to the man but he had to, because he would need him. He would need his radio. It was the only one left. He would need it to let the world know that Charles Girodt was in command of the *Marseille* again, the crisis was over. He stood there in the communications room, waiting for Christain Specht's men to finish hooking up the new antenna to the little gray-and-black transceiver, listening to the distraught young American doctor go on and on. He nodded with proper sympathy and concern, but what he really wanted to do was go on savoring the pleasure he felt at being reborn again, the blood flowing in his veins again, the testicles back in their rightful place. He was the Commandant. There was nobody on board now to stand in his way. And in his pocket he had the reassuring words of Craig Dunleavy's farewell message.

Forgive me for deceiving you, it had said. *When the timers run out at 1600 Zulu, everything will be automatically deactivated, you won't have to do a thing. Do not touch anything. Your ship was going to be out of danger at 1600 Zulu all along, no matter what might have happened to us. Pleasant voyage to all, and my compliments to your chef.*

Who wanted to hear about extermination plans and the danger to two passengers out of two thousand and some vague talk about an urgent warning from California that had not yet been received?

He listened to the man and nodded, but his thoughts were else-where, far below, where fifty-seven members of his crew were standing before fifty-seven softly clicking red boxes, watching them and listening to them but not touching them. In exactly thirty-eight minutes, the clicking would end, and he would be hearing the happy news that it was all over, a thing of the past.

Enough of this anxiety, this negative thinking. Enough.

"You *owe* it to me," the American was insisting. "You owe it to *them* . . ."

"You know how grateful we are, Dr. Berlin . . ."

"Then *do* something about it, goddamn it. Send your men out in the motor launches *now*. Why do you have to wait until maybe it's too late?"

"Because those people are armed," Charles Girodt said, control-ling his impatience. "We are watching the freighter closely. As soon as it gets under way, we will know that the murderers have climbed aboard. We will know then that it is safe to send assistance to your wife and Mr. Columbine without unnecessarily endangering their lives. Please be reasonable, Doctor."

"Reasonable, *shit*." It was like talking to a brick wall. He turned away and saw Christian Specht entering with Yves Chabot.

"It's ready. Have you tried it yet?" the Chief Radio Officer said to Billy.

"No, I've been too busy shouting into the wind."

"And the wind has been telling you to stop worrying about *nothing*," Girodt blurted out angrily.

Muttering to himself, Billy sat down before his transceiver in the ravaged communications room, clamped the earphones on his head and switched the radio on.

Yves Chabot was staring at Girodt. "Are you all right, Com-mandant?" he said.

Girodt grinned suddenly at the Chief Medical Officer, and his voice rose to manic intensity. "Of course I am all right," he chortled. "What kind of idiotic question is that? I have never felt better in my whole life."

And Chabot knew immediately that something was wrong with him. "The passengers have left their cabins, sir. They are happy, but asking questions."

"Good," Girodt cried. "Good. Because now *we* have all the answers."

Chabot stared at him.

"It works," Billy Berlin called out. "It's fine . . ."

Charles Girodt stepped forward quickly. "I want you to try to reach your friend, or anybody else, and have them relay the news to Paris that the *Marseille* is free and out of danger."

Billy turned the gain down and looked up at him. "Is it really, Captain?" There was bitterness in his voice. "I mean, plus or minus a couple of passengers who aren't exactly on board, is the *Marseille* really out of danger?"

Girodt's lips tightened. He was getting fed up with this insolent American. "Here," he said. "Read." He took out Dunleavy's message and thrust it at him.

Billy took the note and read it quickly. 1600 Zulu . . . He glanced at the clock on the wall. Then he looked at Girodt. "It's only 1526 Zulu now. Shouldn't we wait another thirty-four minutes? Aren't you being slightly premature, Captain? Or am I being too technical?"

"Goddamn it, Berlin." Girodt pointed at the radio and his voice shook. "I have given you an order. *Will you do as I say?*"

Yves Chabot and Christain Specht looked at each other quickly.

Billy started to rise, then sat down slowly. What was the use? The man was crazy. He turned the gain up again and started tuning around for Brian Joy. Maybe it would help him to forget Julie out there on the water. But he didn't want to forget her, not really. All he wanted was to have her back with him again. He wanted to be able to start giving her the love that he had somehow withheld from her too long, too long. It was all she had ever needed.

Please, God . . .

She saw it begin a few moments before he did, because his attention was on the dinghy with the lone seaman in it heading out from the freighter. But then he saw it too, the woman half rising to her feet in the cabin, frantically peeling off her rubber mask, tossing it to the cabin floor and rubbing her bare arms and scratching her head, a look of great discomfort on her face, the man sitting next to her, her husband, the man called Kleinfeld, peering at her with a puzzled, inquiring expression, easing her down on the seat again, obviously asking her what was wrong, and she seemed to be crying and shaking her head and mouthing, I don't know, I don't know, Herb, and scratching at her face and her arms with her long finger-

nails over and over again, and then a man not far away from her
tore off his mask and his face was contorted in a grimace of pain
and he bent over in his seat and opened his mouth as though he
wanted to throw up, as though he were seasick or something, and
Julie heard herself whimper and felt Harold's hand covering hers to
reassure her or to reassure himself, she didn't know which, because
his hand was as icy as hers, and then Craig Dunleavy must have
noticed what was happening all around him because suddenly he
was running through the cabin shouting, "Take off your masks,
there must be something wrong with the masks, get rid of the
masks, there's something wrong with the masks," and up onto the
deck shouting the same thing to them, to so many of them who were
coming up out of the cabin into the wind, and when they ripped the
rubber things from their faces their mouths were wide open and
they were gasping for air like fish out of water and holding on to
each other in confusion and terror and hanging over the rail as
though looking for something in the water and slowly sliding to the
deck and lying very still in grotesque positions with contorted faces
and staring eyes, and the sounds that some of the others were
making, the ones on the roof of the cabin, made Julie's hands move
involuntarily to her ears, but Harold swore at her and told her to
keep her hands in her lap and not move, and then she saw Dunleavy's wife stumbling out of the cabin up onto the deck with her
blue eyes all wild and a look of agony on her blood-streaked face,
and Dunleavy started grappling with her crying, don't, Betty, listen
to me, but she kept screaming, I can't stand it, I can't stand it, and
they struggled and she broke from his grasp and ran to the rail and
pulled herself over with her bloody hands and fell into the soothing
waters and vanished beneath the wake of the speeding boat, and
then others were doing the same thing and nobody tried to stop
them because they were too busy trying to tear the burning nerve-
endings from their own tortured bodies, and now Dunleavy turned
with the tears streaming down his cheeks and he came toward Julie
with a lost and hopeless look in his eyes and he looked down at her
and he looked down at Harold and he cried, they did this to us,
didn't they, they did it to us, tell me, and she said nothing and
Harold said nothing, they just looked at him, and he pulled the gun
from his belt crying tell me, I have to know, tell me, and then
suddenly he stiffened and drew in his breath with a great choking
gasp and his mouth opened wide as though he couldn't believe the

enormity of what was happening to him and he began to gulp at the air and his face began to contort in a horrible grimace of agony and she heard Harold saying, *they* didn't, Dunleavy, *I* did, and the man looked at him with dumbstruck, wounded eyes, and he began to sink slowly to his knees gasping, help me, help me, leaning over and down and making his wide-open gasping mouth go down onto the up-pointing barrel of the gun in his hand, and she closed her eyes and heard the muffled sound of his exploding skull and shuddered in the grasp of Harold's comforting arm, and when at last she allowed her eyes to open again she was looking over and beyond what was left of Dunleavy into the cabin where the other man, Kleinfeld, was lying on the floor on top of his wife in the unbreakable embrace of her arms and legs, and it was as though they had just finished making love and were totally spent now, exhausted to death, for they were no longer moving and never would, ever again . . .

At 1531 Zulu, Billy Berlin, sitting in the communications room of the S.S. *Marseille,* established contact with Brian Joy in Beverly Hills, California. Charles Girodt insisted that the conversation be put on the speaker so that he and Christain Specht and Yves Chabot could hear everything that went on.

Billy Berlin told Brian Joy that the conspirators had left the ship, and he told him about the little red boxes that would stop clicking in twenty-nine minutes at 1600 Zulu, and then he read Craig Dunleavy's farewell message over the air, but Charles Girodt kept butting in about notifying Paris and Billy had to ask him to stop talking, please.

Brian Joy sounded very strange when he came back to Billy. He said that he had copied Dunleavy's message down and Maggie was in the room with him and she had someone named Dr. Slocum of the Remo Corporation, a very brilliant man, on the telephone, and she was now reading the message to him.

Why is she doing that? Charles Girodt demanded.

Please, sir, said Yves Chabot.

Why is she doing that, Brian? Billy said into the microphone, even though he had a pretty good idea.

Brian Joy explained that he had been trying to reach Billy for half an hour but Billy had disappeared, what the hell had happened? He said that some of the greatest minds in the whole country wanted the Captain to be warned that any positive statements given to him by the conspirators were not to be trusted, in fact were to be viewed with extreme suspicion, because the conspirators' true intent had always been and probably still was to destroy the ship and everyone on it. Billy could not make out the rest of the transmission because suddenly the three officers behind him were arguing in French in very loud voices about *leaving* or something while there was still *time* and he wished to Christ they *would* get the hell out and leave him because he couldn't hear a goddamn thing and he had to shout at them to stop it stop it and the Captain uttered one last angry *absolument non* before he finally shut up. Please repeat everything after destroy the ship and everyone on it, Billy Berlin said, feeling the fear in his intestines.

At 1534 Zulu, Brian Joy said that Dr. Slocum was calling a Dr. Wibberly or something on his other phone, but was having trouble because Wibberly's wife, or maybe it was Whipperly, didn't want to wake her husband up, but Slocum was working on her.

Well, for Christ's sake, tell him to hurry up, Billy Berlin said.

I want to know what is going on, Charles Girodt said. What are you doing on that radio?

We should give out our position immediately, sir, said Christain Specht.

Stand by, Brian, Billy Berlin said into the microphone.

Girodt said, I want Paris to be notified immediately that the *Marseille* is free and under my command.

Will you please sit down, said Yves Chabot.

What is our position? Christain Specht said to his superior.

Out of danger is our position, the Captain said.

What is our position, sir?

We are at twelve degrees north, forty-eight degrees west and out of danger, Charles Girodt said. Tell them *that*.

Transmit our position please, Christain Specht said quietly to Billy Berlin.

At 1536 Zulu, while the Captain and his Chief Radio Officer were having a heated exchange, Billy Berlin reported the position of the *Marseille* to Brian Joy.

Brian Joy acknowledged the transmission and said that Slocum was now reading Craig Dunleavy's message over the telephone to

Dr. Wibberly, or maybe it was Whipperly, and he went on to add that Slocum and Wibberly were two of the most respected minds in the country, did Billy copy that?

Yes, yes, I copy, will you hurry them up, Brian?

Maggie wants to know how Julie is. Is she all right?

Yes, tell her yes, she couldn't be better, what's going on, for Christ's sake?

At 1539 Zulu, Brian Joy came on in a voice that sounded a little hysterical and said that Dr. Wibberly was not only a world-famous brainstorming type of thinker but also a Nobel Prize winner in physics, and Wibberly was of the firm opinion that Craig Dunleavy's message was a premeditated lie designed to lull the Captain into a false sense of security.

Billy Berlin repeated the transmission to make sure he had received it correctly, what with Christain Specht right behind him having some sort of physical struggle with Girodt, who was protesting angrily about something while Yves Chabot had his arms around the Captain trying to restrain him and force him into a chair, it was noisy as hell and very confusing. Will you hit it harder, Briney? Go ahead.

Dr. Wibberly says that as sure as there are stars in the sky, and Dr. Slocum agrees with him a hundred percent, as sure as there are stars in the sky, when the timers reach 1600 Zulu the *Marseille* will blow up and be destroyed, did you get that, Billy, did you get that?

Billy Berlin pressed the mike button but nothing would come out of his mouth at first and he cleared his throat several times and finally a voice came out that didn't sound like his at all, and it was repeating everything into the microphone about how the *Marseille* would blow up and be destroyed when the timers reached 1600 Zulu, and he yelled for quiet but the Captain was in the chair with his head in his hands sobbing uncontrollably and Christain Specht and Yves Chabot were shouting what sounded like orders to each other and in all the commotion Billy Berlin wasn't sure but he thought he heard Brian Joy's voice coming out of the speaker asking him what time did his clock show out there in the Atlantic, because suddenly there was this great ringing in his ears, but he answered Brian Joy anyway saying, the same time as your clock shows, you dummy, 1543, 1543, say goodbye to my mother for me, and you too, Briney old boy, and then he dropped the microphone and rose to his feet because he couldn't hear a goddamn thing any more anyway, not with all that ringing in his ears . . .

Panos Trimenedes seized him by the collar and cried stop it, stop it, but Nick Moustakos kept gibbering hysterically and the saliva drooled down his chin and it took several hard slaps of his face to get him to quiet down long enough to say, yes, they were dead, all of them on the drifting white boat were dead except the woman sitting at the stern and the man beside her who had tried to keep him from climbing out of the dinghy, waving his arms and yelling at him not to come near, not to climb aboard, but he hadn't listened to him, no he hadn't listened because he had his orders, his Captain had ordered him to find the head man, the leader, the man Dunleavy, and that's why he had to go aboard and look inside the cabin, and it was the expressions on the twisted faces he saw in there that he couldn't stop seeing now, all those people, terrible, terrible, lying together in their own blood and vomit. He started slobbering again, and Panos Trimenedes angrily pushed him aside, knowing now that there never would be a final payment from Otto Laneer, and with a bitter cry he shouted the command that sent the *Angela Gloria* steaming away at full speed to the south, for he wanted distance now between his ship and the great *Marseille,* wanted no one ever to know the true identity of the freighter with the false flag of Liberia and the black paint where its name should have been, especially now that such mysterious death had come to the ones who had hired him, and nothing would get him to slacken the pounding pace of his ship, much less turn her around and go back, not even the burial at sea he would be conducting at full speed ahead a few hours later when Nick Moustakos tore at his flesh for the very last time and took his haunted memory of the terrible faces to a watery grave . . .

They heard the rumble of engines starting up, and knew without turning what it meant. Twisting their bodies carefully on the swaying bench, they took their eyes off the grotesque, lifeless shapes that lay all around them, peered off and saw the freighter turning tail and fleeing to the south. They said nothing. They were alone now on the cold wide sea, trapped in the prison of their own rigidity, fearful of their poisoned vessel.

Its diesels silent, rudder unmanned, the slim white boat pitched and rolled helplessly in the angry swells, moving, with every slosh and slap of the waves against its sides, farther and farther away from the *Marseille,* which was their home, their sanctuary. The big liner stood majestically on the horizon waiting for them, resting large and beautiful against the gray skies, but an eternity away.

Harold Columbine turned his head slightly and glanced at Julie's face and did not like what he saw there. The grim hard set of her mouth and the eyes that stared off without seeing filled him with apprehension. Too long she had held herself together. Too much she had endured for one slim young married lady from Bel Air, California. He was afraid of what might happen if she let her mind open up now, if she looked one more time at the place where Craig Dunleavy's head should have been. He was afraid not just for her but for himself, too. He did not like it. He did not like their chances. Not if all they were going to do was sit there and wait and hope that someone would find them before they drifted into the black hopelessness of night or were capsized by some unfriendly, broadsiding wave.

You're not getting any younger, boychick.

There is no time like the present, and other clever sayings.

Here goes nothing, and other stories, by Harold Columbine.

Why couldn't he remember that girl's last name?

Terri? . . . Terri *what?*

Terri, here ah come.

Slowly, remaining seated, he began to work his arms out of the jacket of his uniform.

"I'm not really that cold," Julie said, looking at him.

"I happen to think you're a very hot number," he said, and got the jacket off and onto his lap. He examined it and saw the seam down the middle leading to a flap. He seized one side of the flap in each hand, pulled sharply with a powerful outward thrust of his triceps and ripped the jacket almost in two. Not for nothing all the mixed doubles and the bullshit on the courts of East Hampton and the Hotel du Cap.

"What are you doing?" Julie said.

"I'm a glove manufacturer," he said.

"You're not going to leave me?"

"Hell no, honey, you're coming along."

"Where to?"

"The *Marseille.* We're going home."

She looked at him with wide blue eyes.

He tore the collar off the jacket and quickly rended the jacket into two halves. He placed one half on Julie's lap beneath her clenched hands. Then, taking his own half, he inserted his left hand into the lower outer pocket of the jacket and his right hand into the armhole of the sleeve, allowing about a foot of the sleeve to dangle.

"Look, Ma, no hands," he said.

Julie stared at him.

"Go on, do it," he said.

She hesitated.

"Do it."

He picked up her hands and took up her half of the jacket and placed one of her hands in the pocket and one in the armhole of the sleeve and showed her how to grasp the material on the inside and flex and unflex her fingers. Then, with his half-jacket held before him encasing his hands, he rose slowly to a standing position, his legs wide apart against the perilous rolling of the boat.

"All right," he said. "Hold on to me, and don't look anywhere but at my back."

She sat there motionless for several moments. Then her lips tightened with determination and she rose to her feet and quickly seized him from behind at his waist.

"Ready?" he said.

"Yes."

"Whither I goest, thou goest," he said.

"Slowly," Julie said in a frightened voice.

He thought at first he would try the helm at the forward end of the cabin, but when they got to the bottom of the steps and he had a good look in there, he knew that it was more than even he could stand. Nothing, not even the biting wind, could cleanse it of the stink and the horror. So he led Julie out onto the swaying deck and picked his way carefully past the tangled bodies, feeling her arms tighten convulsively about him when they got to the worst of it all, the ones on their backs staring sightlessly at the sky who had clawed their own eyeballs out and, Jesus, oh my God, he heard the uncontrollable gasps that escaped from his throat and Julie's moans of disbelief, and he lost his concentration for a moment and stumbled, and she started to go down with him, clinging to his waist, but his hand grabbed at the rail and held on, and the protective sleeve with its fine silk lining was thick enough to keep death from his clutching fingers.

They moved forward slowly, fighting the rise and dip and rolling sway of the boat, and came to the foot of the stairs to the flying bridge. He looked up and saw the steering wheel and the duplicate control panel. Reaching out with his left hand in the pocket of the jacket and with his right hand in the sleeve, he seized the rails on either side of the stairway and started up, with Julie using his body as her guide.

The two women who lay sprawled on the bridge with their heads resting on their arms appeared merely to be sleeping, and the blond-haired one in the tight blue denims had a marvelous grace of form, and he couldn't understand how a woman could look that lovely even in death, or how he could be having such thoughts at a time like this, and he wondered if maybe he was the one who was in bad shape, not Julie.

He darted a glance at her and saw that her lips were bloodless, and she appeared not even to notice the two bodies as they stepped over them. He sat her down on the right-hand seat and took the helmsman's seat behind the wheel. Over his left shoulder he caught a glimpse of the *Marseille* in the distance. Then he located the starters on the control panel in front of him and quickly got the diesels going again. With his protected right hand he slowly shoved the throttles forward until he heard the engines roaring and bur-bling behind him, and he could feel the boat beginning to fight the waves that were buffeting it about. He swung the wheel hard to the left, waited for the *Marseille* to come into view dead ahead, straightened the wheel, then gave the diesels everything he had and felt the thrust of power beneath him. The boat surged forward, gathered speed, and headed for home, slicing and banging through the waves, sending a cold blinding spray into their solemn faces.

He looked at Julie sitting huddled and silent beside him. "Are you okay?" he said.

"I'm fine," she said, her teeth chattering in the wind.

And he realized that it was true.

In her own way, no one else's, more than any woman he had ever known, she was fine. And always would be. And he felt a pang of sadness and loss, knowing he would never be lucky enough to have her for his own, and make something of his fucked-up life.

Maybe he'd be able to do it without her. It seemed worth a try. It did now . . .

They fixed their eyes on the distant *Marseille,* and lost themselves in their own private thoughts of homecoming and warmth and safety, and an end to the whole bloody nightmare. Julie thought of Billy, her Billy boy, with tenderness and longing and an aching desire to make up for the foolishly wasted years, and in her heart, her mind, she felt an open back door quietly closing forever.

They sat side by side on the bucking, charging vessel, willing it toward its destination, peering through the cold spray that obscured their vision, and the biting wind and the waves that burst on their bows, sometimes seeing the topmost part of the big ship clearly, sometimes not at all. They tried not to think of their cargo of death, and peered with eager, anxious eyes through the veil of mist at the haven that awaited them, at the great ocean liner that had brought them together, and soon would carry them away to separate lives, though never truly separate again.

Together, they looked off at their ship, the *Marseille,* and suddenly they heard the thunder, and in their imaginations they saw their ship being seized by a mighty wave and taken from them. They saw their ship rising up out of the swollen sea, trembling and quivering and taking on a blurred, uncertain shape, then falling back into nothingness. They saw all this and heard the deep rolling boom of the thunder repeating itself over and over again, and it was so loud that it rent the air and the sea and filled them with awe, though it could not awaken those who had caused it. They looked at the sky for the bolts of lightning that would surely accompany all the thunder, and saw the lightning rise up from the sea instead in flamelike streaks of orange through black newborn clouds, and then the thunder roared again, reverberated over the waters and finally died away, leaving them in stunned, heart-stopping silence, looking off at their ship, the *Marseille,* and it was no longer there.

The *Marseille* was no longer there.

It had blown apart.

It had moved outward and upward in graceful slow-motion in every direction, then backward and downward upon itself and into itself, to blow up again and cease to exist as a cohesive entity.

It had become random pieces of what had once been something beautiful and whole.

It had not sunk, water had not filled it, for there was nothing to fill. It had simply moved apart and opened up and become one with the sea.

A few moments ago, the *Marseille,* in all its awesome beauty, had dominated their view, commanded their attention, beckoned to them. Now it was gone, and in its place they could see nothing but the boiling, churning sea, nothing but random pieces of flotsam and jetsam bobbing up and down on the waves.

Billy, she cried softly, over and over again, Billy . . . Billy . . .

And Harold Columbine's scalding tears were open and unashamed . . .

Numbed with shock, they stared straight ahead and kept the white boat moving slowly, stubbornly on course toward the now empty horizon, as though they would deny the reality of what they had heard and seen. It had been a vision, a fantasy, it had never happened. In a moment the *Marseille* would be there before them, looming up out of the mist, waiting for them to arrive, waiting to haul them aboard.

Yes, of course, here they were, here were the welcoming boats even now. It had all been in their imaginations. See? Here were boat after boat, filled with men and women calling out to them, welcoming them, cheering them, eager to convoy them to safety. Boat after boat, filled with life-jacketed men and women and children, bobbing up and down on the waves like flotsam and jetsam.

There was Yves Chabot, and Genvieve Bordoni, and Olga Shanneli, and Christain Specht . . . Why, it appeared as though every soul who had been on board the *Marseille* had taken to the lifeboats to come out to welcome them, to rescue them, to help them back onto the ship. And Billy. There was Billy. Calling out to her. Julie. Billy. Tears streaming down his cheeks . . .

What was wrong?

Don't cry, Billy. We're safe. We're all right. The *Marseille* is saved and we're all right. They didn't get away with it after all, we stopped them, we stopped them . . .

She was shivering and crying and Harold was carrying her in his arms down the stairs to the deck and shouting to them not to come too close, not to touch anything, and before he passed her over to their outstretched hands he soothed her and talked to her softly, trying to make her understand why all the lifeboats were coming toward them and why it was so empty, so terribly empty on the horizon, but they were alive, he said, everyone was alive, do you hear me, my love?

We're all alive . . .

THE AFTERMATH

G E O R G E S S A U V I N A G E has lost thirty pounds since becoming Director General of the Compagnie Française Atlantique, following the resignation of Max Dechambre. His most popular act since assuming his new position was his recommendation to the board of directors and to the French government that the S.S. *Bordeaux* be renamed the *Marseille II* before going into service in June.

Aristide Bonnard officially endorsed the proposal, and attended the rechristening ceremonies with Madame Josette Girodt, widow of the late Commandant, who was the only man to go down with the ill-fated ship. However, Bonnard failed in his attempt to retain his presidency, and has retired to his country home in St.-Germain-en-Laye, where he is working on the first volume of his memoirs, with the loving assistance of his wife, Althea. Bonnard has not yet decided how he will deal with his own role in the *Marseille* matter, knowing that as long as Jean-Claude Raffin is alive, there will always be some measure of difficulty in deviating from the truth.

The former President is comforted by the knowledge that he will not have to face that troubling situation until he reaches volume four, which will deal exclusively with the abrupt termination of his public life.

Jean-Claude Raffin survived the hearings in the Chamber of Deputies and returned to his position as Director General of the French Sûreté Nationale, but he was never quite able to overcome his own personal sense of responsibility and failure in the loss of France's gold, if not the *Marseille* itself. Eventually he resigned as head of the Sûreté and moved with his wife and daughter to Pointe-à-Pitre on the island of Guadeloupe in the French West Indies, where he is said to be in the employ of the international police organization, Interpol, though no one has been able to verify this.

Lisa Briande made every effort to do so, hoping to bring the manuscript of her book up to date, but Raffin failed to answer any of her letters of inquiry, nor would he accept her long distance calls. As for Arsène Schreiner, he would give Lisa nothing more than a flat no comment. She had begun work on the book during her stay in the American Hospital at Neuilly-sur-Seine and had completed three fourths of it while awaiting trial for the slaying of Julian Wunderlicht. Soon after her speedy acquittal, the former *Herald Tribune* reporter delivered the finished manuscript to her American publisher, and will sail for New York on the maiden voyage of the *Marseille II* the first week in June to attend a publication party given in her honor. She told Mary Blume, in the interview, that the trip would be strictly for business, not pleasure.

Leonard Ball, never one for believing what he reads in the papers, only what he sees on the tube, turned down the offer from ABC because it would have meant being on the West Coast for the summer. He kind of liked New York when everyone else was out of town. Amanda would be up in Vermont with the children. He'd be saying yes to *one* of the networks by September. Might as well enjoy the quiet of a summer in the city while he could. Especially June.

For no reason at all, Brian Joy suddenly decided to shift the locale of the new series away from Seattle. His executive producer claimed that Brian was doing it just to get a free research trip out of the network, but Brian told the guy he was crazy, why would anyone want to be in New York in June, when it got as hot as all hell there? Maggie Joy asked herself the same question, and decided she'd better go along. According to *Daily Variety*, the trip has been postponed, and the whole decision on the change of locales is now up in the air.

Julie Berlin told Maggie Joy that if Maggie and Brian *did* go to New York, maybe the four of them could have dinner together there, the night before she and Billy left for France on the first eastward sailing of the *Marseille II*. Julie felt they ought to make the trip *now*, while little Harold was still an infant. Billy asked Julie whether she'd mind if he took his microcomputer along. (That's what he's into now, microcomputers.) Julie told Billy he could take anything he wanted along, provided it was small enough to take into bed with them.

The line wasn't Julie's, it was Harold Columbine's. He had used it in his reply to Julie's letter when she had written to him about the new baby. He had told her about his breakup with Terri Montgomery after the fantastic summer on the Costa del Sol, and had sounded lonely and depressed. But that was before he met Delphine, at some nothing party out on the Island. She was no big deal, wide blue eyes, fairly good shape, a little on the diminutive side, worked for a literary agent or something, and nobody who knew Harold Columbine would have predicted that he'd even take her out to dinner, much less marry her within a week. They seem very happy together, and Harold has settled down in a way that disgusts quite a few people around Westport and the Hamptons and in town, particularly some of the higher-priced hookers. His lawyer tells everybody (with that sour expression of his), our Harold is working on a *serious* novel now, something called *The White Boat* . . . but he'll be all right in the morning.

It had drifted away by the time the ships and the planes and the helicopters came. Aimlessly it wanders over the vast, empty reaches of the southern Atlantic, far from the sea lanes of ordinary com-

merce, far from the curious eyes of the winged jets that leave trails in the sky hundreds of miles to the north. Long ago washed clean of its deadly toxins by the breaking waves and the torrential rains, the white boat roams the ocean with the winds and the tides, waiting for an end to its restless journey on the deserted sands of some barren shore, or in the teeth of an angry storm that will send it to a final resting place at the bottom of the sea. Perhaps, some day, some wayfaring sailor will chance across the path of the rudderless craft and circle it slowly with morbid fascination. Perhaps he will even think once or twice of going aboard. But then he will gaze one more time upon its heaped-up decks and the frightful cabin, and with a shake of his head, set his sails and continue onward on his journey, leaving the white boat to drift forever on the boundless sea.

Ernest Lehman, a native of Manhattan, graduated from The City College of New York with a powerful desire to make his way in life as a professional writer. His many subsequent short stories in national magazines, and his two novellas, The Sweet Smell of Success *and* The Comedian, *brought him to the attention of Hollywood, and he was summoned to the West Coast. There, for more than two decades, he has lived with his wife Jacqueline and two sons, Roger and Alan, while writing the screenplays for such notable films as* Executive Suite, The King and I, Somebody Up There Likes Me, North by Northwest, The Sound of Music, West Side Story, *and* Who's Afraid of Virginia Woolf?

The French Atlantic Affair *is Mr. Lehman's first novel.*